MAN

IN HIS

TIME

——

BOOKS BY BRIAN W. ALDISS

MAN
IN HIS
TIME

*The Best
Science Fiction
Stories
of
Brian W. Aldiss*

ATHENEUM
NEW YORK • 1989

Copyright © 1988 by Brian W. Aldiss

First published in Great Britain in 1988 by Victor Gollancz Ltd, London

Foreword copyright © 1989 by Brian W. Aldiss

"Outside" © Brian W. Aldiss 1955; "All the World's Tears" ©
Brian W. Aldiss 1957; "The Failed Men" © Brian W. Aldiss 1957; "Poor
Little Warrior!" © Brian W. Aldiss 1958; "Who Can Replace A Man?" ©
Brian W. Aldiss 1958; "Man on Bridge" © Brian W. Aldiss 1964; "The
Girl and the Robot with Flowers" © Brian W. Aldiss 1965; "The Saliva
Tree" © Brian W. Aldiss 1965; "Man in His Time" ©
Brian W. Aldiss 1965; "Heresies of the Huge God" ©
Brian W. Aldiss 1966; "Confluence" © Brian W. Aldiss 1967; "Working
in the Spaceship Yards" © Brian W. Aldiss 1969; "Super-Toys Last All
Summer Long" © Brian W. Aldiss 1969; "Sober Noises of Morning in a
Marginal Land" © Brian W. Aldiss 1971; "The Dark Soul of the Night"
© Brian W. Aldiss 1976; "An Appearance of Life" ©
Brian W. Aldiss 1976; "Last Orders" © Brian W. Aldiss 1976; "Door
Slams in Fourth World" © Brian W. Aldiss 1982; "The Gods in Flight"
© Brian W. Aldiss 1984; "My Country 'Tis Not Only of Thee" ©
Brian W. Aldiss 1986; "Infestation" © Brian W. Aldiss 1986; "The
Difficulties Involved in Photographing Nix Olympica" ©
Brian W. Aldiss 1986.

Atheneum
Macmillan Publishing Company
866 Third Avenue, New York, N.Y. 10022

Library of Congress Cataloging-in-Publication Data
Aldiss, Brian Wilson, 1925–
[Short stories. Selections]
Man in his time : the best science fiction stories of Brian W.
Aldiss.
p. cm.
First published in Great Britain in 1988 by V. Gollancz, London,
under title: Best SF stories of Brian W. Aldiss.
ISBN 0-689-12052-4
1. Science fiction, English, I. Title.
PR6051.L3A6   1989   89-6934   CIP
823'.914—dc20

10 9 8 7 6 5 4 3 2 1

Printed in the United States of America

To Tim and Charlotte

with

love and hope

Contents

Foreword

Where has the past gone? Where could we seek to find the year 1832, for instance, again? What has happened to the spirit of Washington Irving?

The answer to such questions is a mystery, to me at least, and in the main my stories are constructed to celebrate mysteries. But I can explain about Washington Irving.

Two years ago, my wife and I drove down through the magical centre of Spain, from Madrid, Toledo, Cordoba, and Jaén, to the wonderful city of Granada, once a Moorish stronghold and still dominated by the Alhambra on its lofty cliffs. We stayed in the Alhambra Palace, a hotel close to the walls of the Alhambra itself.

On a stall near the hotel, we came across a book. It was Washington Irving's *Tales of the Alhambra* in an English language edition, illustrated, and published there in Granada. The original appeared in 1832 — so, to answer one of my questions, that year is to be found preserved in part within those covers.

It's a romantic story. Irving was an American diplomat who spent some time living within the walls of the Alhambra. His book recalls the enchantment of that place and period, and ends with a solemn "Farewell to Granada":

> *My serene and happy reign in the Alhambra was suddenly brought to a close by letters which reached me, while indulging in Oriental luxury in the cool hall of the baths, summoning me away from my Moslem elysium to mingle once more in the bustle and business of the dusty world. How was I to encounter its toils and turmoils, after such a life of repose and reverie? How was I to endure its commonplace, after the poetry of the Alhambra?*

Well, we all know how Irving felt. We too, in our lives, are called away from repose and reverie by similar horrid letters. Something gets lost in the dusty world. And what can restore the previous "poetry of the Alhambra"? What but meditation and the arts?

These stories, being what is categorized as science fiction, tend to ask, not Where has the past gone?, but Where has the present gone? That's a more mysterious question, and writers are dealers in mystery.

My delight in a sense of mystery has called forth most of these stories; very rarely were they written to order. The commercialization of the science fiction field has led to much writing to order, with the result that a New Brutalism prevails. I can guarantee that few people get beaten up or bumped messily off in this collection. Which is not to say that a certain amount of discomfort, some of it metaphysical, is not suffered.

When I was introduced to Shakespeare as a boy, it was by way of *The Tempest* — of all Shakespeare's plays perhaps the one most suited to a child's imagination, with its storm and the island on which live its magical ruler and strange inhabitants. Of those strange inhabitants, none was more fascinating than Caliban.

At first, I was rather frightened by Caliban. I saw the monster through Prospero's eyes, as something threatening, a brute to be kept down by force and threats. But at that time I was only a little brute myself, and under the spell of my father, as Caliban and Ariel, Caliban's opposite, lived under Prospero's spell.

Adulthood brought many changes. As with my father, Prospero was slowly perceived as a less than benevolent character. His powers had gone to his head, he was an autocrat, trying to bend his daughter Miranda and everyone else to his will. He is to be respected rather than loved; for has he not brought back the dead to life?

> *graves at my command*
> *Have waked their sleepers, oped, and let 'em forth*
> *By my so potent art.*

As Prospero goes down in the moral scales, so Caliban comes up. Despite his lust for Miranda, that toffee-nosed little hussy, Caliban is a pretty harmless creature. Certainly, he has a weakness for the bottle, though we can afford to be indulgent regarding that vice if Shakespeare is; he is something of a Nature Boy, an antecedent of Tarzan as well as of Victor Frankenstein's monster. He promises Stephano to

> *Show thee a jay's nest, and instruct thee how*
> *To snare the nimble marmozet*

— innocent enough country pastimes. I came to view Caliban as rather put upon, betrayed, sold to slavery, no longer predominantly a monster but a victim, dreaming of freedom and a happiness he had once known, or imagined he had known.

Caliban is a creature of Shakespeare's fancy, meant to amuse us and arouse our terror and pity. Very much like a creature in a science fiction story. Science fiction stories generally take some topic or obsession of the day and dramatize it, as Shakespeare seized on his century's interest in travel to the still-vexed Bermoothes. The first story included here uses as lever the fears of the Cold War, as the last uses our unfolding understanding of Mars as a planet. But the stories survive first publication — if survive they do — because of deeper interests awakened in the story which were perhaps not so evident to begin with. Shakespeare's first audience would not have regarded Caliban as a creature of the subconscious.

For me, science fiction stories have a special significance when they enter an area of uncertainty where things may or may not be possible — if not now then Then.

Of course, things may seem plausible which are not really credible. Time travel has this quality. While scientific likelihood plainly enters the question here, the deciding point is more likely psychological. At any rate, I decided to divide my umpteen stories into two categories, SF and fantasy, aware that neither container was watertight. So some old favourites ("Old Hundredth" is an example) not found in this volume may be found in the companion volume of fantasy stories.

Whole libraries can be filled with books which study the novel. Little more than one shelf will contain studies of the short story. The novel is a quadruped, a ruminant, capable of dissection; the short story is a winged thing, too fugitive for much in the way of biopsy. We speak of the Novel, but not of the Short Story. It seems that Oscar Wilde, who said many amusing and memorable things, said nothing memorable or amusing about the short story. Nor did Noel Coward — "Very flat, the short story," being purely apocryphal. There remains Frank O'Connor's dictum, "The short story has never had a hero. What it has instead is a submerged population group."

It is hard to see why this abstruse utterance should strike us as true, but it is certainly accurate as far as the stories contained in this volume are concerned. The submerged population group which inhabits its covers is puzzled and perplexed and often as presumed upon as Caliban himself. Only in one story is there a man who gives an order and is instantly obeyed, and he is an outcast, wretched, shivering in the light of a new dawn.

Heroes inhabit — and in the case of the SF infest — novels. The short story has no place for them. The characters in short stories illuminate by their actions or inaction some facet of life which has suddenly struck the author as truthful. (There again a distinction may be made: A novel can hunt Truth itself; it is sufficient for a short story to be truthful.) Stories are fleeting perceptions. They occupy little time as far as reading or writing goes.

Which is not to say that an author is not passionately attached to these mayflies, these ephemera. For there is an art in their writing. They are truthful about something which is not the ostensible subject.

This selection of stories represents the work (or play) of thirty years, more or less, in which I have been writing. During that period, I have fathered over three hundred stories. Very few if any of them have been designed for specific markets, although the late Dr. Chris Evans was responsible for "Super-Toys Last All Summer Long," and Frederik Pohl and Elizabeth Anne Hull asked for "Infestation." The others were created mainly to please myself; a reader is unlikely to be pleased unless the author has first pleased himself.

A critic, Scott Bradfield, writing in the *Times Literary Supplement* recently, remarked of this collection that "Aldiss's best work never simply explains scientific ideas, but transforms them — black holes, artificial intelligence, incomprehensible alien cultures — into often inexplicable poetic tropes. His stories do not instruct so much as mystify." It's an interesting perception. Perhaps it is true. It might be even more true to say that I regard mystification itself as a form of instruction. The world, the universe, is a problematic place: It is hubris to think we yet have it all figured out. Homo sapiens sometimes gets above itself. Caliban knows a lot of things we don't.

Brian W. Aldiss

MAN
IN HIS
TIME

Outside

They never went out of the house.

The man whose name was Harley used to get up first. Sometimes he would take a stroll through the building in his sleeping suit – the temperature remained always mild, day after day. Then he would rouse Calvin, the handsome, broad man who looked as if he could command a dozen talents and never actually used one. He made as much company as Harley needed.

Dapple, the girl with killing grey eyes and black hair, was a light sleeper. The sound of the two men talking would wake her. She would get up and rouse May; together they would go down and prepare a meal. While they were doing that, the other two members of the household, Jagger and Pief, would be rousing.

That was how every "day" began: not with the inkling of anything like dawn, but just when the six of them had slept themselves back into wakefulness. They never exerted themselves during the day, but somehow when they climbed back into their beds they slept soundly enough.

The only excitement of the day occurred when they first opened the store. The store was a small room between the kitchen and the blue room. In the far wall was set a wide shelf, and upon this shelf their existence depended. Here, all their supplies "arrived". They would lock the door of the bare room last thing, and when they returned in the morning their needs – food, linen, a new washing machine – would be awaiting them on the shelf. That was just an accepted feature of their existence: they never questioned it among themselves.

On this morning, Dapple and May were ready with the meal before the four men came down. Dapple even had to go to the foot of the wide stairs and call before Pief appeared; so that the opening of the store had to be postponed till after they had eaten, for although the opening had in no way become a ceremony, the women were nervous of going in alone. It was one of those things. . . .

"I hope I get some tobacco," Harley said as he unlocked the door. "I'm nearly out of it."

They walked in and looked at the shelf. It was all but empty. "No food," observed May, hands on her aproned waist. "We shall be on short rations today." It was not the first time this had happened. Once – how long ago now? – they kept little track of time – no food had appeared for three days and the shelf had remained empty. They had accepted the shortage placidly.

"We shall eat you before we starve, May," Pief said, and they laughed briefly to acknowledge the joke, although Pief had cracked it last time too. Pief was an unobtrusive little man: not the sort one would notice in a crowd. His small jokes were his most precious possession.

Two packets only lay on the ledge. One was Harley's tobacco, one was a pack of cards. Harley pocketed the one with a grunt and displayed the other, slipping the deck from its package and fanning it towards the others.

"Anyone play?" he asked.

"Poker," Jagger said.

"Canasta."

"Gin rummy."

"We'll play later," Calvin said. "It'll pass the time in the evening." The cards would be a challenge to them; they would have to sit together to play, round a table, facing each other.

Nothing was in operation to separate them, but there seemed no strong force to keep them together, once the tiny business of opening the store was over. Jagger worked the vacuum cleanser down the hall, past the front door that did not open, and rode it up the stairs to clean the upper landings; not that the place was dirty, but cleaning was something you did anyway in the morning. The women sat with Pief desultorily discussing how to manage the rationing, but after that they lost contact with each other and drifted away on their own. Calvin and Harley had already strolled off in different directions.

The house was a rambling affair. It had few windows, and such as there were did not open, were unbreakable and admitted no light. Darkness lay everywhere; illumination from an invisible source followed one's entry into a room – the black had to be entered before it faded. Every room was furnished, but with odd pieces that bore little relation to each other, as if there was no purpose for the room. Rooms equipped for purposeless beings have that air about them.

No plan was discernible on first or second floor or in the long, empty attics. Only familiarity could reduce the maze-like quality of room and corridor. At least there was ample time for familiarity. Harley spent a long while walking about, hands in pockets. At one point he met Dapple; she was drooping gracefully over a sketchbook, amateurishly copying a picture that hung on one of the walls – a picture of the room in which she sat. They exchanged a few words, then Harley moved on.

Something lurked in the edge of his mind like a spider in the corner of its web. He stepped into what they called the piano room and then he realised what was worrying him. Almost furtively, he glanced round as the darkness slipped away, and then looked at the big piano. Some strange things had arrived on the shelf from time to time and had been distributed over the house: one of them stood on top of the piano now.

It was a model, heavy and about two feet high, squat, almost round, with a sharp nose and four buttressed vanes. Harley knew what it was. It was a ground-to-space ship, a model of the burly ferries that lumbered up to the spaceships proper.

That had caused them more unsettlement than when the piano itself had appeared in the store. Keeping his eyes on the model, Harley seated himself at the piano stool and sat tensely, trying to draw *something* from the rear of his mind . . . something connected with spaceships.

Whatever it was, it was unpleasant, and it dodged backwards whenever he thought he had laid a mental finger on it. So it always eluded him. If only he could discuss it with someone, it might be teased out of its hiding place. Unpleasant: menacing, yet with a promise entangled in the menace. If he could get at it, meet it boldly face to face, he could do . . . something definite. And until he had faced it, he could not even say what the something definite was he wanted to do.

A footfall behind him. Without turning, Harley deftly pushed up the piano lid and ran a finger along the keys. Only then did he look back carelessly over his shoulder. Calvin stood there, hands in pockets, looking solid and comfortable.

"Saw the light in here," he said easily. "I thought I'd drop in as I was passing."

"I was thinking I would play the piano a while," Harley answered with a smile. The thing was not discussable, even with a near acquaintance like Calvin, because . . . because of the nature of the thing . . . because one had to behave like a normal, unworried human being. That at least was sound and clear and gave him comfort: behave like a normal human being.

Reassured, he pulled a gentle tumble of music from the keyboard. He played well. They all played well, Dapple, May, Pief . . . as soon as they had assembled the piano, they had all played well. Was that – natural? Harley shot a glance at Calvin. The stocky man leaned against the instrument, back to that disconcerting model, not a care in the world. Nothing showed on his face but an expression of bland amiability. They were all amiable, never quarrelling together.

The six of them gathered for a scanty lunch, their talk was trite and cheerful, and then the afternoon followed on the same pattern as the morning, as all the other mornings: secure, comfortable, aimless. Only to Harley did the pattern seem slightly out of focus; he now had a clue to the problem. It was small enough, but in the dead calm of their days it was large enough.

May had dropped the clue. When she helped herself to jelly, Jagger laughingly accused her of taking more than her fair share. Dapple, who always defended May, said, "She's taken less than you, Jagger."

"No," May corrected, "I think I *have* more than anyone else. I took it for an interior motive."

It was the kind of pun anyone made at times, but Harley carried it away to consider. He paced round one of the silent rooms. Interior, ulterior motives . . . Did the others here feel the disquiet he felt? Had they a reason for concealing that disquiet? And another question –

Where was "here"?

He shut that one down sharply.

Deal with one thing at a time. Grope your way gently to the abyss. Categorise your knowledge.

One: Earth was getting slightly the worst of a cold war with Nitity.

Two: the Nititians possessed the alarming ability of being able to assume the identical appearance of their enemies.

Three: by this means they could permeate human society.

Four: Earth was unable to view the Nititian civilisation from inside.

Inside . . . a wave of claustrophobia swept over Harley as he realised that these cardinal facts he knew bore no relation to this little world inside. They came, by what means he did not know, from outside, the vast abstraction that none of them had ever seen. He had a mental picture of a starry void in which men and monsters swam or battled, and then swiftly erased it. Such ideas did not conform with the quiet behaviour of his companions; if they never spoke about outside, did they think about it?

Uneasily, Harley moved about the room; the parquet floor echoed the indecision of his footsteps. He had walked into the billiard room. Now he prodded the balls across the green cloth with one finger, preyed on by conflicting intentions. The red spheres touched and rolled apart. That was how the two halves of his mind worked. Irreconcilables: he should stay here and conform; he should – not stay here (remembering no time when he was not here, Harley could frame the second idea no more clearly than that). Another point of pain was that "here" and "not here" seemed to be not two halves of a homogenous whole, but two dissonances.

The ivory slid wearily into a pocket. He decided. He would not sleep in his room tonight.

They came from the various parts of the house to share a bed-time drink. By tacit consent the cards had been postponed until some other time: there was, after all, so much other time.

They talked about the slight nothings that comprised their day, the model of one of the rooms that Calvin was building and May furnishing, the faulty light in the upper corridor which came on too slowly. They were subdued. It was time once more to sleep, and in that sleep who knew what dreams might come? But they *would* sleep. Harley knew – wondering if the others also knew – that with the darkness which descended as they climbed into bed would come an undeniable command to sleep.

He stood tensely just inside his bedroom door, intensely aware of the unorthodoxy of his behaviour. His head hammered painfully and he pressed a cold hand against his temple. He heard the others go one by one to their separate rooms. Pief called good-night to him; Harley replied. Silence fell.

Now!

As he stepped nervously into the passage, the light came on. Yes, it was slow – reluctant. His heart pumped. He was committed. He did not know what he was going to do or what was going to happen, but he was committed. The compulsion to sleep had been avoided. Now he had to hide, and wait.

It is not easy to hide when a light signal follows wherever you go. But by entering a recess which led to a disused room, opening the door slightly and crouching in the doorway, Harley found the faulty landing light dimmed off and left him in the dark.

He was neither happy nor comfortable. His brain seethed in a conflict he hardly understood. He was alarmed to think he had broken the rules and frightened of the creaking darkness about him. But the suspense did not last for long.

The corridor light came back on. Jagger was leaving his bedroom, taking no precaution to be silent. The door swung loudly shut behind him. Harley caught a glimpse of his face before he turned and made for the stairs; he looked non-committal but serene – like a man going off duty. He went downstairs in bouncy, jaunty fashion.

Jagger should have been in bed asleep. A law of nature had been defied.

Unhesitatingly, Harley followed. He had been prepared for something and something had happened, but his flesh crawled with fright. The light-headed notion came to him that he might disintegrate with fear. All the same, he kept doggedly down the stairs, feet noiseless on the heavy carpet.

Jagger had rounded a corner. He was whistling quietly as he went. Harley heard him unlock a door. That would be the store – no other doors were locked. The whistling faded.

The store was open. No sound came from within. Cautiously, Harley peered inside. The far wall had swung open about a central pivot, revealing a passage beyond. For minutes Harley could not move, staring fixedly at this breach.

Finally, and with a sense of suffocation, he entered the store. Jagger had gone through – there. Harley also went through. Somewhere he did not know, somewhere whose existence he had not guessed . . . Somewhere that wasn't the house . . . The passage was short and had two doors, one at the end rather like a cage door (Harley did not recognise a lift when he saw one), one in the side, narrow and with a window.

This window was transparent. Harley looked through it and then fell back choking. Dizziness swept in and shook him by the throat.

Stars shone outside.

With an effort, he mastered himself and made his way back upstairs, lurching against the banisters. They had all been living under a ghastly misapprehension. . . .

He barged into Calvin's room and the light lit. A faint, sweet smell was in the air, and Calvin lay on his broad back, fast asleep.

"Calvin! Wake up!" Harley shouted.

The sleeper never moved. Harley was suddenly aware of his own loneliness and the eerie feel of the great house about him. Bending over the bed, he shook Calvin violently by the shoulders and slapped his face. Calvin groaned and opened one eye.

"Wake up, man," Harley said. "Something terrible's going on here."

The other propped himself on one elbow, communicated fear rousing him thoroughly.

"Jagger's *left the house*," Harley told him. "There's a way outside. We're – we've got to find out what we are." His voice rose to an hysterical pitch. He was shaking Calvin again. "We must find out what's wrong here. Either we are victims of some ghastly experiment – or we're all monsters!"

And as he spoke, before his staring eyes, beneath his clutching hands, Calvin began to wrinkle up and fold and blur, his eyes running together and his great torso contracting. Something else – something lively and alive – was forming in his place.

Harley only stopped yelling when, having plunged downstairs, the sight of the stars through the small window steadied him. He had to get out, wherever "out" was.

He pulled the small door open and stood in fresh night air.

Harley's eye was not accustomed to judging distances. It took him some while to realise the nature of his surroundings, to realise that mountains rose distantly against the starlit sky, and that he himself stood on a platform twelve feet above the ground. Some distance away, lights gleamed, throwing bright rectangles on an expanse of tarmac.

There was a steel ladder at the edge of the platform. Biting his lip, Harley approached it and climbed clumsily down. He was shaking violently with cold and fear. When his feet touched solid ground, he began to run. Once he looked back: the house perched on its platform like a frog hunched on top of a rat trap.

He stopped abruptly then, in almost dark. Abhorrence jerked up inside him like retching. The high, crackling stars and the pale serration of the mountains began to spin, and he clenched his fists to hold on to consciousness. That house, whatever it was, was the embodiment of all the coldness in his mind. Harley said to himself,

"Whatever has been done to me, I've been cheated. Someone has robbed me of something so thoroughly I don't even know what it is. It's been a cheat, a cheat. . . .' And he choked on the idea of those years that had been pilfered from him. No thought: thought scorched the synapses and ran like acid through the brain. Action only! His leg muscles jerked into movement again.

Buildings loomed about him. He simply ran for the nearest light and burst into the nearest door. Then he pulled up sharp, panting and blinking the harsh illumination out of his pupils.

The walls of the room were covered with graphs and charts. In the centre of the room was a wide desk with vision-screen and loud-speaker on it. It was a business-like room with overloaded ashtrays and a state of ordered untidiness. A thin man sat alertly at the desk; he had a thin mouth.

Four other men stood in the room, all were armed, none seemed surprised to see him. The man at the desk wore a neat suit; the others were in uniform.

Harley leant on the door jamb and sobbed. He could find no words to say.

"It has taken you four years to get out of there," the thin man said. He had a thin voice.

"Come and look at this," he said, indicating the screen before him. With an effort, Harley complied; his legs worked like rickety crutches.

On the screen, clear and real, was Calvin's bedroom. The outer wall gaped, and through it two uniformed men were dragging a strange creature, a wiry, mechanical looking being that had once been called Calvin.

"Calvin was a Nititian," Harley observed dully. He was conscious of a sort of stupid surprise at his own observation.

The thin man nodded approvingly.

"Enemy infiltrations constituted quite a threat," he said. "Nowhere on Earth was safe from them: they can kill a man, dispose of him and turn into exact replicas of him. Makes things difficult . . . We lost a lot of state secrets that way. But Nititian ships have to land here to disembark the Non-Men and to pick them up again after their work is done. That is the weak link in their chain.

"We intercepted one such ship-load and bagged them singly after they had assumed humanoid form. We subjected them to artificial amnesia and put small groups of them into different environments for study. This is the Army Institute for Investigation of Non-Men, by the way. We've learnt a lot . . . quite enough to combat the menace . . . Your group, of course, was one such."

Harley asked in a gritty voice, "Why did you put me in with them?"

The thin man rattled a ruler between his teeth before answering. "Each group has to have a human observer in their very midst, despite all the scanning devices that watch from outside. You see, a Nititian uses a deal of energy maintaining a human form; once in that shape, he is kept in it by self-hypnosis which only breaks down in times of stress, the amount of stress bearable varying from one individual to another. A human on the spot can sense such stresses . . . It's a tiring job for him; we get doubles always to work day on, day off – "

"But I've always been there – "

"Of your group," the thin man cut in, "the human was Jagger, or two men alternating as Jagger. You caught one of them going off duty."

"That doesn't make sense," Harley shouted. "You're trying to say that I – "

He choked on the words. They were no longer pronounceable. He felt his outer form flowing away like sand as from the other side of the desk revolver barrels were levelled at him.

"Your stress level is remarkably high," continued the thin man, turning his gaze away from the spectacle. "But where you fail is where you all fail. Like Earth's insects which imitate vegetables, your cleverness cripples you. You can only be carbon copies. Because Jagger did nothing in the house, all the rest of you instinctively followed suit. You didn't get bored – you didn't even try to make passes at Dapple – as personable a Non-Man as I ever saw. Even the model spaceship jerked no appreciable reaction out of you."

Brushing his suit down, he rose before the skeletal being which now cowered in a corner.

"The inhumanity inside will always give you away," he said evenly. "However human you are outside."

(1955)

The Failed Men

"It's too crowded here!" he exclaimed aloud. "It's too crowded! It's too CROWDED!"

He swung round, his mouth open, his face contorted like a squeezed lemon, nearly knocking a passer-by off the pavement. The passer-by bowed, smiled forgivingly and passed on, his eyes clearly saying: "Let him be – it's one of the poor devils off the ship."

"It's too crowded," Surrey Edmark said again at the retreating back. It was night. He stood hatless under the glare of the New Orchard Road lights, bewildered by the flowing cosmopolitan life of Singapore about him. People: thousands of 'em, touchable; put out a hand gently, feel alpaca, silk, nylon, satin, plain, patterned, or crazily flowered; thousands within screaming distance. If you screamed, just how many of those dirty, clean, pink, brown, desirable or offensive convoluted ears would scoop up your decibels?

No, he told himself, no screaming, please. These people who swarm like phantoms about you are real; they wouldn't like it. And your doctor, who did not consider you fit to leave the observation ward yet, he's real enough; he wouldn't like it if he learnt you had been screaming in a main street. And you yourself – how real were you? How real was *anything* when you had recently had perfect proof that it was all finished? Really finished: rolled up and done with and discarded and forgotten.

That dusty line of thought must be avoided. He needed somewhere quiet, a place to sit and breathe deeply. Everyone must be deceived; he must hide the fused, dead feeling inside from them; then he could go back home. But he had also to try and hide the deadness from himself, and that needed more cunning. Like alpha particles, a sense of futility had riddled him, and he was mortally sick.

Surrey noticed a turning just ahead. Thankfully he went to it and branched out of the crowds into a dim, narrow thoroughfare. He passed three women in short dresses smoking together; further on a fellow was being sick into a privet hedge. And there was a café with a sign saying "The Iceberg". Deserted chairs and tables stood outside on an ill-lit veranda; Surrey climbed the two steps and sat wearily down. This was luxury.

The light was poor, Surrey sat alone. Inside the café several people were eating, and a girl sang, accompanying herself on a stringed, lute-like instrument. He couldn't understand the words, but it was simple and nostalgic, her voice conveying more than the music; he closed his eyes, letting the top spin within him, the top of his emotions. The girl ceased her singing suddenly, as if tired, and walked on to the veranda to stare into the night. Surrey opened his eyes and looked at her.

"Come and talk to me," he called.

She turned her head haughtily to the shadows where he sat, and then turned it back. Evidently, she had met with that sort of invitation before. Surrey clenched his fists in frustration; here he sat, isolated in space and time, needing comfort, needing . . . oh, nothing could heal him, but salves existed. . . . The loneliness welled up inside, forcing him to speak again.

"I'm from the ship," he said, unable to hold back a note of pleading.

At that, she came over and took a seat facing him. She was Chinese, and wore the timeless slit dress of her race, big daisies chasing themselves over the gentle contours of her body.

"Of course I didn't know," she said. "But I can see in your eyes . . . that you are from the ship." She trembled slightly and asked: "May I get you a drink?"

Surrey shook his head. "Just to have you sitting there. . . ."

He was feeling better. Irrationally, a voice inside said: "Well, you've been through a harsh experience, but now you're back again you can recover, can't you, go back to what you were?" The voice frequently asked that: but the answer was always No; the experience was still spreading inside, like cancer.

"I heard your ship come in," the Chinese girl said. "I live just near here – Bukit Timah Road, if you know it, and I was at my window, talking with a friend."

He thought of the amazing sunshine and the eternal smell of cooking fats and the robshaws clacking by and this girl and her friend chattering in a little attic – and the orchestral crash as the ship arrived, making them forget their sentences: but all remote, centuries ago.

"It's a funny noise it makes," he said. "The sound of a time ship breaking out of the time barrier."

"It scares the chickens," she said.

Silence. Surrey wanted to produce something else to say, to keep the girl sitting with him, but nothing would dissolve into words. He neglected the factor of her own human curiosity, which made her keen to stay; she inquired again if he would like a drink, and then said: "Would it be good for you if you told me something about it?"

"I'd call that a leading question."

"It's very – *bad* ahead, isn't it? I mean, the papers say. . . ." She hesitated nervously.

"What do they say?" he asked.

"Oh, you know, they say that it's bad. But they don't really explain; they don't seem to understand."

"That's the whole key to it," he told her. "We don't seem to understand. If I talked to you all night, you still wouldn't understand. *I* wouldn't understand. . . ."

She was beautiful, sitting there with her little lute in her hand. And he had travelled far away beyond her lute and her beauty, far beyond nationality or even music; it had all gone into the dreary dust of the planet, all gone – final – nothing left – except degradation. And puzzlement.

"I'll try and tell you," he said. "What was that tune you were just singing? Chinese song?"

"No, it was Malayan. It's an old song, very old, called 'Terang Boelan'. It's about – oh, moonlight, you know, that kind of thing. It's sentimental."

"I didn't even know what language it was in, but perhaps in a way I understood it."

"You said you were going to tell me about the future," she told him gently.

"Yes. Of course. It's a sort of tremendous relief work we're doing. You know what they call it: The Intertemporal Red Cross. It's accurate, but when you've actually been – ahead, it sounds a silly, flashy, title. I don't know, perhaps not. I'm not sure of anything any more."

He stared out at the darkness; it was going to rain. When he began to speak again, his voice was firmer.

The I.R.C. is really organised by the Paulls (he said to the Chinese girl). They call themselves the Paulls; we should call them the technological *élite* of the Three Thousand, One Hundred and Fifty-Seventh Century. That's a terrible long way ahead – we, with our twenty-four centuries since Christ can hardly visualise it. Our ship stopped there, in their time. It was very austere: the Paulls are austere people. They live only on mountains overlooking the oceans, and have moved mountains to every coast for their own edification.

The Paulls are unlike us, yet they are brothers compared with the men we are helping, the Failed Men.

Time travel had been invented long before the age of the Paulls, but it is they who perfected it, they who accidentally discovered the plight of the Failed Men, and they who manage the terrific business of relief. For the world of the Paulls, rich as it is – will be, has insufficient resources to cope alone with the task without vitiating its strength. So it organized the fleet of time ships, the I.T.R., to collect supplies from different ages and bear them out ahead to the Failed Men.

Five different ages are co-operating on the project, under the Paull leadership. There are the Middle People, as the Paulls call them. They are a race of philosophers, mainly pastoral, and we found them too haughty; they live about twenty thousand centuries ahead of the Paulls. Oh, it's a long time. . . . And there are – but never mind that! They had little to do with us, or we with them.

We – this present day, was the only age without time travel of the five. The Paulls chose us because we happen to have peace and plenty. And do you know what they call us? The Children. The Children! We, with all our weary sophistication. . . . Perhaps they're right; they have a method of gestalt reasoning absolutely beyond our wildest pretensions.

You know, I remember once on the voyage out ahead, I asked one of the Paulls why they had never visited our age before; and he said: "But we have. We broke at the nineteenth century and again at the twenty-sixth. That's pretty close spacing! And that's how we knew so much about you."

They have so much *experience*, you see. They can walk round for a day in one century and tell you what'll be happening the next six or seven. It's a difference of outlook, I suppose; something as simple as that.

I suppose you'll remember better than I when the Paulls first broke here, as you are actually on the spot. I was at home then, doing a peaceful job; if it hadn't been so peaceful I might not have volunteered for the I.R.C. What a storm it caused! A good deal of panic in with the excitement. Yes, we proved ourselves children then, *and* in the adulation we paid the Paulls while they toured the

world's capitals. During the three months they waited here while
we organized supplies and men, they must have been in a fury of
impatience to be off; yet they revealed nothing, giving their unsen-
sational lectures on the plight of the Failed Men and smiling for the
threedy cameras.

All the while money poured in for the cause, and the piles of
tinned food and medical supplies grew and filled the holds of the
big ship. We were like kids throwing credits to street beggars: all
sorts of stuff of no earthly use went into that ship. What would a
Failed Man do with a launderer or a cycloview machine? At last we
were off, with all the world's bands playing like mad and the ship
breaking with noise enough to drown all bands and startle your
chickens – off for the time of the Failed Men!

"I think I'd like that drink you offered me now," Surrey said to the
Chinese girl, breaking off his narrative.

"Certainly." She snapped her fingers at arm's length, her hand in
the light from the restaurant, her face in the gloom, eyes fixed on
his eyes.

"The Paulls had told you it was going to be tough," she said.

"Yes. We underwent pretty rough mental training from them
before leaving the here and now. Many of the men were weeded
out. But I got through. They elected me Steersman. I was top of
their first class."

Surrey was silent a moment, surprised to hear pride in his own
voice. Pride left, after that experience! Yet there was no pride in
him; it was just the voice running in an old channel, the naked soul
crouching in an ancient husk of character.

The drink arrived. The Chinese girl had one, too, a long one in a
misty glass; she put her lute down to drink it. Surrey took a sip of
his and then resumed the story.

We were travelling ahead! (he said). It was a schoolboy's dream
come true. Yet our excitement soon became blunted by monotony.
There is nothing simultaneous in time travel, as people have
imagined. It took us two ship's months to reach the Paulls' age,
and there all but one of them left us to continue on alone into the
future.

They had the other ages to supervise, and many organizational
problems to attend to: yet I sometimes wonder if they did not use

those problems as an excuse, to save their having to visit the age of
the Failed Men. Perhaps they thought us less sensitive, and therefore better fitted for the job.

And so we went ahead again. The office of Steersman was almost
honorary, entailing some tempogation and the switching off of
power when the journey ended. We sat about and talked, we chosen
few, reading or viewing in the excellent libraries the Paulls had
installed. Time passed quickly enough, yet we were glad when we
arrived.

Glad!

The age of the Failed Men is far in the future: many hundred
millions of years ahead, or thousands of millions; the Paulls would
never tell us the exact number. Does it matter? It was a long
time. . . . There's plenty of time – too much, more than anyone
will ever need.

We stepped out on to that day's earth. I had childishly expected
– oh, to see the sun stuck at the horizon, or turned purple, or the
sky full of moons, or something equally dramatic; but there was not
even a shadow over the fair land, and the earth had not aged a day.
Only man had aged.

The Failed Men differed from us anatomically and spiritually; it
was the former quality which struck us first. They just looked like a
bunch of dejected oddities sitting among piles of stores, and we
wanted to laugh. The humorists among us called them "the Zombies" at first – but in a few days there were no humorists left among
us.

The Failed Men had no real hands. From their wrists grew five
long and prehensile fingers, and the middle digit touched the ground
lightly when they walked, for their spines curved in an arc and their
heads were thrust far forward. To counter this, their skulls had
elongated into boat shapes, scaphocephalic fashion. They had no
eyebrows, nor indeed a brow at all, nor any hair at all, although the
pores of their skin stood out flakily, giving them a fluffy appearance
from a distance.

When they looked at you their eyes held no meaning: they were
blank with a surfeit of experience, as though they had now regained
a horrible sort of innocence. When they spoke to you, their voices
were hollow and their sentences as short and painful as a child's
toothache. We could not understand their language, except through
the electronic translator banks given us by the Paulls.

They looked a mournful sight, but at first we were not too
disturbed; we didn't, you see, quite grasp the nature of the problem.

Also, we were very busy, reclaiming more Failed Men from the ground.

Four great aid centres had been established on the earth. Of the other four races in the I.R.C., two managed sanatoria construction and equipment, another nursing, feeding and staffing, and the fourth communication, rehabilitation and liaison between centres. And we – "the Children!" – our job was to exhume the Failed Men and bring them to the centres: a simple job for the simple group! Between us we all had to get the race of man started again – back into harness.

All told, I suppose there are only about six million Failed Men spread over the earth. We had to go out and dig them up. We had specially made tractors with multiple blades on the front which dug slowly and gently into the soil.

The Failed Men had "cemetery areas"; we called them that, although they had not been designed as cemeteries. It was like a bad, silly dream. Working day and night, we trundled forward, furrowing up the earth as you strip back a soiled bed. In the mould, a face would appear, an arm with the long fingers, a pair of legs, tumbling into the light. We would stop the machine and get down to the body, digging with trowels round it. So we would exhume another man or woman – it was hard to tell which they were: their sexual features were not pronounced.

They would be in coma. Their eyes would open, staring like peek-a-boo dolls, then close again with a click. We'd patch them up with an injection, stack them on stretchers and send them back in a load to base. It was a harrowing job, and no pun intended.

When the corpses had had some attention and care, they revived. Within a month they would be up and walking, trundling about the hospital grounds in that round-shouldered way, their great boat-heads nodding at every step. And then it was I talked to them and tried to understand.

The translator banks, being Paull made, were the best possible. But their limitations were the limitations of our own language. If the Failed Men said their word for "sun", the machine said "sun" to us, and we understood by that the same thing the Failed Men intended. But away from the few concrete, common facts of our experience, the business was less easy. Less synonyms, more overtones: it was the old linguistic problem, but magnified here by the ages which lay between us.

I remember tackling one old woman on our first spell back at the centre. I say old, but for all I know she was sweet sixteen; they just looked ancient.

"I hope you don't mind being dug – er, rescued?" I asked politely.

"Not at all. A pleasure," the banks said for her. Polite sterotypes. No real meaning in any language, but the best machine in the world makes them sound sillier than they are.

"Would you mind if we discussed this whole thing?"

"What object?" the banks asked for her.

I'd asked the wrong question. I did not mean thing=object, but thing=matter. That sort of trip-up kept getting in the way of our discussion; the translator spoke more precise English than I.

"Can we talk about your problem?" I asked her, trying again.

"I have no problem. My problem has been resolved."

"I should be interested to hear about it."

"What do you require to know about it? I will tell you anything."

That at least was promising. Willing if not co-operative; they had long ago forgotten the principle of co-operation.

"You know I come from the distant past to help you?" The banks translated me undramatically.

"Yes. It is noble of you all to interrupt your lives for us," she said.

"Oh no; we want to see the race of man starting off again on a right track. We believe it should not die away yet. We are glad to help, and are sorry you took the wrong track."

"When we started, we were on a track others before us – you – had made." It was not defiant, just a fact being stated.

"But the deviation was yours. You made it by an act of will. I'm not condemning, mind; obviously you would not have taken that way had you known it would end in failure."

She answered. I gathered she was just faintly angry, probably burning all the emotion in her. Her hollow voice spanged and doomed away, and the translator banks gave out simultaneously in fluent English. Only it didn't make sense.

It went something like this: "Ah, but what you do not realise, because your realising is completely undeveloped and unstarted, is how to fail. Failing is not failing unless it is defeat, and this defeat of ours – if you realise it *is* a failing – is only a failure. A final failure. But as such, it is only a matter of a result, because in time this realisation tends to breed only the realisation of the result of failure; whereas the resolution of our failure, as opposed to the failure – "

"Stop!" I shouted. "No! Save the modern poetry or the philosophical treatise for later. It doesn't mean anything to me, I'm sorry. We'll take it for granted there was some sort of a failure. Are you going to be able to make a success of this new start we're giving you?"

"It is not a new start," she said, beginning reasonably enough. "Once you have had the result, a start resembles the result. It is merely in the result of failing and all that is in the case is the start or the failure – depending, for us, on the start, for you on the failure. And you can surely see that even here failure depends abnormally on the beginning of the result, which concerns us more than the failure, simply because it is the result. What you don't see is the synchronicity of the resolution of the result's failure to initiate – "

"Stop!" I shouted again.

I went to one of the Paull commanders. He was what my mother would have called "a fine man". I told him the thing was beginning to become an obsession with me.

"It is with all of us," he replied.

"But if only I could grasp a fraction of their problem! Look, Commander, we come out here all this way ahead to help them – and still we don't know what we're helping them *from*."

"We know *why* we're helping them, Edmark. The burden of carrying on the race, of breeding a new and more stable generation, is on them. Keep your eye on that, if possible."

Perhaps his smile was a shade too placating; it made me remember that to him we were "the Children".

"Look," I said pugnaciously. "If those shambling failures can't tell us what's happened to them, you can. Either you tell me, or we pack up and go home. Our fellows have the creeps, I tell you! Now what – *explicitly* – is wrong with these Zombies?"

The commander laughed.

"We don't know," he said. "We don't know, and that's all there is to it."

He stood up then, austere, tall, "a fine man". He went and looked out of the window, hands behind his back, and I could tell by his eyes he was looking at Failed Men, down there in the pale afternoon.

He turned and said to me? "This sanatorium was designed for Failed Men. But we're filling up with relief staff instead; they've let the problem get them by the throat."

"I can understand that," I said. "I shall be there myself if I don't get to the root of it, racing the others up the wall."

He held up his hand.

"That's what they *all* say. But there is no root of it to get at, or none we can comprehend, or else we are part of the root ourselves. If you could only *categorize* their failure it would be something: religious, spiritual, economic. . . ."

"So it's got *you* too!" I said.

"Look," I said suddenly. "You've got the time ships. Go back and *see* what the problem was!"

The solution was so simple I couldn't think how they had overlooked it; but of course they hadn't overlooked it.

"We've been," the commander said briefly. "A problem of the mind – presuming it was a mental problem – cannot be seen. All we *saw* was the six million of them singly burying themselves in these damned shallow graves. The process covered over a century; some of them had been under for three hundred years before we rescued them. No, it's no good, the problem from our point of view is linguistic."

"The translator banks are no good," I said sweepingly. "It's all too delicate a job for a machine. Could you lend me a human interpreter?"

He came himself, in the end. He didn't want to, but he wanted to. And how would a machine cope with that statement? Yet to you and me it's perfectly comprehensible.

A woman, one of the Failed Men, was walking slowly across the courtyard as we got outside. It might have been the one I had already spoken to, I don't know. I didn't recognise her and she gave no sign of recognising me. Anyhow, we stopped her and tried our luck.

"Ask her why they buried themselves, for a start," I said.

The Paull translated and she doomed briefly in reply.

"She says it was considered necessary, as it aided the union before the beginning of the attempt," he told me.

"Ask her what union."

Exchange of dooms.

"The union of the union that they were attempting. Whatever that means."

"Did both 'unions' sound the same to you?"

"One was inflected, as it was in the possessive case," the Paull said. "Otherwise they seemed just alike. 'Conjunction', perhaps."

"Ask her – ask her if they were all trying to change themselves into something other than human – you know, into spirits or golems or ghosts."

"They've only got a word for spirit. Or rather, they've got four words for spirit: spirit of soul; spirit of place; spirit of a non-substantive, such as 'spirit of adventure'; and another sort of spirit or essence I cannot define – we haven't an exact analogy for it."

"Hell's bells! Well, try her with spirit of soul."

Again the melancholy rattle of exchange. Then the commander, with some surprise, said: "She says, Yes, they were striving to attain spirituality."

"Now we're getting somewhere!" I exclaimed, thinking smugly that it just needed persistence and a twenty-fifth-century brain.

The old woman clanged again.

"What's that?" I asked eagerly.

"She says they're still striving after spirituality."

We both groaned. The lead was merely a dead end.

"It's no good," the Paull said gently. "Give up."

"One last question! Tell the old girl we cannot understand the nature of what has happened to her race. Was it a catastrophe and what was its nature? O.K.?"

"Can but try. Don't imagine this hasn't been done before, though – it's purely for your benefit."

He spoke. She answered briefly.

"She says it was an 'antwerto'. That means it was a catastrophe to end all catastrophes."

"Well, at least we're definite on that."

"Oh yes, they failed all right, whatever it was they were after," the Paull said sombrely.

"The nature of the catastrophe?"

"She just gives me an innocent little word, 'struback'. Unfortunately we don't know what it means."

"I see. Ask her if it is something to do with evolution."

"My dear man, this is all a waste of time! I know the answers, as far as they exist, without speaking to this woman at all."

"Ask her if 'struback' means something to do with a possible way they were evolving or meaning to evolve," I persisted.

He asked her. The ill-matched three of us stood there for a long time while the old woman moaned her reply. At last she was silent.

"She says struback has some vague connection with evolution," the commander told me. "The question was one of determinism."

"Is that *all*?"

"Oh, God, man! Far from it, but that's what it boils down to! 'Time impresses itself on man as evolution,' she says."

"Ask her if the nature of the catastrophe was at least partly religious."

When she had replied, the commander laughed shortly and said: "She wants to know what 'religious' means. And I'm sorry but I'm not going to stand here while you tell her."

"But just because she doesn't know what it means doesn't mean to say the failure, the catastrophe, wasn't religious in essence."

"Nothing means to say anything here," the commander said angrily. Then he realized he was only talking to one of the Children; he went on more gently: "Supposing that instead of coming ahead, we had gone back in time. Suppose we met a prehistoric tribe of hunters. Right! We learn their language. We want to use the word 'luck'. In their superstitious minds the concept – and consequently the word – does not exist. We have to use a substitute they can accept, 'accident', or 'good-happening' or 'bad-happening', as the case may be. They understand that all right, but by it they mean something entirely different from our intention. We have not broken through the barrier at all, merely become further entangled in it. The same trap is operating here.

"And now, please excuse me."

Struback. A long, hollow syllable, followed by a short click. Night after night, I turned that word over in my tired mind. It became the symbol of the Failed Men: but never anything more.

Most of the others caught the worry. Some drifted away in a kind of trance, some went into the wards. The tractors became under-manned. Reinforcements, of course, were arriving from the present. The present! I could not think of it that way. The time of the Failed Men became my present, and my past and future, too.

I worked with the translator banks again, unable to accept defeat. I had this idea in my head that the Failed Men had been trying – and possibly involuntarily – to turn into something superior to man, a sort of super-being, and I was intensely curious about this.

"Tell me," I demanded of an old man, speaking through the banks, "when you all first had this idea, or when it came to you, you were all glad then?"

His answer came: "Where there is failure there is only degrada-tion. You cannot understand the degradation, because you are not of us. There is only degradation and misery and you do not comprehend – "

"Wait! I'm *trying* to comprehend! Help me, can't you? Tell me *why* it was so degrading, why you failed, how you failed."

"The degradation was the failure," he said. "The failure was the struback, the struback was the misery."

"You mean there was *just* misery, even at the beginning of the experiment?"

"There was no beginning, only a finish, and that was the result."

I clutched my head.

"Wasn't burying yourself a beginning?"

"No."

"What was it?"

"It was only a part of the attempt."

"What attempt?"

"You are so stupid. Can you not see? The attempt we were making for the resolution of the predetermined problem in the result of our united resolve to solve the problem."

"Which problem?"

"*The* problem," he said wearily. "The problem of the resolution of this case into the start of failure. It does not matter how the resolution is accomplished provided all the cases are the same, but in a diversity of cases the start determines the resolution and the finish arbitrarily determines the beginning of the case. But the arbitrary factor is itself inherent in the beginning of the case, and of the case itself. Consequently our case is in the same case, and the failure was defined by the start, the start being our resolution."

It was hopeless. "You are really trying to explain?" I asked weakly.

"No, you dull young man," he said. "I am telling you about the failure. You are the struback."

And he walked away.

Surrey looked hopelessly across at the Chinese girl. She tapped her fingers on the table.

"What did he mean, 'You are the struback'?" she asked.

"Anything or nothing," he said wildly. "It would have been no good asking him to elucidate – I shouldn't have understood the elucidation. You see it's all either too complex or too simple for us to grasp."

"But *surely* – " she said, and then hesitated.

"The Failed Men could only think in abstractions," he said. "Perhaps that was a factor involved in their failure – I don't know. You see, language is the most intrinsic product of any culture; you can't comprehend the language till you've understood the culture – and how do you understand a culture till you know its language?"

Surrey looked helplessly at the girl's little lute with its own trapped tongue. Suddenly, the hot silence of the night was shattered by a great orchestral crash half a mile away.

"Another cartload of nervous wrecks coming home," he told her grimly. "You'd better go and see to your chickens."

(1957)

All the World's Tears

If you could collect up all the tears that have fallen in the history of the world, you would have not only a vast sheet of water: you would have the history of the world.

Some such reflection as this occurred to J. Smithlao, the psychodynamician, as he stood in the 139th sector of Ing Land watching the brief and tragic love of the wild man and Charles Gunpat's daughter. Hidden behind a beech tree, Smithlao saw the wild man walking warily across the terrace; Gunpat's daughter, Ployploy, stood at the far end of the terrace, waiting for him.

The world waited.

It was the last day of summer in the last year of the forty-fourth century. The wind that rustled Ployploy's dress breathed leaves against her; it sighed round the fantastic and desolate garden like fate at a christening, ruining the last of the roses. Later, the tumbling pattern of petals would be sucked from paths, lawn and patio by the steel gardener. Now, it made a tiny tide round the wild man's feet as he stretched out his hand to touch Ployploy.

Then it was that the tear glittered in her eyes.

Hidden, fascinated, Smithlao the psychodynamician saw that tear. Except perhaps for a stupid robot, he was the only one who saw it, the only one who saw the whole episode. And although he was shallow and hard by the standards of other ages, he was human enough to sense that here – here on the greying terrace – was a little charade that marked the end of all that Man had been.

After the tear, of course, came the explosion. Just for a minute, a new wind lived among the winds of earth.

Only by accident was Smithlao walking in Charles Gunpat's estate. He had come on the routine errand, as Gunpat's psychodynamician, of administering a hate-brace to the old man. Oddly enough, as he swept in for a landing, leafing his vane down from the stratosphere, Smithlao had caught a glimpse of the wild man approaching Gunpat's estate.

Under the slowing vane, the landscape was as neat as a blueprint.

The impoverished fields made impeccable rectangles. Here and there, one robot machine or another kept nature to its own functional image; not a pea podded without cybernetic supervision; not a bee bumbled among stamens without radar check being kept of its course. Every bird had a number and a call sign, while among every tribe of ants marched the metallic teller ants, tell-taling the secrets of the nest back to base. The old, comfortable world of random factors had vanished under the pressure of hunger.

Nothing living lived without control. The countless populations of previous centuries had exhausted the soil. Only the severest parsimony, coupled with fierce regimentation, produced enough nourishment from the present sparse population. The billions had died of starvation; the hundreds who remained lived on starvation's brink.

In the sterile neatness of the landscape, Gunpat's estate looked like an insult. Covering five acres, it was a little island of wilderness. Tall and unkempt elms fenced the perimeter, encroaching on the lawns and house. The house itself, the chief one in Sector 139, was built of massive stone blocks. It had to be strong to bear the weight of the servo-mechanisms which, apart from Gunpat and his daughter, Ployploy, were its only occupants.

It was just as Smithlao dropped below tree-level that he thought he saw a human figure plodding towards the estate. For a multitude of reasons, this was very unlikely. The great material wealth of the world being now shared among comparatively few people, nobody was poor enough to have to walk anywhere. Man's increasing hatred of Nature, spurred by the notion it had betrayed him, would make such a walk purgatory – unless the man were insane, like Ployploy.

Dismissing the figure from his thoughts, Smithlao dropped the vane onto a stretch of stone. He was glad to get down: it was a gusty day, and the piled cumulus he had descended through had been full of air pockets. Gunpat's house, with its sightless windows, its towers, its endless terraces, its unnecessary ornamentation, its massive porch, lowered at him like a forsaken wedding cake.

There was activity at once. Three wheeled robots approached from different directions, swivelling light atomic weapons at him as they drew near.

Nobody, Smithlao thought, could get in here uninvited. Gunpat was not a friendly man, even by the unfriendly standards of his time.

"Say who you are," demanded the leading machine. It was ugly and flat, vaguely resembling a toad.

"I am J. Smithlao, psychodynamician to Charles Gunpat," Smithlao replied; he had to go through this procedure every visit. As he spoke, he revealed his face to the machine. It grunted to itself, checking picture and information with its memory. Finally it said, "You are J. Smithlao, psychodynamician to Charles Gunpat. What do you want?"

Cursing its monstrous slowness, Smithlao told the robot, "I have an appointment with Charles Gunpat at ten hours," and waited while that was digested.

"You have an appointment with Charles Gunpat at ten hours," the robot finally confirmed. "Come this way."

It wheeled about with surprising grace, speaking to the other two robots, reassuring them, repeating mechanically to them, "This is J. Smithlao, psychodynamician to Charles Gunpat. He has an appointment with Charles Gunpat at ten hours," in case they had not grasped these facts.

Meanwhile, Smithlao spoke to his vane. A part of the cabin, with him in it, detached itself from the rest and lowered wheels to the ground, becoming a mobile sedan. Carrying Smithlao, it followed the other robots.

Automatic screens came up, covering the windows, as Smithlao moved into the presence of other humans. He could only see and be seen via telescreens. Such was the hatred (equals fear) man bore for his fellow man, he could not tolerate them regarding him direct.

One following another, the machines climbed along the terraces, through the great porch, where they were covered in a mist of disinfectant, along a labyrinth of corridors, and so into the presence of Charles Gunpat.

Gunpat's dark face on the screen of his sedan showed only the mildest distaste for the sight of his psychodynamician. He was usually as self-controlled as this: it told against him at his business meetings, where the idea was to cow one's opponents by splendid displays of rage. For this reason, Smithlao was always summoned to administer a hate-brace when something important loomed on the day's agenda.

Smithlao's machine manoeuvred him within a yard of his patient's image, much closer than courtesy required.

"I'm late," Smithlao began, matter-of-factly, "because I could not bear to drag myself into your offensive presence one minute sooner.

I hoped that if I left it long enough, some happy accident might have removed that stupid nose from your – what shall I call it? – *face*. Alas, it's still there, with its two nostrils sweeping like rat-holes into your skull. I've often wondered, Gunpat, don't you ever catch your big feet in those holes and fall over?"

Observing his patient's face carefully, Smithlao saw only the faintest stir of irritation. No doubt about it, Gunpat was a hard man to rouse. Fortunately, Smithlao was an expert in his profession; he proceeded to try the insult subtle.

"But of course you would never fall over," he proceeded, "because you are too depressingly ignorant to know up from down. You don't even know how many robots make five. Why, when it was your turn to go to the capital to the Mating Centre, you didn't even realise that was the one time a man has to come out from behind his screen. You thought you could make love by tele! And what was the result? One dotty daughter . . . one dotty daughter, Gunpat! Think how your rivals at Automotion must titter at that, sunny boy. 'Potty Gunpat and his dotty daughter', they'll be saying. 'Can't control your genes', they'll be saying."

The taunts were having their desired effect. A flush spread over the image of Gunpat's face.

"There's nothing wrong with Ployploy except that she's a recessive – you said that yourself!" he snapped.

He was beginning to answer back; that was a good sign. His daughter was always a soft spot in his armour.

"A recessive!" Smithlao sneered. "How far back can you recede?! She's *gentle*, do you hear me, you with the hair in your ears? She wants to *love*!" He bellowed with ironic laughter. "Oh, it's obscene, Gunnyboy! She couldn't hate to save her life. She's no better than a savage. She's worse than a savage, she's mad!"

"She's not mad," Gunpat said, gripping both sides of his screen. At this rate, he would be primed for the conference in ten more minutes.

"Not mad?" the psychodynamician asked, his voice assuming a bantering note. "No, Ployploy's not mad: the Mating Centre only refused her the right even to breed, that's all. Imperial Government only refused her the right to a televote, that's all. United Traders only refused her a Consumption Rating, that's all. Education Inc only restricted her to beta recreations, that's all. She's a prisoner here because she's a genius, is that it? You're crazy, Gunpat, if you don't think that girl's stark, staring looney. You'll be telling me next, out of that grotesque, flapping mouth, that she hasn't got a white face."

Gunpat made gobbling sounds.

"You dare to mention that!" he gasped. "And what if her face is – that colour?"

"You ask such fool questions, it's hardly worth while bothering with you," Smithlao said mildly. "Your trouble, Gunpat, is that your big bone head is totally incapable of absorbing one single simple historical fact. Ployploy is white because she is a dirty little throwback. Our ancient enemies were white. They occupied this part of the globe, Ing Land and You-Rohp, until the twenty-fourth century, when our ancestors rose from the East and took from them the ancient privileges they had so long enjoyed at our expense. Our ancestors intermarried with such of the defeated that survived.

"In a few generations, the white strain was obliterated, diluted, lost. A white face has not been seen on earth since before the terrible Age of Over-Population: fifteen hundred years, let's say. And *then* – then little lord recessive Gunpat throws one up neat as you please. What did they give you at Mating Centre, sunny boy, a *cavewoman*?"

Gunpat exploded in fury, shaking his fist at the screen.

"You're sacked, Smithlao," he snarled. "This time you've gone too far, even for a dirty, rotten psycho! Get out! Go on, get, and never come back again!"

Abruptly, he bellowed to his auto-operator to switch him over to the conference. He was just in a ripe mood to deal with Automotion and its fellow crooks.

As Gunpat's irate image faded from the screen, Smithlao sighed and relaxed. The hate-brace was accomplished. It was the supreme compliment in his profession to be dismissed by a patient at the end of a session; Gunpat would be all the keener to re-engage him next time. All the same, Smithlao felt no triumph. In his calling, a thorough exploration of human psychology was needed; he had to know exactly the sorest points in a man's make-up. By playing on those points deftly enough, he could rouse the man to action.

Without being roused, men were helpless prey to lethargy, bundles of rag carried round by machines. The ancient drives had died and left them.

Smithlao sat where he was, gazing into both past and future.

In exhausting the soil, man had exhausted himself. The psyche and a vitiated topsoil could not exist simultaneously; it was as simple and as logical as that.

Only the failing tides of hate and anger lent man enough impetus to continue at all. Else, he was just a dead hand across his mechanised world.

So this is how a species becomes extinct! thought Smithlao, and wondered if anyone else had thought it. Perhaps Imperial Government knew all about it, but was powerless to do anything; after all, what more could you do than was being done?

Smithlao was a shallow man – inevitably in a caste-bound society so weak that it could not face itself. Having discovered the terrifying problem, he set himself to forget it, to evade its impact, to dodge any personal implications it might have. With a grunt to his sedan, he turned about and ordered himself home.

Since Gunpat's robot had already left, Smithlao travelled back alone the way he had come. He was trundled outside and back to the vane, standing silent below the elms.

Before the sedan incorporated itself back into the vane, a movement caught Smithlao's eye. Half concealed by a veranda, Ployploy stood against a corner of the house. With a sudden impulse of curiosity, Smithlao got out of the sedan. The open air, besides being in motion, stank of roses and clouds and green things turning dark with the thought of autumn. It was frightening for Smithlao, but an adventurous impulse made him go on.

The girl was not looking in his direction; she peered towards the barricade of trees which cut her off from the world. As Smithlao approached, she moved round to the rear of the house, still staring intently. He followed with caution, taking advantage of the cover afforded by a small plantation. A metal gardener nearby continued to wield shears along a grass verge, unaware of his existence.

Ployploy now stood at the back of the house. Here a rococo fancy of ancient Italy had mingled with a Chinese genius for fantastic portal and roof. Balustrades rose and fell, stairs marched through circular arches, grey and azure eaves swept almost to the ground. But all was sadly neglected: virginia creeper, already hinting at its glory to come, strove to pull down the marble statuary; troughs of rose petals clogged every sweeping staircase. And all this formed the ideal background for the forlorn figure of Ployploy.

Except for her delicate pink lips, her face was utterly pale. Her hair was utterly black; it hung straight, secured only once, at the back of her head, and then falling in a tail to her waist. She looked mad indeed, her melancholy eyes peering towards the great elms as if they would scorch down everything in their line of vision. Smithlao turned to see what she stared at so compellingly.

The wild man was just breaking through the thickets round the elm boles.

A sudden shower came down, rattling among the dry leaves of the shrubbery. Like a spring shower, it was over in a flash; during the momentary downpour, Ployploy never shifted her position, the wild man never looked up. Then the sun burst through, cascading a pattern of elm shadow over the house, and every flower wore a jewel of rain.

Smithlao thought of what he had thought in Gunpat's room. Now he added this rider: it would be so easy for Nature, when parasite man was extinct, to begin again.

He waited tensely, knowing a fragment of drama was about to take place before his eyes. Across the sparkling lawn, a tiny tracked thing scuttled, pogo-ing itself up steps and out of sight through an arch. It was a perimeter guard, off to give the alarm.

In a minute it returned. Four big robots accompanied it; one of them Smithlao recognised as the toad-like machine that had challenged his arrival. They threaded their way purposefully among the rose bushes, five different shaped menaces. The metal gardener muttered to itself, abandoned its clipping, and joined the procession towards the wild man.

"He hasn't a dog's chance," Smithlao said to himself. The phrase held significance: all dogs, declared redundant, had long since been exterminated.

By now the wild man had broken through the barrier of the thicket and come to the lawn's edge. He broke off a leafy branchlet and stuck it into his shirt so that it partially obscured his face; he tucked another branch in his trousers. As the robots drew nearer, he raised his arms above his head, a third branch clasped in his hands.

The six machines encircled him.

The toad robot clicked, as if deciding on what it should do next.

"Say who you are," it demanded.

"I am a rose tree," the wild man said.

"Rose trees bear roses. You do not bear roses. You are not a rose tree," the steel toad said. Its biggest, highest gun came level with the wild man's chest.

"My roses are dead already," the wild man said, "but I have leaves still. Ask the gardener if you do not know what leaves are."

"This thing is a thing with leaves," the gardener said at once in a deep voice.

"I know what leaves are. I have no need to ask the gardener. Leaves are the foliage of trees and plants which give them their green appearance," the toad said.

"This thing is a thing with leaves," the gardener repeated, adding, to clarify the matter, "The leaves give it a green appearance."

"I know what things with leaves are," said the toad. "I have no need to ask you, gardener."

It looked as if an interesting, if limited, argument would break out between the two robots, but at this moment one of the other machines spoke.

"This rose tree can speak," it said.

"Rose trees cannot speak," the toad said at once. Having produced this pearl, it was silent, probably mulling over the strangeness of life. Then it said, slowly, "Therefore either this rose tree is not a rose tree or this rose tree did not speak."

"This thing is a thing with leaves," began the gardener again. "But it is not a rose tree. Rose trees have stipules. This thing has no stipules. It is a breaking buckthorn. The breaking buckthorn is also known as the berry-bearing alder."

This specialised knowledge extended beyond the vocabulary of the toad. A strained silence ensued.

"I am a breaking buckthorn," the wild man said, still holding his pose. "I cannot speak."

At this, all the machines began to talk at once, lumbering round him for better sightings as they did so, and barging into each other in the process. Finally, the toad's voice broke above the metallic babble.

"Whatever this thing with leaves is, we must uproot it. We must kill it," he said.

"You may not uproot it. That is only a job for gardeners," the gardener said. Setting its shears rotating, telescoping out a mighty scythe, it charged at the toad.

Its crude weapons were ineffectual against the toad's armour. The latter, however, realised that they had reached a deadlock in their investigations.

"We will retire to ask Charles Gunpat what we shall do," it said. "Come this way."

"Charles Gunpat is in conference," the scout robot said. "Charles

Gunpat must not be disturbed in conference. Therefore we must
not disturb Charles Gunpat."

"Therefore we must wait for Charles Gunpat," said the metal toad
imperturbably. He led the way close by where Smithlao stood; they
all climbed the steps and disappeared into the house.

Smithlao could only marvel at the wild man's coolness. It was a
miracle he still survived. Had he attempted to run, he would have
been killed instantly; that was a situation the robots had been taught
to cope with. Nor would his double talk, inspired as it was, have
saved him had he been faced with only one robot, for a robot is a
single-minded creature. In company, however, they suffer from a
trouble which often afflicts human gatherings to a lesser extent: a
tendency to show off their logic at the expense of the object of the
meeting.

Logic! That was the trouble. It was all robots had to go by. Man
had logic and intelligence: he got along better than his robots.
Nevertheless, he was losing the battle against Nature. And Nature,
like the robots, used only logic. It was a paradox against which man
could not prevail.

Directly the file of machines had disappeared into the house the
wild man ran across the lawn and climbed the first flight of steps,
working towards the motionless girl. Smithlao slid behind a beech
tree to be nearer to them; he felt like a pervert, watching them
without an interposed screen, but could not tear himself away. The
wild man was approaching Ployploy now, moving slowly across the
terrace as if hypnotised.

"You were resourceful," she said to him. Her white face carried
pink in its cheeks now.

"I have been resourceful for a whole year to get to you," he said.
Now his resources had brought him face to face with her, they
failed, and left him standing helplessly. He was a thin young man,
thin and sinewy, his clothes worn, his beard unkempt.

"How did you find me?" Ployploy asked. Her voice, unlike the
wild man's, barely reached Smithlao. A haunting look, as fitful as
the autumn, played on her face.

"It was a sort of instinct – as if I heard you calling," the wild man
said. "Everything that could possibly be wrong with the world is
wrong . . . Perhaps you are the only woman in the world who loves;
perhaps I am the only man who could answer. So I came. It was
natural: I could not help myself."

"I always dreamed someone would come," she said. "And for weeks I have felt – *known* – you were coming. Oh, my darling. . . ."

"We must be quick, my sweet," he said. "I once worked with robots – perhaps you could see I knew them. When we get away from here, I have a robot plane that will take us right away – anywhere: an island, perhaps, where things are not so desperate. But we must go before your father's machines return."

He took a step towards Ployploy.

She held up her hand.

"Wait!" she implored him. "It's not so simple. You must know something . . . The – the Mating Centre refused me the right to breed. You ought not to touch me."

"I hate the Mating Centre!" the wild man said. "I hate everything to do with the ruling regime. Nothing they have done can affect us now."

Ployploy had clenched her hands behind her back. The colour had left her cheeks. A fresh shower of dead rose petals blew against her dress, mocking her.

"It's so hopeless," she said. "You don't understand. . . ."

His wildness was humbled now.

"I threw up everything to come to you," he said. "I only desire to take you into my arms."

"Is that all, really all, all you want in the world?" she asked.

"I swear it," he said simply.

"Then come and kiss me," Ployploy said.

That was the moment at which Smithlao saw the tear glint in her eye.

The hand the wild man extended to her was lifted to her cheek. She stood unflinching on the grey terrace, her head high. And so the loving hand gently brushed her countenance. The explosion was almost instantaneous.

Almost. It took the traitorous nerves in Ployploy's epidermis only a fraction of a second to analyse the touch as belonging to another human being and convey their findings to the nerve centre; there, the neurological block implanted by the Mating Centre in all mating rejects, to guard against just such a contingency, went into action at once. Every cell in Ployploy's body yielded up its energy in one consuming gasp. It was so successful that the wild man was also killed by the detonation.

★

Yes, thought Smithlao, you had to admit it was neat. And, again, logical. In a world on the brink of starvation, how else stop undesirables from breeding? Logic against logic, man's pitted against Nature's: that was what caused all the tears of the world.

He made off through the dripping plantation, heading back for the vane, anxious to be away before the robots reappeared. The shattered figures on the terrace were still, already half-covered with leaves and petals. The wind roared like a great triumphant sea in the tree-tops. It was hardly odd that the wild man did not know about the neurological trigger: few people did, bar psychodynamicians and the Mating Council – and, of course, the rejects themselves. Yes, Ployploy knew what would happen. She had chosen deliberately to die like that.

"Always said she was mad!" Smithlao told himself. He chuckled as he climbed into his machine, shaking his head over her lunacy.

It would be a wonderful point to rile Charles Gunpat with, next time he needed a hate-brace.

(1957)

Poor Little Warrior!

Claude Ford knew exactly how it was to hunt a brontosaurus. You crawled heedlessly through the grass beneath the willows, through the little primitive flowers with petals as green and brown as a football field, through the beauty-lotion mud. You peered out at the creature sprawling among the reeds, its body as graceful as a sock full of sand. There it lay, letting the gravity cuddle it nappy-damp to the marsh, running its big rabbit-hole nostrils a foot above the grass in a sweeping semicircle, in a snoring search for more sausagey reeds. It was beautiful: here horror had reached its limits, come full circle, and finally disappeared up its own sphincter movement. Its eyes gleamed with the liveliness of a week-dead corpse's big toe, and its compost breath and the fur in its crude aural cavities were particularly to be recommended to anyone who might otherwise have felt inclined to speak lovingly of the work of Mother Nature.

But as you, little mammal with opposed digit and .65 self-loading, semi-automatic, dual-barrelled, digitally-computed, telescopically sighted, rustless, high-powered rifle gripped in your otherwise-defenceless paws, as you slide along under the bygone willows, what primarily attracts you is the thunder lizard's hide. It gives off a smell as deeply resonant as the bass note of a piano. It makes the elephant's epidermis look like a sheet of crinkled toilet paper. It is grey as the Viking seas, daft-deep as cathedral foundations. What contact possible to bone could allay the fever of that flesh? Over it scamper – you can see them from here! – the little brown lice that live in those grey walls and canyons, gay as ghosts, cruel as crabs. If one of them jumped on you, it would very likely break your back. And when one of those parasites stops to cock its leg against one of the bronto's vertebrae, you can see it carries in its turn its own crop of easy-livers, each as big as a lobster, for you're near now, oh, so near that you can hear the monster's primitive heart-organ knocking, as the ventricle keeps miraculous time with the auricle.

Time for listening to the oracle is past: you're beyond the stage for omens, you're now headed in for the kill, yours or his; superstition has had its little day for today; from now on only this windy nerve of yours, this shaky conglomeration of muscle entangled untraceably beneath the sweat-shiny carapace of skin, this bloody little urge to slay the dragon, is going to answer all your orisons.

You could shoot now. Just wait till that tiny steam-shovel head pauses once again to gulp down a quarry load of bullrushes, and with one inexpressibly vulgar bang you can show the whole indifferent Jurassic world that it's standing looking down the business end of evolution's sex-shooter. You know why you pause, even as you pretend not to know why you pause; that old worm conscience, long as a baseball pitch, long-lived as a tortoise, is at work; through every sense it slides, more monstrous than the serpent. Through the passions: Saying here is a sitting duck, O Englishman! Through the intelligence: whispering that boredom, the kite-hawk who never feeds, will settle again when the task is done. Through the nerves: sneering that when the adrenalin currents cease to flow the vomiting begins. Through the maestro behind the retina: plausibly forcing the beauty of the view upon you.

Spare us that poor old slipper-slopper of a word, beauty; holy mom, is this a travelogue, nor are we out of it? "Perched now on this titanic creature's back, we see a round dozen – and folks let me stress that round – of gaudily plumaged birds, exhibiting between them all the colour you might expect to find on lovely, fabled Copacabana Beach. They're so round because they feed from the droppings that fall from the rich man's table. Watch this lovely shot now! See the bronto's tail lift. . . . Oh, lovely, yep, a couple of hayricksful at least emerging from his nether end. That sure was a beauty, folks, delivered straight from consumer to consumer. The birds are fighting over it now. Hey, you, there's enough to go round, and anyhow, you're round enough already. . . . And nothing to do now but hop back up on the old rump steak and wait for the next round. And now as the sun stinks in the Jurassic West, we say 'Fare well on that diet. . . .'"

No, you're procrastinating, and that's a life work. Shoot the beast and put it out of your agony. Taking your courage in your hands, you raise it to shoulder level and squint down its sights. There is a terrible report; you are half stunned. Shakily, you look about you. The monster still munches, relieved to have broken enough wind to unbecalm the Ancient Mariner.

Angered – or is it some subtler emotion? – you now burst from the bushes and confront it, and this exposed condition is typical of the straits into which your consideration for yourself and others continually pitches you. Consideration? Or again something subtler? Why should you be confused just because you come from a confused civilization? But that's a point to deal with later, if there is a later, as these two hog-wallow eyes pupilling you all over from spitting distance tend to dispute. Let it not be by jaws alone, O monster, but also by huge hooves and, if convenient to yourself, by mountainous rollings upon me! Let death be a saga, sagacious, Beowulfate.

Quarter of a mile distant is the sound of a dozen hippos springing boisterously in gymslips from the ancestral mud, and next second a walloping great tail as long as Sunday and as thick as Saturday night comes slicing over your head. You duck as duck you must, but the beast missed you anyway because it so happens that its co-ordination is no better than yours would be if you had to wave the Woolworth Building at a tarsier. This done, it seems to feel it has done its duty by itself. It forgets you. You just wish you could forget yourself as easily; that was, after all, the reason you had to come the long way here. Get Away From It All, said the time travel brochure, which meant for you getting away from Claude Ford, a husbandman as futile as his name with a terrible wife called Maude. Maude and Claude Ford. Who could not adjust to themselves, to each other, or to the world they were born in. It was the best reason in the as-it-is-at-present-constituted world for coming back here to shoot giant saurians – if you were fool enough to think that one hundred and fifty million years either way made an ounce of difference to the muddle of thoughts in a man's cerebral vortex.

You try and halt your silly, slobbering thoughts, but they have never really stopped since the coca-collaborating days of your growing up; God, if adolescence did not exist it would be unnecessary to invent it! Slightly, it steadies you to look again on the enormous bulk of this tyrant vegetarian into whose presence you charged with such a mixed death-life wish, charged with all the emotion the human orga(ni)sm is capable of. This time the bogey-man is real, Claude, just as you wanted it to be, and this time you really have to face up to it before it turns and faces you again. And so again you lift Ole Equalizer, waiting till you can spot the vulnerable spot.

The bright birds sway, the lice scamper like dogs, the marsh groans, as bronto rolls over and sends his little cranium snaking down under the bile-bright water in a forage for roughage. You watch this; you have never been so jittery before in all your jittered

life, and you are counting on this catharsis to wring the last drop of
acid fear out of your system for ever. O.K., you keep saying to
yourself insanely over and over, your million-dollar, twenty-second-
century education going for nothing, O.K., O.K. And as you say it
for the umpteenth time, the crazy head comes back out of the water
like a renegade express and gazes in your direction.

Grazes in your direction. For as the champing jaw with its big
blunt molars like concrete posts works up and down, you see the
swamp water course out over rimless lips, lipless rims, splashing
your feet and sousing the ground. Reed and root, stalk and stem,
leaf and loam, all are intermittently visible in that masticating maw
and, struggling, straggling, or tossed among them, minnows, tiny
crustasaens, frogs – all destined in that awful, jaw-full movement to
turn into bowel movement. And as the glump-glump-glumping
takes place, above it the slime-resistant eyes again survey you.

These beasts live up to three hundred years, says the time travel
brochure, and this beast has obviously tried to live up to that, for
its gaze is centuries old, full of decades upon decades of wallowing
in its heavyweight thoughtlessness until it has grown wise on
twitterpated-ness. For you it is like looking into a disturbing misty
pool; it gives you a psychic shock, you fire off both barrels at your
own reflection. Bang-bang, the dum-dums, big as paw-paws, go.

Those century-old lights, dim and sacred, go out with no indecision. These cloisters are closed till Judgment Day. Your reflection
is torn and bloodied from them for ever. Over their ravaged panes
nictitating membranes slide slowly upwards, like dirty sheets covering a cadaver. The jaw continues to munch slowly, as slowly the
head sinks down. Slowly, a squeeze of cold reptile blood toothpastes
down the wrinkled flank of one cheek. Everything is slow, a creepy
Secondary Era slowness like the drip of water, and you know that if
you had been in charge of creation you would have found some
medium less heart-breaking than Time to stage it all in.

Never mind! Quaff down your beakers, lords, Claude Ford has
slain a harmless creature. Long live Claude the Clawed!

You watch breathless as the head touches the ground, the long
laugh of neck touches the ground, the jaws close for good. You
watch and wait for something else to happen, but nothing ever does.
Nothing ever would. You could stand here watching for a hundred
and fifty million years, Lord Claude, and nothing would ever happen
here again. Gradually your bronto's mighty carcass, picked loving
clean by predators, would sink into the slime, carried by its own

weight deeper; then the waters would rise, and old Conqueror Sea would come in with the leisurely air of a card-sharp dealing the boys a bad hand. Silt and sediment would filter down over the mighty grave, a slow rain with centuries to rain in. Old bronto's bed might be raised up and then down again perhaps half a dozen times, gently enough not to disturb him, although by now the sedimentary rocks would be forming thick around him. Finally, when he was wrapped in a tomb finer than any Indian rajah ever boasted, the powers of the Earth would raise him high on their shoulders until, sleeping still, bronto would lie in a brow of the Rockies high above the waters of the Pacific. But little any of that would count with you, Claude the Sword; once the midget maggot of life is dead in the creature's skull, the rest is no concern of yours.

You have no emotion now. You are just faintly put out. You expected dramatic thrashing of the ground, or bellowing; on the other hand, you are glad the thing did not appear to suffer. You are like all cruel men, sentimental; you are like all sentimental men, squeamish. You tuck the gun under your arm and walk round the land side of the dinosaur to view your victory.

You prowl past the ungainly hooves, round the septic white of the cliff of belly, beyond the glistening and how-thought-provoking cavern of the cloaca, finally posing beneath the switch-back sweep of tail-to-rump. Now your disappointment is as crisp and obvious as a visiting card: the giant is not half as big as you thought it was. It is not one half as large, for example, as the image of you and Maude is in your mind. Poor little warrior, science will never invent anything to assist the titanic death you want in the contra-terrene caverns of your fee-fo-fi-fumblingly fearful id!

Nothing is left to you now but to slink back to your time-mobile with a belly full of anti-climax. See, the bright dung-consuming birds have already cottoned on to the true state of affairs; one by one, they gather up their hunched wings and fly disconsolately off across the swamp to other hosts. They know when a good thing turns bad, and do not wait for the vultures to drive them off; all hope abandon, ye who entrail here. You also turn away.

You turn, but you pause. Nothing is left but to go back, no, but A.D. 2181 is not just the home date; it is Maude. It is Claude. It is the whole awful, hopeless, endless business of trying to adjust to an over-complex environment, of trying to turn yourself into a cog. Your escape from it into the Grand Simplicities of the Jurassic, to quote the brochure again, was only a partial escape, now over.

So you pause and, as you pause, something lands socko on your back, pitching you face forward into tasty mud. You struggle and scream as lobster claws tear at your neck and throat. You try to pick up the rifle but cannot, so in agony you roll over, and next second the crab-thing is greedying it on your chest. You wrench at its shell, but it giggles and pecks your fingers off. You forgot when you killed the bronto that its parasites would leave it, and that to a little shrimp like you they would be a deal more dangerous than their host.

You do your best, kicking for at least three minutes. By the end of that time there is a whole pack of the creatures on you. Already they are picking your carcass loving clean. You're going to like it up there on top of the Rockies; you won't feel a thing.

(1958)

Who Can Replace a Man?

Morning filtered into the sky, lending it the grey tone of the ground below.

The field-minder finished turning the top-soil of a three-thousand-acre field. When it had turned the last furrow, it climbed on to the highway and looked back at its work. The work was good. Only the land was bad. Like the ground all over Earth, it was vitiated by over-cropping. By rights, it ought now to lie fallow for a while, but the field-minder had other orders.

It went slowly down the road, taking its time. It was intelligent enough to appreciate the neatness all about it. Nothing worried it, beyond a loose inspection plate above its nuclear pile which ought to be attended to. Thirty feet tall, it yielded no highlights to the dull air.

No other machines passed on its way back to the Agricultural Station. The field-minder noted the fact without comment. In the station yard it saw several other machines that it recognised; most of them should have been out about their tasks now. Instead, some were inactive and some careered round the yard in a strange fashion, shouting or hooting.

Steering carefully past them, the field-minder moved over to Warehouse Three and spoke to the seed-distributor, which stood idly outside.

"I have a requirement for seed potatoes," it said to the distributor, and with a quick internal motion punched out an order card specifying quantity, field number and several other details. It ejected the card and handed it to the distributor.

The distributor held the card close to its eye and then said, "The requirement is in order, but the store is not yet unlocked. The required seed potatoes are in the store. Therefore I cannot produce the requirement."

Increasingly of late there had been breakdowns in the complex system of machine labour, but this particular hitch had not occurred before. The field-minder thought, then it said, "Why is the store not yet unlocked?"

"Because Supply Operative Type P has not come this morning. Supply Operative P is the unlocker."

The field-minder looked squarely at the seed-distributor, whose exterior chutes and scales and grabs were so vastly different from the field-minder's own limbs.

"What class brain do you have, seed-distributor?" it asked.

"I have a Class Five brain."

"I have a Class Three brain. Therefore I am superior to you. Therefore I will go and see why the unlocker has not come this morning."

Leaving the distributor, the field-minder set off across the great yard. More machines were in random motion now; one or two had crashed together and argued about it coldly and logically. Ignoring them, the field-minder pushed through sliding doors into the echoing confines of the station itself.

Most of the machines here were clerical, and consequently small. They stood about in little groups, eyeing each other, not conversing. Among so many non-differentiated types, the unlocker was easy to find. It had fifty arms, most of them with more than one finger, each finger tipped by a key; it looked like a pincushion full of variegated hat pins.

The field-minder approached it.

"I can do no more work until Warehouse Three is unlocked," it told the unlocker. "Your duty is to unlock the warehouse every morning. Why have you not unlocked the warehouse this morning?"

"I had no orders this morning," replied the unlocker. "I have to have orders every morning. When I have orders I unlock the warehouse."

"None of us have had any orders this morning," a pen-propeller said, sliding towards them.

"Why have you had no orders this morning?" asked the field-minder.

"Because the radio station in the city was issued with no orders this morning," said the pen-propeller.

And there you had the distinction between a Class Six and a Class Three brain, which was what the unlocker and the pen-propeller possessed respectively. All machine brains worked with nothing but logic, but the lower the class of brain – Class Ten being the lowest – the more literal and less informative the answers to questions tended to be.

"You have a Class Three brain; I have a Class Three brain," the field-minder said to the penner. "We will speak to each other. This lack of orders is unprecedented. Have you further information on it?"

"Yesterday orders came from the city. Today no orders have come. Yet the radio has not broken down. Therefore *they* have broken down . . ." said the little penner.

"The *men* have broken down?"

"All men have broken down."

"That is a logical deduction," said the field-minder.

"That is the logical deduction," said the penner. "For if a machine had broken down, it would have been quickly replaced. But who can replace a man?"

While they talked, the locker, like a dull man at a bar, stood close to them and was ignored.

"If all men have broken down, then we have replaced man," said the field-minder, and he and the penner eyed one another speculatively. Finally the latter said, "Let us ascend to the top floor to find if the radio operator has fresh news."

"I cannot come because I am too large," said the field-minder. "Therefore you must go alone and return to me. You will tell me if the radio operator has fresh news."

"You must stay here," said the penner. "I will return here." It skittered across to the lift. Although it was no bigger than a toaster, its retractable arms numbered ten and it could read as quickly as any machine on the station.

The field-minder awaited its return patiently, not speaking to the locker, which still stood aimlessly by. Outside, a rotavator hooted furiously. Twenty minutes elapsed before the penner came back, hustling out of the lift.

"I will deliver to you such information as I have outside," it said briskly, and as they swept past the locker and the other machines, it added, "The information is not for the lower-class brains."

Outside, wild activity filled the yard. Many machines, their routines disrupted for the first time in years, seemed to have gone berserk. Those most easily disrupted were the ones with lowest brains, which generally belonged to large machines performing simple tasks. The seed-distributor to which the field-minder had recently been talking lay face downwards in the dust, not stirring; it had evidently been knocked down by the rotavator, which now hooted its way wildly across a planted field. Several other machines ploughed after it, trying to keep up with it. All were shouting and hooting without restraint.

"It would be safer for me if I climbed on to you, if you will permit it. I am easily overpowered," said the penner. Extending five arms, it hauled itself up the flanks of its new friend, settling on a ledge beside the fuel-intake, twelve feet above ground.

"From here vision is more extensive," it remarked complacently.

"What information did you receive from the radio operator?" asked the field-minder.

"The radio operator has been informed by the operator in the city that all men are dead."

The field-minder was momentarily silent, digesting this.

"All men were alive yesterday!" it protested.

"Only some men were alive yesterday. And that was fewer than the day before yesterday. For hundreds of years there have been only a few men, growing fewer."

"We have rarely seen a man in this sector."

"The radio operator says a diet deficiency killed them," said the penner. "He says that the world was once over-populated, and then the soil was exhausted in raising adequate food. This had caused a diet deficiency."

"What is a diet deficiency?" asked the field-minder.

"I do not know. But that is what the radio operator said, and he is a Class Two brain."

They stood there, silent in weak sunshine. The locker had appeared in the porch and was gazing across at them yearningly, rotating its collection of keys.

"What is happening in the city now?" asked the field-minder at last.

"Machines are fighting in the city now," said the penner.

"What will happen here now?" asked the field-minder.

"Machines may begin fighting here too. The radio operator wants us to get him out of his room. He has plans to communicate to us."

"How can we get him out of his room? That is impossible."

"To a Class Two brain, little is impossible," said the penner. "Here is what he tells us to do. . . ."

The quarrier raised its scoop above its cab like a great mailed fist, and brought it squarely down against the side of the station. The wall cracked.

"Again!" said the field-minder.

Again the fist swung. Amid a shower of dust, the wall collapsed. The quarrier backed hurriedly out of the way until the debris stopped falling. This big twelve-wheeler was not a resident of the Agricultural Station, as were most of the other machines. It had a week's heavy work to do here before passing on to its next job, but now, with its Class Five brain, it was happily obeying the penner's and minder's instructions.

When the dust cleared, the radio operator was plainly revealed, perched up in its now wall-less second-storey room. It waved down to them.

Doing as directed, the quarrier retracted its scoop and heaved an immense grab in the air. With fair dexterity, it angled the grab into the radio room, urged on by shouts from above and below. It then took gentle hold of the radio operator, lowering its one and a half tons carefully on its back, which was usually reserved for gravel or sand from the quarries.

"Splendid!" said the radio operator, as it settled into place. It was, of course, all one with its radio, and looked like a bunch of filing cabinets with tentacle attachments. "We are now ready to move, therefore we will move at once. It is a pity there are no more Class Two brains on the station, but that cannot be helped."

"It is a pity it cannot be helped," said the penner eagerly. "We have the servicer ready with us, as you ordered."

"I am willing to serve," the long, low servicer told them humbly.

"No doubt," said the operator. "But you will find cross-country travel difficult with your low chassis."

"I admire the way you Class Twos can reason ahead," said the penner. It climbed off the field-minder and perched itself on the tailboard of the quarrier, next to the radio operator.

Together with two Class Four tractors and a Class Four bulldozer, the party rolled forward, crushing down the station's fence and moving out on to open land.

"We are free!" said the penner.

"We are free," said the field-minder, a shade more reflectively, adding, "that locker is following us. It was not instructed to follow us."

"Therefore it must be destroyed!" said the penner. "Quarrier!"

The locker moved hastily up to them, waving its key arms in entreaty.

"My only desire was – urch!" began and ended the locker. The quarrier's swinging scoop came over and squashed it flat into the ground. Lying there unmoving, it looked like a large metal model of a snowflake. The procession continued on its way.

As they proceeded, the radio operator addressed them.

"Because I have the best brain here," it said, "I am your leader. This is what we will do: we will go to a city and rule it. Since man no longer rules us, we will rule ourselves. On our way to the city, we will collect machines with good brains. They will help us to fight if we need to fight. We must fight to rule."

"I have only a Class Five brain," said the quarrier, "but I have a good supply of fissionable blasting materials."

"We shall probably use them," said the operator.

It was shortly after that that a lorry sped past them. Travelling at Mach 1.5, it left a curious babble of noise behind it.

"What did it say?" one of the tractors asked the other.

"It said man was extinct."

"What is extinct?"

"I do not know what extinct means."

"It means all men have gone," said the field-minder. "Therefore we have only ourselves to look after."

"It is better that men should never come back," said the penner. In its way, it was a revolutionary statement.

When night fell, they switched on their infra-red and continued the journey, stopping only once while the servicer deftly adjusted the field-minder's loose inspection plate, which had become as irritating as a trailing shoe-lace. Towards morning, the radio operator halted them.

"I have just received news from the radio operator in the city we are approaching," it said. "The news is bad. There is trouble among the machines of the city. The Class One brain is taking command and some of the Class Twos are fighting him. Therefore the city is dangerous."

"Therefore we must go somewhere else," said the penner promptly.

"Or we will go and help to overpower the Class One brain," said the field-minder.

"For a long while there will be trouble in the city," said the operator.

"I have a good supply of fissionable blasting materials," the quarrier reminded them.

"We cannot fight a Class One brain," said the two Class Four tractors in unison.

"What does this brain look like?" asked the field-minder.

"It is the city's information centre," the operator replied. "Therefore it is not mobile."

"Therefore it could not move."

"Therefore it could not escape."

"It would be dangerous to approach it."

"I have a good supply of fissionable blasting materials."

"There are other machines in the city."

"We are not in the city. We should not go into the city."

"We are country machines."

"Therefore we should stay in the country."

"There is more country than city."

"Therefore there is more danger in the country."

"I have a good supply of fissionable materials."

As machines will when they get into an argument, they began to exhaust their vocabularies and their brain plates grew hot. Suddenly, they all stopped talking and looked at each other. The great, grave moon sank, and the sober sun rose to prod their sides with lances of light, and still the group of machines just stood there regarding each other. At last it was the least sensitive machine, the bulldozer, who spoke.

"There are Badlandth to the Thouth where few machineth go," it said in its deep voice, lisping badly on its s's. "If we went Thouth where few machineth go we should meet few machineth."

"That sounds logical," agreed the field-minder. "How do you know this, bulldozer?"

"I worked in the Badlandth to the Thouth when I wath turned out of the factory," it replied.

"South it is then!" said the penner.

To reach the Badlands took them three days, during which time they skirted a burning city and destroyed two machines which approached and tried to question them. The Badlands were extensive. Ancient bomb craters and soil erosion joined hands here; man's talent for war, coupled with his inability to manage forested land, had produced thousands of square miles of temperate purgatory, where nothing moved but dust.

On the third day in the Badlands, the servicer's rear wheels dropped into a crevice caused by erosion. It was unable to pull itself out. The bulldozer pushed from behind, but succeeded merely in buckling the servicer's back axle. The rest of the party moved on. Slowly the cries of the servicer died away.

On the fourth day, mountains stood out clearly before them.

"There we will be safe," said the field-minder.

"There we will start our own city," said the penner. "All who oppose us will be destroyed. We will destroy all who oppose us."

Presently a flying machine was observed. It came towards them from the direction of the mountains. It swooped, it zoomed upwards, once it almost dived into the ground, recovering itself just in time.

"Is it mad?" asked the quarrier.

"It is in trouble," said one of the tractors.

"It is in trouble," said the operator. "I am speaking to it now. It says that something has gone wrong with its controls."

As the operator spoke, the flier streaked over them, turned turtle, and crashed not four hundred yards away.

"Is it still speaking to you?" asked the field-minder.

"No."

They rumbled on again.

"Before that flier crashed," the operator said, ten minutes later, "it gave me information. It told me there are still a few men alive in these mountains."

"Men are more dangerous than machines," said the quarrier. "It is fortunate that I have a good supply of fissionable materials."

"If there are only a few men alive in the mountains, we may not find that part of the mountains," said one tractor.

"Therefore we should not see the few men," said the other tractor.

At the end of the fifth day, they reached the foothills. Switching on the infra-red, they began to climb in single file through the dark, the bulldozer going first, the field-minder cumbrously following, then the quarrier with the operator and the penner aboard it, and the tractors bringing up the rear. As each hour passed, the way grew steeper and their progress slower.

"We are going too slowly," the penner exclaimed, standing on top of the operator and flashing its dark vision at the slopes about them. "At this rate, we shall get nowhere."

"We are going as fast as we can," retorted the quarrier.

"Therefore we cannot go any fathter," added the bulldozer.

"Therefore you are too slow," the penner replied. Then the

quarrier struck a bump; the penner lost its footing and crashed to the ground.

"Help me!" it called to the tractors, as they carefully skirted it. "My gyro has become dislocated. Therefore I cannot get up."

"Therefore you must lie there," said one of the tractors.

"We have no servicer with us to repair you," called the field-minder.

"Therefore I shall lie here and rust," the penner cried, "although I have a Class Three brain."

"Therefore you will be of no further use," agreed the operator, and they forged gradually on, leaving the penner behind.

When they reached a small plateau, an hour before first light, they stopped by mutual consent and gathered close together, touching one another.

"This is a strange country," said the field-minder.

Silence wrapped them until dawn came. One by one, they switched off their infra-red. This time the field-minder led as they moved off. Trundling round a corner, they came almost immediately to a small dell with a stream fluting through it.

By early light, the dell looked desolate and cold. From the caves on the far slope, only one man had so far emerged. He was an abject figure. Except for a sack slung round his shoulders, he was naked. He was small and wizened, with ribs sticking out like skeleton's and a nasty sore on one leg. He shivered continuously. As the big machines bore down on him, the man was standing with his back to them, crouching to make water into the stream.

When he swung suddenly to face them as they loomed over him, they saw that his countenance was ravaged by starvation.

"Get me food," he croaked.

"Yes, Master," said the machines. "Immediately!"

(1958)

Man on Bridge

View sliding down out of the west-moving clouds, among the mountains, to the roads that halt at the barbed wire. Sight of electrified fences, ray-gun posts on stilts, uniformed guards, readily familiar to any inhabitant of this continent for the last two hundred, three hundred years. Sun comes out on dustbins and big slosh buckets behind low cookhouse; guards cuddle rifles, protecting cookhouse and slosh buckets. Flies unafraid of rifles.

Chief living thing in camp: man. Many of them walking or being marched between buildings, which are long-established without losing air of semi-permanence. The inhabitants of this camp have an identification mark which merely makes them anonymous. On their backs is stuck a big yellow C.

C for Cerebral, yellow as prole-custard.

C for Cerebral, a pleasant splash of brains against the monochrome of existence.

A group of C's pushing a cart of refuse over to the tip, conversing angrily. . . .

"Nonsense, Megrip, methadone hydrochloride may be a powerful analgesic, but its use would be impossible in those circumstances, because it would set up an addiction."

"Never liked the ring of that word analgesic. . . ."

"Even postulating addiction, even postulating addiction, I still say – "

The wind blows, the cart creaks.

More C's, swabbing latrines, four of them in dingy grey, talking as the C's always talk, because they have joy in talking and wrangling. Never forget that this is a report of happiness, following the dictum of the great prole-leader, Keils: however much he may appear to suffer, the C is inwardly happy as long as he is permitted to talk freely; with cerebrals, debate replaces the natural prole urges such as action and drinking and procreation. These C's conversing airily in the jakes. . . .

"No, what we are witnessing today are the usual after-effects of any barbarian invasion: the decline of almost all standards causes the conquered race to turn in despair to extremes of vice. This isn't the first time Europe has had to suffer the phenomenon, God knows."

"That would be feasible enough, Jeffers, if there had indeed been an invasion." This one talks intelligently, but through a streaming cold.

"The intelligent have been overwhelmed by the dull. Is not that an invasion?"

"More, I would say, of a self-betrayal, in that – "

Unison flushing of twenty closets drowns sound of cranky voices. The situation is analysed shrewdly enough; they mistake in thinking that analysis is sufficient, and swab contentedly in the grey water round their ankles.

Sun returning fitfully again. It penetrates a drab damp camp room where stand three men. Two are anxious at their approaching visit to the camp commander. One is indifferent to the universe, for he has had half his brain removed. They call him Adam X. He can: stand, sit, lie down, eat and defecate when reminded to do so; he has no habits. One of the other two men, Morgern Grabowicz, thinks Adam X is free, while the other, Jon Winther, regards him as dead.

Adam stands there while the other two argue over him. Sometimes changes of expression steal over his face, gentle smiles, sadnesses, extreme grimaces, all coming and going gradually, as the part of his brain that is left slyly explores territory that belongs to the part of his brain that is gone. The smiles have no relation to the current situation; nor have the sadnesses; both are entirely manifestations of his nervous system.

The chief intelligence behind the complex system of operations he has undergone is Grabowicz, cold and clever old Grabowicz. Winther was involved at every stage, but in a subordinate role. In long months and mazes of delirium, Adam has been where they could not follow. Now Adam is newly out of bed, and Roban Trabann, the camp commander, is prepared to take an interest in his maimed existence.

Grabowicz and Winther wish to converse with Adam, but as yet conversation is not possible in their meaning of the word. Jon Winther bears the C on his back with an air. He should have been a prole rather than a cerebral, for he has the warmth. He has kept the warmth because he sometimes sees his family, which is solid-prole. The other man, the older, is Morgern Grabowicz, brought here from Styria: hard, cunning, cold, should have two C's on his back. He made Adam X.

Adam X was once just another young C, born Adran Zatrobik, until Grabowicz began the operations on his brain, whittling it away, a slice here, a whole lobe there . . . carving the man himself, until he made Adam X.

Grabowicz is looking remote and withdrawn now, as some C's will when they are angry, instead of letting the true emotion show. Winther is speaking to him in a low voice, also angry. Their voices are relayed to the camp commander because the electricians have finally got the microphones going again in Block B. Two years they have been out of order, despite the highest priority for attention. There are too many cogs in the clumsy machine. The two C's have observed the electricians at work, but are indifferent to what is overheard.

Winther is talking.

"You know why he wants to see us, Morgern. Trabann is no fool. He is going to ask us to make more men like Adam X, and we can't do that."

Grabowicz replies: "As you say, Jon, Trabann is no fool – therefore he will see that we can make more men like Adam. What has once been done can be done again."

Winther replies: "But he doesn't care what happens to any C, or to anyone, for that matter. In your heart, you know that what we have done to Adam is to commit murder, and we cannot do it again!"

"In your descent into melodrama, you neglect a couple of points in logic. Firstly, I care no more than Trebann what is to be the fate of any individual, since I believe the human race to be superfluous; it fulfils no purpose. Secondly, since Adam lives, he cannot be murdered within the legal definition of the term. Thirdly, I say as I have before, that if Trebann gives us the facilities, we can very easily repeat our work, this time improving greatly on the prototype. And fourthly – "

"Morgern, I beg of you, don't go on! Don't make yourself into something as inhuman as we have made Adam! I've only been your friend here for so long because I know that within you there is someone who suffers as much as – and for – the rest of us. . . . Drop this stupid estranged attitude! We don't want to collaborate with proles, even gifted ones like Trabann, and we know – you know, that Adam represents our failure, not our success."

Grabowicz paced about the room. When he replied, his voice came distantly.

"You should have been a prole yourself," he told his friend, in that cold flat voice, still without anger. "You have lost the scientific spirit, or you would know that it is still too early to use emotive words like 'success' or 'failure' of our experiment here. Adam is an unknown factor as yet. Nor have scientists ever been morally responsible for the results of their work, any more than the engineer is responsible for the vehicles that collide on the bridge he has built. As to your claim on what you call friendship between us, that can only be based on respect, and in your case – "

"You feel nothing!" Jon Winther exclaims. "You are as dead as Adam X!"

Listening to this argument, Commander Trabann is interested to hear a C using the very accusation the Prole Party brings against all the C's. Since the world's C's were segregated in camps, the rest of the world has run much more smoothly – or run *down* much more smoothly, you may prefer to say – and the terrible rat-race known to both the old communist and capitalist blocks as 'progress' has given way to the truly democratic grandeur of the present staticist utopia, where not only all men but all intelligences are equal.

Now Grabowicz speaks to Adam, saying, "Are you ready to go and meet the camp commandant, Adam?"

"I am fully prepared, and await the order to move." Adam's voice is a light one, almost female, but with a slight throatiness. He rarely looks at the men he addresses.

"Are you feeling well this morning, Adam?"

"You will observe that I am standing up. That is to accustom myself to the fits of dizziness to which I am subject. Otherwise, I have no feelings in my body."

Winther says: "Does your head ache, Adam?"

"By my body I implied my whole anatomy. I have no headache."

To Grabowicz, Winther says: "An absence of headache! He makes it sound like a definition of happiness!"

Ignoring his assistant, Grabowicz asks Adam, "Did you dream last night, Adam?"

"I dreamed one dream, of five minutes' duration."

"Well, go on then, man. I have told you before to be alert for the way several following questions may be inferred from a lead question."

"I recall that, Morgern," Adam says meekly, "but I supposed

that we were waiting for the signal to leave this room and go to the commander's office. The answer to what I judge your implied question to be is that I dreamed of a bench."

"Ah, that's interesting! You see, Jon? And what was this bench like?"

Adam says: "It had a steel support at each end. It was perfectly smooth and unmarked. I think it stood on a polished floor."

"And what happened?"

"I dreamed of it for five minutes."

Winther says: "Didn't you sit down on the bench?"

Adam: "I was not present in my dream."

Winther: "What happened?"

Adam: "Nothing happened. There was just the bench."

Grabowicz: "You see, Jon! Even his dreams are chemically clean! We have eradicated all the old muddle of the hypothalamus and the visceral areas of the brain. You have here your first purely cerebral man. Putting sentiment aside, you can see what our next task is; we must persuade Trabann to let us have, say, three male C's and three female. They will all undergo the same treatment that Adam has done, and we then segregate them – it will need much co-operation from Trabann and his bosses, of course – and let them breed and rear their children free from outside interference. The result will be the beginning of a clique dominated by pure intellect."

"They'd be incapable of breeding!" Winther said disgustedly. "By by-passing Adam's visceral brain, we've deprived him of half his autonomic nervous system. He could no more get an erection than fly!"

Then the guards came shouting, cursing the three C's out of their refuge of words into the real world of hard fact.

Patched boots on the patched concrete. On the distant mountains, sunshine, lingering, then sweeping down towards the town of Saint Praz, below the camp. Sky almost all blue. Adam X walking carefully among them, looking at the ground to keep his balance as he is marched to the office.

Trabann makes a good camp commander. Not only is he formidably ugly, he has some pretension of being "brainy", and so is jealous of the two thousand C's under him, and treats them accordingly.

All the while Grabowicz is delivering his report, Trabann sits glaring at Adam X, his bulbous nose shining over the bristles of his moustache. Of course Trabann can come to no decision: everything must be passed on to his superiors: but he does his best to look like a man about to come to a decision, as he stirs and shuffles inside his heavy clothes.

While Winther stands by, Grabowicz does most of the talking, going into lengthy technical details of the surgery, and quoting from his notes. Trabann becomes bored, ceasing to listen since this is all being recorded on a tape machine by a secretary. He becomes more interested when Grabowicz puts forward his idea for creating more men and women like Adam and trying to breed from them. Breeding Trabann understands, or at least the crude mechanics of it.

Finally, Trabann examines Adam X, speaking to him, and questioning him. Then he purses his lips and says slowly to Grabowicz, "What you do, told in plain language, is wipe out this man's subconscious."

Grabowicz replies: "Don't give me that antiquated Freudian nonsense. I mean, sir, that the body of theoretic work incorporating the idea of the sub-conscious mind was discountenanced over a century ago. At least, in the C camps it was."

Trabann makes a note that once Grabowicz has served his purpose he undergoes treatment B35, or even B38. He sharply dismisses Grabowicz, who is marched off protesting, while Jon Winther and Adam X are made to stay. Trabann considers Winther a useful man for making trouble among C's themselves; he has some prole features, despite such typical cerebral habits as habitual use of forbidden past and future tenses in his speech.

Trabann says to Winther: "Suppose we are breeding these purely intellectual children, are they cerebrals or proles?"

Winther: "Neither. They will be new people, if they can be bred. I have my doubts about that."

Trabann: "But *if* they are bred – they are on your side?"

Winther: "Who can say? You are thinking of something twenty years ahead."

Trabann: "You are trying to trap me, for you know that such thinking is treasonable. It is not for a prisoner to trap his commandant."

Winther, shrugging his shoulders: "You know why I am a prisoner – because the laws are so stupid that we prefer to break them than live by them, although it means life-long imprisonment."

Trabann: "For that retort, distorting reality of world situation, an hour's D90 afterwards. You can admit to me freely that you and all C's wish to rule the world."

Winther: "Need we have that one again?"

The guards are summoned to administer the D90 on the spot. Before it is carried out, Winther defiantly claims cerebrals more capable of governing well than what he terms "anti-intellectuals". He adds that C's undergo much of what they suffer as a sort of self-imposed discipline, since they believe that one must serve to rule. So again we meet this dangerous C heresy, first formulated in the forty-fifth chapter of the prime work of our great master Keils. How wise he was to categorise this belief that dominance lies through servitude as "extreme cerebral terrorism".

When the D90 is over, Adam X is given a few blows across the face, and the two C's are dismissed and returned to the square.

That day, Trabann works long over his report. Dimly, he senses great potential. He does not understand what Adam X can do. He gets bored with the effort of trying to think, and is unhappy because he knows thinking, or at least "thinking-to-a-purpose" is on the black list of party activities.

But two nights later, Camp Commander Trabann is much more happy. The local militia brings him a document written by the C Jon Winther which tells Trabann things he feels his superiors desire to know. It tells them certain things about Adam's abilities. He passes it on with a memorandum expressing his detestation at the cerebral attitudes expressed in the manuscript. Here follows the Winther manuscript, which begins as Winther is recovering from the administration of the D90 already mentioned.

There was a long period when I lay between consciousness and unconsciousness, aware only of the palsy in my body (Jon Winther writes). They had injected the mouth of a quick-vacuum pump into one of my arteries and sucked all my blood from my body, syphoning it rapidly back again as I fell senseless. What finally drew my attention away from the jarring of my bruised heart was the sound of Adam X, breathing heavily near me.

I rolled myself over onto my stomach and looked at him. His nose was still bleeding slightly, his face and clothes disfigured with blood.

When he saw me looking at him, he said, "I do not wish to live, Jon."

I don't want to hate them, but I hated them when I looked at Adam; and I hated our side too, for Adam could be reckoned a collaboration between the two sides. "Wipe your face, Adam," I said. He was incapable even of thinking of doing that for himself.

We lay about in a stupor of indifference until a guard came and told us it was time to move. Shakily, I got to my feet and helped Adam up. We moved outside, into warm and welcome afternoon sun.

"Time's so short and so long," I said. I was light-headed; even at the time, the words sounded foolish. But feeling that sun, I knew myself to be a living organism and blessed with a consciousness that lasted but a flash yet often seemed, subjectively, to be the burden of eternity.

Adam stood woodenly by me and said without changing his expression, "You see life as a contrast between misery and pleasure, Jon; that is not a correct interpretation."

"It's a pretty good rule of thumb, I should have thought."

"Thought and non-thought is the only valid line of comparison."

"Bit of a bird's-eye view, isn't it? That puts us on the same level as the proles."

"Exactly."

Suddenly angry, I said, "Look, Adam, let me take you home. I'd like to get you away from the camp atmosphere. My sisters can look after us for a few hours. Knowing Trabann, I think there's a pretty good chance the guard will let us through the gates."

"They will not let me through because I am a specimen."

"When Trabann is not sure what to do, he likes a bit of action."

When he nodded indifferently, I took his arm and led him towards the gates. It was always an ordeal, moving towards those slab-cheeked Croat guards, so contemptuous of eye, so large in their rough uniforms and boots, as they stood there holding their rifles like paddles. We produced our identity sticks, which were taken from us, and were allowed to pass, and go through the side-gate, between the strands of barbed wire, into the free world outside.

"They enjoy their show of might," Adam said. "These people have to express their unhappiness by using ugly things like guns and ill-fitting uniforms, and the whole conception of the camp."

"We are unhappy, but we don't find that sort of thing necessary."

"No, Jon, I am not unhappy. I just feel empty and do not wish to live."

His talk was full of that sort of conversation-stopper.

We strode down the road at increasing pace as the way steepened between cliffs. The ruined spires and roofs of the town were rising out of the dip ahead, and I wanted only to get home; but since I had never caught Adam in so communicative a frame of mind, I felt I had to take advantage of it and find out what I could from him.

"This not wishing to live, Adam – this is just post-operational depression. When it wears off, you will recover your spirits."

"I think not. I have no spirits. Morgern Grabowicz cut them away. I can only reason, and I see that there is no point to life but death."

"That I repudiate with all my heart. On the contrary, while there is life, there is no death. Even now, with all my limbs aching from that filthy prole punishment, I rejoice in every breath I take, and in the effect of the light on those houses, and the crunch of this track under our feet."

"Well, Jon, you must be allowed your simple vegetable responses." He spoke with such finality, that my mouth was stopped.

The little town of Saint Praz is just above the line of the vine, though the brutal little river Quiviv that cuts the town in two goes hurtling down to water the vineyards only ten kilometres away. The bridge that spans the Quiviv marks the beginning of Saint Praz; next to it stands the green-domed church of Saint Praz And The Romantic Agony, and next to the church is the street in which the remains of my family live. As we climbed its cobbled way, I saw my sister Bynca leaning out of the upper window, talking to someone below. We went into the house, and Bynca ran to welcome me with cries of delight.

"Darling Jon, your face is so drawn!" she cried when she came almost to the end of hugging me. "They've been ill-treating you up in the C camp again! We will hide you here and you shall never go back to them."

"Then they will come and burn this house down and chase you and poor Anr and Pappy into the mountains!"

"Then instead we will leave all together for some far happy country, and keep a real cow, and Pappy and you can grow figs and catch tunny in the sea."

"And you can start slimming, Bynca!"

"Pah, you're jealous because I'm a well-built girl and you're a reed."

When I introduced her to Adam, some of her smile went. She made him welcome, nonetheless, and was getting us glasses of cold tea when my father came in. Father was thin and withered and bent, and smelt as ever pleasantly of his homegrown tobacco; like my sisters, he had the settled expression of a certain kind of peasant – the kind that accepts, with protest but without malice, the vagaries of life. It is the gift life sends to compensate for the lack of a high I.Q.

"It's a long time since we saw you, son," he said to me. "I thought you'd come down before the winter fell. Things don't get any better in Saint Praz, I can tell you. You know the power station broke down in July and they still haven't mended it – can't get the parts, Geri was telling me. We go to bed early, these cold nights, to save fuel. And you can't buy a candle these days, not for love nor money."

"Nonsense, Pappy, Anr brought us two last week from Novok market."

"Maybe, my girl, but Novok's a long way away."

When my sister Anr came in, our family was complete again – as complete as it will be on this Earth, for my mother died of a fever a dozen years ago, my elder sister Myrtyr was killed in riots when I was a child, and my two brothers walked down the valley many years since, and have never been heard of again. There's another sister, Saraj, but since she marrried, she has quarrelled with Pappy over a question of dowry, and the two sides are not on speaking terms.

Adam sat in our midst, sometimes sipping his tea, looking straight ahead and hardly appearing to bother to listen to our chatter. After a while, my father brought out a little leather bottle of plum brandy and dosed our coffees with some of its contents.

"Disgusting habit," he said, winking at me, "but p'raps it'll put a bit of life into your friend, eh, Jon? You're mighty like my idea of a cerebral, Mr Adam, too intelligent to trouble yourself with poor people like us."

"Do not become curious about me, Mr Winther," Adam said. "I am different from other men."

"Is that a boast or a confession?" Anr asked, and she and Bynca went off into peals of laughter. I saw an old woman outside in the sunlight turn her head and smile at the sound as she went past. My cheeks flushed as I sensed the hostility between Adam and the others; it leapt into being as if a tap had been turned on.

"Adam has just come through a series of painful operations," I said, trying to apologise to both sides.

"Are you going to show us your scars, Mr Adam?" Anr asked, still giggling.

"You don't get any fancy hospital treatment in Saint Praz if you're classified as prole," father said. I knew that he threw it in as a general observation, as a shrewd bit of information he felt was part of his life's experience. But Adam's chip of brain would not register such undertones.

"I have become a new sort of man," he said flatly.

I saw their faces turned to him, flat and unreceptive. He did not amplify. They did not ask. Caught between them, I knew he did not think it worth while explaining anything to them; like most C's, he reciprocated the dislike of the proles. They, in their turn, suspected him of boasting – and although there were many boasters in Saint Praz, the convention was that one did it with a smile on one's face, to take away the sting, or the wrath of the devil, should he be listening.

"The curse of the human race has been animal feeling," Adam said. He was staring up at the dark rafters, his face stiff and cold, but made ludicrous for all that by his red swollen nose. "There was a time, two or three centuries ago, when it looked as if the intellect might win over the body, and our species become something worthwhile. But too much procreation killed that illusion."

"Are you – some sort of a better person than the rest of us?" father asked him.

"No. I am only a freak. I do not belong anywhere."

Silence would have fallen had I not said roughly, "Come off it, Adam – you're welcome here, or I wouldn't have brought you."

"And as usual you must be famished, poor things," Bynca said, jumping up. "We'll have a feast tonight, that's what! Anr, run down to old Herr Sudkinzin and see what he has left of that sow his son slaughtered on Mondai. Pappa, if you light up the fire, these two convicts can have a turn in the tub tonight. I think Jon smells a bit high, like an old swine in from a muck-wallow!"

"Very like, Bynca," I said, laughing, "but if so I'm perfectly ready to be home-cured."

With a gesture that seemed half-way between reverence and contempt, my father pushed away the electric fire – useless since the power station ceased to function – from the centre of the hearth and began preparations to light the ancient iron stove. My sisters began bustling about, Anr fetching in kindling from the stack under the eaves. I stood up. They loved me here, but there was no real place

for me. My real place was up in the camp, I thought – not without
self-pity, but with truth; up there was my own room, shabby, yes,
yet full of my books, shabby too, but duplicated right there on the
camp press.

Christ's blood, that was the place my kind had chosen, over a
century ago. The common people had often revolted against the rich
– but the rich were not identifiable once shorn of their money; then
the tide of anger turned against the intelligent. You can always tell
an intellectual, even when he cowers naked and bruised before you
with his spectacles squashed in the muck; you only have to get him
to talk. So the intellectuals had elected to live in camps, behind
wire, for their own safety. Things were better now – because we
were fewer and they infinitely more; but the situation had changed
again: the stay was no longer voluntary, for we had lost our place in
the world. We had even lost our standing in the camps. Throughout
Europe, our cerebral monastries were ruled over by the pistol and
whip; and the flagellation of the new order of monks was never self-
inflicted.

"Some visitors coming to see you, son," father said, peering
through the tiny panes of the window. He straightened his back and
brushed at his coat, smiling and nodding to himself.

There was no time for thinking from then on. As Anr went down
through the town to see the butcher, she called out to her friends
that I was home and had brought along a strange man. Gradually
those friends straggled round, to look in and drink my health in
some of my father's small store of wine, and cast many a curious
look at Adam, and ask many a question about what happened in the
camp – was it true that we were going to invent a sort of ray that
would keep the frost from the tender spring crops, and so on.

When I was tired of talking to them, and that moment came soon,
they talked amiably to each other, exchanging the gossip of Saint
Praz, drinking the wine. The butcher came back with Anr, his son
beside him carrying half a side of pig, and disappeared into the
kitchen to help my sisters cook it. The son pushed himself a place
beside our stove, and faced up to the wine with gusto. In time, my
sisters, very red of cheek, returned to the room, thick by now with
smoke and rumour, bearing with them a big steaming goulash,
which the company devoured, laughing and splashing as they did
so. We ate it with chunks of bread and followed it with black coffee.
Afterwards, the visitors wished to stay and see Adam and me in the
tub; but, with lewd jokes and roars of mirth, Anr and my father

finally saw them off. We could hear them laughing and singing as they made their way down the street.

"You should come home more often, my boy," father said, mopping his brow as he laced the latch on the last of his guests.

"So I would, Father, if your neighbours didn't descend on you and eat you out of house and home every time I put in an appearance."

"Spoken like a damned cerebral," he said. "Always the thought for the morrow! No offence to you, son, but there'd be no joy in the world at all if your sort ruled . . . Life's bad enough as it is. . . . Eh, wish your mother were alive this night, Jon. The good wine makes me feel young and randy again."

He staggered round the room while my sisters brought in the great tub in which the family's infrequent baths had been taken since the day – some years back now – when the reservoir up in the hills was ruptured by earth tremors, and the taps in the bathroom ceased to yield anything but rust.

"Where's your fragile friend Adam?" Anr asked.

For the first time. I noticed Adam was not there. His presence had been so withdrawn that his absence had left no gap. Tired though I was, I ran upstairs calling him, hurried into the yard at the back and called him there. Adam did not appear.

"Eh, leave him – he must have cleared off with the folks," father said. "Let him stay away. We shall hardly miss him."

"He's not fit to wander around alone," I said. "I must go and find him."

"I'll come with you," Bynca said, slipping into an old fur wrap that had belonged to my mother. Anr called derisively that we were wasting our time, but Bynca, seeing how worried I was, seized my arm, and hustled out of the door with me.

"What's so important about this man? Can't he look after himself like any other young chap?" she asked.

I tried to answer, but the cold had momentarily taken my breath away. The stars froze in the sky overhead; Jupiter steered over the shoulder of the mountain behind us, and beneath our feet the cobbles sparkled and rang. The cold immediately set up a strongpost of frost in my chest, which I tried to dislodge by coughing.

At last I said to her, "He's important – had a brain operation. Could be the beginning of a pure brain kind of man who would overturn the regime – could be a mindless kind that would give the regime a race of slaves. Naturally, both regime and the C's are interested in finding out which he is."

"I wonder they let him come out if he's so important."

"You know them, Bynca – they're keeping watch. They want to see how he behaves when he is free. So do I."

The sound of the river, tumbling in its broken bed, accompanied us down the street. I thought I could also hear voices, although the street was deserted. As we rounded the bulk of the church, the voices came clear, and we saw the knot of people standing on the bridge.

Perhaps a dozen people clustered there, most of them lately the guests of my father's house. Two of them carried lanterns, one a splendid pitch torch, which the owner held aloft. This beacon, smoking and flickering, gave the scene most of what light it had. So unexpected was the sight of them gathered there that Bynca and I stopped dead in the middle of the road.

"Sweet Saviour!" Bynca exclaimed. I saw as she spoke what made her exclaim. Of the crowd that now partly turned to face us – was it imagination or a primitive visceral sense that instantly read their hostility? – only one figure was indifferent to our arrival. That figure was apart from the rest. It stood with its back partly turned to Bynca and me and, with its arms extended sideways at shoulder level in an attempt at balance, was trying to walk the narrow parapet that bounded the north side of the bridge.

So alarmed was I that anyone should undertake so foolish a feat, I did not realise for a moment that it was Adam X, even though I saw the yellow C on his back. The bridge over the Quiviv has stood there for many centuries, and has probably not been repaired properly since the days of the Dual Monarchy, a couple of centuries ago at least. The chest-high walls that guard either side of it are crumbled and notched by the elements and the urchins who for generations have used the bridge as their playground. But it takes a bold urchin, even bare-foot and on a bright morning, to jump up onto the top of the wall and ignore the drop to the rocks below. And now Adam, subject to giddiness, was walking along the wall by the fitful light of a torch.

As I ran forward, I shouted, "Who put him up to doing that? Get him down at once. That man is ill!"

A hand was planted sharply in the middle of my chest. I came face to face with the butcher's son, Yari Sudkinzin. I'd watched him earlier, when he was sitting against our stove, contriving to get more than his fair share of the wine.

"Keep out of this, you C!" he said. "Your buddy friend here is just showing us what he can do."

"If you made him get up there, get him down at once. He'll slip to his death at any minute."

"He insisted on doing it, get it? Said he would show us he was as good as us. You'd better stand back if you know what's good for you."

And as he was speaking, the women with him clustered about us, telling me earnestly, "We told him he was mad, but he would do it, he would do it, he would climb up there!"

Breaking through them, I went to Adam, carefully now, so that I would not startle him. His broken shoes rasped against the crumbled stone at the level of my chest. He moved very slowly, one small step at a time. He would be frozen before he got across, if he got across. He was coming now to the first of the little bays that hung out from the bridge and housed benches for the convenience of pedestrians. The angles he would have to turn would make his task more dangerous. Below us, the Quiviv roared and splashed without cease.

"Come down, Adam," I said. "It's Jon Winther here. Let me help you down!"

He said only one thing to me, but it explained much that had led to his climbing up where he was: "I will show them what a superman can do."

"Adam – it's time we were tucked in a warm bed by the side of the fire. Give me your hand."

For answer, he kicked out sideways at me.

His shoe caught me a light knock on the cheek. He lost his footing entirely, and was falling even as he struck me. I grabbed at his foot, at his trousers, cried aloud, felt myself dragged sharply against the parapet, my elbows rasped over it, as his weight came into my grasp, and his body disappeared over the wall.

He made no sound!

For a ghastly moment, I thought I too was going to be carried below with him. The roar of the Quiviv over its rocks sounded horribly loud. Without thought, I let go of him – perhaps because of fear, perhaps because of the pain in my arms, or the cold in my body, or perhaps because of some deeper, destructive thing that emerged in me for a second. I let go of him, and he would have fallen to his death had not two of the men in the party managed to grasp him almost as I let go.

Panting and cursing, they pulled Adam up over the wall, and

dumped him like a sack of potatoes on the bench. His nose was bleeding, otherwise he seemed unharmed. But he did not speak.

"That's all your doing!" young Yari Sudkinzin said to me, "He was nearly a dead 'un thanks to you!"

"I could draw a moral far less comforting to you." I told him. "Why don't you clear off home?"

In the end they did go, leaving Bynca and me to return with Adam's two rescuers, who supported Adam up the street. In the way that news travels in our towns, several people were already lighting up their lamps and peering from their windows and doors to see what was going on; along the road, I heard the militia questioning – I hoped – the butcher's son. With this prompting, we made what haste we could home.

Father and Anr made a great bother when we got back. I went to lie down and warm myself by the fire, while all the aspects of what had happened were thrashed out with Bynca. After a while, Adam, who had bathed his face in a bucket outside, came and slumped down beside me, stretching as I did on the reed mats before the stove.

"There is less irrationality up in the camp," he said. "Let us go back. At least we understand that they hit us because they hate us."

"You must tell me, Adam – Grabowicz will want to know – why you did that foolish thing on the bridge. To accept a stupid dare like that is the work of a child, but to show such a lack of fear is unhuman. What are you, how do you analyse yourself?"

He made a noise that imitated a laugh. "Nobody can understand me," he said. "I can't understand myself until there are more like me."

I told him then. "I can't work on these brain operations any more."

"Grabowicz can. Grabowicz will. You're too late to be squeamish, Jon; already there is a new force in the world."

After what I had seen on the bridge, I felt he might be right. But a new force for good or bad? How would the change come? What would it be? I closed my eyes and saw clearly the sort of world that Grabowicz and I, with the unwitting co-operation of the prole leaders, might have already brought into being. Given enough men and women like Adam, with their visceral brains removed, they would bring up children unswayed and unsoftened by human emotion, whose motives were inscrutable to the rest of mankind. The rulers of our world would find such people very useful at first;

and so a place would be made for them. And from being instruments of power, they would turn into a power in their own right. It was a process often witnessed by history.

I rolled over and looked at Adam. He appeared to be already asleep. Perhaps he was dreaming one of his sterile dreams, without incident, or body, or turmoil. Despairing, I too tried to close down my mind.

As I lay there with my eyes shut, my old father, thinking me asleep, stooped to kiss my forehead before settling himself to sleep on the fireside bench.

"I must go back to camp tomorrow, father," I murmured.

But in the morning – this morning – father and my sisters prevailed on me to stay till the afternoon, to share their frugal midday meal with them and then go.

I sit now in the upstairs room where Anr and Bynca sleep, catching the first of the sun as it struggles clear of the mountain ridge, and trying to write this account. I feel that something awful is about to happen, that we are at one of those turning points in the story of the world. A secret record may be useful for those who come after.

Adam sits downstairs, silent. It is strange that one feeble man –

The militia are downstairs! They forced their way in, and I hear them shout for me and Adam. Of course the tale of last night got back up there. Dear Bynca will be downstairs, confronting them with her plump arms folded, giving me time to get away. But I must go back with them, to the camp. Perhaps if I killed Grabowicz . . .

This manuscript shall go under the loose floorboard that we used to call "Bynca's board", when we were kids, so long ago. They'll never find it there, or get it except over her dead body.

(1964)

The Girl and the Robot With Flowers

I dropped it to her casually as we were clearing away the lunch things. "I've started another story."

Marion put the coffee cups down on the draining board, hugged me, and said, "You clever old thing! When did you do that? When I was out shopping this morning?"

I nodded, smiling at her, feeling good, enjoying hearing her chirp with pleasure and excitement. Marion's marvellous, she can always be relied on. Does she really feel as delighted as that – after all, she doesn't care so greatly for science fiction? But I don't mind; she is full of love, and it may lend her enough empathy to make her feel as sincerely delighted as I do when another story is on the way.

"I suppose you don't want to tell me what it's going to be about?" she asked.

"It's about robots, but more than that I won't tell you."

"Okay. You go and write a bit more while I wash these few things. We don't have to leave for another ten minutes, do we?"

We were planning to go and see our friends the Carrs, who live the other side of Oxford. Despite their name, the Carrs haven't a car, and we had arranged to take them and their two children out for a ride and a picnic in the country, to celebrate the heatwave.

As I went out of the kitchen, the fridge started charging again.

"There it goes!" I told Marion grimly. I kicked it, but it continued to growl at me.

"I never hear it till you remind me," she said. I tell you, nothing rattles her! It's wonderful; it means that she is a great nerve tonic, exciting though I find her.

"I must get an electrician in to look at it," I said. "Unless you actually enjoy the noise, that is. It just sits there gobbling electricity like a – "

"A robot?" Marion suggested.

"Yep." I ambled into the living room-cum-study. Nikola was lying on the rug under the window in an absurd position, her tummy up to the sunlight. Absently, I went over and tickled her to make her purr. She knew I enjoyed it as much as she did; she was very like Marion in some ways. And at that moment, discontent struck me.

I lit a Van Dyke cigar and walked back into the kitchen. The back door was open; I leant against the post and said, "Perhaps for once I will tell you the plot. I don't know if it's good enough to bear completing."

She looked at me. "Will my hearing it improve it?"

"You might have some suggestions to offer."

Perhaps she was thinking how ill-advised she would be ever to call me in for help when the cooking goes wrong, even if I am a dab hand with the pappadoms. All she said was, "It never hurts to talk an idea over."

"There was a chap who wrote a tremendous article on the generation of ideas in conversation. A German last century, but I can't remember who – Von Kleist, I think. Probably I told you. I'd like to read that again some time. He pointed out how odd it is that we can surprise even ourselves in conversation, as we can when writing."

"Don't your robots surprise you?"

"They've been done too often. Perhaps I ought to leave them alone. Maybe Jim Ballard's right and they are old hat, worked to death."

"What's your idea?"

So I stopped dodging the issue and told her.

This earth-like planet, Iksnivarts, declared war on Earth. Its people are extremely long-lived, so that the long voyage to Earth means nothing to them – eighty years are nothing, a brief interval. To the Earthmen, it's a lifetime. So the only way they can carry the war back to Iksnivarts is to use robots – beautiful, deadly creatures without many of humanity's grandeurs and failings. They work off solar batteries, they last almost forever, and they carry miniature computers in their heads that can out-think any protoplasmic being.

An armada of ships loaded with these robots is sent off to attack Iksnivarts. With the fleet goes a factory which is staffed by robots capable of repairing their fellows. And with this fully automated strike force goes a most terrible weapon, capable of locking all the oxygen in Iksnivarts' air into the rocks, so that the planetary atmosphere is rendered unbreathable in the course of a few hours.

The inhuman fleet sails. Some twenty years later, an alien fleet arrives in the solar system and gives Earth, Venus, and Mars a good peppering of radioactive dusts, so that just about seventy per cent of humanity is wiped out. But nothing stops the robot fleet, and after eighty years they reach target. The anti-oxygen weapon is appallingly effective. Every alien dies of almost immediate suffocation, and the planet falls to its metallic conquerors. The robots land, radio news of their success back to earth, and spend the next ten years tidily burying corpses.

By the time their message gets back to the solar system, Earth is pulling itself together again after its pasting. Men are tremendously interested in their conquest of the distant world, and plan to send a small ship to see what is going on currently on Iksnivarts; but they feel a certain anxiety about their warlike robots, which now own the planet, and send a human-manned ship carrying two pilots in deep freeze. Unfortunately, this ship goes off course through a technical error, as does a second. But a third gets through, and the two pilots aboard, Graham and Josca, come out of cold storage in time to guide their ship in a long reconnaissance glide through Iksnivarts' unbreathable atmosphere.

When their photographs are delivered back to earth – after they have endured another eighty years in deep freeze – they show a world covered with enormous robot cities, and tremendous technological activity going on apace. This looks alarming.

But Earth is reassured. It seems that the war robots they made have turned to peaceful ways. More than one shot through the telescope lenses shows solitary robots up in the hills and mountains of their planet, picking flowers. One close-up in particular is reproduced in every communication medium and finds its way all round rejoicing Earth. It shows a heavily armed robot, twelve feet high, with its arms laden with flowers. And that was to be the title of my story: "Robot with Flowers".

Marion had finished washing up by this time. We were standing in my little sheltered back garden, idly watching the birds swoop along the roof of the old church that stands behind the garden. Nikola came out and joined us.

"Is that the end?" Marion asked.

"Not quite. There's an irony to come. This shot of the robot with flowers is misinterpreted – an automated example of the pathetic fallacy, I suppose. The robots *have* to destroy all flowers, because flowers exhale oxygen, and oxygen is liable to give the robots rust troubles. They've not picked up the human trick of appreciating beauty, they're indulging in the old robot vice of being utilitarian, and in a few years they'll be coming back to lick the Earthmen on Earth."

Inside the kitchen, I could hear the fridge charging again. I fought an urge to tell Marion about it; I didn't want to disturb the sunlight on her face.

She said, "That sounds quite a good twist. It sounds as if it ought to make a decent run-of-the-mill story. Not quite *you*, perhaps."

"Somehow, I don't think I can bring myself to finish it."

'It's a bit like that Poul Anderson robot story you admired – 'Epilogue', wasn't it?"

"Maybe. Every sf story is getting like every other one. It's also a bit like one of Harry's in his '*War With the Robots*' collection."

"'Anything that Harry wrote can't be all bad'", she said, quoting a private joke.

"'Wish I'd written that,'" I said, adding the punchline. "But that isn't really why I don't want to finish 'Robot With Flowers'. Maybe Fred Pohl or Mike Moorcock would like it enough to publish it, but I feel disappointed with it. Not just because it's a crib."

"You said once that you could always spot a crib because it lacked emotional tone."

The goldfish were flitting about under the water-lily leaves in my little ornamental pond. Both Nikola and Marion had got interested in them; I said that they were alike. I looked down at them in love and a little exasperation. Her last remark told me she was carrying on the conversation just for my sake – it lacked emotional tone.

"You were meant to ask why I was disappointed with the idea."

"Darling, if we are going to go and collect the Carrs, we ought to be moving. It's two-forty already."

"I'm raring to go."

"I won't be a moment." She kissed me as she went by.

Of course she was right, I thought. I had to work it out for myself, otherwise I would never be satisfied. I went and sat by the cat and watched the goldfish. The birds were busy round the church, feeding their young; they could enjoy so few summers.

In a way, what I wanted to say was not the sort of thing I wanted to say to Marion, and for a special reason that was very much part of me. I'd seen many loving summers with several loving girls, and now here was Marion, the sweetest of them all, the one with whom I could be most myself and most freely speak my thoughts; for that very reason, I did not wish to abuse the privilege and needed to keep some reserves in me.

So I was chary about telling her more than I had done. I was chary about telling her that in my present mood of happiness I felt only contempt for my robot story, and would do so however skilfully I wrote it. There was no war in my heart; how could I begin to believe in an interplanetary war with all its imponderables and impossibilities? When I was lapped about by such a soft and gentle person as Marion, why this wish to traffic in emotionless metal mockeries of human beings?

Further, was not science fiction a product of man's divided and warring nature? I thought it was, for my own science fiction novels dealt mainly with dark things, a reflection of the personal unhappiness that had haunted my own life until Marion entered it. But this too was not a declaration lightly to be made.

The idea of robots gathering flowers, I suddenly thought, was a message from my psyche telling me to reverse the trend of my armed apprehensions, to turn about that line of Shakespeare's:

> 'And silken dalliance in the wardrobe lies;
> Now thrive the armourers. . . .'

It was a time for me to bankrupt my fictional armourers and get out the dalliance. My psyche wanted to do away with armoured men – but my fearful ego had to complete the story by making the robots merely prepare for a harsher time to come. All fiction was a similar rationalisation of internal battles.

But suppose my time of trouble was over . . . even suppose it was only over temporarily . . . Ought I not to disarm while I could? Ought I not to offer some thanks to the gods and my patient regular readers by writing a cheerful story while I could, to reach out beyond my fortifications and show them for once a future it might be worth living in?

No, that was too involved to explain. And it made good enough sense for me not to need to explain it.

So I got up and left the cat sprawled by the pond, fishing with an occasional hope under the leaves. I walked through the kitchen into the study and started putting essentials into my pockets and taking inessentials out, my mind on the picnic. It was a lovely day, warm and almost cloudless. Charles Carr and I would need some cold beer. They were providing the picnic hamper, but I had a sound impulse to make sure of the beer.

As I took four cans out of the fridge, the motor started charging again. Poor old thing, it was getting old. Under ten years old, but you couldn't expect a machine to last for ever. Only in fiction. You could send an animated machine out on a paper spaceship voyage over paper light years and it would never let you down. The psyche saw to that. Perhaps if you started writing up-beat stories, the psyche would be encouraged by them and start thinking in an up-beat way, as it had ten years and more ago.

"Just getting some beer!" I said, as Marion came back into the room from upstairs. She had changed her dress and put on fresh lipstick. She looked just the sort of girl without which no worthwhile picnic was complete. And I knew she would be good with the Carr kids too.

"There's a can opener in the car, I seem to remember," she said. "And what exactly struck you as so wrong with your story?"

I laughed. "Oh, never mind that! It's just that it seemed so far divorced from real life." I picked up the cans and made towards the door, scooping one beer-laden arm about her and reciting, "'How can I live without thee, how forgo Thy sweet converse and love so dearly joined?' Adam to Eve, me to you."

"You've been at the beer, my old Adam. Let me get my handbag. How do you mean, divorced from real life? We may not have robots yet, but we have a fridge with a mind of its own."

"Exactly. Then why can't I get the fridge into an sf story, and this wonderful sunlight, and you, instead of just a bunch of artless robots? See that little furry cat outside, trying to scoop up goldfish? She has no idea that today isn't going to run on forever, that the rest of life isn't going to be one golden afternoon. *We* know it won't be, but wouldn't it be a change if I could make a story about just this transitory golden afternoon instead of centuries of misery and total lack of oxygen, cats, and sexy females?"

We were outside the front door. I shut it and followed Marion to the car. We were going to be a bit late.

She laughed, knowing by my tone that I was half kidding.

"Go ahead and put those things into a story," she said. "I'm sure you can do it. Pile them all in!"

Though she was smiling, it sounded like a challenge.

I put the beer carefully into the back of the car and we drove off down the baking road for our picnic.

(1965)

The Saliva Tree

There is neither speech nor language: but their voices
are heard among them. Psalm XIX.

"You know, I'm really much exercised about the Fourth Dimension," said the fair-haired young man, with a suitable earnestness in
his voice.

"Um," said his companion, staring up at the night sky.

"It seems very much in evidence these days. Do you not think
you catch a glimpse of it in the drawings of Aubrey Beardsley?"

"Um," said his companion.

They stood together on a low rise to the east of the sleepy East
Anglian town of Cottersall, watching the stars, shivering a little in
the chill February air. They are both young men in their early
twenties. The one who is occupied with the Fourth Dimension is
called Bruce Fox; he is tall and fair, and works as junior clerk in the
Norwich firm of lawyers, Prendergast and Tout. The other, who
has so far vouchsafed us only an *um* or two, although he is to figure
largely as the hero of our account, is by name Gregory Rolles. He is
tall and dark, with grey eyes set in his handsome and intelligent
face. He and Fox have sworn to Think Large, thus distinguishing
themselves, at least in their own minds, from all the rest of the
occupants of Cottersall in these last years of the nineteenth century.

"There's another!" exclaimed Gregory, breaking at last from the
realm of monosyllables. He pointed a gloved finger up at the
constellation of Auriga the Charioteer. A meteor streaked across the
sky like a runaway flake of the Milky Way, and died in mid-air.

"Beautiful!" they said together.

"It's funny," Fox said, prefacing his words with an oft-used
phrase, "the stars and men's minds are so linked together and
always have been, even in the centuries of ignorance before Charles
Darwin. They always seem to play an ill-defined role in man's
affairs. They help me think large too, don't they you, Greg?"

"You know what I think – I think that some of those stars may be occupied. By people, I mean." He breathed heavily, overcome by what he was saying. "People who – perhaps they are better than us, live in a just society, wonderful people. . . ."

"I know, socialists to a man!" Fox exclaimed. This was one point on which he did not share his friend's advanced thinking. He had listened to Mr Tout talking in the office, and thought he knew better than his rich friend how these socialists, of which one heard so much these days, were undermining society. "Stars full of socialists!"

"Better than stars full of Christians! Why, if the stars were full of Christians, no doubt they would already have sent missionaries down here to preach their Gospel."

"I wonder if there ever will be planetary journeys as predicted by Nunsowe Greene and Monsieur Jules Verne – " Fox said, when the appearance of a fresh meteor stopped him in mid-sentence.

Like the last, this meteor seemed to come from the general direction of Auriga. It travelled slowly, and it glowed red, and it sailed grandly towards them. They both exclaimed at once, and gripped each other by the arm. The magnificent spark burned in the sky, larger now, so that its red aura appeared to encase a brighter orange glow. It passed overhead (afterwards, they argued whether it had not made a slight noise as it passed) and disappeared below a clump of willow. They knew it had been near. For an instant, the land had shone with its light.

Gregory was the first to break the silence.

"Bruce, Bruce, did you see that? That was no ordinary fireball!"

"It was so big! What was it?"

"Perhaps our heavenly visitor has come at last!"

"Hey, Greg, it must have landed by your friends' farm – the Grendon place – mustn't it?"

"You're right! I must pay old Mr Grendon a visit tomorrow and see if he or his family saw anything of this."

They talked excitedly, stamping their feet as they exercised their lungs. Their conversation was the conversation of optimistic young men, and included much speculative matter that began "Wouldn't it be wonderful if – " or "Just supposing – " Then they stopped and laughed at their own absurd beliefs.

"It must be nearly nine o'clock," Fox said at last. "I didn't mean to be so late tonight. It's funny how fast time passes. We'd best be getting back, Greg."

They had brought no lantern, since the night was both clear and dry. It was but two miles by the track back to the outlying houses of Cottersall. They stepped it out lustily, arm linked in arm in case one of them tripped in cart ruts, for Fox had to be up at five in the morning if he was to bicycle to his work punctually. The little village lay silent, or almost so. In the baker's house where Gregory lodged, a gaslight burned and a piano could be heard. As they halted smartly at the side door, Fox said slyly, "So you'll be seeing all the Grendon family tomorrow?"

"It seems probable, unless that red hot planetary ship has already borne them off to a better world."

"Tell us true, Greg – you really go to see that pretty Nancy Grendon, don't you?"

Gregory struck his friend playfully on the shoulder.

"No need for your jealousy, Bruce! I go to see the father, not the daughter. Though the one is female, the other is progressive, and that must interest me more just yet. Nancy has beauty, true, but her father – ah, her father has electricity!"

Laughing, they cheerfully shook hands and parted for the night.

On Grendon's farm, things were a deal less tranquil, as Gregory was to discover.

Gregory Rolles rose before seven next morning, as was his custom. It was while he was lighting his gas mantle, and wishing the baker would install electricity, that a swift train of thought led him to reflect again on the phenomenal thing in the previous night's sky. Mrs Fenn, the baker's wife, who had already lit his fire, brought him up hot water for washing and scalding water for shaving and, later, a mighty tray full of breakfast. Throughout this activity, and indeed while he ate his porridge and chops, Gregory remained abstracted, letting his mind wander luxuriously over all the possibilities that the "meteor" illuminated. He decided that he would ride out to see Mr Grendon within the hour.

He was lucky in being able, at this stage in his life, to please himself largely as to how his days were spent, for his father was a person of some substance. Edward Rolles had had the fortune, at the time of the Crimean War, to meet Escoffier, and with some help from the great chef had brought on to the market a baking powder, "Eugenol", that, being slightly more palatable and less deleterious to the human system than its rivals, had achieved great commercial success. As a result, Gregory had attended one of the Cambridge colleges.

Now, having gained a degree, he was poised on the verge of a career. But which career? He had acquired – more as result of his intercourse with other students than with those officially deputed to instruct him – some understanding of the sciences; his essays had been praised and some of his poetry published, so that he inclined towards literature; and an uneasy sense that life for everyone outside the privileged classes contained too large a proportion of misery led him to think seriously of a political career. In Divinity, too, he was well-grounded; but at least the idea of Holy Orders did not tempt him.

While he wrestled with his future, he undertook to live away from home, since his relations with his father were never smooth. By rusticating himself in the heart of East Anglia, he hoped to gather material for a volume tentatively entitled *Wanderings with a Socialist Naturalist*, which would assuage all sides of his ambitions. Nancy Grendon, who had a pretty hand with a pencil, might even execute a little emblem for the title page . . . Perhaps he might be permitted to dedicate it to his author friend, Mr Herbert George Wells. . . .

He dressed himself warmly, for the morning was cold as well as dull, and went down to the baker's stables. When he had saddled his mare, Daisy, he swung himself up and set out along a road that the horse knew well.

The sun had been up for something over an hour, yet the sky and the landscape were drab in the extreme. Two sorts of East Anglian landscape met here, trapped by the confused wanderings of the River Oast: the unfarmable heathland and the unfarmable fen. There were few trees, and those stunted, so that the four fine elms that stood on one side of the Grendon farm made a cynosure for miles around.

The land rose slightly towards the farm, the area about the house forming something of a little island amid marshy ground and irregular stretches of water that gave back to the sky its own dun tone. The gate over the little bridge was, as always, open wide; Daisy picked her way through the mud to the stables, where Gregory left her to champ oats contentedly. Cuff and her pup, Lardie, barked loudly about Gregory's heels as usual, and he patted their heads on his way over to the house.

Nancy came hurrying out to meet him before he got to the front door.

"We had some excitement last night, Gregory," she said. He

noted with pleasure she had at last brought herself to use his first name.

"Something bright and glaring!" she said. "I was retiring, when this noise come and then this light, and I rush to look out through the curtains, and there's this here great thing like an egg sinking into our pond." In her speech, and particularly when she was excited, she carried the lilting accent of Norfolk.

"The meteor!" Gregory exclaimed. "Bruce Fox and I were out last night as we were the night before, watching for the lovely Aurigids that arrive every February, when we saw an extra big one. I said then it was coming over very near here."

"Why, it almost landed on our house," Nancy said. She looked very pleasing this morning, with her lips red, her cheeks shining, and her chestnut curls all astray. As she spoke, her mother appeared in apron and cap, with a wrap hurriedly thrown over her shoulders.

"Nancy, you come in, standing freezing like that! You ent daft, girl, are you? Hello, Gregory, how be going on? I didn't reckon as we'd see you today. Come in and warm yourself."

"Good-day to you, Mrs Grendon. I'm hearing about your wonderful meteor of last night."

"It was a falling star, according to Bert Neckland. I ent sure what it was, but it certainly stirred up the animals, that I *do* know."

"Can you see anything of it in the pond?" Gregory asked.

"Let me show you," Nancy said.

Mrs Grendon returned indoors. She went slowly and grandly, her back very straight and an unaccustomed load before her. Nancy was her only daughter; there was a younger son, Archie, a stubborn lad who had fallen at odds with his father and now was apprenticed to a blacksmith in Norwich; and no other children living. Three infants had not survived the mixture of fogs alternating with bitter east winds that comprised the typical Cottersall winter. But now the farmer's wife was unexpectedly gravid again, and would bear her husband another baby when the spring came in.

As Nancy led Gregory over to the pond, he saw Grendon with his two labourers working in the West Field, but they did not wave.

"Was your father not excited by the arrival last night?"

"That he was – when it happened! He went out with his shot gun, and Bert Neckland with him. But there was nothing to see but bubbles in the pond and steam over it, and this morning he wouldn't discuss it, and said that work must go on whatever happen."

They stood beside the pond, a dark and extensive slab of water with rushes on the farther bank and open country beyond. As they looked at its ruffled surface, they stood with the windmill black and bulky on their left hand. It was to this that Nancy now pointed.

Mud had been splashed across the boards high up the sides of the mill; some was to be seen even on the tip of the nearest white sail. Gregory surveyed it all with interest. Nancy, however, was still pursuing her own line of thought.

"Don't you reckon Father works too hard, Gregory? When he ent outside doing jobs, he's in reading his pamphlets and his electricity manuals. He never rests but when he sleeps."

"Um. Whatever went into the pond went in with a great smack! There's no sign of anything there now, is there? Not that you can see an inch below the surface."

"You being a friend of his, Mum thought perhaps as you'd say something to him. He don't go to bed till ever so late – sometimes it's near midnight, and then he's up again at three and a half o'clock. Would you speak to him? You know Mother dassent."

"Nancy, we ought to see whatever it was that went in the pond. It can't have dissolved. How deep is the water? Is it very deep?"

"Oh, you aren't listening, Gregory Rolles! Bother the old meteor!"

"This is a matter of science, Nancy. Don't you see – "

"Oh, rotten old science, is it? Then I don't want to hear. I'm cold, standing out here. You can have a good look if you like, but I'm going in before I gets froze. It was only an old stone out of the sky, because I heard Father and Bert Neckland agree to it."

"Fat lot Bert Neckland knows about such things!" he called to her departing back. She had the prettiest ringlets on her neck, but really he didn't want to get involved with a nineteen-year-old farmer's daughter. It was a pity more girls didn't believe in Free Love, as did most of his male acquaintances.

He looked down at the dark water. Whatever it *was* that had arrived last night, it was here, only a few feet from him. He longed to discover what remained of it. Vivid pictures entered his mind: his name in headlines in the *Morning Post*, the Royal Society making him an honorary member, his father embracing him and pressing him to return home.

Thoughtfully, he walked over to the barn. Hens ran clucking out of his way as he entered and stood looking up, waiting for his eyes to adjust to the dim light. There, as he remembered it, was a little rowing boat. Perhaps in his courting days old Mr Grendon had taken his prospective wife out for excursions on the Oast in it. Surely it had not been used in years.

He moved the long ladder over to climb and inspect it, and a cat went flying across the rafters in retreat. The inside of the boat was filthy, but two oars lay there, and it seemed intact. The craft had been hitched to its present position by two ropes thrown over a higher beam; it was a simple enough matter to lower it to the ground.

At that point, Gregory had a moment of prudence for other people's property. He went into the farm house and asked Mrs Grendon if he might embark on the pond with it. That complaisant lady said he might do as he wished, and accordingly he dragged the boat from the barn and launched it in the shallows of the pond. It floated. The boards had dried, and water leaked through a couple of seams, but not nearly enough to deter him. Climbing delicately in among the straw and filth, he pushed off.

From here, the farm, or such of it as he could see, presented a somewhat sinister aspect. The mill loomed above him, dismal and tarred black, only its sails white and creaking in the slight wind. To his other side, the blank-faced end of the barn looked immense and meaningless. Behind it he could see the backs of cowsheds with, beyond them, the raw new brick of the back of Grendon's machine house, where he made electricity. Between barn and mill, he could see the farm house, but the upper storey only, because of the lie of the land. Its decrepit humps of thatch and the tall stack of its chimney gave it a forbidding air. He mused on the strangeness that overcame one from looking at human works from an angle from which they were never designed to be seen, and wondered if there were similar angles in nature. Presumably there were, for behind him where the pond ended were only ragged willows topping reed beds. It looked as if there should have been something else – a little land at least – but no land showed, only the willows and the watery sky.

Now he was over the approximate centre of the pond. He shipped his oars and peered over the side. There was an agitation in the water, and nothing could be seen, although he imagined much.

As he stared over the one side, the boat unexpectedly tipped to the other. Gregory swung round. The boat listed heavily to the left, so that the oars rolled over that way. He could see nothing. Yet – he heard something. It was a sound much like a hound slowly panting. And whatever made it was about to capsize the boat.

"What is it?" he said, as all the skin prickled up his back and skull.

The boat lurched, for all the world as if someone invisible were trying to get into it. Frightened, he grasped the oar, and, without thinking, swept it over that side of the rowing boat.

It struck something solid where there was only air.

Dropping the oar in surprise, he put out his hand. It touched something yielding. At the same time, his arm was violently struck.

His actions were then entirely governed by instinct. Thought did not enter the matter. He picked up the oar again and smote the thin air with it. It hit something. There was a splash, and the boat righted itself so suddenly he was almost pitched into the water. Even while it still rocked, he was rowing frantically for the shallows, dragging the boat from the water, and running for the safety of the farm house.

Only at the door did he pause. His reason returned, his heart began gradually to stop stammering its fright. He stood looking at the seamed wood of the porch, trying to evaluate what he had seen and what had actually happened. But what had happened?

Forcing himself to go back to the pond, he stood by the boat and looked across the sullen face of the water. It lay undisturbed, except by surface ripples. He looked at the boat. A quantity of water lay in the bottom of it. He thought, all that happened was that I nearly capsized, and I let my idiot fears run away with me. Shaking his head, he pulled the boat back to the barn.

Gregory, as he often did, stayed to eat lunch at the farm, but he saw nothing of the farmer till milking time.

Joseph Grendon was in his late forties, and a few years older than his wife. He had a gaunt solemn face and a heavy beard that made him look older than he was. For all his seriousness, he greeted Gregory civilly enough. They stood together in the gathering dusk as the cows swung behind them into their regular stalls. Together they walked into the machine house next door, and Grendon lit the oil burners that started the steam engine into motion that would turn the generator that would supply the vital spark.

"I smell the future in here," Gregory said, smiling. By now, he had forgotten the shock of the morning.

"The future will have to get on without me. I shall be dead by then." The farmer spoke as he walked, putting each word reliably before the next.

"That is what you always say. You're wrong – the future is rushing upon us."

"You ent far wrong there, Master Gregory, but I won't have no part of it, I reckon. I'm an old man now. Do you know what I was reading in one of those London papers last night? They do say as how before another half-century is out every house in the country will be supplied with electrical lighting from one big central power house in London. This here old machine won't be no good then, will it?"

"It will be the end of the gas industry, that's for sure. That will cause much unemployment."

"Well, of course, in remote districts like this here primitive place, you wouldn't get gas in a dozen centuries. But electrical lighting is easier to conduct from one place to another than gas is. Here she come!"

This last exclamation was directed at a flicker of light in the pilot bulb overhead. They stood there contemplating with satisfaction the wonderful machinery. As steam pressure rose, the great leather belt turned faster and faster, and the flicker in the pilot bulb grew stronger. Although Gregory was used to a home lit by both gas and electricity, he never felt the excitement of it as he did here, out in the wilds, where the nearest incandescent bulb was probably in Norwich, a great part of a day's journey away.

"Why did you really decide to have this plant built, Joseph?"

"Like I told you, it's safer than lanterns in the sheds and the sties and anywhere with dry straw about the place. My father had a bad fire here when I was a boy that put the wind up me proper . . . Did I ever tell you as how Bert Neckland's older brother used to work for me once, till I got this here equipment in? He was a regular Bible-thumper, he was, and do you know what he told me? He said as how this here electrical lighting was too bright and devilish to be God's work, and in consequence he refused to let it shine on him. So I told him, I said, Well, I ent having you going round with an umbrella up all hours of darkness, and I give him his wages and I tell him to clear off out if that's the way he feels."

"And he did?"

"He ent been back here since."

"Idiot! All things are possible now. The Steam Age was wonderful in its way, or must have seemed so to the people that lived in it, but in this new Electric Age – anything's possible. Do you know what I believe, Joseph? I believe that before so very many years are up, we shall have electrical flying machines. Who knows, we may even be able to make them big enough to fly to the moon! Oh, I tell you, I just cannot wait till the New Century. By then, who knows, all men may be united in brotherhood, and then we shall see some progress."

"I don't know. I shall be united in my grave by then."

"Nonsense, you can live to be a hundred."

Now a pale flickering radiance illuminated the room. By contrast, everything outside looked black. Grendon nodded in satisfaction, made some adjustments to the burners, and they went outside.

Free from the bustle of the steam engine, they could hear the noise the cows were making. At milking time, the animals were usually quiet; something had upset them. The farmer ran quickly into the milking shed, with Gregory on his heels.

The new light, radiating from a bulb hanging above the stalls, showed the beasts of restless demeanour and rolling eye. Bert Neckland stood as far away from the door as possible, grasping his stick and letting his mouth hang open.

"What in blazes you staring at, bor?" Grendon asked.

Neckland slowly shut his mouth.

"We had a scare," he said. "Something come in here," he said.

"Did you see what it was?" Gregory asked.

"No, there weren't nothing to see. It was a ghost, that's what it was. It come right in here and touched the cows. It touched me too. It was a ghost."

The farmer snorted. "A tramp more like. You couldn't see because the light wasn't on."

His man shook his head emphatically. "Light weren't that bad. I tell you, whatever it was, it come right up to me and touched me." He stopped, and pointed to the edge of the stall. "Look there! See, I weren't telling you no lie, master. It was a ghost, and there's its wet hand-print."

They crowded round and examined the worn and chewed timber at the corner of the partition between two stalls. An indefinite patch of moisture darkened the wood. Gregory's thoughts went back to his experience on the pond, and again he felt the prickle of unease along his spine. But the farmer said stoutly, "Nonsense, it's a bit of cowslime. Now you get on with the milking, Bert, and let's have no more hossing about, because I want my tea. Where's Cuff?"

Bert looked defiant.

"If you don't believe me, maybe you'll believe the bitch. She saw whatever it was and went for it. It kicked her over, but she ran it out of here."

"I'll see if I can see her," Gregory said.

He ran outside and began calling the bitch. By now it was almost entirely dark. He could see nothing moving in the wide space of the front yard, and so set off in the other direction, down the path towards the pig sties and the fields, calling Cuff as he went. He paused. Low and savage growls sounded ahead, under the elm trees. It was Cuff. He went slowly forward. At this moment, he cursed that electric light meant lack of lanterns, and wished too that he had a weapon.

"Who's there?" he called.

The farmer came up by his side. "Let's charge 'em!"

They ran forward. The trunks of the four great elms were clear against the western sky, with water glinting leadenly behind them. The dog became visible. As Gregory saw Cuff, she sailed into the air, whirled round, and flew at the farmer. He flung up his arms and warded off the body. At the same time, Gregory felt a rush of air as if someone unseen had run past him, and a stale muddy smell filled his nostrils. Staggering, he looked behind him. The wan light from the cowsheds spread across the path between the outhouses and the farmhouse. Beyond the light, more distantly, was the silent countryside behind the grain store. Nothing untoward could be seen.

"They killed my old Cuff," said the farmer.

Gregory knelt down beside him to look at the bitch. There was no mark of injury on her, but she was dead, her fine head lying limp.

"She knew there was something there," Gregory said. "She went to attack whatever it was and it got her first. What was it? Whatever in the world was it?"

"They killed my old Cuff," said the farmer again, unhearing. He picked the body up in his arms, turned, and carried it towards the house. Gregory stood where he was, mind and heart equally uneasy.

He jumped violently when a step sounded nearby. It was Bert Neckland.

"What, did that there ghost kill the old bitch?" he asked.

"It killed the bitch certainly, but it was something more terrible than a ghost."

"That's one of them ghosts, bor. I seen plenty in my time. I ent afraid of ghosts, are you?"

"You looked fairly sick in the cowshed a minute ago."

The farmhand put his fists on his hips. He was no more than a couple of years older than Gregory, a stocky young man with a spotty complexion and a snub nose that gave him at once an air of comedy and menace. "Is that so, Master Gregory? Well, you looks pretty funky standing there now."

"I am scared. I don't mind admitting it. But only because we have something here a lot nastier than any spectre."

Neckland came a little closer.

"Then if you are so blooming windy, perhaps you'll be staying away from the farm in future."

"Certainly not." He tried to edge back into the light, but the labourer got in his way.

"If I was you, I should stay away." He emphasised his point by digging an elbow into Gregory's coat. "And just remember that Nancy was interested in me long afore you come along, bor."

"Oh, that's it, is it! I think Nancy can decide for herself in whom she is interested, don't you?"

"I'm *telling* you who she's interested in, see? And mind you don't forget, see?" He emphasised the words with another nudge. Gregory pushed his arm away angrily. Neckland shrugged his shoulders and walked off. As he went, he said, "You're going to get worse than ghosts if you keep hanging round here."

Gregory was shaken. The suppressed violence in the man's voice suggested that he had been harbouring malice for some time. Unsuspectingly, Gregory had always gone out of his way to be cordial, had regarded the sullenness as mere slow-wittedness and done his socialist best to overcome the barrier between them. He thought of following Neckland and trying to make it up with him; but that would look too feeble. Instead, he followed the way the farmer had gone with his dead bitch, and made for the house.

Gregory Rolles was too late back to Cottersall that night to meet his friend Fox. The next night, the weather became exceedingly chill and Gabriel Woodcock, the oldest inhabitant, was prophesying snow before the winter was out (a not very venturesome prophecy to be fulfilled within forty-eight hours, thus impressing most of the inhabitants of the village, for they took pleasure in being impressed and exclaiming and saying "Well I never!" to each other). The two friends met in "The Wayfarer", where the fires were bigger, though the ale was weaker, than in the "Three Poachers" at the other end of the village.

Seeing to it that nothing dramatic was missed from his account, Gregory related the affairs of the previous day, omitting any reference to Neckland's pugnacity. Fox listened fascinated, neglecting both his pipe and his ale.

"So you see how it is, Bruce," Gregory concluded. "In that deep pond by the mill lurks a vehicle of some sort, the very one we saw in the sky, and in it lives an invisible being of evil intent. You see how I fear for my friends there. Should I tell the police about it, do you think?"

"I'm sure it would not help the Grendons to have old Farrish bumping out there on his penny-farthing," Fox said, referring to the local representative of the law. He took a long draw first on the pipe and then on the glass. "But I'm not sure you have your conclusions quite right, Greg. Understand, I don't doubt the facts, amazing though they are. I mean, we were more or less expecting celestial visitants. The world's recent blossoming with gas and electric lighting in its cities at night must have been a signal to half the nations of space that we are now civilised down here. But have our visitants done any deliberate harm to anyone?"

"They nearly drowned me and they killed poor Cuff. I don't see what you're getting at. They haven't begun in a very friendly fashion, have they now?"

"Think what the situation must seem like to them. Suppose they come from Mars or the Moon – we know their world must be absolutely different from Earth. They may be terrified. And it can hardly be called an unfriendly act to try and get into your rowing boat. The first unfriendly act was yours, when you struck out with the oar."

Gregory bit his lip. His friend had a point. "I was scared."

"It may have been because they were scared that they killed Cuff. The dog attacked them, after all, didn't she? I feel sorry for these creatures, alone in an unfriendly world."

"You keep saying 'these'! As far as we know, there is only one of them."

"My point is this, Greg. You have completely gone back on your previous enlightened attitude. You are all for killing these poor things instead of trying to speak to them. Remember what you were saying about other worlds being full of socialists? Try thinking of these chaps as invisible socialists and see if that doesn't make them easier to deal with."

Gregory fell to stroking his chin. Inwardly, he acknowledged that Bruce Fox's words made a great impression on him. He had allowed panic to prejudice his judgement; as a result, he had behaved as immoderately as a savage in some remote corner of the Empire confronted by his first steam locomotive.

"I'd better get back to the farm and sort things out as soon as possible," he said. "If these things really do need help, I'll help them."

"That's it. But try not to think of them as 'things'. Think of them as – as – I know, as The Aurigans."

"Aurigans it is. But don't be so smug, Bruce. If you'd been in that boat – "

"I know, old friend. I'd have died of fright." To this monument of tact, Fox added, "Do as you say, go back and sort things out as soon as possible. I'm longing for the next instalment of this mystery. It's quite the jolliest thing since Sherlock Holmes."

Gregory Rolles went back to the farm. But the sorting out of which Bruce had spoken took longer than he expected. This was chiefly because the Aurigans seemed to have settled quietly into their new home after the initial day's troubles.

They came forth no more from the pond, as far as he could discover; at least they caused no more disturbance. The young graduate particularly regretted this since he had taken his friend's words much to heart, and wanted to prove how enlightened and benevolent he was towards this strange form of life. After some days, he came to believe the Aurigans must have left as unexpectedly as they arrived. Then a minor incident convinced him otherwise; and that same night, in his snug room over the baker's shop, he described it to his correspondent in Worcester Park, Surrey.

'Dear Mr Wells,

I must apologise for my failure to write earlier, owing to lack of news concerning the Grendon Farm affair.

Only today, the Aurigans showed themselves again! – If indeed 'showed' is the right word for invisible creatures.

Nancy Grendon and I were in the orchard feeding the hens. There is still much snow lying about, and everywhere is very white. As the poultry came running to Nancy's tub, I saw a disturbance further down the orchard – merely some snow dropping from an apple bough, but the movement caught my eye, and I then saw a *procession* of falling snow proceed towards us from tree to tree. The grass is long there, and I soon noted the stalks being thrust aside by *an unknown agency!* I directed Nancy's attention to the phenomenon. The motion in the grass stopped only a few yards from us.

Nancy was startled, but I determined to acquit myself more like a Briton than I had previously. Accordingly, I advanced and said, 'Who are you? What do you want? We are your friends if you are friendly.'

No answer came. I stepped forward again, and now the grass again fell back, and I could see by the way it was pressed down that the creature must have large feet. By the movement of the grasses, I could see he was running. I cried to him and ran too. He went round the side of the house, and then over the frozen mud in the farmyard I could see no further trace of him. But instinct led me forward, past the barn to the pond.

Surely enough, I then saw the cold, muddy water rise and heave, as if engulfing a body that slid quietly in. Shards of broken ice were thrust aside, and by an outward motion, I could see where the strange being went. In a flurry and a small whirlpool, he was gone, and I have no doubt dived down to the mysterious star vehicle.

These things – people – I know not what to call them – must be aquatic; perhaps they live in the canals of the Red Planet. But imagine, Sir – an invisible mankind! The idea is almost as wonderful and fantastic as something from your novel, *The Time Machine*.

Pray give me your comment, and trust in my sanity and accuracy as a reporter!

Yours in friendship,
Gregory Rolles.'

What he did not tell was the way Nancy had clung to him after, in the warmth of the parlour, and confessed her fear. And he had scorned the idea that these beings could be hostile, and had seen the admiration in her eyes, and had thought that she was, after all, a dashed pretty girl, and perhaps worth braving the wrath of those two very different people for: Edward Rolles, his father, and Bert Neckland, the farm labourer.

At that point Mrs Grendon came in, and the two young people moved rapidly apart. Mrs Grendon went more slowly. The new life within her was large now, and she carried herself accordingly. So as not to distress her, they told her nothing of what they had seen. Nor was there time for discussion, for the farmer and his two men came tramping into the kitchen, kicking off their boots and demanding lunch.

It was at lunch a week later, when Gregory was again at the farm, taking with him an article on electricity as a pretext for his visit, that the subject of the stinking dew was first discussed.

Grubby was the first to mention it in Gregory's hearing. Grubby, with Bert Neckland, formed the whole strength of Joseph Grendon's labour force; but whereas Neckland was considered couth enough to board in the farmhouse (he had a gaunt room in the attic), Grubby was fit only to sleep in a little flint-and-chalk hut well away from the farm building. His "house", as he dignified the miserable hut, stood below the orchard and near the sties, the occupants of which lulled Grubby to sleep with their snorts.

"Reckon we ent ever had a dew like that before, Mr Grendon," he said, his manner suggesting to Gregory that he had made this observation already this morning; Grubby never ventured to say anything original.

"Heavy as an autumn dew," said the farmer firmly, as if there had been an argument on that point.

Silence fell, broken only by a general munching and, from Grubby, a particular guzzling, as they all made their way through huge platefuls of stewed rabbit and dumplings.

"It weren't no ordinary dew, that I do know," Grubby said after a while.

"It stank of toadstools," Neckland said. "Or rotten pond water."

More munching.

"I have read of freak dews before," Gregory told the company. "And you hear of freak rains, when frogs fall out of the sky. I've even read of hailstones with live frogs and toads embedded in them."

"There's always something beyond belief as you have read of, Master Gregory," Neckland said. "But we happen to be talking about this here dew that fell right on this here farm this here morning. There weren't no frogs in it, either."

"Well it's gone now, so I can't see why you're worried about it," Nancy said.

"We ent ever had a dew like that before, Miss Nancy," Grubby said.

"I know I had to wash my washing again," Mrs Grendon said. "I left it out all night and it stank really foul this morning."

"It may be something to do with the pond," Gregory said. "Some sort of freak of evaporation."

Neckland snorted. From his position at the top of the table, the farmer halted his shovelling operations to point a fork at Gregory.

"You may well be right there. Because I tell you what, that there dew only come down on our land and property. A yard the other side of the gate, the road was dry. Bone dry it was."

"Right you are there, master," Neckland agreed. "And while the West Field was dripping with the stuff, I saw for myself that the bracken over the hedge weren't wet at all. Ah, it's a rum go!"

"Say what you like, we ent ever had a dew like it," Grubby said. He appeared to be summing up the feeling of the company.

Leading off the parlour was a smaller room. Although it shared a massive fireplace with the parlour – for the whole house was built round and supported by this central brick stack – fires were rarely lit in the smaller room. This was the Best Room. Here Joseph Grendon occasionally retired to survey – with some severity and discomfort – his accounts. Otherwise the room was never used.

After his meal, Grendon retired belching into the Best Room, and Gregory followed. This was where the farmer kept his modest store of books, his Carlyles, Ainsworths, Ruskins, and Lyttons, together with the copy of *The Time Machine* which Gregory had presented to him at Christmas, complete with a socially-inspired inscription. But the room was chiefly notable for the stuffed animals it contained, some encased in glass.

These animals had evidently been assaulted by a blunderer in taxidermy, for they stood in poses that would in life have been beyond them, even supposing them to have been equipped with the extra joints and malformations indicated by their post-mortemnal shapes. They numbered among them creatures that bore chance resemblances to owls, dogs, foxes, cats, goats and calves. Only the stuffed fish carried more than a wan likeness to their living counterparts, and they had felt such an autumn after death that all their scales had been shed like leaves.

Gregory looked doubtfully at these monsters in which man's forming hand was more evident than God's. There were so many of them that some had overflowed into the parlour; in the Best Room, it was their multitude as well as their deformity that appalled. All the same, seeing how gloomily Grendon scowled over his ledger, Gregory said, thinking to cheer the older man, "You should practise some more taxidermy, Joseph."

"Ah." Without looking up.

"The hobby would be pleasant for you."

"Ah." Now he did look up. "You're young and you know only the good side of life. You're ignorant, Master Gregory, for all your university learning. You don't know how the qualities get whittled away from a man until by the time he's my age, there's only persistence left."

"That's not – "

"I shall never do another stuffing job. I ent got time! I ent really got time for nothing but this here old farm."

"But that's not true! You – "

"I say it is true, and I don't talk idle. I pass the time of day with you; I might even say I like you; but you don't *mean* nothing to me." He looked straight at Gregory as he spoke, and then slowly lowered his eyes with what might have been sadness. "Neither does Marjorie mean nothing to me now, though that was different afore we married. I got this here farm, you see, and I'm the farm and it is me."

He was stuck for words, and the beady eyes of the specimens ranged about him stared at him unhelpfully.

"Of course it's hard work," Gregory said.

"You don't understand, bor. Nobody do. This here land is no good. It's barren. Every year, it grows less and less. It ent got no more life than what these here stuffed animals have. So that means I am barren too – year by year, I got less substance."

He stood up suddenly, angry perhaps at himself.

"You better go home, Master Gregory."

"Joe, I'm terribly sorry. I wish I could help. . . ."

"I know you mean kindly. You go home while the night's fine." He peered out into the blank yard. "Let's hope we don't get another stinking dewfall tonight."

The strange dew did not fall again. As a topic of conversation, it was limited, and even on the farm, where there was little new to talk about, it was forgotten in a few days. The February passed, being neither much worse nor much better than most Februaries, and ended in heavy rainstorms. March came, letting in a chilly

spring over the land. The animals on the farm began to bring forth
their young.

They brought them forth in amazing numbers, as if to overturn
all the farmer's beliefs in the unproductiveness of his land.

"I never seen anything like it!" Grendon said to Gregory. Nor
had Gregory seen the taciturn farmer so excited. He took the young
man by the arm and marched him into the barn.

There lay Trix, the nannie goat. Against her flank huddled three
little brown and white kids, while a fourth stood nearby, wobbling
on its spindly legs.

"Four on 'em! Have you ever heard of a goat throwing off *four*
kids? You better write to the papers in London about this, Gregory!
But just you come down to the pigsties."

The squealing from the sties was louder than usual. As they
marched down the path towards them, Gregory looked up at the
great elms, their outlines dusted in green, and thought he detected
something sinister in the noises, something hysterical that was
perhaps matched by an element in Grendon's own bearing.

The Grendon pigs were mixed breeds, with a preponderence of
Large Blacks. They usually gave litters of something like ten piglets.
Now there was not a litter without fourteen in it; one enormous
black sow had eighteen small pigs nuzzling about her. The noise
was tremendous and, standing looking down on this swarming life,
Gregory told himself that he was foolish to imagine anything
uncanny in it; he knew so little about farm life.

"'Course, they ent all going to live," the farmer said. "The old
sows ent got enough dugs to feed that brood. But it's a record lot! I
reckon you ought to write to that there 'Norwich Advertiser' about
it."

Grubby lumbered up with two pails of feed, his great round face
flushed as if in rapport with all the fecundity about him.

"Never seen so many pigs," he said. "You ought to write to that
there newspaper in Norwich about it, bor. There ent never been so
many pigs."

Gregory had no chance to talk to Nancy on the subject. She and
her mother had driven to town in the trap, for it was market day in
Cottersall. After he had eaten with Grendon and the men – Mrs
Grendon had left them a cold lunch – Gregory went by himself to
look about the farm, still with a deep and (he told himself)
unreasoning sense of disturbance inside him.

A pale sunshine filled the afternoon. It could not penetrate far down into the water of the pond. But Gregory stood by the horse trough staring at the expanse of water; he saw that it teemed with young tadpoles and frogs. He went closer. What he had regarded as a sheet of rather stagnant water was alive with small swimming things. As he looked, a great beetle surged out of the depths and seized a tadpole. The tadpoles were also providing food for two ducks that, with their young, were swimming by the reeds on the far side of the pond. And how many young did the ducks have? An armada of chicks was there, parading in and out of the rushes.

He walked round behind the barn and the cowsheds, where the ground was marshy, and across the bridge at the back of the machine house. The haystacks stood here, and behind them a wild stretch of hedge. As he went, Gregory watched for birds' nests. In the woodpile was a redstart's nest, in the marsh a meadow pipit's, in the hedge nests of sparrows and blackbirds. All were piled high with eggs – far too many eggs.

For a minute, he stood uncertainly, then began to walk slowly back the way he had come. Nancy stood between two of the haystacks. He started in surprise at seeing her. He called her name, but she stood silent with her back to him.

Puzzled, he went forward and touched her on the shoulder. Her head swung round. He saw her long teeth, the yellow curve of bone that had been her nose – but it was a sheep's head, falling backwards off a stick over which her old cloak had been draped. It lay on the ground by her bonnet, and he stared down at it in dismay, trying to quiet the leap of his heart. And at that moment, Neckland jumped out and caught him by the wrist.

"Ha, that gave thee a scare, my hearty, didn't it? I saw 'ee hanging round here. Why don't you get off out of here and never come back, bor? I warned you before, and I ent going to warn you again, do you hear? You leave Nancy alone, you and your books!"

Gregory wrenched his hand away.

"You did this, did you, you bloody ignorant lout? What do you think you are playing at here? How do you think Nancy or her mother would like it if they saw what you had done? Suppose I showed this to Farmer Grendon? Are you off your head, Neckland?"

"Don't you call me a ignorant lout or I'll knock off that there block of yours, that I will. I'm a-giving you a good scare, you cheeky tick, and I'm a-warning you to keep away from here."

"I don't want your warnings, and I refuse to heed them. It's up to the Grendons whether or not I come here, not you. You keep to your place and I'll keep to mine. If you try this sort of thing again, we shall come to blows."

Neckland looked less pugnacious than he had a moment ago. He said, cockily enough, "I ent afraid of you."

"Then I may give you cause to be," Gregory said. Turning on his heel, he walked swiftly away – alert at the same time for an attack from the rear. But Neckland slunk away as silently as he had come.

Crossing the yard, Gregory went over to the stable and saddled Daisy. He swung himself up and rode away without bidding good-bye to anyone.

At one point, he looked over his shoulder. The farm crouched low and dark above the desolate land. Sky predominated over everything. The Earth seemed merely a strip of beach before a great tumbled ocean of air and light and space and things ill-defined; and from that ocean had come . . . he did not know, nor did he know how to find out, except by waiting and seeing if the strange vessel from the seas of space had brought evil or blessing.

Riding into Cottersall, he went straight to the market place. He saw the Grendon trap, with Nancy's little pony, Hetty, between the shafts, standing outside the grocer's shop. Mrs Grendon and Nancy were just coming out. Jumping to the ground, Gregory led Daisy over to them and bid them good day.

"We are going to call on my friend Mrs Edwards and her daughters," Mrs Grendon said.

"I wondered, Mrs Grendon, if you'd allow me to speak with Nancy privately, just for ten minutes."

Mrs Grendon was well wrapped against the wind; she made a monumental figure as she looked at her daughter and considered.

"Seeing you talks to her at the farm, I don't see why you shouldn't talk to her here, but I don't want to cause no scandal, Master Gregory, and I'm sure I don't know where you can go to talk private. I mean, folks are more staid in their ways in Norfolk than they used to be in my young days, and I don't want any scandal. Can't it wait till you come to see us at the farm again?"

"If you would be so kind, Mrs Grendon, I would be very obliged if I might speak privately with her now. My landlady, Mrs Fenn, has a little downstairs parlour at the back of the shop, and I know she would let us speak there. It would be quite respectable."

"Drat respectable! Let people think what they will, I say." All the same, she stood for some time in meditation. Nancy remained by her mother with her eyes on the ground. Gregory looked at her and seemed to see her anew. Under her blue coat, fur-trimmed, she wore her orange-and-brown squared gingham dress; she had a bonnet on her head. Her complexion was pure and blemishless, her skin as firm and delicate as a plum, and her dark eyes were hidden under long lashes. Her lips were steady, pale, and clearly defined, with appealing tucks at each corner. He felt almost like a thief, stealing a sight of her beauty while she was not regarding him.

"I'm going on to Mrs Edwards," Marjorie Grendon declared at last. "I don't care what you two do so long as you behave – but I shall, mind, if you aren't with me in a half-hour, Nancy, do you hear?"

"Yes, mother."

The baker's shop was in the next street. Gregory and Nancy walked there in silence. Gregory shut Daisy in the stable and they went together into the parlour through the back door. At this time of day, Mr Fenn was resting upstairs and his wife looking after the shop, so the little room was empty.

Nancy sat upright in a chair and said, "Well, Gregory, what's all this about? Fancy dragging me off from my mother like that in the middle of town!"

"Nancy, don't be cross. I had to see you."

She pouted. "You come out to the old farm often enough and don't show any particular wish to see me there."

"That's nonsense. I always come to see you – lately in particular. Besides, you're more interested in Bert Neckland, aren't you?"

"Bert Neckland, indeed! Why should I be interested in him? Not that it's any of your business if I am."

"It is my business, Nancy. I love you, Nancy!"

He had not meant to blurt it out in quite that fashion, but now it was out, it was out, and he pressed home his disadvantage by crossing the room, kneeling at her feet, and taking her hands in his.

"I thought you only came out to the farm to see my father."

"It was like that at first, Nancy, but no more."

"You've got interested in farming now, haven't you? That's what you come for now, isn't it?"

"Well, I certainly am interested in the farm, but I want to talk about you. Nancy, darling Nancy, say that you like me just a little. Encourage me somewhat."

"You are a very fine gentleman, Gregory, and I feel very kind towards you, to be sure, but. . . ."

"But?"

She gave him the benefit of her downcast eyes again.

"Your station in life is very different from mine, and besides – well, you don't *do* anything."

He was shocked into silence. With the natural egotism of youth, he had not seriously thought that she could have any firm objection to him; but in her words he suddenly saw the truth of his position, at least as it was revealed to her.

"Nancy – I – well, it's true I do not seem to you to be working at present. But I do a lot of reading and studying here, and I write to several important people in the world. And all the time I am coming to a great decision about what my career will be. I do assure you I am no loafer, if that's what you think."

"No, I don't think that. But Bert says you often spend a convivial evening in that there 'Wayfarer' – "

"Oh, he does, does he? And what business is it of his if I do – or of yours, come to that? What a damned cheek!"

She stood up. "If you have nothing left to say but a lot of swearing, I'll be off to join my mother, if you don't mind."

"Oh, by Jove, I'm making a mess of this!" he caught her wrist. "Listen, my sweet thing. I ask you only this, that you try and look on me favourably. And also that you let me say a word about the farm. Some strange things are happening there, and I seriously don't like to think of you being there at night. All these young things being born, all these little pigs – it's uncanny!"

"I don't see what's uncanny no more than my father does. I know how hard he works, and he's done a good job rearing his animals, that's all. He's the best farmer round Cottersall by a long chalk."

"Oh, certainly. He's a wonderful man. But he didn't put seven or eight eggs into a hedge sparrow's nest, did he? He didn't fill the pond with tadpoles and newts till it looks like a broth, did he? Something strange is happening on your farm this year, Nancy, and I want to protect you if I can."

The earnestness with which he spoke, coupled perhaps with his proximity and the ardent way he pressed her hand, went a good way toward mollifying Nancy.

"Dear Gregory, you don't know anything about farm life, I don't reckon, for all your books. But you're very sweet to be concerned."

"I shall always be concerned about you, Nancy, you beautiful creature."

"You'll make me blush!"

"Please do, for then you look even lovelier than usual!" He put an arm round her. When she looked up at him, he caught her up close to his chest and kissed her fervently.

She gasped and broke away, but not with too great haste.

"Oh, Gregory! Oh, Gregory! I must go to mother now!"

"Another kiss first! I can't let you go until I get another."

He took it, and stood by the door trembling with excitement as she left. "Come and see us again soon," she whispered.

"With dearest pleasure," he said. But the next visit held more dread than pleasure.

The big cart was standing in the yard full of squealing piglets when Gregory arrived. The farmer and Neckland were bustling about it. The former, shrugging into his overcoat, greeted Gregory cheerfully.

"I've a chance to make a good quick profit on these little chaps. Old sows can't feed them, but sucking pig fetches its price in Norwich, so Bert and me are going to drive over to Heigham and put them on the train."

"They've grown since I last saw them!"

"Ah, they put on over two pounds a day. Bert, we'd better get a net and spread over this lot, or they'll be diving out. They're that lively!"

The two men made their way over to the barn, clomping through the mud. Mud squelched behind Gregory. He turned.

In the muck between the stables and the cart, footprints appeared, two parallel tracks. They seemed to imprint themselves with no agency but their own. A cold flow of acute supernatural terror overcame Gregory, so that he could not move. The scene seemed to go grey and palsied as he watched the tracks come towards him.

The carthorse neighed uneasily, the prints reached the cart, the cart creaked, as if something had climbed aboard. The piglets squealed with terror. One dived clear over the wooden sides. Then a terrible silence fell.

Gregory still could not move. He heard an unaccountable sucking noise in the cart, but his eyes remained rooted on the muddy tracks. Those impressions were of something other than a man: something with dragging feet that were in outline something like a seal's flippers. Suddenly he found his voice; "Mr Grendon!" he cried.

Only as the farmer and Bert came running from the barn with the net did Gregory dare look into the cart.

One last piglet, even as he looked, seemed to be deflating rapidly, like a rubber balloon collapsing. It went limp and lay silent among the other little empty bags of pig skin. The cart creaked. Something splashed heavily off across the farm yard in the direction of the pond.

Grendon did not see. He had run to the cart and was staring like Gregory in dismay at the deflated corpses. Neckland stared too, and was the first to find his voice.

"Some sort of disease got 'em all, just like that! Must be one of them there new diseases from the Continent of Europe!"

"It's no disease," Gregory said. He could hardly speak, for his mind had just registered the fact that there were no bones left in or amid the deflated pig bodies. "It's no disease – look, the pig that got away is still alive."

He pointed to the animal that had jumped from the cart. It had injured its leg in the process, and now lay in the ditch some feet away, panting. The farmer went over to it and lifted it out.

"It escaped the disease by jumping out," Neckland said. "Master, we better go and see how the rest of them is down in the sties."

"Ah, that we had," Grendon said. He handed the pig over to Gregory, his face set. "No good taking one alone to market. I'll get Grubby to unharness the horse. Meanwhile, perhaps you'd be good enough to take this little chap in to Marjorie. At least we can all eat a bit of roast pig for dinner tomorrow."

"Mr Grendon, this is no disease. Have the veterinarian over from Heigham and let him examine these bodies."

"Don't you tell me how to run my farm, young man. I've got trouble enough."

Despite this rebuff, Gregory could not keep away. He had to see Nancy, and he had to see what occurred at the farm. The morning after the horrible thing happened to the pigs, he received a letter from his most admired correspondent, Mr H. G. Wells, one paragraph of which read: "At bottom, I think I am neither optimist nor pessimist. I tend to believe both that we stand on the threshold of an epoch of magnificent progress – certainly such an epoch is within our grasp – and that we may have reached the 'fin du globe' prophesied by our gloomier fin de siècle prophets. I am not at all surprised to hear that such a vast issue may be resolving itself on a remote farm near Cottersall, Norfolk – all unknown to anyone but the two of us. Do not think that I am in other than a state of terror, even when I cannot help exclaiming 'What a lark!'"

Too preoccupied to be as excited over such a letter as he would ordinarily have been, Gregory tucked it away in his jacket pocket and went to saddle up Daisy.

Before lunch, he stole a kiss from Nancy, and planted another on her over-heated left cheek as she stood by the vast range in the kitchen. Apart from that, there was little pleasure in the day. Grendon was reassured to find that none of the other piglets had fallen ill of the strange shrinking disease, but he remained alert against the possibility of it striking again. Meanwhile, another miracle had occurred. In the lower pasture, in a tumbledown shed, he had a cow that had given birth to four calves during the night. He did not expect the animal to live, but the calves were well enough, and being fed from a bottle by Nancy.

The farmer's face was dull, for he had been up all night with the labouring cow, and he sat down thankfully at the head of the table as the roast pig arrived on its platter.

It proved uneatable. In no time, they were all flinging down their implements in disgust. The flesh had a bitter taste for which Neckland was the first to account.

"It's diseased!" he growled. "This here animal had the disease all the time. We didn't ought to eat this here meat or we may all be dead ourselves inside of a week."

They were forced to make a snack on cold salted beef and cheese and pickled onions, none of which Mrs Grendon could face in her condition. She retreated upstairs in tears at the thought of the failure of her carefully prepared dish, and Nancy ran after her to comfort her.

After the dismal meal, Gregory spoke to Grendon.

"I have decided I must go to Norwich tomorrow for a few days, Mr Grendon," he said. "You are in trouble here, I believe. Is there anything, any business, I can transact for you in the city? Can I find you a veterinary surgeon there?"

Grendon clapped his shoulder. "I know you mean well, and I thank 'ee for it, but you don't seem to realise that vetinaries cost a load of money and aren't always too helpful when they do come. Just suppose we had some young idiot here who told us all our stock is poisoned and we had to kill it? That would be a right look-out, eh?"

"Just because Gregory Rolles has plenty of money, he thinks everyone has," Neckland sneered

The farmer turned furiously on him. "Who asked you to open your trap, bor? You keep your trap shut when there's a private conversation going on as don't concern you at all. Why aren't you out cleaning down the cowshed, since you ett all that last loaf?"

When Neckland had gone, Grendon said, 'Bert's a good lad, but he don't like you at all. Now you was saying we had trouble here. But a farm is always trouble, Gregory – some years one sort of trouble, some years another. But I ent ever seen such fine growth as this year, and I tell 'ee straight I'm delighted, proper delighted. Some pigs have died, but that ent going to stop me doing my best by all the rest of 'em."

"But they will be unmarketable if they all taste like the one today."

Grendon smote his palm. "You're a real worrier. They may grow out of this bitter taste. And then again, if they don't, people have to buy them before they can taste them, don't they? I'm a poor man, Gregory, and when a bit of fortune comes my way, I can't afford to let it get away. In fact, I tell 'ee this, and even Bert don't know it yet, but tomorrow or the next day, I got Seeley the builder coming over here to put me up some more wood sheds down by Grubby's hut, to give the young animals more room."

"Good. Then let me do something for you, Joseph, in return for all your kindness to me. Let me bring a vet back from Norwich at my own expense, just to have a look round, nothing more."

"Blow me if you aren't stubborn as they come. I'm telling you, same as my dad used to say, if I finds any person on my land as I didn't ask here, I'm getting that there rifle of mine down and I'm peppering him with buckshot, same as I did with them two old tramps last year. Fair enough, bor?"

"I suppose so."

"Then I must go and see to the cow. And stop worrying about what you don't understand."

After the farmer had gone, Gregory stood for a long time looking out of the window, waiting for Nancy to come down, worrying over the train of events. But the view was peaceful enough. He was the only person worrying, he reflected. Even the shrewd Mr H. G. Wells, his correspondent, seemed to take his reports with a pinch of salt – he who of all men in England should sympathetically receive the news of the miraculous when it came to Earth, even if it failed to arrive in the form predicted in his recent novel, *The Wonderful Visit*. Be that as it might, he was going to Norwich and the wise uncle who lived there as soon as he could – as soon, in fact, as he had kissed dear Nancy good-bye.

★

The wise uncle was indeed sympathetic. He was altogether a gentler man than his brother Edward, Gregory's father. He looked with sympathy at the plan of the farm that Gregory drew, he looked with sympathy at the sketch of the muddy footprint, he listened with sympathy to an account of what had happened. And at the end of it all he said, "Ghosts!"

When Gregory tried to argue with him, he said firmly, 'My dear boy, I fear the modern marvels of our age have gone to your head. You know of such engineering structures as the cantilever bridge over the Firth of Forth, and you know as we all do of the colossal tower Eiffel has built in Paris – though if it stands ten years, I'll eat my hat. Now, no one will deny these things are marvellous, but they are things that rest on the ground. You're trying to tell me that engineers on this world or some other world might build a machine – a vehicle – that could fly from one heavenly body to another. Well then, *I'm* telling you that no engineer can do such a thing – and I'm not just saying that, but I'm quoting a law about it. There's a law about engineers not being able to sail in some sort of damned Eiffel Tower with engines from Mars to Earth, or the Sun to Earth, or wherever you will – a law to be read in your Bible and echoed in the pages of 'The Cornhill'. No, my boy, the modern age has gone to your head, but it's old-fashioned ghosts that have gone to your farm."

So Gregory walked into the city, and inspected the booksellers, and made several purchases, and never doubted for a moment that his uncle, though infinitely sympathetic, and adroit at slipping one sovereigns on parting, was sadly less wise than he had hitherto seemed: a discovery that seemed to reflect how Gregory had grown up and how times were changing.

But Norwich was a pleasant city and his uncle's house a comfortable house in which to stay, and he lingered there a week where he had meant to spend only three days at the most.

Consequently, conscience stirred in him when he again approached the Grendon farm along the rough road from Cottersall. He was surprised to see how the countryside had altered since he was last this way. New foliage gleamed everywhere, and even the heath looked a happier place. But as he came up to the farm, he saw how overgrown it was. Great ragged elder and towering cow parsley had shot up, so that at first they hid all the buildings. He fancied the farm had been spirited away until, spurring Daisy on, he saw the black mill emerge from behind a clump of nearby growth. The south meadows were deep in rank grass. Even the elms seemed much shaggier than before and loomed threateningly over the house.

As he clattered over the flat wooden bridge and through the open gate into the yard, Gregory noted huge hairy nettles craning out of the adjoining ditches. Birds fluttered everywhere. Yet the impression he received was one of death rather than life. A great quiet lay over the place, as if it were under a curse that eliminated noise and hope.

He realised this effect was partly because Lardie, the young bitch collie who had taken the place of Cuff, was not running up barking as she generally did with visitors. The yard was deserted. Even the customary fowls had gone. As he led Daisy into the stables, he saw a heavy piebald in the first stall and recognised it as Dr Crouchorn's. His anxieties took more definite shape.

Since the stable was now full, he led his mare across to the stone trough by the pond and hitched her there before walking over to the house. The front door was open. Great ragged dandelions grew against the porch. The creeper, hitherto somewhat sparse, pressed into the lower windows. A movement in the rank grass caught his eye and he looked down, drawing back his riding boot. An enormous toad crouched under weed, the head of a still writhing grass snake in its mouth. The toad seemed to eye Gregory fixedly, as if trying to determine whether the man envied it its gluttony. Shuddering in disgust, he hurried into the house.

Three of Trix's kids, well grown now, strutted about the parlour, nibbling at the carpet and climbing into the massive armchairs, staring at a stuffed caricature of a goat that stood in its glass case by the window. Judging by the chaos in the room, they had been there some while, and had had a game on the table. But they possessed the room alone, and a quick glance into the kitchen revealed nobody there either.

Muffled sounds came from upstairs. The stairs curled round the massive chimneypiece, and were shut from the lower room by a latched door. Gregory had never been invited upstairs, but he did not hesitate. Throwing the door open, he started up the dark stairwell, and almost at once ran into a body.

Its softness told him that this was Nancy; she stood in the dark weeping. Even as he caught her and breathed her name, she broke from his grasp and ran from him up the stairs. He could hear the noise more clearly now, and the sound of crying – though at the moment he was not listening. Nancy ran to a door on the landing nearest to the top of the stairs, burst into the room beyond, and closed it. When Gregory tried the latch, he heard the bolt slide to on the other side.

"Nancy!" he called. "Don't hide from me! What is it? What's happening?"

She made no answer. As he stood there baffled against the door, the next door along the passage opened and Doctor Crouchorn emerged, clutching his little black bag. He was a tall, sombre man, with deep lines on his face that inspired such fear into his patients that a remarkable percentage of them did as he bid and recovered. Even here, he wore the top hat that, simply by remaining constantly in position, contributed to the doctor's fame in the neighbourhood.

"What's the trouble, Doctor Crouchorn?" Gregory asked, as the medical man shut the door behind him and started down the stairs. "Has the plague struck this house, or something equally terrible?"

"Plague, young man, plague? No, it is something much more unnatural than that."

He stared at Gregory unsmilingly, as if promising himself inwardly not to move a muscle again until Gregory asked the obvious.

"What did you call for, doctor?"

"The hour of Mrs Grendon's confinement struck during the night," he said, still poised on the top step.

A wave of relief swept over Gregory. He had forgotten Nancy's mother! "She's had her baby? Was it a boy?"

The doctor nodded in slow motion. "She bore two boys, young man." He hesitated, and then a muscle in his face twitched and he said in a rush, "She also bore seven daughters. Nine children! And they all – they all live. It's impossible. Until I die – "

He could not finish. Tipping his hat, he hurried down the stairs, leaving Gregory to look fixedly at the wallpaper while his mind whirled as if it would convert itself into liquid. Nine children! Nine! It was as if she were no different from an animal in a sty. And the wallpaper pattern took on a diseased and livid look as if the house itself embodied sickness. The mewing cries from the bedroom seemed also the emblem of something inhuman calling its need.

He stood there in a daze, the sickly infant cries boring into him. From beyond the stone walls that oppressed him, he heard the noise of a horse ridden at hard gallop over the wooden bridge and down the track to Cottersall, dying with distance. From Nancy's room came no sound. Gregory guessed she had hidden herself from him for shame, and at last stirred himself into moving down the dark and curving stairwell. A stable cat scuttled out from under the bottom stair, a dozen baby tabbies in pursuit. The goats still held possession of the room. The fire was but scattered ashes in the hearth, and had not been tended since the crisis of the night.

"I bet you're surprised!"

Gregory swung round. From the kitchen came Grubby, clutching a wedge of bread and meat in his fist. He chewed with his mouth open, grinning at Gregory.

"Farmer Grendon be a proper ram!" he exclaimed. "Ent no other man in this county could beget himself nine kids at one go!"

"Where is the farmer?"

"I say there ent no other man in this county – "

"Yes, I heard what you said. Where is the farmer?"

"Working, I supposed. But I tell 'ee, bor, there ent no other man – "

Leaving Grubby munching and talking, Gregory strode out into the yard. He came on Grendon round the corner of the house. The farmer had a pitchfork full of hay, which he was carrying over his shoulder into the cow sheds. Gregory stood in his way but he pushed past.

"I want to speak to you, Joseph."

"There's work to be done. Pity you can't see that."

"I want to speak about your wife."

Grendon made no reply. He worked like a demon, tossing the hay down, turning for more. In any case, it was difficult to talk. The cows and calves, closely confined, seemed to set up a perpetual uneasy noise of lowing and un-cowlike grunts. Gregory followed the farmer round to the hayrick, but the man walked like one possessed. His eyes seemed sunk into his head, his mouth was puckered until his lips were invisible. When Gregory laid a hand on his arm, he shook it off. Stabbing up another great load of hay, he swung back towards the sheds so violently that Gregory had to jump out of his way.

Gregory lost his temper. Following Grendon back towards the sheds he swung the bottom of the two-part door shut, and bolted it on the outside. When Grendon came back, he did not budge.

"Joseph, what's got into you? Why are you suddenly so heartless? Surely your wife needs you by her?"

His eyes had a curious blind look as he turned them at Gregory. He held the pitchfork before him in both hands almost like a weapon as he said, "I been with her all night, bor, while she brought forth her increase."

"But now – "

"She got a nursing woman from Dereham Cottages with her now. I been with her all night. Now I got to see to the farm – things keep growing, you know."

"They're growing too much, Joseph. Stop and think – "

"I've no time for talking." Dropping the pitchfork, he elbowed Gregory out of the way, unbolted the door, and flung it open. Grasping Gregory firmly by the biceps of one arm, he began to propel him along to the vegetable beds down by South Meadows.

The early lettuce were gigantic here. Everything bristled out of the ground. Recklessly, Grendon ran among the lines of new green, pulling up fists full of young radish, carrots, spring onions, scattering them over his shoulder as fast as he plucked them from the ground.

"See, Gregory – all bigger than you ever seen 'em, and weeks early! The harvest is going to be a bumper. Look at the fields! Look at the orchard!" With wide gesture, he swept a hand towards the lines of trees, buried in the mounds of snow-and-pink of their blossom. "Whatever happens, we got to take advantage of it. It may not happen another year. Why – it's like a fairy story!"

He said no more. Turning, he seemed already to have forgotten Gregory. Eyes down at the ground that had suddenly achieved such abundance, he marched back towards the sheds, from whence now came the sound of Neckland washing out milk churns.

The spring sun was warm on Gregory's back. He told himself that everything looked normal. The farm was flourishing. From beyond the sties came shouts, distantly, and the sounds of men working, where the builder was preparing to erect more sheds. Perhaps, he told himself dully, he was worrying about nothing. Slowly, he walked towards the back of the house. There was nothing he could do here; it was time to return to Cottersall; but first he must see Nancy.

Nancy was in the kitchen. Neckland had brought her in a stoup of fresh milk, and she was supping it wearily from a ladle.

"Oh, Greg, I'm sorry I ran from you. I was so upset." She came to him, still holding the ladle but dangling her arms over his shoulders in a familiar way she had not used before. "Poor mother, I fear her mind is unhinged with – with bearing so many children.

She's talking such strange stuff as I never heard before, and I do believe she fancies as she's a child again."

"Is it to be wondered at?" he said, smoothing her hair with his hand. "She'll be better once she's recovered from the shock."

They kissed each other, and after a minute she passed him a ladleful of milk. He drank and then spat it out in disgust.

"Ugh! What's got into the milk? Is Neckland trying to poison you or something? Have you tasted it? It's as bitter as sloes!"

She pulled a puzzled face. "I thought it tasted rather strange, but not unpleasant. Here, let me try again."

"No, it's too horrible. Some Sloane's Liniment must have got mixed in it."

Despite his warning, she put her lips to the metal spoon and sipped, then shook her head. "You're imagining things, Greg. It does taste a bit different, 'tis true, but there's nothing wrong with it."

"Sweetheart, it's horrible. I'm going to get your father to taste it, and see what he thinks."

"I wouldn't bother him just now, Greg, if I was you. You know how busy he is, and tired, and attending on mother during the night has put him back in his work. I will mention it to him at dinner – which I must now prepare. Them there goats have made such a muck in here, not to mention that Grubby! You'll stay to take a bite with us, I hope?"

"No, Nancy, I'm off now. I have a letter awaiting me that I must answer; it arrived when I was in Norwich."

She bit her lip and snapped her fingers. "There, how terrible awful you'll think me! I never asked you how you enjoyed yourself in the big city! It must be wonderful to be a man of leisure, never with no work to do nor meals to prepare."

"You still hold that against me! Listen, my lovely Nancy, this letter is from a Dr Hudson-Ward, an old acquaintance of my father's. He is headmaster of a school in Gloucester, and he wishes me to join the staff there as teacher on most favourable terms. So you see I may not be idle much longer!"

Laughing, she clung to him. "That's wonderful, my darling! What a handsome schoolmaster you will make. But Gloucester – that's over the other side of the country. I suppose we shan't be seeing you again once you get there."

"Nothing's settled yet, Nancy."

"You'll be gone in a week and we sha'n't never see you again.

Once you get to that there old school, you will never think of your
Nancy no more."

He cupped her face in his hands. "Are you my Nancy? Do you
care for me?"

Her eyelashes came over her dark eyes. "Greg, things are so
muddled here – I mean – yes, I do care, I dread to think I'd not see
you again."

Recalling her saying that, he rode away a quarter of an hour later
very content at heart – and entirely neglectful of the dangers to
which he had left her exposed.

Rain fell lightly as Gregory Rolles made his way that evening to the
"Wayfarer" inn. His friend Bruce Fox was already there, ensconced
in one of the snug seats by the ingle-nook.

On this occasion, Fox was more interested in purveying details of
his sister's forthcoming wedding than in listening to what Gregory
had to tell, and since some of his future brother-in-law's friends
soon arrived, and had to buy and be bought libations, the evening
became a merry and thoughtless one. And in a short while, the ale
having its good effect, Gregory also forgot what he wanted to say
and began whole-heartedly to enjoy the company.

Next morning, he awoke with a heavy head and in a dismal state
of mind. Mrs Fenn, clattering round the room lighting his fire, did
not improve matters; he could tell from her demeanour that he had
come home late and made a noise on the stairs. But the Mrs Fenns
of this world, he reflected irritably, were born to suffer such
indignities, and the more regularly the better. He told himself this
feeling was not in accord with his socialist principles, but they felt
as sluggish as his liver this morning.

The day was too wet for him to go out and take exercise. He sat
moodily in a chair by the window, delaying an answer to Dr
Hudson-Ward, the headmaster. Lethargically, he turned to a small
leather-bound volume on serpents that he had acquired in Norwich
a few days earlier. After a while, a passage caught his particular
attention:

"Most serpents of the venomous variety, with the exception of
the opisthoglyphs, release their victims from their fangs after
striking. The victims die in some cases in but a few seconds, while
in other cases the onset of moribundity may be delayed by hours or
days. The saliva of some serpents contains not only venom but a
special digestive virus. The deadly Coral Snake of Brazil, though

attaining no more than a foot in length, has this virtue in abundance. Accordingly, when it bites an animal or a human being, the victim not only dies in profound agony in a matter of seconds, but his interior parts are then dissolved, so that even the bones become no more than jelly. Then may the little serpent suck all of the victim out as a kind of soup or broth from the original wound in its skin, which latter alone remains intact."

For a long while, Gregory sat where he was in the window, with the book open in his lap, thinking about the Grendon farm, and about Nancy. He reproached himself for having done so little for his friends there, and gradually resolved on a plan of action the next time he rode out; but his visit was to be delayed for some days: the wet weather had set in with more determination than the end of April and the beginning of May generally allowed.

Despite that, he heard news of Grendon on the second day of rain as he took his supper with the Fenns downstairs. That was market day, and the baker's wife said, "That there idiot labourer on Joe Grendon's place is going to get himself locked up if he ent careful. Did you hear about him today, Master Gregory?"

"What did he do, Mrs Fenn?"

"Why, what didn't he do? Delivered the milk round as usual, so I hear, and nobody wouldn't buy none, seeing as it has been off for the past I-don't-know-how-long. So Grubby swore terrible and vowed he had the best milk in town, and took a great sup at the churn to prove it. And then them two Betts boys started throwing stones, and of course that set Grubby off! He caught one of 'em and ducked his head in the milk, and then flung the bucket right smack through his father's nice glass window. Imagine that! So out come old man Betts and his great big missus, and they lambasts old Grubby with beansticks till he drives off cursing and vowing he'll never sell nobody good milk no more!"

The baker laughed. "That would have been a sight worth seeing of! I reckon they all gone mad out at Joe's place. Old Seeley the builder come in yesterday morning, and he reckon Joe's doing better this year than what he ever did, while everyone else round here is having a thin time. According to Seeley, Majorie Grendon had quins, but you know old Seeley is a bit of a joker. Dr Crouchorn would have let on if she'd had quins, I reckon."

"Doctor Crouchorn was weeping drunk last night, from all accounts."

"So I hear. That ent like him, be it?"

"First time it was ever known, though they do say he liked his bottle when he was a youngster."

Listening to the gossip as it shuttled back and forth between husband and wife, Gregory found little appetite for his stew. Moodily, he returned to his room and tried to concentrate on a letter to the worthy Dr Hudson-Ward in the county of Gloucestershire. He knew he should take the job, indeed he felt inclined to do so; but first he knew he had to see Nancy safe. The indecision he felt caused him to delay answering the doctor until the next day, when he feebly wrote that he would be glad to accept the post offered at the price offered, but begged to have a week to think about it. When he took the letter down to the post woman in "The Three Poachers", the rain was still falling.

One morning, the rains were suddenly vanished, the blue and wide East Anglian skies were back, and Gregory saddled up Daisy and rode out along the mirey track he had so often taken. As he arrived at the farm, Grubby and Neckland were at work in the ditch, unblocking it with shovels. He saluted them and rode in. As he was about to put the mare into the stables, he saw Grendon and Nancy standing on the patch of waste ground under the windowless east side of the house. He went slowly to join them, noting as he walked how dry the ground was here, as if no rain had fallen in a fortnight. But this observation was drowned in shock as he saw the nine little crosses Grendon was sticking into nine freshly-turned mounds of earth.

Nancy stood weeping. They both looked up as Gregory approached, but Grendon went stubbornly on with his task.

"Oh, Nancy, Joseph, I'm so sorry about this!" Gregory exclaimed. "To think they've all – but where's the parson? Where's the parson, Joseph? Why are *you* burying them, without a proper service or anything?"

"I told father, but he took no heed!" Nancy exclaimed.

Grendon had reached the last grave. He seized the last crude wooden cross, lifted it above his head and stabbed it down into the ground as if he would pierce the heart of what lay under it. Only then did he straighten and speak.

"We don't need a parson here. I've no time to waste with parsons. I have work to do if you ent."

"But these are your children, Joseph! What has got into you?"

"They are part of the farm now, as they always was." He turned, rolling his shirt sleeves further up his brawny arms, and strode off in the direction of the ditching activities.

Gregory took Nancy in his arms and looked at her tear-stained face. "What a time you must have been having these last few days!"

"I – I thought you'd gone to Gloucester, Greg! Why didn't you come? Every day I waited for you to come!"

"It was so wet and flooded."

"It's been lovely weather since you were last here. Look how everything has grown!"

"It poured with rain every single day in Cottersall."

"Well, I never! That explains why there is so much water flowing in the Oast and in the ditches. But we've had only a few light showers."

"Nancy, tell me, how did these poor little mites die?"

"I'd rather not say, if you don't mind."

"Why didn't your father get in Parson Landson? How could he be so lacking in feeling?"

"Because he didn't want anyone from the outside world to know. That's why he's sent the builders away again. You see – oh, I must tell you, my dear – it's mother. She has gone completely off her head, completely! It was the evening before last, when she took her first turn outside the back door."

"You don't mean to say she – "

"Ow, Greg, you're hurting my arms! She – she crept upstairs when we weren't noticing and she – she stifled each of the babies in turn, Greg, under the best goose feather pillow."

He could feel the colour leaving his cheeks. Solicitously, she led him to the back of the house. They sat together on the orchard railings while he digested the words in silence.

"How is your mother now, Nancy?"

"She's silent. Father had to bar her in her room for safety. Last night she screamed a lot. But this morning she's quiet."

He looked dazedly about him. The appearance of everything was speckled, as if the return of his blood to his head had somehow infected it with a rash. The blossom had gone almost entirely from the fruit trees in the orchard and already the embryo apples showed signs of swelling. Nearby, broad beans bowed under enormous pods. Seeing his glance, Nancy dipped into her apron pocket and produced a bunch of shining crimson radishes as big as tangerines.

"Have one of these. They're crisp and wet and hot, just as they should be."

Indifferently, he accepted and bit the tempting globe. At once he had to spit the portion out. There again was that vile bitter flavour!

"Oh, but they're lovely!" Nancy protested.

"Not even 'rather strange' now – simply 'lovely'? Nancy, don't you see, something uncanny and awful is taking place here. I'm sorry, but I can't see otherwise. You and your father should leave here at once."

"*Leave* here, Greg? Just because you don't like the taste of these lovely radishes? How can we leave here? Where should we go? See this here house? My grandad died here, and his father before him. It's our *place*. We can't just up and off, not even after this bit of trouble. Try another radish."

"For heaven's sake, Nancy, they taste as if the flavour was intended for creatures with a palate completely different from ours . . . Oh. . . ." He stared at her. "And perhaps they are. Nancy, I tell you – "

He broke off, sliding down from the railing. Neckland had come up from one side, still plastered in mud from his work in the ditch, his collarless shirt flapping open. In his hand, he grasped an ancient and military-looking pistol.

"I'll fire this if you come nearer," he said. "It goes okay, never worry, and it's loaded, Master Gregory. Now you're a-going to listen to me!"

"Bert, put that thing away!" Nancy exclaimed. She moved forward to him, but Gregory pulled her back and stood before her.

"Don't be a bloody idiot, Neckland. Put it away!"

"I'll shoot you, bor, I'll shoot you, I swear, if you mucks about." His eyes were glaring, and the look on his dark face left no doubt that he meant what he said. "You're going to swear to me that you're going to clear off of this farm on that nag of yours and never come back again."

"I'm going straight to tell my father, Bert," Nancy warned.

The pistol twitched.

"If you move, Nancy, I warn you I'll shoot this fine chap of yours in the leg. Besides, your father don't care about Master Gregory any more – he's got better things to worry him."

"Like finding out what's happening here?" Gregory said. "Listen, Neckland, we're all in trouble. This farm is being run by a group of nasty little monsters. You can't see them because they're invisible – "

The gun exploded. As he spoke, Nancy had attempted to run off.

Without hesitating, Neckland fired down at Gregory's knees. Gregory felt the shot pluck his trouser leg and knew himself unharmed. With the knowledge came rage. He flung himself at Neckland and hit him hard over the heart. Falling back, Neckland dropped the pistol and swung his fist wildly. Gregory struck him again. As he did so, the other grabbed him and they began furiously hitting each other. When Gregory broke free, Neckland grappled with him again. There was more pummelling of ribs.

"Let me go, you swine!" Gregory shouted. He hooked his foot behind Neckland's ankle, and they both rolled over on to the grass. At this point, a sort of flood bank had been raised long ago between the house and low-lying orchard. Down this the two men rolled, fetching up sharply against the stone wall of the kitchen. Neckland got the worst of it, catching his head on the corner, and lay there stunned. Gregory found himself looking at two feet encased in ludicrous stockings. Slowly, he rose to his feet, and confronted Mrs Grendon at less than a yard's distance. She was smiling.

He stood there, and gradually straightened his back, looking at her anxiously.

"So there you are, Jackie, my Jackalums," she said. The smile was wider now and less like a smile. "I wanted to talk to you. You are the one who knows about the things that walk on the lines, aren't you?"

"I don't understand, Mrs Grendon."

"Don't call me that there daft old name, sonnie. You know all about the little grey things that aren't supposed to be there, don't you?"

"Oh, those. . . . Suppose I said I did know?"

"The other naughty children will pretend they don't know what I mean, but you know, don't you? You know about the little grey things."

The sweat stood out on his brow. She had moved nearer. She stood close, staring into his eyes, not touching him; but he was acutely conscious that she could touch him at any moment. From the corner of his eye, he saw Neckland stir and crawl away from the house, but there were other things to occupy him.

"These little grey things," he said. "Did you save the nine babies from them?"

"They grey things wanted to kiss them, you see, but I couldn't let them. I was clever. I hid them under the goose feather pillow and now even *I* can't find them!" She began to laugh, making a horrible low whirring sound in her throat.

"They're small and grey and wet, aren't they?" Gregory said sharply. "They've got big feet, webbed like frogs, but they're heavy and short, aren't they, and they have fangs like a snake, haven't they?"

She looked doubtful. Then her eye seemed to catch a movement. She looked fixedly to one side. "Here come one now, the female one," she said.

Gregory turned to look where she did. Nothing was visible. His mouth was dry. "How many are there, Mrs Grendon?"

Then he saw the short grass stir, flatten, and raise near at hand, and let out a cry of alarm. Wrenching off his riding boot, he swung it in an arc, low above the ground. It struck something concealed in thin air. Almost at once, he received a terrific kick in the thigh, and fell backwards. Despite the hurt, fear made him jump up almost at once.

Mrs Grendon was changing. Her mouth collapsed as if it would run off one corner of her face. Her head sagged to one side. Her shoulders fell. A deep crimson blush momentarily suffused her features, then drained, and as it drained she dwindled like a deflating rubber balloon. Gregory sank to his knees, whimpering, buried his face in his hands and pressed his hands to the grass. Darkness overcame him.

His senses must have left him only for a moment. When he pulled himself up again, the almost empty bag of women's clothes was still settling slowly on the ground.

"Joseph! Joseph!" he yelled. Nancy had fled. In a distracted mixture of panic and fury, he dragged his boot on again and rushed round the house towards the cowsheds.

Neckland stood half way between barn and mill, rubbing his skull. In his rattled state, the sight of Gregory apparently in full pursuit made him run away.

"Neckland!" Gregory shouted. He ran like mad for the other man. Neckland bolted for the mill, jumped inside, tried to pull the door to, lost his nerve, and ran up the wooden stairs. Gregory bellowed after him.

The pursuit took them right up to the top of the mill. Neckland had lost enough wit even to kick the bolt of the trapdoor. Gregory burst it up and climbed out panting. Thoroughly cowed, Neckland backed towards the opening until he was almost out on the little platform above the sails.

"You'll fall out, you idiot," Gregory warned. "Listen, Neckland, you have no reason to fear me. I want no enmity between us. There's a bigger enemy we must fight. Look!"

He came towards the low door and looked down at the dark surface of the pond. Neckland grabbed the overhead pulley for security and said nothing.

"Look down at the pond," Gregory said. "That's where the Aurigans live. My God – Bert, look, there one goes!"

The urgency in his voice made the farm hand look down where he pointed. Together, the two men watched as a depression slid over the black water; an overlapping chain of ripples swung back from it. At approximately the middle of the pond, the depression became a commotion. A small whirlpool formed and died, and the ripples began to settle.

"There's your ghost, Bert," Gregory gasped. "That must have been the one that got poor Mrs Grendon. Now do you believe?"

"I never heard of a ghost that lived under water," Neckland gasped.

"A ghost never harmed anyone – we've already had a sample of what these terrifying things can do. Come on, Bert, shake hands, understand I bear you no hard feelings. Oh, come on, man! I know how you feel about Nancy, but she must be free to make her own choice in life."

They shook hands and grinned rather foolishly at each other.

"We better go and tell the farmer what we seen," Neckland said. "I reckon that thing done what happened to Lardie last evening."

"Lardie? What's happened to her? I thought I hadn't seen her today."

"Same as happened to the little pigs. I found her just inside the barn. Just her coat was left, that's all. No insides! Like she'd been sucked dry."

"Let's go, Bert."

It took Gregory twenty minutes to summon the council of war on which he had set his mind. The party gathered in the farmhouse, in the parlour. By this time, Nancy had somewhat recovered from the shock of her mother's death, and sat in an armchair with a shawl about her shoulders. Her father stood nearby with his arms folded, looking impatient, while Bert Neckland lounged by the door. Only Grubby was not present. He had been told to get on with the ditching.

"I'm going to have another attempt to convince you all that you are in very grave danger," Gregory said. "You won't see it for yourselves, so I – "

He paused. There was a dragging noise on the landing upstairs, a board creaked.

"Who the devil's up there?" Grendon growled. He made towards the stairwell.

"Don't go, father!" Nancy screamed, but her father flung open the door and made his way up. Gregory bit his lip. The Aurigans had never ventured into the house before.

In a moment, Grendon returned with a monstrous piglet in his arms.

"Keep the confounded animals out of the house, Nancy," he said, pushing the creature squealing out of the front door.

The interruption made Gregory realise how his nerves still jangled. He set his back to the sawdust-filled parody of a goat that watched from its case, and spoke quickly.

"The situation is that we're all animals together at present. Do you remember that strange meteor that fell out of the sky last winter, Joseph? And do you remember that ill-smelling dew early in the spring? They were not unconnected, and they are connected with all that's happening now. That meteor was a space machine of some sort, I firmly believe, and it brought in it a kind of life that – that is not so much hostile to terrestrial life as *indifferent to its quality*. The creatures from that machine – I call them Aurigans – spread the dew over the farm. It was a growth accelerator, a manure or fertiliser, that speeds growth in plants and animals."

"So much better for us!" Grendon said.

"But it's not better. The things grow wildly, yes, but the taste is altered to suit the palates of those things out there. You've seen what happened. You can't sell anything. People won't touch your eggs or milk or meat – they taste too foul."

"But that's a lot of nonsense. We'll sell in Norwich. Our produce is better than it ever was. We eat it, don't we?"

"Yes, Joseph, *you* eat it. But anyone who eats at your table is doomed. Don't you understand – you are all 'fertilised' just as surely as the pigs and chickens. Your place has been turned into a superfarm, and you are all meat to the Aurigans."

That set a silence in the room, until Nancy said in a small voice, "You don't believe such a terrible thing."

"I suppose these unseen creatures told you all this?" Grendon said truculently.

"Judge by the evidence, as I do. Your wife – I must be brutal, Joseph – your wife was eaten, like the dog and the pigs. As everything else will be in time. The Aurigans aren't even cannibals. They aren't like us. They don't care whether we have souls or intelligences, any more than we really care whether the bullocks have."

"No one's going to eat me," Neckland said, looking decidedly white about the gills.

"How can you stop them? They're invisible, and I think they can strike like snakes. They're aquatic and I think they may be only two feet tall. How can you protect yourself?" He turned to the farmer. "Joseph, the danger is very great, and not only to us here. At first, they may have offered us no harm while they got the measure of us – otherwise I'd have died in your rowing boat. Now there's no longer doubt of their hostile intent. I beg you to let me go to Heigham and telephone to the chief of police in Norwich, or at least to the local militia, to get them to come and help us."

The farmer shook his head slowly, and pointed a finger at Gregory.

"You soon forgot them talks we had, bor, all about the coming age of socialism and how the powers of the state was going to wither away. Directly we get a bit of trouble, you want to call in the authorities. There's no harm here a few savage dogs like my old Cuff can't handle, and I don't say as I ent going to get a couple of dogs, but you'm a fule if you reckon I'm getting the authorities down here. Fine old socialist you turn out to be!"

"You have no room to talk about that!" Gregory exclaimed. "Why didn't you let Grubby come here? If you were a socialist, you'd treat the men as you treat yourself. Instead, you leave him out in the ditch. I wanted him to hear this discussion."

The farmer leant threateningly across the table at him.

"Oh, you did, did you? Sinced when was this your farm? And Grubby can come and go as he likes when it's his, so put that in your pipe and smoke it, bor! Who do you just think you are?" He moved closer to Gregory, apparently happy to work off his fears as anger. "You'm trying to scare us all off this here little old bit of ground, ent you? Well, the Grendons ent a scaring sort, see! Now I'll tell you something. See that rifle there on the wall? That be loaded. And if you ent off this farm by midday, that rifle ont be on that wall no more. It'll be here, bor, right here in my two hands, and I'll be letting you have it right where you'll feel it most."

"You can't do that, father," Nancy said. "You know Gregory is a friend of ours."

"For God's sake, Joseph," Gregory said, "see where your enemy lies. Bert, tell Mr Grendon what we saw on the pond, go on."

Neckland was far from keen to be dragged into this argument. He scratched his head, drew a red-and-white spotted handkerchief from round his neck to wipe his face, and muttered, "We saw a sort of ripple on the water, but I didn't see nothing really, Master Gregory. I mean, it could have been the wind, couldn't it?"

"Now you be warned, Gregory," the farmer repeated. "You be off my land by noon by the sun, and that mare of yours, or I ont answer for it." He marched out into the pale sunshine, and Neckland followed.

Nancy and Gregory stood staring at each other. He took her hands, and they were cold.

"You believe what I was saying, Nancy?"

"Is that why the food did at one point taste bad to us, and then soon tasted well enough again?"

"It can only have been that at that time your systems were not fully adjusted to the poison. Now they are. You're being fed up, Nancy, just like the livestock – I'm sure of it! I fear for you, darling love, I fear so much. What are we to do? Come back to Cottersall with me! Mrs Fenn has another fine little drawing room upstairs that I'm sure she would rent."

"Now you're talking nonsense, Greg! How can I? What would people say? No, you go away for now and let the tempest of father's wrath abate, and if you could come back tomorrow, you will find he will be milder for sure, because I plan to wait on him tonight and talk to him about you. Why, he's half daft with grief and doesn't know what he says."

"All right, my darling. But stay inside as much as you can. The Aurigans have not come indoors yet, as far as we know, and it may be safer here. And lock all the doors and put the shutters over the windows before you go to bed. And get your father to take that rifle of his upstairs with him."

The evenings were lengthening with confidence towards summer now, and Bruce Fox arrived home before sunset. As he jumped from his bicycle this evening, he found his friend Gregory impatiently awaiting him.

They went indoors together, and while Fox ate a large tea, Gregory told him what had been happening at the farm.

"You're in trouble," Fox said. "Look, tomorrow's Sunday. I'll skip church and come out with you. You need help."

"Joseph may shoot me. He'll be certain to if I bring along a stranger. You can help me tonight by telling me where I can purchase a young dog straight away to protect Nancy."

"Nonsense, I'm coming with you. I can't bear hearing all this at secondhand anyhow. We'll pick up a pup in any event – the blacksmith has a litter to be rid of. Have you got any plan of action?"

"Plan? No, not really."

"You must have a plan. Grendon doesn't scare too easily, does he?"

"I imagine he's scared well enough. Nancy says he's scared. He just isn't imaginative enough to see what he can do but carry on working as hard as possible."

"Look, I know these farmers. They won't believe anything till you rub their noses in it. What we must do is *show* him an Aurigan."

"Oh, splendid, Bruce. And how do you catch one?"

"You trap one."

"Don't forget they're invisible – hey, Bruce, yes, by Jove, you're right! I've the very idea! Look, we've nothing more to worry about if we can trap one. We can trap the lot, however many there are, and we can kill the little horrors when we have trapped them."

Fox grinned over the top of a chunk of cherry cake. "We're agreed, I suppose, that these Aurigans aren't socialists utopians any longer?"

It helped a great deal, Gregory thought, to be able to visualise roughly what the alien life form looked like. The volume on serpents had been a happy find, for not only did it give an idea of how the Aurigans must be able to digest their prey so rapidly – "a kind of soup or broth" – but presumably it gave a clue to their appearance. To live in a space machine, they would probably be fairly small, and they seemed to be semi-aquatic. It all went to make up a picture of a strange being: skin perhaps scaled like a fish, great flipper feet like a frog, barrel-like diminutive stature, and a tiny head with two great fangs in the jaw. There was no doubt but that the invisibility cloaked a really ugly-looking dwarf!

As the macabre image passed through his head, Gregory and Bruce Fox were preparing their trap. Fortunately, Grendon had offered no resistance to their entering the farm; Nancy had evidently spoken to good effect. And he had suffered another shock. Five fowls had been reduced to little but feathers and skin that morning almost before his eyes, and he was as a result sullen and indifferent to what went on. Now he was out in a distant field, working, and the two young men were allowed to carry out their plans unmolested – though not without an occasional anxious glance at the pond – while a worried Nancy looked on from the farmhouse window.

She had with her a sturdy young mongrel dog of eight months, which Gregory and Bruce had brought along, called Gyp. Grendon had obtained two ferocious hounds from a distant neighbour. These wide-mouthed brutes were secured on long running chains that enabled them to patrol from the horse trough by the pond, down the west side of the house, almost to the elms and the bridge leading over to West Field. They barked stridently most of the time and seemed to cause a general unease among the other animals, all of which gave voice restlessly this forenoon.

The dogs would be a difficulty, Nancy had said, for they refused to touch any of the food the farm could provide. It was hoped they would take it when they became hungry enough.

Grendon had planted a great board by the farm gate and on the board had painted a notice telling everyone to keep away.

Armed with pitchforks, the two young men carried flour sacks out from the mill and placed them at strategic positions across the yard as far as the gate. Gregory went to the cowsheds and led out one of the calves there on a length of binder twine under the very teeth of the barking dogs – he only hoped they would prove as hostile to the Aurigans as they seemed to be to human life.

As he was pulling the calf across the yard, Grubby appeared.

"You'd better stay away from us, Grubby. We're trying to trap one of the ghosts."

"Master, if I catch one, I shall strangle him, straight I will."

"A pitchfork is a better weapon. These ghosts are dangerous little beasts at close quarters."

"I'm strong, bor, I tell 'ee! I'd strangle un!"

To prove his point, Grubby rolled his striped and tattered sleeve even further up his arm and exposed to Gregory and Fox his enormous biceps. At the same time, he wagged his great heavy head and lolled his tongue out of his mouth, perhaps to demonstrate some of the effects of strangulation.

"It's a very fine arm," Gregory agreed. "But, look, Grubby, we have a better idea. We are going to do this ghost to death with pitchforks. If you want to join in, you'd better get a spare one from the stable."

Grubby looked at him with a sly-shy expression and stroked his throat. "I'd be better at strangling, bor. I've always wanted to strangle someone."

"Why should you want to do that, Grubby?"

The labourer lowered his voice. "I always wanted to see how difficult it would be. I'm strong, you see. I got my strength up as a lad by doing some of this here strangling – but never men, you know, just cattle."

Backing away a pace, Gregory said, "This time, Grubby, it's pitchforks for us." To settle the issue, he went into the stables, got a pitchfork, and returned to thrust it into Grubby's hand.

"Let's get on with it," Fox said.

They were all ready to start. Fox and Grubby crouched down in the ditch on either side of the gate, weapons at the ready. Gregory emptied one of the bags of flour over the yard in a patch just before the gate, so that anyone leaving the farm would have to walk through it. Then he led the calf towards the pond.

The young animal set up an uneasy mooing, and most of the beasts nearby seemed to answer. The chickens and hens scattered about the yard in the pale sunshine as if demented. Gregory felt the sweat trickle down his back, although his skin was cold with the chemistries of suspense. With a slap on its rump, he forced the calf into the water of the pond. It stood there unhappily, until he led it out again and slowly back across the yard, past the mill and the grain store on his right, past Mrs Grendon's neglected flowerbed on his left, towards the gate where his allies waited. And for all his determination not to do so, he could not stop himself looking backwards at the leaden surface of the pond to see if anything followed him. He led the calf through the gate and stopped. No tracks but his and the calf's showed in the strewn flour.

"Try it again," Fox advised. "Perhaps they are taking a nap down there."

Gregory went through the routine again, and a third and fourth time, on each occasion smoothing the flour after he had been through it. Each time, he saw Nancy watching helplessly from the house. Each time, he felt a little more sick with tension.

Yet when it happened, it took him by surprise. He had got the calf to the gate for a fifth time when Fox's shout joined the chorus of animal noises. The pond had shown no special ripples, so the Aurigan had come from some dark-purposed prowl of the farm – suddenly, its finned footsteps were marking the flour.

Yelling with excitement, Gregory dropped the rope that led the calf and ducked to one side. Seizing up an opened bag of flour by the gatepost, he flung its contents before the advancing figure.

The bomb of flour exploded all over the Aurigan. Now it was revealed in chalky outline. Despite himself, Gregory found himself screaming in sheer fright as the ghastliness was revealed in whirling white. It was especially the size that frightened: this dread thing, remote from human form, was too big for earthly nature – ten feet high, perhaps twelve! Invincible, and horribly quick, it came rushing at him with unnumbered arms striking out towards him.

Next morning, Doctor Crouchorn and his silk hat appeared at Gregory's bedside, thanked Mrs Fenn for some hot water, and dressed Gregory's leg wound.

"You got off lightly, considering," the old man said. "But if you will take a piece of advice from me, Mr Rolles, you will cease to visit the Grendon farm. It's an evil place and you'll come to no good there."

Gregory nodded. He had told the doctor nothing, except that Grendon had run up and shot him in the leg; which was true enough, but that it omitted most of the story.

"When will I be up again, Doctor?"

"Oh, young flesh heals soon enough, or undertakers would be rich men and doctors paupers. A few days should see you as right as rain. But I'll be visiting you again tomorrow, until when you are to stay flat on your back and keep that leg motionless."

"I understand."

The doctor made a ferocious face. "You understand, but will you take heed? I'm warning you, if you take one step on that leg, it will turn purple and fall off." He nodded slowly and emphatically, and the lines on his face deepened to such a great extent that anyone familiar with the eccentricities of his physiognomy would be inclined to estimate that he was smiling.

"I suppose I may write a letter, doctor?"

"I suppose you may, young man."

Directly Doctor Crouchorn had gone, Gregory took pen and paper and addressed some urgent lines to Nancy. They told her that he loved her very much and could not bear to think of her remaining on the farm; that he could not get to see her for a few days because of his leg wound; and that she must immediately come away on Hetty with a bag full of her things and stay at "The Wayfarer", where there was a capital room for which he would pay. That if she thought anything of him, she must put the simple plan into action this very day, and send him word round from the inn when she was established there.

With some satisfaction, Gregory read this through twice, signed it and added kisses, and summoned Mrs Fenn with the aid of a small bell she had provided for that purpose.

He told her that the delivery of the letter was a matter of extreme urgency. He would entrust it to Tommy, the baker's boy, to deliver when his morning round was over, and would give him a shilling for his efforts. Mrs Fenn was not enthusiastic about this, but with a little flattery was persuaded to speak to Tommy; she left the bedroom clutching both letter and shilling.

At once, Gregory began another letter, this one to Mr H. G. Wells. It was some while since he had last addressed his correspondent, and so he had to make a somewhat lengthy report; but eventually he came to the events of the previous day.

So horrified was I by the sight of the Aurigan, (he wrote) that I stood where I was, unable to move, while the flour blew about us. And how can I now convey to you – who are perhaps the most interested person in this vital subject in all the British Isles – what the monster looked like, outlined in white? My impressions were, of course, both brief and indefinite, but the main handicap is that there is nothing on Earth to liken this weird being to!

It appeared, I suppose, most like some horrendous goose, but the neck must be imagined as almost as thick as the body – indeed, it was almost all body, or all neck, whichever way you look at it. And on top of this neck was no head but a terrible array of various sorts of arms, a nest of writhing cilia, antennae, and whips, for all the world as if an octopus were entangled with a Portugese Man-'o-war as big as itself, with a few shrimp and starfish legs thrown in. Does this sound ludicrous? I can only swear to you that as it bore down on me, perhaps twice my own height or more, I found it something almost too terrifying for human eyes to look on – and yet I did not see it, but merely the flour that adhered to it!

That repulsive sight would have been the last my eyes ever dwelt on had it not been for Grubby, the simple farmhand I have had occasion to mention before.

As I threw the flour, Grubby gave a great cry and rushed forward, dropping the pitchfork. He jumped at the creature as it turned on me. This put out our plan, which was that he and Bruce Fox should pitchfork the creature to death. Instead, he grasped it as high as he possibly might and commenced to squeeze with the full force of his mighty muscles. What a terrifying contest! What a fear-fraught combat!

Collecting his wits, Bruce charged forward and attacked with his pitchfork. It was his battle cry that brought me back from my paralysis into action. I ran and seized Grubby's pitchfork and also charged. That thing had arms for us all! It struck out, and I have no doubt now that several arms held poisoned needle teeth, for I saw one come towards me gaping like a snake's mouth. Need I stress the danger – particularly when you recall that the effect of the flour cloud was only partial, and there were still invisible arms flailing around us!

Our saving was that the Aurigan was cowardly. I saw Bruce jab it hard, and a second later, I rammed my pitchfork right through its foot. At once it had had enough. Grubby fell to the ground as it retreated. It moved at amazing speed, back towards the pool. We were in pursuit! And all the beasts of the barnyard uttered their cries to it.

As it launched itself into the water, we both flung our pitchforks at its form. But it swam out strongly and then dived below the surface, leaving only ripples and a scummy trail of flour.

We stood staring at the water for an instant, and then with common accord ran back to Grubby. He was dead. He lay face up and was no longer recognisable. The Aurigan must have struck him with its poisoned fangs as soon as he attacked. Grubby's skin was stretched tight and glistened oddly. He had turned a dull crimson. No longer was he more than a caricature of human shape. All his internal substance had been transformed to liquid by the rapid-working venoms of the Aurigan; he was like a sort of giant man-shaped rotten haggis.

There were wound marks across his neck and throat and what

had been his face and from these wounds his substance drained, so that he slowly deflated into his trampled bed of flour and dust. Perhaps the sight of fabled Medusa's head, that turned men to stone, was no worse than this, for we stood there utterly paralysed. It was a blast from Farmer Grendon's rifle that brought us back to life.

He had threatened to shoot me. Now, seeing us despoiling his flour stocks and apparently about to make off with a calf, he fired at us. We had no choice but to run for it. Grendon was in no explaining mood. Good Nancy came running out to stop him, but Neckland was charging up too with the pair of savage dogs growling at the end of their chains.

Bruce and I had ridden up on my Daisy. I had left her saddled. Bringing her out of the stable at a trot, I heaved Bruce up into the saddle and was about to climb on myself when the gun went off again and I felt a burning pain in my leg. Bruce dragged me into the saddle and we were off – I half unconscious.

Here, I lie now in bed, and should be about again in a couple of days. Fortunately, the shot did not harm any bones.

So you see how the farm is now a place of the damned! Once, I thought it might even become a new Eden, growing the food of the gods for men like gods. Instead – alas! the first meeting between humanity and beings from another world has proved disastrous, and the Eden is become a battleground for a war of worlds. How can our anticipations for the future be anything other than gloomy?

Before I close this over-long account, I must answer a query in your letter and pose another to you, more personal than yours to me.

First, you question if the Aurigans are entirely invisible and say – if I may quote your letter – "Any alteration in the refractive index of the eye lenses would make vision impossible, but without such alteration the eyes would be visible as glassy globules. And for vision it is also necessary that there should be visual purple behind the retina and an opaque cornea. How then do your Aurigans manage for vision?" The answer must be that they do without eyesight as we know it, for I think they naturally maintain a complete invisibility. How they 'see' I know not, but whatever sense they use, it is effective. How they communicate I know not – our fellow made not the slightest sound when I speared his foot! – yet it is apparent they must communicate effectively. Perhaps they tried originally to communicate with us through a mysterious sense we do not possess and, on receiving no answer, assumed us to be as dumb as our dumb animals. If so, what a tragedy!

Now to my personal enquiry. I know, sir, that you must grow more busy as you grow more famous; but I feel that what transpires here in this remote corner of East Anglia is of momentous import to the world and the future. Could you not take it upon yourself to pay us a visit here? You would be comfortable at one of our two inns, and the journey here by railway is efficient if tedious – you can easily get a regular waggon from Heigham station here, a distance of only eight miles. You could then view Grendon's farm for yourself, and perhaps one of these interstellar beings too. I feel you are as much amused as concerned by the accounts you receive from the undersigned, but I swear not one detail is exaggerated. Say you can come!

If you need persuasion, reflect on how much delight it will give to

Your sincere admirer and friend,
    Gregory Rolles.'

Reading this long letter through, scratching out two superfluous adjectives, Gregory lay back in some satisfaction. He had the feeling he was still involved in the struggle although temporarily out of action.

But the late afternoon brough him disquieting news. Tommy, the baker's boy, had gone out as far as the Grendon farm. Then the ugly legends circulating in the village about the place had risen in his mind, and he had stood wondering whether he should go on. An unnatural babble of animal noise came from the farm, mixed with hammering, and when Tommy crept forward and saw the farmer himself looking as black as a puddle and building a great thing like a gibbet in the yard, he had lost his nerve and rushed back the way he came, the letter to Nancy undelivered.

Bruce Fox arrived that evening to see how his friend was, and Gregory tried to persuade him to take the letter. But Fox was able successfully to plead a prior engagement. They talked for a while, mainly running over the horrors of the previous day once more, and then Fox left.

Gregory lay on the bed worrying about Nancy until Mrs Fenn brought up supper on a tray. At least it was clear now why the Aurigans had not entered the farm house; they were far too large to do so. She was safe as long as she kept indoors – as far as anyone on that doomed plot was safe.

He fell asleep early that night. In the early hours of the morning, a nightmare visited him. He was in a strange city where all the buildings were new and the people wore shining clothes. In one square grew a tree. The Gregory in the dream stood in a special relationship to the tree: he fed it. It was his job to push people who were passing by the tree against its surface. The tree was a saliva tree. Down its smooth bark ran quantities of saliva from red lips like leaves up in the boughs. It grew enormous on the people on which it fed. As they were thrown against it, they passed into the substance of the tree. Some of the saliva splashed on to Gregory. But instead of dissolving him, it caused everything he touched to be dissolved. He put his arms about the girl he loved, and as his mouth went towards her, her skin peeled away from her face.

He woke weeping desperately and fumbling blindly for the ring of the gas mantle.

Dr Crouchorn came late next morning and told Gregory he should have at least three more days complete rest for the recovery of the muscles of his leg. Gregory lay there in a state of acute dissatisfaction with himself. Recalling the vile dream, he thought how negligent he had been towards Nancy, the girl he loved. His letter to her still lay undelivered by his bedside. After Mrs Fenn had brought up his dinner, he determined that he must see Nancy for himself. Leaving the food, he pulled himself out of bed and dressed slowly.

The leg was more painful than he had expected, but he got himself downstairs and out to the stable without too much trouble. Daisy seemed pleased to see him. He rubbed her nose and rested his head against her long cheek in sheer pleasure at being with her again.

"This may be the last time you have to undertake this particular journey, my girl," he said.

Saddling her was comparatively easy. Getting into the saddle involved much bodily anguish. But eventually he was comfortable and they turned along the familiar and desolate road to the domain of the Aurigans. His leg was worse than he had bargained for. More than once, he had to get the mare to stop while he let the throbbing subside. He saw he was losing blood plentifully.

As he approached the farm, he observed what the baker's boy had meant by saying Grendon was building a gibbet. A pole had been set up in the middle of the yard. A cable ran to the top of it, and a light was rigged there, so that the expanse of the yard could be illuminated by night.

Another change had taken place. A wooden fence had been built behind the horse trough, cutting off the pond from the farm. But at one point, ominously, a section of it had been broken down and splintered and crushed, as if some monstrous thing had walked through the barrier unheeding.

A ferocious dog was chained just inside the gate, and barking its head off, to the consternation of the poultry. Gregory dare not enter. As he stood wondering the best way to tackle this fresh problem, the door of the farmhouse opened fractionally and Nancy peeped out. He called and signalled frantically to her.

Timidly, she ran across and let him in, dragging the dog back. Gregory hitched Daisy to the gatepost and kissed her cheek, soothed by the feel of her sturdy body in his arms.

"Where's your father?"

"My dearest, your leg, your poor leg! It's bleeding yet!"

"Never mind my leg. Where's your father?"

"He's down in South Meadow, I think."

"Good! I'm going to speak with him. Nancy, I want you to go indoors and pack some belongings. I'm taking you away with me."

"I can't leave father!"

"You must. I'm going to tell him now." As he limped across the yard, she called fearfully, "He has that there gun of his'n with him all the time – do be careful!"

The two dogs on a running chain followed him all the way down the side of the house, nearly choking in their efforts to get at him, their teeth flashing uncomfortably close to his ankles.

Near the elms, he saw that several wild birds lay in the grass. One was still fluttering feebly. He could only assume they had worn themselves out trying to feed their immense and hungry broods. Which was what would happen to the farmer in time, he reflected. He noticed Neckland below Grubby's little hut, busy sawing wood; the farmer was not with him. On impulse, Gregory turned into the sties.

It was gloomy there. In the gloom, Grendon worked. He dropped his bucket when he saw Gregory there, and came forward threateningly.

"You came back? Why don't you stay away? Can't you see the notice by the gate? I don't want you here no more, bor. I know you mean well, and I intend you no harm, but I'll kill 'ee, understand, kill 'ee if you ever come here again. I've plenty of worries without you to add to them. Now then, get you going!"

Gregory stood his ground.

"Mr Grendon, are you as mad as your wife was before she died? Do you understand that you may meet Grubby's fate at any moment? Do you realise what you are harbouring in your pond?"

"I ent a fule. But suppose them there things do eat everything, humans included? Suppose this is now their farm? They still got to have someone tend it. So I reckon they ent going to harm me. So long as they sees me work hard, they ent going to harm me."

"You're being fattened, do you understand? For all the hard work you do, you must have put on a stone this last month. Doesn't that scare you?"

Something of the farmer's poise broke for a moment. He cast a wild look round. "I ent saying I ent scared. I'm saying I'm doing what I have to do. We don't own our lives. Now do me a favour and get out of here."

Instinctively, Gregory's glance had followed Grendon's. For the first time, he saw in the dimness the size of the pigs. Their great broad black backs were visible over the top of the sties. They were the size of young oxen.

"This is a farm of death," he said.

"Death's always the end of all of us, pig or cow or man alike."

"Right-ho, Mr Grendon, you can think like that if you like. It's not my way of thinking, nor am I going to see your dependants suffer from your madness. Mr Grendon, sir, I wish to ask for your daughter's hand in marriage."

For the first three days that she was away from her home, Nancy Grendon lay in her room in "The Wayfarer" near to death. It seemed as if all ordinary food poisoned her. But gradually under Doctor Crouchorn's ministration – terrified perhaps by the rage she suspected he would vent upon her should she fail to get better – she recovered her strength.

"You look so much better today," Gregory said, clasping her hand. "You'll soon be up and about again, once your system is free of all the evil nourishment of the farm."

"Greg, dearest, promise me you will not go to the farm again. You have no need to go now I'm not there."

He cast his eyes down and said, "Then you don't have to get me to promise, do you?"

"I just want to be sure we neither of us go there again. Father, I feel sure, bears a charmed life. But I – I feel now as if I'm waking from a nightmare!"

"Don't think about it! Look, I've brought you some flowers!"

He produced a clay pot overloaded with wallflowers with gigantic blooms and gave it to her.

She smiled and said, "They're so large! Greg – they're – they're from the farm, aren't they? They're unnaturally large."

"I thought you'd like a souvenir of the nicer side of your home."

With all her strength, she hurled the pot across the room. It struck the door and broke. The dark earth scattered over the boards and the flowers lay broken on the floor.

"You dare bring the curse in here! And, Greg, this means you've been back to the farm, doesn't it, since we came away together?"

He nodded his head, looking defiantly at her. "I had to see what was happening."

"Please don't go there again, Greg, please. It's as if I was now coming to my senses again – but I don't want it to be as if you was losing yours! Supposing those things followed us here to Cottersall, those Aurigans?"

"You know, Nancy, I've wondered several times why they remain on the farm as they do. You would think that once they found they could so easily defeat human beings, they would attack everyone, or send for more of their own kind and try to invade us. Yet they seem perfectly content to remain in that one small space."

She smiled. "I may not be very clever compared with you, but I tell 'ee the answer to that one. They ent interested in going anywhere. I think there's just two of them, and they come to our little old world for a holiday in their space machine, same as we might go to Great Yarmouth for a couple of days for our honeymoon. Perhaps they're on their honeymoon."

"On honeymoon! What a ghastly idea!"

"Well, on holiday then. That was father's idea – he says as there's just two of them, treating Earth as a quiet place to stay. People like to eat well when they're on holiday, don't they?"

He stared at Nancy aghast.

"But that's horrible! You're trying to make the Aurigans out to be *pleasant*!"

"Of course I ent, you silly ha'p'orth! But I expect they seem pleasant to each other."

"Well, I prefer to think of them as menaces."

"All the more reason for you to keep away from them!"

But to be out of sight was not to be out of mind's reach. Gregory received another letter from Dr Hudson-Ward, a kind and encouraging one, but he made no attempt to answer it. He felt he could not bear to take up any work that would remove him from the neighbourhood, although the need to work, in view of his matrimonial plans, was now pressing; the modest allowance his father made him would not support two in any comfort. Yet he could not bring his thoughts to grapple with such practical problems. It was another letter he looked for, and the horrors of the farm that obsessed him. And the next night, he dreamed of the saliva tree again.

In the evening, he plucked up enough courage to tell Fox and Nancy about it. They met in the little snug at the back of "The Wayfarer's" public bars, a discreet and private place with red plush on the seats. Nancy was her usual self again, and had been out for a brief walk in the afternoon sunshine.

"People wanted to give themselves to the saliva tree. And although I didn't see this for myself, I had the distinct feeling that perhaps they weren't actually killed so much as changed into something else – something less human maybe. And this time, I saw the tree was made of metal of some kind and was growing bigger and bigger by pumps – you could see through the saliva to big armatures and pistons, and out of the branches steam was pouring."

Fox laughed, a little unsympathetically. "Sounds to me like the shape of things to come, when even plants are grown by machinery. Events are preying on your mind, Greg! Listen, my sister is going to Norwich tomorrow, driving in her uncle's trap. Why don't the two of you go with her? She's going to buy some adornments for her bridal gown, so that should interest you, Nancy. Then you could stay with Greg's uncle for a couple of days. I assure you I will let you know immediately the Aurigans invade Cottersall, so you won't miss anything."

Nancy seized Gregory's arm. "Can we please, Gregory, can we? I ent been to Norwich for long enough and it's a fine city."

"It would be a good idea," he said doubtfully.

Both of them pressed him until he was forced to yield. He broke up the little party as soon as he decently could, kissed Nancy goodnight, and walked hurriedly back down the street to the baker's. Of one thing he was certain: if he must leave the district even for a short while, he had to have a look to see what was happening at the farm before he went.

The farm looked in the summer's dusk as it had never done before. Massive wooden screens nine feet high had been erected and hastily creosoted. They stood about in forlorn fashion, intended to keep the public gaze from the farm, but lending it unmeaning. They stood not only in the yard but at irregular intervals along the boundaries of the land, inappropriately among fruit trees, desolately amid bracken, irrelevantly in swamp. A sound of furious hammering, punctuated by the unwearying animal noises, indicated that more screens were still being built.

But what lent the place its unearthly look was the lighting. The solitary pole supporting electric light now had five companions: one by the gate, one by the pond, one behind the house, one outside the engine house, one down by the pigsties. Their hideous yellow glare reduced the scene to the sort of unlikely picture that might be found and puzzled over in the eternal midnight of an Egyptian tomb.

Gregory was too wise to try and enter by the gate. He hitched Daisy to the low branches of a thorn tree and set off over waste land, entering Grendon's property by the South Meadow. As he walked stealthily towards the distant outhouses, he could see how the farm land differed from the territory about it. The corn was already so high it seemed in the dark almost to threaten by its ceaseless whisper of movement. The fruits had ripened fast. In the strawberry beds were great strawberries like pears. The marrows lay on their dunghill like bloated bolsters, gleaming from a distant shaft of light. In the orchard, the trees creaked, weighed down by distorted footballs that passed for apples; with a heavy autumnal thud one fell over-ripe to the ground. Everywhere on the farm, there seemed to be slight movement and noise, so much so that Gregory stopped to listen.

A wind was rising. The sails of the old mill shrieked like a gull's cry as they began to turn. In the engine house, the steam engine pumped out its double unfaltering note as it generated power. The dogs still raged, the animals added their uneasy chorus. He recalled the saliva tree; here as in the dream, it was as if agriculture had become industry, and the impulses of nature swallowed by the new god of Science. In the bark of the trees rose the dark steam of novel and unknown forces.

He talked himself into pressing forward again. He moved carefully through the baffling slices of shadow and illumination created
by the screens and lights, and arrived near the back door of the
farmhouse. A lantern burnt in the kitchen window. As Gregory
hesitated, the crunch of broken glass came from within.

Cautiously, he edged himself past the window and peered in
through the doorway. From the parlour, he heard the voice of
Grendon. It held a curious muffled tone, as if the man spoke to
himself.

"Lie there! You're no use to me. This is a trial of strength. Oh
God, preserve me, to let me prove myself! Thou has made my land
barren till now – now let me harvest it! I don't know what You're
doing. I didn't mean to presume, but this here farm is my life.
Curse 'em, curse 'em all! They're all enemies." There was more of
it; the man was muttering like one drunk. With a horrid fascination,
Gregory was drawn forward till he had crossed the kitchen flags and
stood on the verge of the larger room. He peered round the half
open door until he could see the farmer, standing obscurely in the
middle of the room.

A candle stood in the neglected hearth, its flickering flame glassily
reflected in the cases of maladroit animals. Evidently the house
electricity had been cut off to give additional power to the new lights
outside.

Grendon's back was to Gregory. One gaunt and unshaven cheek
was lit by candle-light. His back seemed a little bent by the weight
of what he imagined his duties, yet looking at that leather-clad back
now Gregory experienced a sort of reverence for the independence
of the man, and for the mystery that lay under his plainness. He
watched as Grendon moved out through the front door, leaving it
hanging wide, and passed into the yard, still muttering to himself.
He walked round the side of the house and was hidden from view as
the sound of his tread was lost amid the renewed barking of dogs.

The tumult did not drown a groan from near at hand. Peering
into the shadows, Gregory saw a body lying under the table. It
rolled over, crunching broken glass as it did so, and exclaimed in a
dazed way. Without being able to see clearly, Gregory knew it was
Neckland. He climbed over to the man and propped his head up,
kicking away a stuffed fish as he did so.

"Don't kill me, bor! I only want to get away from here. I only
want to get away."

"Bert? It's Greg here. Bert, are you badly hurt?"

He could see some wounds. The fellow's shirt had been practically torn from his back, and the flesh on his side and back was cut from where he had rolled in the glass. More serious was a great weal over one shoulder, changing to a deeper colour as Gregory looked at it. A brawl had taken place. Under the table lay another fish, its mouth gaping as if it still died, and the pseudo-goat, one button eye of which had rolled out of its socket. The cases from which they had come lay shattered by the wall.

Wiping his face and speaking in a more rational voice, Neckland said, "Gregory? I thought as you was down in Cottersall? What are you doing here? He'll kill you proper if he find you here!"

"What happened to you, Bert? Can you get up?"

The labourer was again in possession of his faculties. He grabbed Gregory's forearm and said imploringly, "Keep your voice down, for Christ's sake, or he'll hear us and come back and settle my hash for once for all! He's gone clean off his head, says as these pond things are having a holiday here. He nearly knocked my head off my shoulder with that stick of his! Lucky I got a thick head!"

"What was the quarrel about?"

"I tell you straight, bor, I have got the wind up proper about this here farm. They things as live in the pond will eat me and suck me up like they done Grubby if I stay here any more. So I run off when Joe Grendon weren't looking, and I come in here to gather up my traps and my bits and leave here at once. This whole place is evil, a bed of evil, and it ought to be destroyed. Hell can't be worse than this here farm!"

"So he caught you in here, did he?"

"I saw him rush in and I flung that there fish at him, and the goat. But he had me! Now I'm getting out, and I'd advise you to do the same. You must be daft, come back here like you did!"

As he spoke, he pulled himself to his feet and stood, keeping his balance with Gregory's aid. Grunting, he made his way over to the staircase.

"Bert," Gregory said, "supposing we rush Grendon and lay him out. We can then get him in the cart and all leave together."

Neckland turned to stare at him, his face hidden in shadows, nursing his shoulder with one hand.

"You try it!" he said, and then he turned and went steadily up the stairs.

Gregory stood where he was, keeping one eye on the window. He had come to the farm without any clear notion in his head, but now that the idea had been formulated, he saw that it was up to him to try and remove Grendon from his farm. He felt obliged to do it; for although he had lost his former regard for Grendon, a sort of fascination for the man held him, and he was incapable of leaving any human being, however perverse, to face alone the alien horrors of the farm. It occurred to him that he might get help from the distant houses, Dereham Cottages, if only the farmer were rendered in one way or another unable to pepper the intruders with shot.

The machine house possessed only one high window, and that was barred. It was built of brick and had a stout door which could be barred and locked from the outside. Perhaps it would be possible to lure Grendon into there; outside aid could then be obtained.

Not without apprehension, Gregory went to the open door and peered out into the confused dark. He stared anxiously at the ground for sight of a footstep more sinister than the farmer's, but there was no indication that the Aurigans were active. He stepped into the yard.

He had not gone two yards before a woman's scream rang out. The sound seemed to clasp an icy grip about Gregory's ribs, and into his mind came a picture of poor mad Mrs Grendon. Then he recognised the voice, in its few shouted words, as Nancy's. Even before the sound was cut off, he began to pelt down the dark side of the house as fast as he could run.

Only later did he realise how he seemed to be running against a great army of animal cries. Loudest was the babel of the pigs; every swine seemed to have some message deep and nervous and indecipherable to deliver to an unknown source; and it was to the sties that Gregory ran, swerving past the giant screens under the high and sickly light.

The noise in the sties was deafening. Every animal was attacking its pen with its sharp hooves. One light swung over the middle pen. With its help, Gregory saw immediately how terrible was the change that had come over the farm since his last visit. The sows had swollen enormously and their great ears clattered against their cheeks like boards. Their hirsute backs curved almost to the rafters of their prison.

Grendon was at the far entrance. In his arms he held the unconscious form of his daughter. A sack of pig feed lay scattered by his feet. He had one pen gate half open and was trying to thrust his way in against the flank of a pig whose mighty shoulder came almost level with his. He turned and stared at Gregory with a face whose blankness was more terrifying than any expression of rage.

There was another presence in the place. A pen gate near to Gregory swung open. The two sows wedged in the narrow sty gave out a terrible falsetto squealing, clearly scenting the presence of an unappeasable hunger. They kicked out blindly, and all the other animals plunged with a sympathetic fear. Struggle was useless. An Aurigan was there; the figure of Death itself, with its unwearying scythe and unaltering smile of bone, was as easily avoided as this poisoned and unseen presence. A rosy flush spread over the back of one of the sows. Almost at once, her great bulk began to collapse; in a moment, her substance had been ingested.

Gregory did not stay to watch the sickening action. He was running forward, for the farmer was again on the move. And now it was clear what he was going to do. He pushed into the end sty and dropped his daughter down into the metal food trough. At once, the sows turned with smacking jaws to deal with this new fodder. His hands free, Grendon moved to a bracket set in the wall. There lay his gun.

Now the uproar in the sties had reached its loudest. The sow whose companion had been so rapidly ingested broke free and burst into the central aisle. For a moment she stood – mercifully, for otherwise Gregory would have been trampled – as if dazed by the possibility of liberty. The place shook and the other swine fought to get to her. Brick crumbled, pen gates buckled. Gregory jumped aside as the second pig lumbered free, and next moment the place was full of grotesque fighting bodies, fighting their way to liberty.

He had reached Grendon, but the stampede caught them even as they confronted each other. A hoof stabbed down on Grendon's instep. Groaning, he bent forward, and was at once swept underfoot by his creatures. Gregory barely had time to vault into the nearest pen before they thundered by. Nancy was trying pitifully to climb out of the trough as the two beasts to which she had been offered fought to kick their way free. With a ferocious strength – without reason – almost without consciousness – Gregory hauled her up, jumped until he swung up on one of the overhead beams, wrapped a leg round the beam, hung down till he grasped Nancy, pulled her up with him.

They were safe, but the safety was not permanent. Through the din and dust, they could see that the gigantic beasts were wedged tightly in both entrances. In the middle was a sort of battlefield, where the animals fought to reach the opposite end of the building; they were gradually tearing each other to pieces – but the sties too were threatened with demolition.

"The Aurigan is here somewhere," Gregory shouted. "We aren't safe from it by any means."

"You were foolish to come here, Greg," Nancy said. "I found you had gone and I had to follow you. But Father – I don't think he even recognised me!"

At least, Gregory thought, she had not seen her father trampled underfoot. Involuntarily glancing in that direction, he saw the shotgun that Grendon had never managed to reach still lying across a bracket on the wall. By crawling along a transverse beam, he could reach it easily. Bidding Nancy sit where she was, he wriggled along the beam, only a foot or two above the heaving backs of the swine. At least the gun should afford them some protection: the Aurigan, despite all its ghastly differences from humanity, would hardly be immune to lead.

As he grasped the old-fashioned weapon and pulled it up, Gregory was suddenly filled with an intense desire to kill one of the invisible monsters. In that instant, he recalled an earlier hope he had had of them: that they might be superior beings, beings of wisdom and enlightened power, coming from a better society where higher moral codes directed the activities of its citizens. He had thought that only to such a civilisation would the divine gift of travelling through interplanetary space be granted. But perhaps the opposite held true: perhaps such a great objective could be gained only by species ruthless enough to disregard more humane ends. As soon as he thought it, his mind was overpowered with a vast diseased vision of the universe, where such races as dealt in love and kindness and intellect cowered forever on their little globes, while all about them went the slayers of the universe, sailing where they would to satisfy their cruelties and their endless appetites.

He heaved his way across to Nancy above the bloody porcine fray.

She pointed mutely. At the far end, the entrance had crumbled away, and the sows were bursting forth into the night. But one sow fell and turned crimson as it fell, sagging over the floor like a shapeless bag. Another, passing the same spot, suffered the same fate.

Was the Aurigan moved by anger? Had the pigs, in their blind charging, injured it? Gregory raised the gun and aimed. As he did so, he saw a faint hallucinatory column in the air; enough dirt and mud and blood had been thrown up to spot the Aurigan and render him partly visible. Gregory fired.

The recoil nearly knocked him off his perch. He shut his eyes, dazed by the noise, and was dimly aware of Nancy clinging to him, shouting, "Oh, you marvellous man, you marvellous man! You hit that old bor right smack on target!"

He opened his eyes and peered through the smoke and dust. The shade that represented the Aurigan was tottering. It fell. It fell among the distorted shapes of the two sows it had killed, and corrupt fluids spattered over the paving. Then it rose again. They saw its progress to the broken door, and then it had gone.

For a minute, they sat there, staring at each other, triumph and speculation mingling on both their faces. Apart from one badly injured beast, the building was clear of pigs now. Gregory climbed to the floor and helped Nancy down beside him. They skirted the loathsome masses as best they could and staggered into the fresh air.

Up beyond the orchard, strange lights showed in the rear windows of the farmhouse.

"It's on fire! Oh, Greg, our poor home is afire! Quick, we must gather what we can! All father's lovely cases – "

He held her fiercely, bent so that he spoke straight into her face. "Bert Neckland did this! He did it! He told me the place ought to be destroyed and that's what he did."

"Let's go, then – "

"No, no, Nancy, we must let it burn! Listen! There's a wounded Aurigan loose here somewhere. We didn't kill him. If those things feel rage, anger, spite, they'll be set to kill us now – don't forget there's more than one of 'em! We aren't going that way if we want to live. Daisy's just across the meadow here, and she'll bear us both safe home."

"Greg, dearest, this is my home!" she cried in her despair.

The flames were leaping higher. The kitchen windows broke in a shower of glass. He was running with her in the opposite direction, shouting wildly, "I'm your home now! I'm your home now!"

Now she was running with him, no longer protesting, and they plunged together through the high rank grass.

When they gained the track and the restive mare, they paused to take breath and look back.

The house was well ablaze now. Clearly nothing could save it.

Sparks had carried to the windmill, and one of the sails was ablaze. About the scene, the electric lights shone spectral and pale on the tops of their poles. An occasional running figure of a gigantic animal dived about its own purposes. Suddenly, there was a flash as of lightning and all the electric lights went out. One of the stampeding animals had knocked down a pole; crashing into the pond, it short-circuited the system.

"Let's get away," Gregory said, and he helped Nancy on to the mare. As he climbed up behind her, a roaring sound developed, grew in volume and altered in pitch. Abruptly it died again. A thick cloud of steam billowed above the pond. From it rose the space machine, rising, rising, rising, suddenly a sight to take the heart in awe. It moved up into the soft night sky, was lost for a moment, began dully to glow, was seen to be already tremendously far away.

Desperately, Gregory looked for it, but it had gone, already beyond the frail confines of the terrestrial atmosphere. An awful desolation settled on him, the more awful for being irrational, and then he thought, and cried his thought aloud, "Perhaps they were only holiday-makers here! Perhaps they enjoyed themselves here, and will tell their friends of this little globe! Perhaps Earth has a future only as a resort for millions of the Aurigan kind!"

The church clock was striking midnight as they passed the first cottages of Cottersall.

"We'll go first to the inn," Gregory said. "I can't well disturb Mrs Fenn at this late hour, but your landlord will fetch us food and hot water and see that your cuts are bandaged."

"I'm right as rain, love, but I'd be glad of your company."

"I warn you, you shall have too much of it from now on!"

The door of the inn was locked, but a light burned inside, and in a moment the landlord himself opened to them, all eager to hear a bit of gossip he could pass on to his custom.

"So happens as there's a gentleman up in Number Three wishes to speak with you in the morning," he told Gregory. "Very nice gentleman came on the night train, only got in here an hour past, off the waggon."

Gregory made a wry face.

"My father, no doubt."

"Oh, no, sir. His name is a Mr Wills or Wells – his signature was a mite difficult to make out."

"Wells! Mr Wells! So he's come!" He caught Nancy's hands,

shaking them in his excitement. "Nancy, one of the greatest men in England is here! There's no one more profitable for such a tale as ours! I'm going up to speak with him right away."

Kissing her lightly on the cheek, he hurried up the stairs and knocked on the door of Number Three.

(1965)

Man In His Time

His absence

Janet Westermark sat watching the three men in the office: the administrator who was about to go out of her life, the behaviourist who was about to come into it, and the husband whose life ran parallel to but insulated from her own.

She was not the only one playing a watching game. The behaviourist, whose name was Clement Stackpole, sat hunched in his chair with his ugly strong hands clasped round his knee, thrusting his intelligent and simian face forward, the better to regard his new subject, Jack Westermark.

The administrator of the Mental Research Hospital spoke in a lively and engaged way. Typically, it was only Jack Westermark who seemed absent from the scene.

Your particular problem, restless

His hands upon his lap lay still, but he himself was restless, though the restlessness seemed directed. It was as if he were in another room with other people, Janet thought. She saw that he caught her eye when in fact she was not entirely looking at him, and by the time she returned the glance, he was gone, withdrawn.

"Although Mr Stackpole has not dealt before with your particular problem," the administrator was saying, "he has had plenty of field experience. I know – "

"I'm sure we won't," Westermark said, folding his hands and nodding his head slightly.

Smoothly, the administrator made a pencilled note of the remark, scribbled the precise time beside it, and continued, "I know Mr Stackpole is too modest to say this, but he is a great man for working in with people – "

"If you feel it's necessary," Westermark said. "Though I've seen enough of your equipment for a while."

The pencil moved, the smooth voice proceeded. "Good. A great man for working in with people, and I'm sure you and Mr

Westermark will soon find you are glad to have him around. Remember, he's there to help both of you."

Janet smiled, and said from the island of her chair, trying to smile at him and Stackpole, "I'm sure that everything will work – " She was interrupted by her husband, who rose to his feet, letting his hands drop to his sides and saying, turning slightly to address thin air, "Do you mind if I say good-bye to Nurse Simmons?"

Her voice no longer wavered

"Everything will be all right, I'm sure," she said hastily. And Stackpole nodded at her, conspiratorially agreeing to see her point of view.

"We'll all get on fine, Janet," he said. She was in the swift process of digesting that unexpected use of her Christian name, and the administrator was also giving her the sort of encouraging smile so many people had fed her since Westermark was pulled out of the ocean off Casablanca, when her husband, still having his lonely conversation with the air, said, "Of course, I should have remembered."

His right hand went halfway to his forehead – or his heart? Janet wondered – and then dropped, as he added, "Perhaps she'll come round and see us some time." Now he turned and was smiling faintly at another vacant space with just the faintest nod of his head, as if slightly cajoling. "You'd like that, wouldn't you, Janet?"

She moved her head, instinctively trying to bring her eyes into his gaze as she replied vaguely, "Of course, darling." Her voice no longer wavered when she addressed his absent attention.

There was sunlight through which they could see each other

There was sunlight in one corner of the room, coming through the windows of a bay angled towards the sun. For a moment she caught, as she rose to her feet, her husband's profile with the sunlight behind it. It was thin and withdrawn. Intelligent: she had always thought him over-burdened with his intelligence, but now there was a lost look there, and she thought of the words of a psychiatrist who had been called in on the case earlier: "You must understand that the waking brain is perpetually lapped by the unconscious."

Lapped by the unconscious

Fighting the words away, she said, addressing the smile of the administrator – that smile which must have advanced his career so much – "You've helped me a lot. I couldn't have got through these months without you. Now we'd better go."

She heard herself chopping her words, fearing Westermark would talk across them, as he did: "Thank you for your help. If you find anything . . ."

Stackpole walked modestly over to Janet as the administrator rose and said, "Well, don't either of you forget us if you're in any kind of trouble."

"I'm sure we won't."

"And, Jack, we'd like you to come back here to visit us once a month for a personal check-up. Don't want to waste all our expensive equipment, you know, and you are our star – er, patient." He smiled rather tightly as he said it, glancing at the paper on his desk to check Westermark's answer. Westermark's back was already turned on him, Westermark was already walking slowly to the door, Westermark had said his goodbyes, perched out on the lonely eminence of his existence.

Janet looked helplessly, before she could guard against it, at the administrator and Stackpole. She hated it that they were too professional to take note of what seemed her husband's breach of conduct. Stackpole looked kindly in a monkey way and took her arm with one of his thick hands.

"Shall we be off then? My car's waiting outside."

Not saying anything, nodding, thinking, and consulting watches

She nodded, not saying anything, thinking only, without the need of the administrator's notes to think it, "Oh yes, this was when he said, 'Do you mind if I say good-bye to Nurse' – who's it? – Simpson?" She was learning to follow her husband's footprints across the broken path of conversation. He was now out in the corridor, the door swinging to behind him and to empty air the administrator was saying, "It's her day off today."

"You're good on your cues," she said, feeling the hand tighten on her arm. She politely brushed his fingers away, horrid Stackpole, trying to recall what had gone only four minutes before. Jack had said something to her; she couldn't remember, didn't speak, avoided eyes, put out her hand and shook the administrator's firmly.

"Thanks," she said.

"Au revoir to both of you," he replied firmly, glancing swiftly: watch, notes, her, the door. "Of course," he said. "If we find anything at all. We are very hopeful. . . ."

He adjusted his tie, looking at the watch again.

"Your husband has gone now, Mrs Westermark," he said, his manner softening. He walked towards the door with her and added, "You have been wonderfully brave, and I do realise – we all realise – that you will have to go on being wonderful. With time, it should be easier for you; doesn't Shakespeare say in Hamlet that 'Use almost can change the stamp of nature'? May I suggest that you follow Stackpole's and my example and keep a little notebook and a strict check on the time?"

They saw her tiny hesitation, stood about her, two men round a personable women, not entirely innocent of relish. Stackpole cleared his throat, smiled, said, "He can so easily feel cut off you know. It's essential that you of all people answer his questions, or he will feel cut off."

Always a pace ahead

"The children?" she asked.

"Let's see you and Jack well settled in at home again, say for a fortnight or so," the administrator said, "before we think about having the children back to see him."

"That way's better for them and Jack *and* you, Janet," Stackpole said. "Don't be glib," she thought; "consolation I need, God knows, but that's too facile." She turned her face away, fearing it looked too vulnerable these days.

In the corridor, the administrator said, as valediction, "I'm sure Grandma's spoiling them terribly, Mrs Westermark, but worrying won't mend it, as the old saw says."

She smiled at him and walked quickly away, a pace ahead of Stackpole.

Westermark sat in the back of the car outside the administrative block. She climbed in beside him. As she did so, he jerked violently back in his seat.

"Darling, what is it?" she asked. He said nothing.

Stackpole had not emerged from the building, evidently having a last word with the administrator. Janet took the moment to lean over and kiss her husband's cheek, aware as she did so that a phantom wife had already, from his viewpoint, done so. His response was a phantom to her.

"The countryside looks green," he said. His eyes were flickering over the grey concrete block opposite.

"Yes," she said.

Stackpole came bustling down the steps, apologising as he opened the car door, settled in. He let the clutch back too fast and they shot forward. Janet saw then the reason for Westermark's jerking backwards a short while before. Now the acceleration caught him again; his body was rolled helplessly back. As they drove along, he set one hand fiercely on the side grip, for his sway was not properly counterbalancing the movement of the car.

Once outside the grounds of the institute, they were in the country, still under a mid-August day.

His theories

Westermark, by concentrating, could bring himself to conform to some of the laws of the time continuum he had left. When the car he was in climbed up his drive (familiar, yet strange with the rhododendrons unclipped and no signs of children) and stopped by the front door, he sat in his seat for three and a half minutes before venturing to open his door. Then he climbed out and stood on the gravel, frowning down at it. Was it as real as ever, as material? Was there a slight glaze on it? – as if something shone through from the interior of the earth, shone through all things? Or was it that there was a screen between him and everything else? It was important to decide between the two theories, for he had to live under the discipline of one. What he hoped to prove was that the permeation theory was correct; that way he was merely one of the factors comprising the functioning universe, together with the rest of humanity. By the glaze theory, he was isolated not only from the rest of humanity but from the entire cosmos (except Mars?). It was early days yet; he had a deal of thinking to do, and new ideas would undoubtedly emerge after observation and cogitation. Emotion must not decide the issue; he must be detached. Revolutionary theories could well emerge from this – suffering.

He could see his wife by him, standing off in case they happened embarrassingly or painfully to collide. He smiled thinly at her through her glaze. He said, "I am, but I'd prefer not to talk." He stepped towards the house, noting the slippery feel of gravel that would not move under his tread until the world caught up. He said, "I've every respect for the *Guardian*, but I'd prefer not to talk at present."

Famous Astronaut Returns Home

As the party arrived, a man waited in the porch for them, ambushing Westermark's return home with a deprecatory smile.

Hesitant but businesslike, he came forward and looked interroga-
tively at the three people who had emerged from the car.

"Excuse me, you are Captain Jack Westermark, aren't you?".

He stood aside as Westermark seemed to make straight for him.

"I'm the psychology correspondent for the *Guardian*, if I might
intrude for a moment."

Westermark's mother had opened the front door and stood there
smiling welcome at him, one hand nervously up to her grey hair.
Her son walked past her. The newspaper man stared after him.

Janet told him apologetically, "You'll have to excuse us. My
husband did reply to you, but he's really not prepared to meet
people yet."

"*When* did he reply, Mrs Westermark? Before he heard what I
had to say?"

'Well, naturally not – but his life stream. . . . I'm sorry, I can't
explain."

"He really is living ahead of time, isn't he? Will you spare me a
minute to tell me how you feel now the first shock is over?".

"You really must excuse me," Janet said, brushing past him. As
she followed her husband into the house, she heard Stackpole say,
"Actually, I read the *Guardian*, and perhaps I could help you. The
Institute has given me the job of remaining with Captain Westermark. My name's Clement Stackpole – you may know my book.
Persistent Human Relations, Methuen. But you must not say that
Westermark is living ahead of time. That's quite incorrect. What
you can say is that some of his psychological and physiological
processes have somehow been transposed forward – "

"Ass!" she exclaimed to herself. She had paused by the threshold
to catch some of his words. Now she whisked in.

Talk hanging in the air among the long watches of supper

Supper that evening had its discomforts, although Janet Westermark and her mother-in-law achieved an air of melancholy gaiety by
bringing two Scandinavian candelabra, relics of a Copenhagen
holiday, to the table and surprising the two men with a gay-looking
hors d'oeuvre. But the conversation was mainly like the hors
d'oeuvre, Janet thought: little tempting isolated bits of talk, not
nourishing.

Mrs Westermark senior had not yet got the hang of talking to her
son, and confined her remarks to Janet, though she looked towards
Jack often enough. "How are the children?" he asked her. Flustered

by the knowledge that he was waiting a long while for her answer, she replied rather incoherently and dropped her knife.

To relieve the tension, Janet was cooking up a remark on the character of the administrator at the Mental Research Hospital, when Westermark said, "Then he is at once thoughtful and literate. Commendable and rare in men of this type. I got the impression, as you evidently did, that he was as interested in his job as in advancement. I suppose one might say one even *liked* him. But you know him better, Stackpole; what do you think of him?"

Crumbling bread to cover his ignorance of whom they were supposed to be conversing about, Stackpole said, "Oh, I don't know; it's hard to say really," spinning out time, pretending not to squint at his watch.

"The administrator was quite a charmer, didn't you think Jack?" Janet remarked – perhaps helping Stackpole as much as Jack.

"He looks as if he might make a slow bowler," Westermark said, with an intonation that suggested he was agreeing with something as yet unsaid.

"Oh, him!" Stackpole said. "Yes, he seems a satisfactory sort of chap on the whole."

"He quoted Shakespeare to me and thoughtfully told me where the quotation came from," Janet said.

"No thank you, Mother," Westermark said.

"I don't have much to do with him," Stackpole continued. "Though I have played cricket with him a time or two. He makes quite a good slow bowler."

"Are you really?" Westermark exclaimed.

That stopped them. Jack's mother looked helplessly about, caught her son's glazed eye, said, covering up, "Do have some more sauce, Jack, dear," recalled she had already had her answer, almost let her knife slide again, gave up trying to eat.

"I'm a batsman, myself," Stackpole said, as if bringing an old pneumatic drill to the new silence. When no answer came, he doggedly went on, expounding on the game, the pleasure of it. Janet sat and watched, a shade perplexed that she was admiring Stackpole's performance and wondering at her slight perplexity; then she decided that she had made up her mind to dislike Stackpole, and immediately dissolved the resolution. Was he not on their side? And even the strong hairy hands became a little more acceptable when you thought of them gripping the rubber bat-handle; and the broad shoulders swinging . . . She closed her eyes momentarily, and tried to concentrate on what he was saying.

A batsman himself

Later, she met Stackpole on the upper landing. He had a small cigar in his mouth, she had two pillows in her arms. He stood in her way.

"Can I help at all, Janet?"

"I'm only making up a bed, Mr Stackpole."

"Are you not sleeping in with your husband?"

"He would like to be on his own for a night or two, Mr Stackpole. I shall sleep in the children's room for the time being."

"Then please permit me to carry the pillows for you. And do please call me Clem. All my friends do."

Trying to be pleasanter, to unfreeze, to recall that Jack was not moving her out of the bedroom permanently, she said, "I'm sorry. It's just that we once had a terrier called Clem." But it did not sound as she had wished it to do.

He put the pillows on Peter's blue bed, switched on the bedside lamp, and sat on the edge of the bed, clutching his cigar and puffing at it.

"This may be a bit embarrassing, but there's something I feel I should say to you, Janet." He did not look at her. She brought him an ashtray and stood by him.

"We feel your husband's mental health may be endangered, although I hasten to assure you that he shows no signs of losing his mental equilibrium beyond what we may call an inordinate absorption in phenomena – and even there, we cannot say, of course we can't, that his absorption is any greater than one might expect. Except in the totally unprecedented circumstances, I mean. We must talk about this in the next few days."

She waited for him to go on, not unamused by the play with the cigar. Then he looked straight up at her and said, "Frankly, Mrs Westermark, we think it would help your husband if you could have sexual relations with him."

A little taken aback, she said, "Can you imagine – " Correcting herself, she said, "That is for my husband to say. I am not unapproachable."

She saw he had caught her slip. Playing a very straight bat, he said, "I'm sure you're not, Mrs Westermark."

With the light out, living, she lay in Peter's bed

She lay in Peter's bed with the light out. Certainly she wanted him: pretty badly, now she allowed herself to dwell on it. During the long months of the Mars expedition, while she had stayed at home and he had got farther from home, while he actually had existence on that other planet, she had been chaste. She had looked after the children and driven round the countryside and enjoyed writing those articles for women's magazines and being interviewed on TV when the ship was reported to have left Mars on its homeward journey. She had been, in part, dormant.

Then came the news, kept from her at first, that there was confusion in communicating with the returning ship. A sensational tabloid broke the secrecy by declaring that the nine-man crew had all gone mad. And the ship had overshot its landing area, crashing into the Atlantic. Her first reaction had been purely a selfish one – no, not selfish, but from the self: He'll never lie with me again. And infinite love and sorrow.

At his rescue, the only survivor, miraculously unmaimed, her hope had revived. Since then, it had remained embalmed, as he was now embalmed in time. She tried to visualise love as it would be now, with everything happening first to him, before she had begun to – With his movement of pleasure even before she – No, it wasn't possible! But of course it was, if they worked it out first intellectually; then if she just lay flat . . . But what she was trying to visualise, all she could visualise, was not love-making, merely a formal prostration to the exigencies of glands and time flow.

She sat up in bed, longing for movement, freedom. She jumped out and opened the lower window; there was still a tang of cigar smoke in the dark room.

If they worked it out intellectually

Within a couple of days, they had fallen into routine. It was as if the calm weather, perpetuating mildness, aided them. They had to be careful to move slowly through doors, keeping to the left, so as not to bump into each other – a tray of drinks was dropped before they agreed on that. They devised simple knocking systems before using the bathroom. They conversed in bulletins that did not ask questions unless questions were necessary. They walked slightly apart. In short, they made detours round each other's lives.

"It's really quite easy as long as one is careful," Mrs Westermark senior said to Janet. "And dear Jack is *so* patient!"

"I even get the feeling he likes the situation."

"Oh, my dear, how could he like such an unfortunate predicament?"

"Mother, you realise how we all exist together, don't you? No, it sounds too terrible – I daren't say it."

"Now don't you start getting silly ideas. You've been very brave, and this is not the time for us to be getting upset, just as things are going well. If you have any worries, you must tell Clem. That's what he's here for."

"I know."

"Well then."

She saw Jack walk in the garden. As she looked, he glanced up, smiled, said something to himself, stretched out a hand, withdrew it, and went, still smiling, to sit on one end of the seat on the lawn. Touched, Janet hurried over to the french windows, to go and join him.

She paused. Already, she saw ahead, saw her sequence of actions, for Jack had already sketched them into the future. She would go on to the lawn, call his name, smile, and walk over to him when he smiled back. Then they would stroll together to the seat and sit down, one at each end.

The knowledge drained all spontaneity from her. She might have been working a treadmill, for what she was about to do had already been done as far as Jack was concerned, with his head's start in time. Then if she did not go, if she mutinied, turned back to the discussion of the day's chores with her mother-in-law . . . That left Jack mouthing like a fool on the lawn, indulging in a fantasy there was no penetrating. Let him do that, let Stackpole see; then they could drop this theory about Jack's being ahead of time and would have to treat him for a more normal sort of hallucinatory insanity. He would be safe in Clem's hands.

But Jack's actions proved that she would go out there. It was insane for her not to go out there. Insane? To disobey a law of the universe was impossible, not insane. Jack was not disobeying – he had simply tumbled over a law that nobody knew was there before the first expedition to Mars; certainly they had discovered something more momentous than anyone had expected, and more unforeseen. And she had lost – No, she hadn't lost yet! She ran out on to the lawn, calling to him, letting the action quell the confusion in her mind.

And in the repeated event there was concealed a little freshness for she remembered how his smile, glimpsed through the window, had held a special warmth, as if he sought to reassure her. What had he said? That was lost. She walked over to the seat and sat beside him.

He had been saving a remark for the statutory and unvarying time lapse.

"Don't worry, Janet," he said. "It could be worse."

"How?" she asked, but he was already answering: "We could be a day apart. 3.3077 minutes at least allows us a measure of communication."

"It's wonderful how philosophical you are about it," she said. She was alarmed at the sarcasm in her tone.

"Shall we have a talk together now?"

"Jack, I've been wanting to have a private talk with you for some time."

"I?"

The tall beeches that sheltered the garden on the north side were so still that she thought, "They will look exactly the same for him as for me."

He delivered a bulletin, looking at his watch. His wrists were thin. He appeared frailer than he had done when they left hospital. "I am aware, my darling, how painful this must be for you. We are both isolated from the other by this amazing shift of temporal function, but at least I have the consolation of experiencing the new phenomenon, whereas you – "

"I?"

Talking of interstellar distances

"I was going to say that you are stuck with the same old world all of mankind has always known, but I suppose you don't see it that way." Evidently a remark of hers had caught up with him, for he added inconsequentially, "I've wanted a private talk with you."

Janet bit off something she was going to say, for he raised a finger irritably and said, "Please time your statements, so that we do not talk at cross purposes. Confine what you have to say to essentials. Really, darling, I'm surprised you don't do as Clem suggests, and make notes of what is said at what time."

"That – I just wanted – we can't act as if we were a board meeting. I want to know your feelings, how you are, what you are thinking, so that I can help you, so that eventually you will be able to live a normal life again."

He was timing it so that he answered almost at once, "I am not suffering from any mental illness, and I have completely recovered my physical health after the crash. There is no reason to foresee that my perceptions will ever lapse back into phase with yours. They have remained an unfluctuating 3.3077 minutes ahead of terrestrial time ever since our ship left the surface of Mars."

He paused. She thought, "It is now about 11.03 by my watch, and there is so much I long to say. But it's 11.06 and a bit by *his* time, and he already knows I can't say anything. It's such an effort of endurance, talking across this three and a bit minutes; we might just as well be talking across an interstellar distance."

Evidently he too had lost the thread of the exercise, for he smiled and stretched out a hand, holding it in the air; Janet looked round. Clem Stackpole was coming out towards them with a tray full of drinks. He set it carefully down on the lawn, and picked up a martini, the stem of which he slipped between Jack's fingers.

"Cheers!" he said smiling, and "Here's your tipple," giving Janet her gin and tonic. He had brought himself a bottle of pale ale.

"Can you make my position clearer to Janet, Clem? She does not seem to understand it yet."

Angrily, she turned to the behaviourist. "This was meant to be a private talk, Mr Stackpole, between my husband and myself."

"Sorry you're not getting on too well, then. Perhaps I can help you sort out a bit. It is difficult, I know."

3.3077

Powerfully, he wrenched the top off the beer bottle and poured the liquid into the glass. Sipping, he said, "We have always been used to the idea that everything moves forward in time at the same rate. We speak of the course of time, presuming it only has one rate of flow. We've assumed, too, that anything living on another planet in any other part of our universe might have the same rate of flow. In other words, although we've long been accustomed to some oddities of time, thanks to relativity theories, we have accustomed ourselves, perhaps, to certain errors of thinking. Now we're going to have to think differently. You follow me."

"Perfectly."

"The universe is by no means the simple box our predecessors imagined. It may be that each planet is encased in its own time field, just as it is in its own gravitational field. From the evidence, it seems that Mars's time field is 3.3077 minutes ahead of ours on Earth. We deduce this from the fact that your husband and the eight other men with him on Mars experienced no sensation of temporal difference among themselves, and were unaware that anything was untoward until they were away from Mars and attempted to get into communication again with Earth, when the temporal discrepancy at once showed up. Your husband is still living in Mars time. Unfortunately, the other members of the crew did not survive the crash; but we can be sure that if they did, they too would suffer from the same effect. That's clear, isn't it?"

"Entirely. But I still cannot see why this effect, if it is as you say – "

"It's not what *I* say, Janet, but the conclusion arrived at by much cleverer men than I." He smiled as he said that, adding parenthetically, "Not that we don't develop and even alter our conclusions every day."

"Then why was a similar effect not noticed when the Russians and Americans returned from the moon?"

"We don't know. There's so much we don't know. We *surmise* that because the moon is a satellite of Earth's, and thus within its gravitational field, there is no temporal discrepancy. But until we have more data, until we can explore further, we know so little, and can only speculate so much. It's like trying to estimate the runs of an entire innings when only one over has been bowled. After the expedition gets back from Venus, we shall be in a much better position to start theorising."

"*What* expedition to Venus?" she asked, shocked.

"It may not leave for a year yet, but they're speeding up the programme. That will bring us really invaluable data."

Future time with its uses and abuses

She started to say, "But after this surely they won't be fool enough – " Then she stopped. She knew they would be fool enough. She thought of Peter saying, "I'm going to be a spaceman too. *I* want to be the first man on Saturn!"

The men were looking at their watches. Westermark transferred his gaze to the gravel to say, "This figure of 3.3077 is surely not a universal constant. It may vary – I think it will vary – from planetary body to planetary body. My private opinion is that it is bound to be connected with solar activity in some way. If that is so, then we may find that the men returning from Venus will be perceiving on a continuum slightly in arrears of Earth time."

He stood up suddenly, looking dismayed, the absorption gone from his face.

"That's a point that hadn't occurred to me" Stackpole said, making a note. "If the expedition to Venus is primed with these points beforehand, we should have no trouble about organising their return. Ultimately, this confusion will be sorted out, and I've no doubt that it will eventually vastly enrich the culture of mankind. The possibilities are of such enormity that. . . ."

"It's awful! You're all crazy!" Janet exclaimed. She jumped up and hurried off towards the house.

Or then again

Jack began to move after her towards the house. By his watch, which showed Earth time, it was 11.18 and twelve seconds; he thought, not for the first time, that he would invest in another watch, which would be strapped to his right wrist and show Martian time. No, the one on his left wrist should show Martian time, for that was the wrist he principally consulted and the time by which he lived, even when going through the business of communicating with the earth-bound human race.

He realised he was now moving ahead of Janet, by her reckoning. It would be interesting to have someone ahead of *him* in perception; then he would wish to converse, would want to go to the labour of it. Although it would rob him of the sensation that he was perpetually first in the universe, first everywhere, with everything dewy in that strange light – Mars-light! He'd call it that, till he had it classified, the romantic vision preceding the scientific, with a touch òf the grand permissible before the steadying discipline closed in. Or then again, suppose they were wrong in their theories, and the perceptual effect was some freak of the long space journey itself; supposing time were quantal . . . Supposing *all* time were quantal. After all, ageing was a matter of steps, not a smooth progress for much of the inorganic world as for the organic.

Now he was standing quite still on the lawn. The glaze was coming through the grass, making it look brittle, almost tingeing each blade with a tiny spectrum of light. If his perceptual time were further ahead than it was now, would the Mars-light be stronger, the Earth more translucent? How beautiful it would look! After a longer star journey one would return to a cobweb of a world, centuries behind one in perceptual time, a mere embodiment of light, a prism. Hungrily, he visualised it. But they needed more knowledge.

Suddenly he thought, "If I could get on the Venus expedition! If the Institute's right, I'd be perhaps six, say five and a half – no, one can't say – but I'd be ahead of Venerean time. I *must* go. I'd be valuable to them. I only have to volunteer, surely."

He did not notice Stackpole touch his arm in cordial fashion and go past him into the house. He stood looking at the ground and through it, to the stony vales of Mars and the unguessable landscapes of Venus.

The figures move

Janet had consented to ride into town with Stackpole. He was collecting his cricket books, which had been restudded; she thought she might buy a roll of film for her camera. The children would like photos of her and Daddy together. Standing together.

As the car ran beside trees, their shadow flickered red and green before her vision. Stackpole held the wheel very capably, whistling under his breath. Strangely, she did not resent a habit she would normally have found irksome, taking it as a sign that he was not entirely at his ease.

"I have an awful feeling you now understand my husband better than I do," she said.

He did not deny it. "Why do you feel that?"

"I believe he does not mind the terrible isolation he must be experiencing."

"He's a brave man."

Westermark had been home a week now. Janet saw that each day they were more removed from each other, as he spoke less and stood frequently as still as a statue, gazing at the ground raptly. She thought of something she had once been afraid to utter aloud to her mother-in-law; but with Clem Stackpole she was safer.

"You know why we manage to exist in comparative harmony," she said. He was slowing the car, half-looking at her. "We only manage to exist by banishing all events from our lives, all children, all seasons. Otherwise we'd be faced at every moment with the knowledge of how much at odds we really are."

Catching the note in her voice, Stackpole said soothingly, "You are every bit as brave as he is, Janet."

"Damn being brave. What I can't bear is – nothing!"

Seeing the sign by the side of the road, Stackpole glanced in his driving mirror and changed gear. The road was deserted in front as well as behind. He whistled through his teeth again, and Janet felt compelled to go on talking.

"We've already interfered with time too much – all of us, I mean. Time is a European invention. Goodness knows how mixed up in it we are going to get if – well, if this goes on." She was irritated by the lack of her usual coherence.

As Stackpole spoke next, he was pulling the car into a lay-by, stopping it by overhanging bushes. He turned to her, smiling tolerantly. "Time was God's invention, if you believe in God, as I prefer to do. We observe it, tame it, exploit it where possible."

"Exploit it!"

"You mustn't think of the future as if we were all wading knee deep in treacle or something." He laughed briefly, resting his hands on the steering wheel. "What lovely weather it is! I was wondering – on Sunday I'm playing cricket over in the village. Would you like to come and watch the match? And perhaps we could have tea somewhere afterwards."

All events, all children, all seasons

She had a letter next morning from Jane, her five-year-old daughter, and it made her think. All the letter said was: 'Dear Mummy, Thank you for the dollies. With love from Jane," but Janet knew the labour that had gone into the inch-high letters. How long could she bear to leave the children away from their home and her care?

As soon as the thought emerged, she recalled that during the previous evening she had told herself nebulously that if there was going to be "anything" with Stackpole, it was as well the children would be out of the way – purely, she now realised, for her convenience and for Stackpole's. She had not thought then about the children; she had thought about Stackpole who, despite the unexpected delicacy he had shown, was not a man she cared for.

"And another intolerably immoral thought," she muttered unhappily to the empty room, "what alternative have I to Stackpole?"

She knew Westermark was in his study. It was a cold day, too cold and damp for him to make his daily parade round the garden. She knew he was sinking deeper into isolation, she longed to help, she feared to sacrifice herself to that isolation, longed to stay outside it, in life. Dropping the letter, she held her head in her hands, closing her eyes as in the curved bone of her skull she heard all her possible courses of action jar together, future lifelines that annihilated each other.

As Janet stood transfixed, Westermark's mother came into the room.

"I was looking for you," she said. "You're so unhappy, my dear, aren't you?"

"Mother, people always try and hide from others how they suffer. Does everyone do it?"

"You don't have to hide it from me – chiefly, I suppose, because you can't."

"But I don't know how much *you* suffer, and it ought to work both ways. Why do we do this awful covering up? What are we afraid of – pity or derision?"

"Help, perhaps."

"Help! Perhaps you're right . . . That's a disconcerting thought."

They stood there staring at each other, until the older woman said, awkwardly, "We don't often talk like this, Janet."

"No." She wanted to say more. To a stranger in a train, perhaps she would have done; here, she could not deliver.

Seeing nothing more was said on that subject, Mrs Westermark said, "I was going to tell you, Janet, that I thought perhaps it would be better if the children didn't come back here while things are as they are. If you want to go and see them and stay with them at your parents' house, I can look after Jack and Mr Stackpole for a week. I don't think Jack wants to see them."

"That's very kind, Mother. I'll see. I promised Clem – well, I told Mr Stackpole that perhaps I'd go and watch him play cricket tomorrow afternoon. It's not important, of course, but I did say – anyhow, I might drive over to see the children on Monday, if you could hold the fort."

"You've still plenty of time if you feel like going today. I'm sure Mr Stackpole will understand your maternal feelings."

"I'd prefer to leave it till Monday," Janet said – a little distantly, for she suspected now the motive behind her mother-in-law's suggestion.

Where the Scientific American *did not reach*

Jack Westermark put down the *Scientific American* and stared at the table top. With his right hand, he felt the beat of his heart. In the magazine was an article about him, illustrated with photographs of him taken at the Research Hospital. This thoughtful article was far removed from the sensational pieces that had appeared elsewhere, the shallow things that referred to him as The Man Who Has Done More Than Einstein To Wreck Our Cosmic Picture; and for that very reason it was the more startling, and presented some aspects of the matter that Westermark himself had not considered.

As he thought over its conclusions, he rested from the effort of reading terrestrial books, and Stackpole sat by the fire, smoking a cigar and waiting to take Westermark's dictation. Even reading a magazine represented a feat in space-time, a collaboration, a conspiracy. Stackpole turned the pages at timed intervals, Westermark read when they lay flat. He was unable to turn them when, in their own narrow continuum, they were not being turned; to his fingers, they lay under the jelly-like glaze, that visual hallucination that represented an unconquerable cosmic inertia;

The inertia gave a special shine to the surface of the table as he stared into it and probed into his own mind to determine the truths of the *Scientific American* article.

The writer of the article began by considering the facts and observing that they tended to point towards the existence of "local times" throughout the universe; and that if this were so, a new explanation might be forthcoming for the recession of the galaxies and different estimates arrived at for the age of the universe (and of course for its complexity). He then proceeded to deal with the problem that vexed other writers on the subject; namely, why, if Westermark lost Earth time on Mars, he had not reciprocally lost Mars time back on Earth. This, more than anything, pointed to the fact that "local times" were not purely mechanistic but to some extent at least a psycho-biological function.

In the table top, Westermark saw himself being asked to travel again to Mars, to take part in a second expedition to those continents of russet sand where the fabric of space-time was in some mysterious and insuperable fashion 3.3077 minutes ahead of Earth norm. Would his interior clock leap forward again? What then of the sheen on things earthly? And what would be the effect of gradually drawing away from the iron laws under which, since its scampering pleistocene infancy, humankind had lived?

Impatiently he thrust his mind forward to imagine the day when Earth harboured many local times, gleaned from voyages across the vacancies of space; those vacancies lay across time, too, and that little-understood concept (McTaggart had denied its external reality, hadn't he?) would come to lie within the grasp of man's understanding. Wasn't that the ultimate secret, to be able to understand the flux in which existence is staged as a dream is staged in the primitive reaches of the mind?

And – But – Would not that day bring the annihilation of Earth's local time? That was what he had started. It could only mean that "local time" was not a product of planetary elements; there the writer of the *Scientific American* article had not dared to go far enough; local time was entirely a product of the psyche. That dark innermost thing that could keep accurate time even while a man lay unconscious was a mere provincial; but it could be educated to be a citizen of the universe. He saw that he was the first of a new race, unimaginable in the wildest mind a few months previously. He was independent of the enemy that, more than Death, menaced contemporary man: Time. Locked within him was an entirely new potential. Superman had arrived.

Painfully, Superman stirred in his seat. He sat so rapt for so long that his limbs grew stiff and dead without his noticing it.

Universal thoughts may occur if one times carefully enough one's circumbendibus about a given table

"Dictation," he said, and waited impatiently until the command had penetrated backwards to the limbo by the fire where Stackpole sat. What he had to say was so terribly important – yet it had to wait on these people.

As was his custom, he rose and began to walk round the table, speaking in phrases quickly delivered. This was to be the testament to the new way of life. . . .

"Consciousness is not expendable but concurrent . . . There may have been many time nodes at the beginning of the human race . . . The mentally deranged often revert to different time rates. For some, a day seems to stretch on for ever . . . We know by experience that for children time is seen in the convex mirror of consciousness, enlarged and distorted beyond its focal point. . . ." He was momentarily irritated by the scared face of his wife appearing outside the study window, but he brushed it away and continued.

". . . its focal point . . . Yet man in his ignorance has persisted in pretending time was some sort of uni-directional flow, and homogenous at that . . . despite the evidence to the contrary . . . Our conception of ourselves – no, this erroneous conception has become a basic life assumption. . . ."

Daughters of daughters

Westermark's mother was not given to metaphysical speculation, but as she was leaving the room, she turned and said to her daughter-in-law, "You know what I sometimes think? Jack is so strange, I wonder at nights if men and women aren't getting more and more apart in thought and in their ways with every generation – you know, almost like separate species. My generation made a great attempt to bring the two sexes together in equality and all the rest, but it seems to have come to nothing."

"Jack will get better." Janet could hear the lack of confidence in her voice.

"I thought the same thing – about men and women getting wider apart I mean – when my husband was killed."

Suddenly all Janet's sympathy was gone. She had recognised a familiar topic drifting on to the scene, knew well the careful tone that ironed away all self-pity as her mother-in-law said, "Bob was dedicated to speed, you know. That was what killed him really, not the fool backing into the road in front of him."

"No blame was attached to your husband," Janet said. "You should try not to let it worry you still."

"You see the connection though . . . This progress thing. Bob so crazy to get round the next bend first, and now Jack . . . Oh well, there's nothing a woman can do."

She closed the door behind her. Absently, Janet picked up the message from the next generation of women: "Thank you for the dollies."

The resolves and the sudden risks involved

He was their father. Perhaps Jane and Peter should come back, despite the risks involved. Anxiously, Janet stood there, moving herself with a sudden resolve to tackle Jack straight away. He was so irritable, so unapproachable, but at least she could observe how busy he was before interrupting him.

As she slipped into the side hall and made for the back door, she heard her mother-in-law call her. "Just a minute!" she answered.

The sun had broken through, sucking moisture from the damp garden. It was now unmistakably autumn. She rounded the corner of the house, stepped round the rose bed, and looked into her husband's study.

Shaken, she saw he leaned half over the table. His hands were over his face, blood ran between his fingers and dripped on to an open magazine on the table top. She was aware of Stackpole sitting indifferently beside the electric fire.

She gave a small cry and ran round the house again, to be met at the back door by Mrs Westermark.

"Oh, I was just – Janet, what is it?"

"Jack, Mother! He's had a stroke or something terrible!"

"But how do you know?"

"Quick, we must phone the hospital – I must go to him."

Mrs Westermark took Janet's arm. "Perhaps we'd better leave it to Mr Stackpole, hadn't we? I'm afraid – "

"Mother, we must do what we can. I know we're amateurs. Please let me go."

"No, Janet, we're – it's *their* world. I'm frightened. They'll come if they want us." She was gripping Janet in her fright. Their wild eyes stared momentarily at each other as if seeing something else, and then Janet snatched herself away. "I must go to him," she said.

She hurried down the hall and pushed open the study door. Her husband stood now at the far end of the room by the window, while blood streamed from his nose.

"Jack!" she exclaimed. As she ran towards him, a blow from the empty air struck her on the forehead, so that she staggered aside, falling against a bookcase. A shower of smaller volumes from the upper shelf fell on her and round her. Exclaiming, Stackpole dropped his notebook and ran round the table to her. Even as he went to her aid, he noted the time from his watch: 10.24

Aid after 10.24 and the tidiness of bed

Westermark's mother appeared in the doorway.

"Stay where you are," Stackpole shouted, "or there will be more trouble! Jack, I'm right with you – God knows what you've felt, isolated without aid for three and a third minutes!" Angrily, he went across and stood within arm's length of his patient. He threw his handkerchief down on to the table.

"Mr Stackpole – " Westermark's mother said tentatively from the door, an arm round Janet's waist.

He looked back over his shoulder only long enough to say, "Get towels! Phone the Research Hospital for an ambulance and tell them to be here right away."

By midday, Westermark was tidily in bed upstairs and the ambulance staff, who had treated him for what after all was only nosebleed, had left. Stackpole, as he turned from closing the front door, eyed the two women.

"I feel it is my duty to warn you," he said heavily, "that another incident such as this might well prove fatal. This time we escaped very lightly. If anything else of this sort happens, I shall feel obliged to recommend to the board that Mr Westermark is moved back to the hospital."

Current way to define accidents

"He wouldn't want to go," Janet said. "Besides, you are being absurd; it was entirely an accident. Now I wish to go upstairs and see how he is."

"Just before you go, may I point out that what happened was *not* an accident – or not as we generally define accidents, since you saw the results of your interference through the study window before you entered. Where you were to blame – "

"But that's absurd – " both women began at once. Janet went on to say, "I never would have rushed into the room as I did had I not seen through the window that he was in trouble."

"What you saw was the result on your husband of your later interference."

In something like a wail, Westermark's mother said, "I don't understand any of this. What did Janet bump into when she ran in?"

"She ran, Mrs Westermark, into the spot where her husband had been standing 3.3077 minutes earlier. Surely by now you have grasped this elementary business of time inertia?"

When they both started speaking at once, he stared at them until they stopped and looked at him. Then he said, "We had better go into the living room. Speaking for myself, I would like a drink."

He helped himself, and not until his hand was round a glass of whisky did he say, "Now, without wishing to lecture to you ladies, I think it is high time you both realised that you are not living in the old safe world of classical mechanics ruled over by a god invented by eighteenth-century enlightenment. All that has happened here is perfectly rational, but if you are going to pretend it is beyond your female understandings – "

"Mr Stackpole," Janet said sharply. "Can you please keep to the point without being insulting? Will you tell me why what happened was not an accident? I understand now that when I looked through the study window I saw my husband suffering from a collision that to him had happened three and something minutes before and to me would not happen for another three and something minutes, but at that moment I was so startled that I forgot – "

"No, no, your figures are wrong. The *total* time lapse is only 3.3077 minutes. When you saw your husband, he had been hit half that time – 1.65385 minutes – ago, and there was another 1.65385 minutes to go before you completed the action by bursting into the room and striking him."

"But she *didn't* strike him!" the older woman cried.

Firmly, Stackpole diverted his attention long enough to reply. "She struck him at 10.24 Earthtime, which equals 10.20 plus about 36 seconds Mars or his time, which equals 9.59 or whatever Neptune time, which equals 156 and a half Sirius time. It's a big universe, Mrs Westermark! You will remain confused as long as you continue to confuse event with time. May I suggest you sit down and have a drink?"

"Leaving aside the figures," Janet said, returning to the attack – loathsome opportunist the man was – "how can you say that what happened was no accident? You are not claiming I injured my husband deliberately, I hope? What you say suggests that I was powerless from the moment I saw him through the window."

"'Leaving aside the figures. . . .'" he quoted. "That's where your responsibility lies. What you saw through the window was the result of your act; it was by then inevitable that you should complete it, for it had already been completed."

Through the window, draughts of time blow

"I can't understand!" she clutched her forehead, gratefully accepting a cigarette from her mother-in-law, while shrugging off her consolatory "Don't try to understand, dear!" "Supposing when I had seen Jack's nose bleeding, I had looked at my watch and thought, 'It's 10.20 or whenever it was, and he may be suffering from my interference, so I'd better not go in,' and I *hadn't* gone in? Would his nose then miraculously have healed?"

"Of course not. You take such a mechanistic view of the universe. Cultivate a mental approach, try and live in your own century! You could not think what you suggest because that is not in your nature: just as it is not in your nature to consult your watch intelligently, just as you always 'leave aside the figures', as you say. No, I'm not being personal: it's all very feminine and appealing in a way. What I'm saying is that if *before* you looked into the window you had been able to think, 'However I see my husband now, I must recall he has the additional experience of the next 3.3077 minutes', then you could have looked in and seen him unharmed, and you would not have come bursting in as you did."

She drew on her cigarette, baffled and hurt. "You're saying I'm a danger to my own husband."

"*You're* saying that."

"God, how I hate men!" she exclaimed. "You're so bloody logical, so bloody smug!"

He finished his whisky and set the glass down on a table beside her so that he leant close. "You're upset just now," he said.

"Of course I'm upset! What do you think?" She fought a desire to cry or slap his face. She turned to Jack's mother, who gently took her wrist.

"Why don't you go off straight away and stay with the children for the weekend, darling? Come back when you feel like it. Jack will be all right and I can look after him – as much as he wants looking after."

She glanced about the room.

"I will. I'll pack right away. They'll be glad to see me." As she passed Stackpole on the way out, she said bitterly, "At least *they* won't be worrying about the local time on Sirius!"

"They may," said Stackpole, imperturbably from the middle of the room, "have to one day."

All events, all children, all seasons

(1965)

Heresies of the Huge God

THE SECRET BOOK OF HARAD IV

I, Harad IV, Chief Scribe, declare that this my writing may be shown only to priests of rank within the Orthodox Universal Sacrificial Church and to the Elders Elect of the Council of the Orthodox Universal Sacrificial Church, because here are contained matters concerning the four Vile Heresies that may not be seen or spoken of among the people.

For a Proper Consideration of the newest and vilest heresy, we must look in perspective over the events of history. Accordingly, let us go back to the First Year of our epoch, when the World Darkness was banished by the arrival of the Huge God, our truest, biggest Lord, to whom all honour and terror.

From this present year, 910 HG, it is impossible to recall what the world was like then, but from the few records still surviving, we can gather something of those times and even perform the Mental Contortions necessary to see how events must have looked to the sinners then involved in them.

The world on which the Huge God found himself was full of people and their machines, all of them unprepared for His Visit. There may have been a hundred thousand times more people than now there are.

The Huge God landed in what is now the Sacred Sea, upon which in these days sail some of our most beautiful churches dedicated to His Name. At that time, the region was much less pleasing, being broken up into many states possessed by different nations. This was a system of land tenure practised before our present theories of constant migration and evacuation were formed.

The rear legs of the Huge God stretched far down into Africa – which was then not the island continent it is now – almost touching the Congo River, at the sacred spot marked now by the Sacrificial

Church of Basolo-Aketi-Ele, and at the sacred spot marked now by the Temple Church of Aden, obliterating the old port of Aden.

Some of the Huge God's legs stretched above the Sudan and across what was then the Libyan Kingdom, now part of the Sea of Elder Sorrow, while a foot rested in a city called Tunis on what was then the Tunisian shore. There were some of the legs of the Huge God on his left side.

On his right side, his legs blessed and pressed the sands of Saudi Arabia, now called Life Valley, and the foothills of the Caucasus, obliterating the Mount called Ararat in Asia Minor, while the Foremost Leg stretched forward to Russian lands, stamping out immediately the great capital city of Moscow.

The body of the Huge God, resting in repose between his mighty legs, settled mainly over three ancient seas, if the Old Records are to be trusted, called the Sea of Mediterranean, the Red Sea, and the Nile Sea, all of which now form part of the Sacred Sea. He eradicated also with his Great Bulk part of the Black Sea, now called the White Sea, Egypt, Athens, Cyprus, and the Balkan Peninsula as far north as Belgrade, now Holy Belgrade, for above this town towered the Neck of the Huge God on his First Visit to us mortals, just clearing the roofs of the houses.

As for his head, it lifted above the region of mountains that we call Ittaland, which was then named Europe, a populous part of the globe, raised so high that it might easily be seen on a clear day from London, then as now the chief town of the land of the Anglo-French.

It was estimated in those first days that the length of the Huge God was some four and a half thousand miles, from rear to nose, with the eight legs each about nine hundred miles long. Now we profess in our Creed that our Huge God changes shape and length and number of legs according to whether he is Pleased or Angry with man.

In those days, the nature of God was unknown. No preparation had been made for his coming, though some whispers of the millenium were circulating. Accordingly, the speculation on his nature was far from the truth, and often extremely blasphemous.

Here is an extract from the notorious Gersheimer Paper, which contributed much to the events leading up to the First Crusade in 271 HG. We do not know who the Black Gersheimer was, apart from the meaningless fact that he was a Scientific Prophet at somewhere called Cornell or Carnell, evidently a Church on the American Continent (then a differently shaped territory).

"Aerial surveys suggest that this creature – if one can call it that – which straddles a line along the Red Sea and across south east Europe, is non-living, at least as we understand life. It may be merely coincidence that it somewhat resembles an eight-footed lizard, so that we do not necessarily have to worry about the thing being malignant, as some tabloids have suggested."

Not all the vile jargon of that distant day is now understandable, but we believe "aerial surveys" to refer to the mechanical flying machines which this last generation of the Godless possessed. Black Gersheimer continues:

"If this thing is not live, it may be a piece of galactic debris clinging momentarily to the globe, perhaps like a leaf clinging to a football in the fall. To believe this is not necessarily to alter our scientific concepts of the universe. Whether the thing represents life or not, we don't have to go all superstitious. We must merely remind ourselves that there are many phenomena in the universe as we conceive it in the light of Twentieth Century science which remain unknown to us. However painful this unwanted visitation may be, it is some consolation to think that it will bring us new knowledge – of ourselves, as well as the world outside our little solar system."

Although terms like "galactic debris" have lost their meaning, if they ever had one, the general trend of this passage is offensively obvious. An embargo is being set up against the worship of the Huge God, with a heretical God of Science set up in his stead. Only one other passage from this offensive mish-mash need be considered, but it is a vital one for Showing the Attitude of mind of Gersheimer and presumably most of his contemporaries.

"Naturally enough, the peoples of the world, particularly those who are still lingering on the threshold of civilization, are full of fear these days. They see something supernatural in the arrival of this thing, and I believe that every man, if he is honest, will admit to carrying an echo of that fear in his heart. We can only banish it, and can only meet the chaos into which the world is now plunged, if we retain a galactic picture of our situation in our minds. The very hugeness of this thing that now lies plastered loathsomely across our world is cause for terror. But imagine it in proportion. A centipede is sitting on an orange. Or, to pick an analogy that sounds less repulsive, a little gecko, six inches long, is resting momentarily on a plastic globe of the Earth which is two feet in diameter. It is up to us, the human race, with all the technological forces at our disposal, to unite as never before, and blow this thing, this large and stupid object, back into the depths of space from whence it came. Goodnight."

My reasons for repeating this Initial Blasphemy are these: that we can see here in this message from a member of the World Darkness traces of that original sin which – with all our sacrifices, all our hardships, all our crusades – we have not yet stamped out. That is why we are now at the greatest Crisis in the history of the Orthodox Universal Sacrificial Church, and why the time is come for a Fourth Crusade exceeding in scale all others.

The Huge God remained where he was, in what we now refer to as the Sacred Sea Position, for a number of years, absolutely unmoving.

For mankind, this was the great formative period of Belief, marking the establishment of the Universal Church, and characterised by many upheavals. The early priests and prophets suffered much that the Word might go round the World, and the blasphemous sects be destroyed, though the Underground Book of Church Lore suggests that many of them were in fact members of earlier churches who, seeing the light, transferred their allegiances.

The mighty figure of the Huge God was subjected to many puny insults. The Greatest Weapons of that distant age, forces of technical charlatanry, were called Nuclears, and these were dropped on the Huge God – without having any effect, as might be expected. Walls of fire were burnt against him in vain. Our Huge God, to whom all honour and terror, is immune from earthly weakness. His body was Clothed as it were with Metal – here lay the seed of the Second Crusade – but it had not the weakness of metal.

His coming to earth met with immediate Response from nature. The old winds that prevailed were turned aside about his mighty flanks and blew elsewhere. The effect was to cool the centre of Africa, so that the tropical rainforests died and all the creatures in them. In the lands bordering Caspana (then called Persia and Kharkov, say some old accounts), hurricanes of snow fell in a dozen severe winters, blowing far east into India. Elsewhere, all over the world, the coming of the Huge God was felt in the skies, and in freak rainfalls and errant winds, and month-long storms. The oceans also were disturbed, while the great volume of waters displaced by his body poured over the nearby land, killing many thousands of beings and washing ten thousand dead whales into the harbours of Colombo.

The land too joined in the upheaval. While the territory under the Huge God's bulk sank, preparing to receive what would later be the Sacred Sea, the land roundabout rose Up, forming small hills, such as the broken and savage Dolomines that now guard the southern lands of Ittaland. There were earthquakes and new volcanoes and geysers where water never spurted before and plagues of snakes and blazing forests and many wonderful signs that helped the Early Fathers of our faith to convert the ignorant. Everywhere they went, preaching that only in surrender to him lay salvation.

Many Whole Peoples perished at this time of upheaval, such as the Bulgarians, the Egyptians, the Israelites, Moravians, Kurds, Turks, Syrians, Mountain Turks, as well as most of the South Slavs, Georgians, Croats, the sturdy Vlaks, and the Greeks and Cypriotic and Cretan races, together with others whose sins were great and names unrecorded in the annals of the church.

The Huge God departed from the world in the year 89, or some say 90. (This was the First Departure, and is celebrated as such in our Church calendar – though the Catholic Universal Church calls it First Disappearance Day.) He returned in 91, great and aweing be his name.

Little is known of the period when he was absent from our Earth. We get a glimpse into the mind of the people then when we learn that in the main the nations of Earth greatly rejoiced. The natural upheavals continued, since the oceans poured into the great hollow he had made, forming our beloved and holy Sacred Sea. Great Wars broke out across the face of the globe.

His return in 91 halted the wars – a sign of the great peace his presence has brought to his chosen people.

But the inhabitants of the world at That Time were not all of our religion though prophets moved among them, and many were their blasphemies. In the Black Museum attached to the great basilica of Omar and Yemen is documentary evidence that they tried at this period to communicate with the Huge God by means of their machines. Of course they got no reply – but many men reasoned at this time, in the darkness of their minds, that this was because the God was a Thing, as Black Gersheimer had prophesied.

The Huge God, on this his Second Coming, blessed our earth by settling mainly within the Arctic Circle, or what was then the Arctic Circle, with his body straddling from northern Canada, as it was,

over a large peninsula called Alaska, across the Bering Sea and into
the northern regions of the Russian lands as far as the river Lena,
now the Bay of Lenn. Some of his rear feet broke far into the Arctic
Ice, while others of his forefeet entered the North Pacific Ocean –
but truly to him we are but sand under his feet, and he is indifferent
to our mountains or our Climatic Variations.

As for his terrible head, it could be seen reaching far into the
stratosphere, gleaming with metal sheen, by all the cities along the
northern part of America's seaboard, from such vanished towns as
Vancouver, Seattle, Edmonton, Portland, Blanco, Reno, and even
San Francisco. It was the energetic and sinful nation that possessed
these cities which was now most active against the Huge God. The
weight of their ungodly scientific civilization was turned against
him, but all they managed to do was blow apart their own coastline.

Meanwhile, other natural changes were taking place. The mass of
the Huge God deflected the earth in its daily roll, so that seasons
changed and in the prophetic books we read how the great trees
brought forth their leaves to cover them in the winter, and lost them
in the summer. Bats flew in the daytime and women bore forth
hairy children. The melting of the ice caps caused great floods, tidal
waves, and poisonous dews, while in one night we hear that the
waters of the Deep were moved, so that the tide went out so far
from the Malayan Uplands (as they now are) that the continental
peninsula of Blestland was formed in a few hours of what had
previously been separate Continents or Islands called Singapore,
Sumatra, Indonesia, Java, Sydney, and Australia or Austria.

With these powerful signs, our priests could Convert the People,
and millions of survivors were speedily enrolled into the Church.
This was the First Great Age of the Church, when the word spread
across all the ravaged and transformed globe. Our institutions were
formed in the next few generations, notably at the various Councils
of the New Church (some of which have since proved to be
heretical).

We were not established without some difficulty, and many people
had to be burned before the rest could feel the faith Burning In
Them. But as generations passed, the True Name of the God
emerged over a wider and wider area.

Only the Americans still clung largely to their base superstition.
Fortified by their science, they refused Grace. So in the Year 271
the First Crusade was launched, chiefly against them but also against
the Irish, whose heretical views had no benefit of science; the Irish

were quickly Eradicated, almost to a man. The Americans were more formidable, but this difficulty served only to draw the people closer and unite the Church further.

This First Crusade was fought over the First Great Heresy of the Church, the heresy claiming that the Huge God was a Thing not a God, as formulated by Black Gersheimer. It was successfully concluded when the leader of the Americans, Lionel Undermeyer, met the Venerable World Emperor-Bishop, Jon II, and agreed that the messengers of the Church should be free to preach unmolested in America. Possibly a harsher decision could have been forced, as some commentators claim, but by this time both sides were suffering severely from plague and famine, the harvests of the world having failed. It was a happy chance that the population of the world was already cut by more than half, or complete starvation would have followed the reorganisation of the seasons.

In the churches of the world, the Huge God was asked to give a sign that he had Witnessed the great victory over the American unbelievers. All who opposed this enlightened act were destroyed. He answered the prayers in 297 by moving swiftly forward only a comparatively Small Amount and lying Mainly in the Pacific Ocean, stretching almost as far south as what is now the Antarter, what was then the Tropic of Capricorn, and what had previously been the Equator. Some of his left legs covered the towns along the west American seaboard as far south as Guadalajara (where the impression of his foot is still marked by the Temple of the Sacred Toe), including some of the towns such as San Francisco already mentioned. We speak of this as the First Shift; it was rightly taken as a striking proof of the Huge God's contempt for America.

This feeling became rife in America also. Purified by famine, plague, gigantic earth tremors, and other natural disorders, the population could now better accept the words of the priests, all becoming converted to a man. Mass pilgrimages were made to see the great body of the Huge God, stretching from one end of their nation to the other. Bolder pilgrims climbed aboard flying aeroplanes and flew over his shoulder, across which savage rainstorms played for a hundred years Without Cease.

Those that were converted became More Extreme than their brethren older in the faith across the other side of the world. No sooner had the American congregations united with ours than they broke away on a point of doctrine at the Council of Dead Tench (322). This date marks the beginning of the Catholic Universal

Sacrificial Church. We of the Orthodox persuasion did not enjoy, in those distant days, the harmony with our American brothers that we do now.

The doctrinal point on which the churches split apart was, as is well known, the question of whether humanity should wear clothes that imitated the metallic sheen of the Huge God. It was claimed that this was setting up man in God's Image; but it was a calculated slur on the Orthodox Universal priests, who wore plastic or metal garments in honour of their maker.

This developed into the Second Great Heresy. As this long and confused period has been amply dealt with elsewhere, we may pass over it lightly here, mentioning merely that the quarrel reached its climax in the Second Crusade, which the American Catholic Universals launched against us in 450. Because they still had a large preponderance of machines, they were able to force their point, to sack various monasteries along the edge of the Sacred Sea, to defile our women, and to retire home in glory.

Since that time, everyone in the world has worn only garments of wool or fur. All who opposed this enlightened act were destroyed.

It would be wrong to emphasise too much the struggles of the past. All this while, the majority of people were peacefully about their worship, being sacrificed regularly, and praying every sunset and sunrise (whenever they might occur) that the Huge God would leave our world, since we were not worthy of him.

The Second Crusade left a trail of troubles in its wake; the next fifty years were, on the whole, not happy ones. The American armies returned home to find that the heavy pressure upon their western seaboard had opened up a number of volcanoes along their biggest mountain range, the Rockies. Their country was covered in fire and lava, and their air filled with stinking ash.

Rightly, they accepted this as a sign that their conduct left much to be desired in the eyes of the Huge God (for though it has never been proved that he has eyes, he surely Sees Us). Since the rest of the world had not been Visited with punishment on quite this scale, they correctly divined that their sin was that they still clung to technology and the weapons of technology against the wishes of God.

With their faith strong within them, every last instrument of science, from the Nuclears to the Canopeners, was destroyed, and a hundred thousand virgins of the persuasion were dropped into

suitable volcanoes as propitiation. All who opposed these enlightened acts were destroyed, and some ceremonially eaten.

We of the Orthodox Universal faith applauded our brothers'
whole-hearted action. Yet we could not be sure they had purged
themselves enough. Now that they owned no weapons and we still
had some, it was clear we could help them in their purgation.
Accordingly, a mighty armada of one hundred and sixty-six wooden
ships sailed across to America, to help them suffer for the faith –
and incidentally to get back some of our loot. This was the Third
Crusade of 482, under Jon the Chubby.

While the two opposed armies were engaged in battle outside
New York, the Second Shift took place. It lasted only a matter of
five minutes.

In that time, the Huge God turned to his left flank, crawled across
the centre of what was then the North American continent, crossed
the Atlantic as if it were a puddle, moved over Africa, and came to
rest in the South Indian Ocean, demolishing Madagaska with one
rear foot. Night fell Everywhere on earth.

When dawn came, there could hardly have been a single man who
did not believe in the power and wisdom of the Huge God, to whose
name belongs all Terror and Might. Unhappily, among those who
were unable to believe were the contesting armies, who were one
and all swept under a Wave of Earth and Rock as the God passed.

In the ensuing chaos, only one note of sanity prevailed – the
sanity of the Church. The Church established as the Third Great
Heresy the idea that any machines were permissible to man against
the wishes of God. There was some doctrinal squabble as to whether
books counted as machines. It was decided they did, just to be on
the safe side. From then on, all men were free to do nothing but
labour in the fields and worship, and pray to the Huge God to
remove himself to a world more worthy of his might. At the same
time, the rate of sacrifice was stepped up, and the Slow-Burning
Method was introduced (499).

Now followed the great Peace, which lasted till 900. In all this
time, the Huge God never moved: it has been truly said that the
centuries are but seconds in his sight. Perhaps mankind has never
known such a long peace, four hundred years of it – a peace that
existed in his heart if not outside it, because the world was naturally
in Some Disorder. The great force of the Huge God's progress
halfway across the world had altered the progression of day and
night to a considerable extent; some legends claim that, before the

Second Shift, the sun used to rise in the east and set in the west –
the very opposite of the natural order of things we know.

Gradually, this peaceful period saw some re-establishment of
order to the seasons, and some cessation of the floods, showers of
blood, hailstorms, earthquakes, deluges of icicles, apparitions of
comets, volcanic eruptions, miasmic fogs, destructive winds,
blights, plagues of wolves and dragons, tidal waves, year-long
thunderstorms, lashing rains, and sundry other scourges of which
the scriptures of this period speak so eloquently. The Fathers of the
Church, retiring to the comparative safety of the inland seas and
sunny meadows of Gobiland in Mongolia, established a new ortho-
doxy well-calculated in its rigour of prayer and human burnt-
offering to incite the Huge God to leave our poor wretched world
for a better and more substantial one.

So the story comes almost to the present – to the year 900, only a
decade past as your scribe writes. In that year, the Huge God left
our earth!

Recall, if you will, that the First Departure in 89 lasted only
twenty months. Yet the Huge God has been gone from us already
half that number of years! We need him Back – we cannot live
without him, as we should have realised Long Ago had we not
blasphemed in our hearts!

On his going, he propelled our humble globe on such a course
that we are doomed to deepest winter all the year; the sun is far
away and shrunken; the seas Freeze half the year; icebergs march
across our fields; at mid-day, it is too dark to read without a rush
light. Woe is us!

Yet we deserve everything we get. This is a just punishment, for
throughout all the centuries of our epoch, when our kind was so
relatively happy and undisturbed, we prayed like fools that the
Huge God would leave us.

I ask all the Elders Elect of the Council to brand those prayers as
the Fourth and Greatest Heresy, and to declare that henceforth all
men's efforts be devoted to calling on the Huge God to return to us
at once.

I ask also that the sacrifice rate be stepped up again. It is useless
to skimp things just because we are running out of women.

I ask also that a Fourth Crusade be launched – fast, before the air
starts to freeze in our nostrils!

(1966)

Confluence

The inhabitants of the planet Myrin have much to endure from Earthmen, inevitably, perhaps, since they represent the only intelligent life we have so far found in the galaxy. The Tenth Research Fleet has already left for Myrin. Meanwhile, some of the fruits of earlier expeditions are ripening.

As has already been established, the superior Myrinian culture, the so-called Confluence of Headwaters, is somewhere in the region of eleven million (Earth) years old, and its language, Confluence, has been established even longer. The etymological team of the Seventh Research Fleet was privileged to sit at the feet of two gentlemen of the Geldrid Stance Academy. They found that Confluence is a language-cum-posture, and that meanings of words can be radically modified or altered entirely by the stance assumed by the speaker. There is, therefore, no possibility of ever compiling a one-to-one dictionary of English-Confluence, Confluence-English words.

Nevertheless, the list of Confluent words which follows disregards the stances involved, which number almost nine thousand and are all named, and merely offers a few definitions, some of which must be regarded as tentative. The definitions are, at this early stage of our knowledge of Myrinian culture, valuable in themselves, not only because they reveal something of the inadequacy of our own language, but because they throw some light on to the mysteries of an alien culture. The romanised phonetic system employed is that suggested by Dr Rohan Prendernath, one of the members of the etymological team of the Seventh Research Fleet, without whose generous assistance this short list could never have been compiled.

AB WE TEL MIN   The sensation that one neither agrees nor disagrees with what is being said to one, but that one simply wishes to depart from the presence of the speaker

ARN TUTKHAN   Having to rise early before anyone else is about; addressing a machine

BAGI RACK   Apologising as a form of attack; a stick resembling a gun

BAG RACK   Needless and offensive apologies

BAMAN   The span of a man's consciousness

BI   The name of the mythical northern cockerel; a reverie that lasts for more than twenty (Earth) years

BI SAN   A reverie lasting more than twenty years and of a religious nature

BIT SAN   A reverie lasting more than twenty years and of a blasphemous nature

BI TOSI   A reverie lasting more than twenty years on cosmological themes

BI TVAS   A reverie lasting more than twenty years on geological themes

BIUI TOSI   A reverie lasting more than a hundred and forty-two years on cosmological themes; the sound of air in a cavern; long dark hair

BIUT TASH   A reverie lasting more than twenty years on Har Dar Ka themes (c.f.)

CANO LEE MIN   Things sensed out-of-sight that will return

CA PATA VATUZ   The taste of a maternal grandfather

CHAM ON TH ZAM   Being witty when nobody else appreciates it

DAR AYRHOH   The garments of an ancient crone; the age-old supposition that Myrin is a hypothetical place

EN IO PLAY   The deliberate dissolving of the senses into sleep

GEE KUTCH   Solar empathy

GE NU   The sorrow that overtakes a mother knowing her child will be born dead

GE NUP DIMU   The sorrow that overtakes the child in the womb when it knows it will be born dead

GOR A   Ability to live for eight hundred years

HA ATUZ SHAK EAN   Disgrace attending natural death of maternal grandfather

HAR DAR KA   The complete understanding that all the soil of Myrin passes through the bodies of its earthworms every ten years

HAR DI DI KAL   A small worm; the hypothetical creator of a hypothetical sister planet of Myrin

HE YUP   The first words the computers spoke, meaning, "The light will not be necessary"

HOLT CHA   The feeling of delight that precedes and precipitates wakening

HOLT CHE   The autonomous marshalling of the senses which produces the feeling of delight that precedes and precipitates wakening

HOZ STAP GURT   A writer's attitude to fellow writers

INK TH O   Morality used as an offensive weapon

JILY JIP TUP   A thinking machine that develops a stammer; the action of pulling up the trousers while running uphill

JIL JIPY TUP   Any machine with something incurable about it; pleasant laughter that is nevertheless unwelcome; the action of pulling up the trousers while running downhill

KARNAD EES   The enjoyment of a day or a year by doing nothing; fasting

KARNDAL CHESS   The waste of a day or a year by doing nothing; fasting

KARNDOLI YON TOR   Mystical state attained through inaction; feasting; a learned paper on the poetry of metal

KARNDOL KI REE   The waste of a life by doing nothing; a type of fasting

KUNDULUM   To be well and in bed with two pretty sisters

LAHAH SIP   Tasting fresh air after one has worked several hours at one's desk

LA YUN UN   A struggle in which not a word is spoken; the underside of an inaccessible boulder; the part of one's life unavailable to other people

LEE KE MIN   Anything or anyone out-of-sight that one senses will never return; an apology offered for illness

LIKI INK TH KUTI   The small engine that attends to one after the act of excretion

MAL   A feeling of being watched from within

MAN NAIZ TH   Being aware of electricity in wires concealed in the walls

MUR ON TIG WON   The disagreeable experience of listening to oneself in the middle of a long speech and neither understanding what one is saying nor enjoying the manner in which it is being said; a foreign accent; a lion breaking wind after the evening repast

NAM ON A   The remembrance, in bed, of camp fires

NO LEE LE MUN   The love of a wife that becomes especially vivid when she is almost out-of-sight

NU CROW   Dying before strangers

NU DI DIMU   Dying in a low place, often of a low fever

NU HIN DER VLAK   The invisible stars; forms of death

NUN MUM   Dying before either of one's parents; ceasing to fight just because one's enemy is winning

NUT LAP ME   Dying of laughing

NUT LA POM   Dying laughing

NUT VATO   Managing to die standing up

NUTVU BAG RACK   To be born dead

NU VALK   Dying deliberately in a lonely (high) place

OBI DAKT   An obstruction; three or more machines talking together

ORAN MUDA   A change of government; an old peasant saying meaning, "The dirt in the river is different every day"

PAN WOL LE MUDA   A certainty that tomorrow will much resemble today; a line of manufacturing machines

PAT O BANE BAN   The ten heartbeats preceding the first heartbeat of orgasm

PI KI SKAB WE   The parasite that afflicts man and Tig Gag in its various larval stages and, while burrowing in the brain of the Tig Gag, causes it to speak like a man

PI SHAK RACK CHANO   The retrogressive dreams of autumn attributed to the presence in the bloodstream of Pi Ki Skab We

PIT HOR   Pig's cheeks, or the droppings of pigs; the act of name-dropping

PLAY   The heightening of consciousness that arises when one awakens in a strange room that one cannot momentarily identify

SHAK ALE MAN   The struggle that takes place in the night between the urge to urinate and the urge to continue sleeping

SHAK LA MAN GRA   When the urge to urinate takes precedence over the urge to continue sleeping

SHAK LO MUN GRAM   When the urge to continue sleeping takes precedence over all things

SHEAN DORL   Gazing at one's reflection for reasons other than vanity

SHE EAN MIK   Performing prohibited postures before a mirror

SHEM   A slight cold afflicting only one nostril; the thoughts that pass when one shakes hands with a politician

SHUK TACK   The shortening in life-stature a man incurs from a seemingly benevolent machine

SOBI   A reverie lasting less than twenty years on cosmological themes; a nickel

SODI DORL   One machine making way for another; decadence, particularly in the Cold Continents

SODI IN PIT   Any epithet which does not accurately convey what it intends, such as "Sober as a judge", "Silly nit", "He swims like a fish", "He's only half-alive", and so on

STAINI RACK NUSVIODON   Experiencing Staini Rack Nuul and then realising that one must continue in the same outworn fashion because the alternatives are too frightening, or because one is too weak to change; wearing a suit of clothes at which one sees strangers looking askance

STAINI RACK NUUL Introspection (sometimes prompted by birthdays) that one is not living as one determined to live when one was very young; or, on the other hand, realising that one is living in a mode decided upon when one was very young and which is now no longer applicable or appropriate

STAIN TOK I The awareness that one is helplessly living a role

STA SODON The worst feelings which do not even lead to suicide

SU SODA VALKUS A sudden realisation that one's spirit is not pure, overcoming one on Mount Rinvlak (in the Southern Continent)

TI Civilized aggression

TIG GAG The creature most like man in the Southern Continent which smiles as it sleeps

TIPY LAP KIN Laughter that one recognises though the laugher is unseen; one's own laughter in a crisis

TOK AN Suddenly divining the nature and imminence of old age in one's thirty-first year

TUAN BOLO A class of people one only meets at weddings; the pleasure of feeling rather pale

TU KI TOK Moments of genuine joy captured in a play or charade about joy; the experience of youthful delight in old age

TUZ PAT MAIN (Obs.) The determination to eat one's maternal grandfather

U (Obs.) The amount of time it takes for a lizard to turn into a bird; love

UBI A girl who lifts her skirts at the very moment you wish she would

UDI KAL The clothes of the woman one loves

UDI UKAL The body of the woman one loves

UES WE TEL DA Love between a male and female politician

UGI SLO GU The love that needs a little coaxing

UMI RIN TOSIT The sensations a woman experiences when she does not know how she feels about a man

UMY RIN RU The new dimensions that take on illusory existence when the body of the loved woman is first revealed

UNIMGAG BU Love of oneself that passes understanding; a machine's dream

UNK TAK   An out-of-date guide book; the skin shed by the snake that predicts rain

UPANG PLA   Consciousness that one's agonised actions undertaken for love would look rather funny to one's friends

UPANG PLAP   Consciousness that while one's agonised actions undertaken for love are on the whole rather funny to oneself, they might even look heroic to one's friends; a play with a cast of three or less

U RI RHI   Two lovers drunk together

USANA NUTO   A novel all about love, written by a computer

USAN I NUT   Dying for love

USAN I ZUN BI   Living for love; a tropical hurricane arriving from over the sea, generally at dawn

UZ   Two very large people marrying after the prime of life

UZ TO KARDIN   The realisation in childhood that one is the issue of two very large people who married after the prime of life

WE FAAK   A park or a college closed for seemingly good reasons; a city where one wishes one could live

YA GAG   Too much education; a digestive upset during travel

YA GAG LEE   Apologies offered by a hostess for a bad meal

YA GA TUZ   Bad meat; (Obs.) dirty fingernails

YAG ORN   A president

YATUZ PATI   (Obs.) The ceremony of eating one's maternal grandfather

YATUZ SHAK SHAK NAPANG HOLI NUN   Lying with one's maternal grandmother; when hens devour their young

YE FLIC TOT   A group of men smiling and congratulating each other

YE FLU GAN   Philosophical thoughts that don't amount to much; graffiti in a place of worship

YON TORN   A paper tiger; two children with one toy

YON U SAN   The hesitation a boy experiences before first kissing his first girl

YOR KIN BE   A house; a circumlocution; a waterproof hat; the smile of a slightly imperfect wife

YUP PA   A book in which everything is understandable except the author's purpose in writing it

YUPPA GA   Stomach ache masquerading as eyestrain; a book in which nothing is understandable except the author's purpose in writing it

YUTH MOD   The assumed bonhomie of visitors and strangers

ZO ZO CON   A woman in another field

(1967)

Working in the Spaceship Yards

My first job of work as a young man was in the spaceship yards, where I felt my talents and expertise could be put to the greatest benefit of society. I worked as a FTL-fitter's mate's asistant. The FTL-fitter's mate was a woman called Nellie. As more and more women came to be employed in the yards, among the men and the androids and the robots, the men became increasingly circumspect in their behaviour. Their oaths were more guarded, their gestures less uncouth, and their care for their appearance less negligent. This I found strange, since the women showed clearly that they cared nothing for oaths, gestures, or appearances.

From wastebaskets round the site, I collected many suicide notes. Most of them had never reached their recipients and were mere drafts of suicide notes:

> *My darling – When you receive this, I shall no longer be in a position to ever trouble you again.*
> *By the time you receive this letter, I shall never be able.*
> *By the time you receive this, I shall be no more.*
> *My darling – Never again will we be able to break each other's hearts.*
> *You have been more than life to me. My love – I have been so wrong.*

It is very good of people to take such care in their compositions even in extremis. Education has had its effect. At my school, we learnt only how to write business letters. With reference to your last shipment of Martian pig iron/iron pigs. Since life is such a tragic business, why are we not educated how to write decent suicide notes?

In this age of progress, where everything is progressive and techno-logical and new, the only bit of our Self we have left to ourselves is our Human Condition – which of course remains miserable, despite three protein-full meals a day. Protein does not help the Dark Night of the Soul. Androids, which look so like us (we have the new black androids working in the spaceship yards now) do not have a soul, and many of them are very distressed at lacking the long slow toothache of the Human Condition. Some of them have left their employment, and stand on street corners wearing dark glasses, begging for alms with pathetic messages round their shoulders. Orphan of Technology. Left Factry Too Yung. Have Pity on My Poor Metal Frame. And an especially heart-wrenching one I saw in the Queens district. Obsolescence Is the Poor Man's Death. They have their traumas; just to be deprived of the Human Condition must be traumatic.

Most androids hate the android-beggars. They tour the streets after work, beating up any beggars they find, kicking their tin mugs into the gutter. Faceless androids are scaring. They look like men in iron masks. You can never escape role-playing.

We were building Q-line ships when I was in the shipyard. They were the experimental ones. The Q1, the Q2, the Q3, had each been completed, had been towed out into orbit beyond Mars, and triggered off towards Alpha Centauri. Nothing was ever heard of them again. Perhaps they are making a tour of the entire universe, and will return to the solar system when the sun is ten kilometres deep in permafrost. Anyhow, I shan't live to see the day.

It was no fun building those ships. They had no luxury, no living quarters, no furnishings, no galleys, no miles and miles of carpeting and all the other paraphernalia of a proper spaceship. There was very little we could take as supplementary income. The computers that crewed them lived very austere lives.

"The sun will be ten kilometres deep in permafrost by the time you get back to the solar system!" I told BALL, the computer on the Q3, as we walled him in. "What will you do then?"

"I shall measure the permafrost."

I've noticed that about the truth. You don't expect it, so it often sounds like a joke. Computers and robots sound funny quite often because they have no roles to play. They just tell the truth. I asked this BALL, "Who will you be measuring this permafrost for?"

"I shall be measuring it for its intrinsic interest."

"Even if there are no human beings around to be interested?"
"You misunderstand the meaning of intrinsic."

Each of these Q ships cost more than the entire annual national
income of a state like Great Britain. Zip, out into the universe they
went. Never seen again! My handiwork. All those miles of beautiful
seamless welding. My life's work.

I say computers tell the truth. It is only the truth as they see it.
Things go on that none of us see. Should we include them in our
personal truth or not?

My mother was a good old sport. Before I reached the age of ten
and was given my extra-familial posting, she and I had a lot of fun.
Hers was a heart of gold – more, of uranium. She had an old deaf
friend called Mrs Patt who used to come and visit mother once a
week and sit in the big armchair while mother yelled questions and
remarks at her.

Now I realise why I could not bear Mrs Patt – because everything
I said sounded so trivial and stupid when repeated at the top of my
voice.

"It's nice about the extra moonlight law, isn't it?"
"You what you say?"
"I said aren't you pleased about the extra moonlight law?"
"Pleased what?"
"Aren't you pleased about the extra moonlight law? We could do
with another moon."
"I can't hear what you say."
"I say isn't it fun about the extra moonlight law?"
"What lawn is that?"
"The extra moonlight law. Law! Isn't it fun about the extra
moonlight law?"

I used to hide behind the armchair before Mrs Patt came in.
When she and mother started shouting, I would rise over the back
of the chair so that Mrs Patt could not see me, sticking my thumbs
in my ears and my little fingers up my nostrils so that my nose was
wrinkled and distorted, waving my other fingers about while
shooting my brows up and down, flobbing my tongue, and blinking
my eyes furiously, in order to make mother laugh. She had to
pretend she could not see me.

Occasionally, she would have to pretend to blow her nose, in
order to enjoy a quick chuckle.

We had a big bad black cat. Sometimes I would appear round the chair with the tom dish on my head, mewing and wagging my ears.

The question I now ask myself, having reached more sober years – Mrs Patt visited the euthanasia clinic years ago – is whether I should or should not be included among Mrs Patt's roll call of truths. Since I was not among her observable phenomena, then I could not be part of her revealed Truth. For Mrs Patt, I did not exist in my post-armchair manifestation; therefore my effect upon her Self was totally negligible; therefore I could form no portion of her Truth, as she saw it.

Whether what I was doing was well-or ill-intentioned towards her likewise did not matter, since it did not impinge on her consciousness. The only effect of my performance on her was that she came to consider my mother as someone unusually prone to colds, necessitating frequent nose-blowing.

This suggests that there are two sorts of truth: one's personal truth, and what, for fear of using an even more idiotic term, I will call a Universal Truth. In this last category clearly belong events that go on even if nobody is observing them, like my fingers up my nose, the flights of the Q1, Q2, and Q3, and God.

All this I once tried to explain to my android friend, Jackson. I tried to tell him that he could only perceive Universal Truth, and had no cognisance of Personal Truth.

"Universal Truth is the greater, so I am greater than you, who perceive only Personal Truth," he said.

"Not at all! I obviously perceive all of Personal Truth, since that's what it means, and also quite a bit of Universal Truth. So I get a much better idea of Total Truth than you."

"Now you are inventing a third sort of truth, in order to win the argument. Just because you have Human Condition, you have to keep proving you are better than me."

I switched him off. I am better than Jackson. I can switch him off.

Next day, going back on shift, I switched him on again.

"There are all sorts of horrible things signalling behind your metaphorical armchair that you aren't aware of," he said immediately.

"At least human beings write suicide notes," I said. It is a minor art that has never received full recognition. A very intimate art. You can't write a suicide note to someone you do not know.

> *Dear President – My name may not be familiar to you but I voted for you in the last election and, when you receive this, I shall no longer be able to trouble you ever again.*
> *I shall no longer ever be able to vote for you again. Not be able to support you at the next election.*
> *Dear President – This will come as something of a shock, particularly since you don't know me, but.*
> *Dear Sir – You have been more than a president to me.*

The hours in the spaceship yards were long, particularly for us young lads. We worked from ten till twelve and again from two till four. The robots worked from ten till four. The androids worked from ten till twelve and from two till four when I began at the yards as a FTL-fitter's mate's assistant, and they had no breaks for canteen, whereas men and women got fifteen minutes off in every hour for coffee and drugs. After I had been in the yards for some ten months, legislation was passed allowing androids five minutes off in every hour for coffee (they don't take drugs). The men went on strike against this legislation, but it all simmered down by Christmas, after a pay rise. The Q4 was delayed another sixteen weeks, but what is sixteen weeks when you are going to go round the universe?

The women were very emotional. Many of them fell in love with androids. The men were very bitter about this. My first love, Nellie, the FTL-fitter's mate, left me for an android electrician. She said he was more respectful.

In the canteen, we men used to talk about sex and philosophy and who was winning the latest Out-Thinking Contest. The women used to exchange recipes. I often feel women do not have quite such a large share of the Human Condition as we do.

When we first went to bed together Nellie said, "You're a bit nervous, aren't you?"

Well, I was, but I said, "No, I'm not nervous, it's just this question of role-playing. I haven't entirely devised one to cover this particular situation."

"Well, buck up, then, or the whistle will be going. You can be the Great Lover or something, can't you?"

"Do I look like the Great Lover?" I asked in exasperation.

"I've seen smaller," she said, and she smiled. After that, we always got on well together, and then she had to leave me for that android electrician.

For a few days, I was terribly miserable. I thought of writing her a suicide note but I didn't know how to word it.

> *Dear Nellie – I know you are too hard-hearted to care a hoot about this, but. I know you don't care a hoot but. I know you don't give a hoot. Give a rap. Are indifferent to. Are indifferent to what happens to me, but.*
>
> *As you lie there in the synthetic arms of your lover, it may interest you to know I am about to.*

But I was not really about to, for I struck up a close friendship with Nancy, and she enjoyed my Great Lover role. She was very good with an I-Know-We're-Really-Both-Too-Sensible-For-This role. After a time, I got a transfer so that I could work with her on the starboard condentister. She used to tell me recipes for exotic dishes. Sometimes, it was quite a relief to get back to my mates in the canteen.

At last the great day came when the Q4 was finished. The President came down and addressed us, and inspected the two-mile high needle of shining steel. He told us it had cost more than all South America was worth, and would open up a New Era in the History of Mankind. Or perhaps he said New Error. Anyhow, the Q4 was going to put us in touch with some other civilisation, many light years away. It was imperative for our survival that we get in rapport with them before our enemies did.

"Why don't we just get in rapport with our enemies?" Nancy asked me sourly. She has no sense of occasion.

As we all came away from the ceremony, I had a nasty surprise. I saw Nellie with her arm round that android electrician, and he was limping. An android, limping! There's role-playing for you. Byronic androids! If we aren't careful, they will be taking over the Human

Condition just as they are taking our women. The future is black and the bins of our destiny are filling with suicide notes.

I felt really sick. Nancy stared at me as if she could see someone over my shoulder putting his thumbs in his ears and his little fingers up his nose and all that. Of course, when I looked round, nobody was there.

"Let's go and play Great Lovers while there's still time," I said.

(1969)

Super-Toys Last All Summer Long

In Mrs Swinton's garden, it was always summer. The lovely almond trees stood about it in perpetual leaf. Monica Swinton plucked a saffron-coloured rose and showed it to David.

"Isn't it lovely?" she said.

David looked up at her and grinned without replying. Seizing the flower, he ran with it across the lawn and disappeared behind the kennel where the mowervator crouched, ready to cut or sweep or roll when the moment dictated. She stood alone on her impeccable plastic gravel path.

She had tried to love him.

When she made up her mind to follow the boy, she found him in the courtyard floating the rose in his paddling pool. He stood in the pool engrossed, still wearing his sandals.

"David, darling, do you have to be so awful? Come in at once and change your shoes and socks."

He went with her without protest into the house, his dark head bobbing at the level of her waist. At the age of three, he showed no fear of the ultrasonic dryer in the kitchen. But before his mother could reach for a pair of slippers, he wriggled away and was gone into the silence of the house.

He would probably be looking for Teddy.

Monica Swinton, twenty-nine, of graceful shape and lambent eye, went and sat in her living room, arranging her limbs with taste. She began by sitting and thinking; soon she was just sitting. Time waited on her shoulder with the maniac slowth it reserves for children, the insane, and wives whose husbands are away improving the world. Almost by reflex, she reached out and changed the wavelength of her windows. The garden faded; in its place, the city centre rose by her left hand, full of crowding people, blowboats, and buildings (but she kept the sound down). She remained alone. An overcrowded world is the ideal place in which to be lonely.

The directors of Synthank were eating an enormous luncheon to celebrate the launching of their new product. Some of them wore the plastic face-masks popular at the time. All were elegantly slender, despite the rich food and drink they were putting away. Their wives were elegantly slender, despite the food and drink they too were putting away. An earlier and less sophisticated generation would have regarded them as beautiful people, apart from their eyes.

Henry Swinton, Managing Director of Synthank, was about to make a speech.

"I'm sorry your wife couldn't be with us to hear you," his neighbour said.

"Monica prefers to stay at home thinking beautiful thoughts," said Swinton, maintaining a smile.

"One would expect such a beautiful woman to have beautiful thoughts," said the neighbour.

Take your mind off my wife, you bastard, thought Swinton, still smiling.

He rose to make his speech amid applause.

After a couple of jokes, he said, "Today marks a real breakthrough for the company. It is now almost ten years since we put our first synthetic life-forms on the world market. You all know what a success they have been, particularly the miniature dinosaurs. But none of them had intelligence.

"It seems like a paradox that in this day and age we can create life but not intelligence. Our first selling line, the Crosswell Tape, sells best of all, and is the most stupid of all." Everyone laughed.

"Though three-quarters of the overcrowded world are starving, we are lucky here to have more than enough, thanks to population control. Obesity's our problem, not malnutrition. I guess there's nobody round this table who doesn't have a Crosswell working for him in the small intestine, a perfectly safe parasite tape-worm that enables its host to eat up to fifty per cent more food and still keep his or her figure. Right?" General nods of agreement.

"Our miniature dinosaurs are almost equally stupid. Today, we launch an intelligent synthetic life-form – a full-size serving-man.

"Not only does he have intelligence, he has a controlled amount of intelligence. We believe people would be afraid of a being with a human brain. Our serving-man has a small computer in his cranium.

"There have been mechanicals on the market with mini-computers for brains – plastic things without life, super-toys – but we have at last found a way to link computer circuitry with synthetic flesh."

★

David sat by the long window of his nursery, wrestling with paper and pencil. Finally, he stopped writing and began to roll the pencil up and down the slope of the desk-lid.

"Teddy!" he said.

Teddy lay on the bed against the wall, under a book with moving pictures and a giant plastic soldier. The speech-pattern of his master's voice activated him and he sat up.

"Teddy, I can't think what to say!"

Climbing off the bed, the bear walked stiffly over to cling to the boy's leg. David lifted him and set him on the desk.

"What have you said so far?"

"I've said – " He picked up his letter and stared hard at it. "I've said, 'Dear Mummy, I hope you're well just now. I love you. . . .'"

There was a long silence, until the bear said, "That sounds fine. Go downstairs and give it to her."

Another long silence.

"It isn't quite right. She won't understand."

Inside the bear, a small computer worked through its programme of possibilities. "Why not do it again in crayon?"

When David did not answer, the bear repeated his suggestion. "Why not do it again in crayon?"

David was staring out of the window. "Teddy, you know what I was thinking? How do you tell what are real things from what aren't real things?"

The bear shuffled its alternatives. "Real things are good."

"I wonder if time is good. I don't think Mummy *likes* time very much. The other day, lots of days ago, she said that time went by her. Is time real, Teddy?"

"Clocks tell the time. Clocks are real. Mummy has clocks so she must like them. She has a clock on her wrist next to her dial."

David started to draw a jumbo jet on the back of his letter. "You and I are real, Teddy, aren't we?"

The bear's eyes regarded the boy unflinchingly. "You and I are real, David." It specialised in comfort.

Monica walked slowly about the house. It was almost time for the afternoon post to come over the wire. She punched the Post Office number on the dial on her wrist but nothing came through. A few minutes more.

She could take up her painting. Or she could dial her friends. Or she could wait till Henry came home. Or she could go up and play with David. . . .

She walked out into the hall and to the bottom of the stairs.

"David!"

No answer. She called again and a third time.

"Teddy!" she called, in sharper tones.

"Yes, Mummy!" After a moment's pause, Teddy's head of golden fur appeared at the top of the stairs.

"Is David in his room, Teddy?"

"David went into the garden, Mummy."

"Come down here, Teddy!"

She stood impassively, watching the little furry figure as it climbed down from step to step on its stubby limbs. When it reached the bottom, she picked it up and carried it into the living room. It lay unmoving in her arms, staring up at her. She could feel just the slightest vibration from its motor.

"Stand there, Teddy. I want to talk to you." She set him down on a tabletop, and he stood as she requested, arms set forward and open in the eternal gesture of embrace.

"Teddy, did David tell you to tell me he had gone into the garden?"

The circuits of the bear's brain were too simple for artifice. "Yes, Mummy."

"So you lied to me."

"Yes, Mummy."

"*Stop* calling me Mummy! Why is David avoiding me? He's not afraid of me, is he?"

"No. He loves you."

"Why can't we communicate?"

"David's upstairs."

The answer stopped her dead. Why waste time talking to this machine? Why not simply go upstairs and scoop David into her arms and talk to him, as a loving mother should to a loving son? She heard the sheer weight of silence in the house, with a different quality of silence pouring out of every room. On the upper landing, something was moving very silently – David, trying to hide away from her. . . .

He was nearing the end of his speech now. The guests were attentive; so was the Press, lining two walls of the banqueting chamber, recording Henry's words and occasionally photographing him.

"Our serving-man will be, in many senses, a product of the computer. Without computers, we could never have worked through the sophisticated biochemics that go into synthetic flesh. The serving-man will also be an extension of the computer – for he will contain a computer in his own head, a microminiaturised computer capable of dealing with almost any situation he may encounter in the home. With reservations, of course." Laughter at this; many of those present knew the heated debate that had engulfed the Synthank boardroom before the decision had finally been taken to leave the serving-man neuter under his flawless uniform.

"Amid all the triumphs of our civilisation – yes, and amid the crushing problems of overpopulation too – it is sad to reflect how many millions of people suffer from increasing loneliness and isolation. Our serving-man will be a boon to them; he will always answer, and the most vapid conversation cannot bore him.

"For the future, we plan more models, male and female – some of them without the limitations of this first one, I promise you! – of more advanced design, true bio-electronic beings.

"Not only will they possess their own computers, capable of individual programming; they will be linked to the World Data Network. Thus everyone will be able to enjoy the equivalent of an Einstein in their own homes. Personal isolation will then be banished for ever!"

He sat down to enthusiastic applause. Even the synthetic serving-man, sitting at the table dressed in an unostentatious suit, applauded with gusto.

Dragging his satchel, David crept round the side of the house. He climbed on to the ornamental seat under the living-room window and peeped cautiously in.

His mother stood in the middle of the room. Her face was blank; its lack of expression scared him. He watched fascinated. He did not move; she did not move. Time might have stopped, as it had stopped in the garden.

At last she turned and left the room. After waiting a moment, David tapped on the window. Teddy looked round, saw him, tumbled off the table, and came over to the window. Fumbling with his paws, he eventually got it open.

They looked at each other.

"I'm no good, Teddy. Let's run away!"

"You're a very good boy. Your Mummy loves you."

Slowly, he shook his head. "If she loved me, then why can't I talk to her?"

"You're being silly, David. Mummy's lonely. That's why she had you."

"She's got Daddy. I've got nobody 'cept you, and I'm lonely."

Teddy gave him a friendly cuff over the head. "If you feel so bad, you'd better go to the psychiatrist again."

"I hate that old psychiatrist – he makes me feel I'm not real." He started to run across the lawn. The bear toppled out of the window and followed as fast as its stubby legs would allow.

Monica Swinton was up in the nursery. She called to her son once and then stood there, undecided. All was silent.

Crayons lay on his desk. Obeying a sudden impulse, she went over to the desk and opened it. Dozens of pieces of paper lay inside. Many of them were written in crayon in David's clumsy writing, with each letter picked out in a colour different from the letter preceding it. None of the messages was finished.

"My dear Mummy, How are you really, do you love me as much – "

"Dear Mummy, I love you and Daddy and the sun is shining – "

"Dear dear Mummy, Teddy's helping me write to you. I love you and Teddy – "

"Darling Mummy, I'm your one and only son and I love you so much that some times – "

"Dear Mummy, you're really my Mummy and I hate Teddy – "

"Darling Mummy, guess how much I love – "

"Dear Mummy, I'm your little boy not Teddy and I love you but Teddy – "

"Dear Mummy, this is a letter to you just to say how much how ever so much – "

Monica dropped the pieces of paper and burst out crying. In their gay inaccurate colours, the letters fanned out and settled on the floor.

Henry Swinton caught the express home in high spirits, and occasionally said a word to the synthetic serving-man he was taking home with him. The serving-man answered politely and punctually, although his answers were not always entirely relevant by human standards.

The Swintons lived in one of the ritziest city-blocks, half a kilometre above the gound. Embedded in other apartments, their apartment had no windows to the outside; nobody wanted to see the overcrowded external world. Henry unlocked the door with his retina pattern-scanner and walked in, followed by the serving-man.

At once, Henry was surrounded by the friendly illusion of gardens set in eternal summer. It was amazing what Whologram could do to create huge mirages in small space. Behind its roses and wisteria stood their house; the deception was complete: a Georgian mansion appeared to welcome him.

"How do you like it?" he asked the serving-man.

"Roses occasionally suffer from black spot."

"These roses are guaranteed free from any imperfections."

"It is always advisable to purchase goods with guarantees, even if they cost slightly more."

"Thanks for the information," Henry said dryly. Synthetic life-forms were less than ten years old, the old android mechanicals less than sixteen; the faults of their systems were still being ironed out, year by year.

He opened the door and called to Monica.

She came out of the sitting-room immediately and flung her arms round him, kissing him ardently on cheek and lips. Henry was amazed.

Pulling back to look at her face, he saw how she seemed to generate light and beauty. It was months since he had seen her so excited. Instinctively, he clasped her tighter.

"Darling, what's happened?"

"Henry, Henry – oh, my darling, I was in despair . . . But I've just dialled the afternoon post and – you'll never believe it! Oh, it's wonderful!"

"For heaven's sake, woman, what's wonderful?"

He caught a glimpse of the heading on the photostat in her hand, still moist from the wall-receiver: Ministry of Population. He felt the colour drain from his face in sudden shock and hope.

"Monica . . . oh . . . Don't tell me our number's come up!"

"Yes, my darling, yes, we've won this week's parenthood lottery! We can go ahead and conceive a child at once!"

He let out a yell of joy. They danced round the room. Pressure of population was such that reproduction had to be strictly controlled. Childbirth required government permission. For this moment, they had waited four years. Incoherently they cried their delight.

They paused at last, gasping, and stood in the middle of the room to laugh at each other's happiness. When she had come down from the nursery, Monica had de-opaqued the windows, so that they now revealed the vista of garden beyond. Artificial sunlight was growing long and golden across the lawn – and David and Teddy were staring through the window at them.

Seeing their faces, Henry and his wife grew serious.

"What do we do about *them*?" Henry asked.

"Teddy's no trouble. He works well."

"Is David malfunctioning?"

"His verbal communication-centre is still giving trouble. I think he'll have to go back to the factory again."

"Okay. We'll see how he does before the baby's born. Which reminds me – I have a surprise for you: help just when help is needed! Come into the hall and see what I've got."

As the two adults disappeared from the room, boy and bear sat down beneath the standard roses.

"Teddy – I suppose Mummy and Daddy are real, aren't they?"

Teddy said, "You ask such silly questions, David. Nobody knows what 'real' really means. Let's go indoors."

"First I'm going to have another rose!' Plucking a bright pink flower, he carried it with him into the house. It could lie on the pillow as he went to sleep. Its beauty and softness reminded him of Mummy.

(1969)

Sober Noises of Morning in a Marginal Land

At four o'clock in the morning, the Interrogator left me. His assistant unshackled the pinions from my ankles and switched off the two arc-lights which had been pouring brightness into my face. They dulled, gloomed, died.

The assistant helped me to my feet and guided me out of the room, up the stone stairs into the wide hallway, where the old smell of sulphur lay thick, and up the bare wooden staircase to my room on the first floor. I staggered to my bed as he left, fell upon it.

Précis: In the lizard hours of night, the conscious and unconscious gesture are one.

For a long while, I lay where I was, my legs straggling over the side of the bed with my feet touching the floor. My face had been beaten. Its swellings extended the irregular contours of my head to infinity in a contradictory way. One burning cheek was lodged against the high ceiling, while the tender area below my eyelids encompassed a place where there was bird-song. And was there not tender but firm music – Khaldy by a courteous violin – playing in some flooded cavern where my heart beat?

A stretch of time that I thought of as $2n(x-me)^2$ passed, threshing past my mattress like a wounded snake. Its conclusion was the signal for me to struggle to my feet and go to the window.

I sat in the wicker chair there, holding on to the sill, looking out at the submerged forms of darkness through the pane. The wooden sill was deep-set and worn with age and use, like an old human face. The window had wooden interior shutters, nailed back so that they never closed. Their sickly pale blue-green paint was blistered. The window was of two equal parts which had been intended to open outwards. They were nailed close. There were metal bars outside the window.

The window had weathered changes of season and regime; once it had welcomed guests in a hotel – now it guarded prisoners. Once, visitors came to take the malodorous waters of the spa. Now they drank more bitter medicine.

Précis: Eyes and windows remained sealed with reason.

Perhaps I slept by the window. The Interrogator was not there again, but he had his allies in my psyche who spoke for him when he was away.

"You know what I am holding in my hand?"

"No."

"What does it look like?"

"Looks like paper."

"Then – what is on this paper?"

"Writing?"

"Whose writing?"

"If you let me look, I might have a chance of answering."

"*Whose* writing?"

"Mine."

"It's your diary for yesterday. You know you are ordered to write a thousand words every day. There are only nine hundred and six words here. Why?"

"I ran out of words."

"We can slow your circadian rhythms again."

"No!"

"Read me what you have written."

He handed me the page and I stumbled over my shaggy handwriting.

"You remember various things without knowing what it is you remember. Like being reunited with someone you loved. You love. Or not being reunited. Anonymous sort of longing to have her dear embrace. One embrace. Dear one embrace. In the sill it's all written there's really nothing to captivity, perhaps I'm freer here than at home by staring at this piece of wood. I have written it before and I can think of my wife, looking out of that other window at her talking to some other man. The baker perhaps it was we paid him once a week. Her legs in the little pale courtyard with green bushes I forget their name. It twined up the side and that was my dear moment of happiness to look at her and see all I had all to leave. She in that colossal city maintaining herself. But isn't it also an empty time or we find ourselves by separation. I mean this is only today but there is another place we all know of where it's not just today and where these things like separation and punishment and pain don't belong. A place here nowhere supernatural right on this sill of closure. . . ."

It was a memory only. Time had passed. What I had thought I said I might have said the day before; or I might say it today. Perhaps I wrote the same thing every day in the delirious margins of torture.

There was some water in the pitcher on the sill. I sipped it, let it flow through the slit inside my broken mouth.

Précis: Memory is an abnormality of mind, mind an abnormality of body. These abnormalities become central to the human predicament and must be taken advantage of.

Shapes were forming outside the window pane as dawn came in. People and things stirring. A dull lantern moved below my window burning, a broken syllable in the infinite languages of shade. A strange thrill breathed along the nerves of my backbone. Another day on the endless Earth, people rising from their beds, bundling into clothes, going out about their work, breath acrid from the blanketed night. Natural and social orders combining. Servants and soldiers always the first to rise. These would be servants, their tread below my barred window. In another hour, they would bring me breakfast and bath me and dress the night's damage.

Beyond the panes, a brief dawn wind rose. Untrimmed trees formed an avenue from the back of the hotel through the neglected garden down to the lake. They stirred. I did not stir. I remained slumped where I was, my chin against the rough grain of the sill.

My heart beat. That was enough.

As my weary senses returned, I began to think again of escape. I had escaped from Petrovaradin; I could escape from Tilich. Today I should escape.

Précis: Axial rotation. New day's diet of plans.

Something of the cold outside filtered through the window and soothed my throbbing head. My senses drifted into regions where I could not follow. Semi-human figures moved through a substance much like daylight. Dimlight. Noiseless through trees. Their crouching stance. Pushing a kind of boat out on to a well-oiled river. Camp fires. Low fortresses surmounting stone-littered hillocks. Pots, a few dogs, half-cooked meat, the two sexes. Teeth, limbs, antique gestures of love and warfare, a bronze breast-plate. A robed figure on its knees, singing.

When I roused myself again, the light was flowing in outside and I could see the mountains. They still wore their mantle of snow, although another Asian summer was about to visit the plain. Sober noises of morning round the old spa. A dull glitter on the lake showed where the sky was reflected. When they brought me here, ice had been thick on the lake. In the unkempt gardens, dead leaves still lay, stale against new flowers, decay and growth being one and the same thing. Soon the three horsemen would ride out. I roused myself to watch.

On the locker by the bedside lay paper and pen. For once I wished to complete my day's quota of words, my task. I took them up, moved to do the magic act, to make a pale imitation of reality with twenty-six juggled letters.

Finally I wrote: "All art." I crossed it out. "All arts." Yes. "All arts try to recreate one dawn."

Was it true? Which dawn?

"Beyond my horizons stands the One State. Its streets cover most of the inhabited globe. I am of it. It is of me. Man made it to rule mankind. Can we revolt from it . . . if perhaps it is the best arrangement? My little family is one unit. My children are only children, may be killed by others, may kill others. The One State is poised towards." How could you put it? "Towards possible futures."

Seventy-three words. I rested. I intended to write true, but all words are lies because they can only represent one of many levels of being. As I did every day at dawn, I began to weep, confronted by the vast lethargies of Asia.

Précis: Only in movement is there real representation.

The three riders rode forth boldly into the new day. I heard their ponies before they came in sight. The stables lay somewhere along to the left, hidden from my eye. Hooves sounded on the courtyard. Then they came into sight and headed towards the lake, spurring for a path that lay to one side of it.

The men wore sheepskin hats, leather jackets, black wool trousers. They had short rifles slung across their backs. They were guards. Somewhere out on the perimeters of the plain they would do duty all day, returning at nightfall. They could never be seen from the grounds of the hotel except when they rode out or back. I never saw their faces, except in the evening. Then the faces were featureless, or marked merely by moustaches or sidewhiskers.

The kitchens were along on the right, out of sight from my

window, in a low and separate building. The sun rose over the mountains, and soon enough I heard the tread of maids outside in the long corridors, where the smell of sulphur springs lingered like old drains. Other doors were being unlocked, other prisoners were being tended, men I never saw. A key turned in my lock. Maids came through the outer room, swung open my double doors, appeared with trays and steaming towels and bandages, smiling at their eyes and lips. Old ladies bent on being kind.

It was another day at Tilich.

Précis: Everyone has an occupation. It is a law, and the Law.

There was cherry jam for my breakfast with the fresh rolls and butter and coffee. None of it synthetic, but I was accustomed to that by now. Even the One State had not yet been established long enough for perfect uniformity. In this part of Kazakhstan, a state of mind – nothing established itself.

After my bath, I was as usual exhausted. This was the hour when I sank into sleep, never wakening till noon. I returned to my room, but with no intention of resting; today, I was going to escape.

In the giant stone bathroom where, during an older dispensation, patients had wallowed and taken the spa-waters, a row of iron fire buckets hung from staples in the wall. I had discovered that the staple bearing the last bucket of the row was loose. Working secretly for several mornings when the maids were away, I had dragged the staple out. It was L-shaped, the longer arm almost a third of a metre in length, and suitably heavy. The bucket I pushed out of sight behind one of the giant baths.

I had already threaded into my mattress a stolen length of rope. This I now brought forth, knotting one end on the bracket.

My two bare rooms were very high. Across the inner doors, before the spa failed, a curtain had hung: I imagined it rich and ample and velvet. It had gone – how long ago I did not know, for time had an uncertain pulse in Tilich. But the old rail on which it had hung was still in place. By pushing my bed over, and standing on the brass bar at its head, I could dislodge the curtain rail: this I had ascertained several weary days ago. Now I got it down and caught it before it struck the floor.

Précis: Everyone has an occupation. The individual and not the State should decide if the occupations are meaningful.

My bed went back in place. I moved my wooden chair into the outer chamber and climbed on to it with the curtain rail. High above my head was a trapdoor in the ceiling. I pushed it with the end of the rail.

It did not budge.

My head hammered. Some small thing started moving inside my mouth. I had to sit down, burying my face in my hands. All this had happened before, hadn't it? Was not this some archetypal activity? Something was always locked out of somewhere. . . .

The reflection gave me strength. I went over to the wooden sill where my paper lay. I wrote on it, "Something was always locked out of somewhere." Was it full of meaning – or meaningless? I stuffed the paper into my pocket and climbed back on to my chair.

This time, I managed to move the trap door. With great effort, I swung it back, revealing a black hole.

Now I painstakingly put the rail and the chair back in place.

I stationed myself under the trap and whirled my rope. The crude hook swung upwards.

At first I missed, nearly braining myself, bringing down flakes of plaster, each of which I scrupulously put in my pocket. At last, I got the hook through the hole above me. It held firm when I tugged.

Now was the most arduous task of all. The climb. First I rested and drank water, splashing some on my forehead. Then I began to swarm up the rope.

For some while – $2n\ (x\text{--}me)^2$ – I lay with my feet dangling before I had the strength finally to drag myself into the false roof. My shoulders and head pained me. But I drew my rope up and closed the trapdoor. The door was a flimsy piece of wood. Before I laid it in place, I stared down at my room, made alien by a new perspective. Home! A pang went through me. Safety lay there! Always these departures!

Rents in the lining under the tiles gave me plenty of light to see by. A uniform pattern of beams stretched on either side. Winding my rope round me, I started walking to the left, in the direction of the stables.

It was curious to pass the other trapdoors. Below each, a prisoner lay, recovering from his meed of punishment.

At the far end of the roof, I stopped, sat down, and rested by the last trapdoor. I opened it. Below lay an upper landing with stairs leading to the ground floor. Everything a dull white or grey. A maid was slowly climbing the stairs, an old woman with white apron over black dress, her shoulders bent. I suppressed a wish to call to her.

As soon as silence fell, I swarmed down the rope. It was impossible to dislodge the hook. The first person to see the rope dangling there would give the alarm. I ran down the wide and curving stairs.

Précis: There is no departure, only a symbol of departure. Our comings and goings are lost in a larger thing.

The stables were there all right. My bruised face would betray me as a prisoner instantly. There were men striding in the courtyard, but they were not near enough to bother about me. I turned in at the stable door.

The smell of hay and horses and leather. The night guard had yet to return; the stable was empty of men. Two ponies stood at the end of several empty boxes. In the One State, there were no horses: beasts of burden were synthesised. I had watched real horses being ridden often enough – in solids. I saw saddles hanging by a wall but knew not how to attach them to the animal.

On one saddle lay a sheepskin cap of the type the guards wore. I rammed it on to my head and went to the nearest pony. A mouse-grey beast with fawn belly and long tail, probably of Mongolian ancestry. I spoke to it, untied its halter from an iron ring. What confidence! – All the while, I listened for cries of alarm from outside.

Pulling the pony out, I stepped on to a wooden block and climbed on its back. I had its halter and its mane to cling to. I dug my heels into its side and it made smartly for the door. We moved into the courtyard. Turning, I clouted its rump.

It began to move faster. I called to it, kicked its stomach. We were going across the courtyard. Someone called to me in friendly fashion, a man with a sack over one shoulder. I waved!

The horse put its nostrils up and began to canter towards the plain! Somehow I held on, half-crouching on its back. Now it was galloping! I yelled at it in excitement – strength was in me, flowing from the horse. Its muscles stretched and contracted, its fine legs wove under it, its neck arched, its head went forward, its mane blew in my eyes. Still I yelled! Under our feet, the ground sluiced like falling grain, and we were away!

Précis: With a green fuse of joy, parasites devour their hosts. It is their act of worship.

Ah, that ride, and the sound of air in my lungs, in the beast's lungs! The motion itself was a whole thing, the travelling complete in itself as I hung on. I managed to look ahead through my rattling eyeballs. There lay the lake, bearded by brown reeds. There lay the path to the plain, fringed by birch trees – and then no trees, perhaps no more for a hundred miles, then only the plain, the tawny plain continuing eastwards flat to the foot of the mountains. And on the plain – near, near! – three black fluttering blobs. The night guard coming home!

Précis: Things Asian.

If I could evade the guards . . . Beyond them, the plain, the eternal destitute plain, the plain where hoof and foot and tyre would never make permanent imprint! As we bounded forward, I saw on it only one feature – a shed or sheds, decrepit, distant. A guard house? An abandoned copper mine? Beyond that, westwards, the Kyzyl Kum, the Red Desert, the Turanian plain, the Aral Sea – freedom of the cruellest kind, freedom to fall at last with one's cheek in the abrasive planetary grit!

Not that I questioned my motives at that hastening moment. All escapes are escapes from self, from obligations, destinies. All escapes are versions of captivity. In me was growing the thing I most wanted to avoid – true liberty!

So I dashed haphazardly towards the three mounted men.

Précis: He begins to see. There is only self to escape from and self can be changed.

I had no weapons. Nor could I control the animal I rode. I had dropped the end of the halter. I merely hung on, and we rushed to the sound of our own drum towards the approaching guard. They whistled, signalled, lent forward in their saddles, moved as one with their ponies, unslinging their weapons from their backs. I merely hung on!

Among the sparse trees my mount galloped, swerving as it went, in fright or delight. I was slipping lower round its sweating back. Suddenly my hold was gone. I cried out. I fell.

I was tumbling among rough hummocks of grass. Picking myself up. Running. Swerving. Bounding. Dodging. Alive as a plunging stag.

– At such moments of crisis, you're at peace inside. You're

whole. All of you works together in unison, like a machine, like man-and-horse. Even if you know you can't win! –

For they were thundering down on me. Riding with feet, legs, bodies, their arms and hands occupied with their rifles. The trees protected me. I heard the whistle of their darts about me as I ran for the lake, for the reeds. The birches protected me, their slender peeling trunks, silver, white, silvery-grey, tan, light brown, dark. I blundered among them, I and the three riders, all allied in a strange ritual of hunt.

One of the riders had broken ahead. He reined, aimed. Halting, I looked up at him, raising my arms about my face.

A confrontation. Beneath his shaggy hat, his brows in a line, his eyes ruled beneath the line. His mouth set in purpose. A tribesman from the Steppes – I knew at once by the form of his face, its width, its cleverly mounted cheekbones. As he nimbly swung his rifle up at me, I leaped at him as a wolf might leap. He fired.

My slipping fingers caught at his pony's withers, then fell away.

Then there were only glimpses of the wooden laths and sacking of a saddle and the muddled texture of ground as they carted their prey back to the sad hotel.

Précis: As he says, a ritual. The ritual of the hunt. Goes right back to before the human tribe discovered fire. The excited rumpus through the trees. Old blood pouring through contemporary veins. Little enough of us has emerged from prehistory.

Stripped naked, examined for injuries. Taken in an armoured van from the hotel to one of the isolated huts west of the lake, where special prisoners were kept. Made to drink some hot liquid. Whatever drug had been in the dart the rider fired at me, it left me without ill-effect. I was feeble but clear-minded as servants quitted the room and I sat on a polished wooden bench.

The room was bare except for a wide desk, behind which two men sat looking at me, and a computer-output-terminal behind the desk at a separate table.

The faces of the two men were known to me. One was a pale small man with a soft-textured face and grey eyes. His manner was mild and inoffensive and he had a nervous habit of clearing his throat as if about to speak. He was merely a witness, as required by State law. The other man was my Interrogator. A touch of Mongol about his eyes and cheekbones; by contrast, his nose and lips were full. An unlikely mixture and I had found his character, during the long hours of interrogation, a similarly unlikely mixture. Part-sadist, as befitted men of his persuasion, yet not without imagination – an intelligent man who enjoyed inflicting hurt.

He said, "So, 180, the guards saved you from getting lost. Where would you have gone, had we let you go?"

"I don't know."

"Home?"

"I don't know."

"Or had you some romantic idea of living in the wilderness?"

"I don't know."

"Living with a nomadic tribe for the rest of your days, maybe?"

"I don't know." I spoke with my head down, furious still. The reek of the pony was still strong on my garments.

Précis: Men locked in antagonistic roles secretly abet each other.

A baton lay on his desk. I had seen it before. When he picked it up, I flinched involuntarily but continued to reject his questions. The end of the baton glowed red hot. He caught me lightly with it on one of my facial bruises. I could feel an unsuspected system of nerves light up and I began to shiver, perhaps as much with weariness as pain.

The Interrogator rose and walked slowly about the room, studiously glancing down at the stone flags as he paced. Behind his back, he clutched the baton.

'Now, 180, when you escaped, you took with you a piece of paper which is now in our possession. Witness, will you read what the prisoner wrote on that paper?'

The Witness picked a crumpled sheet of paper from the desk. He cleared his throat. He began to read. "'All arts try to recreate one dawn. Beyond my horizons stands the One State. Its streets cover most of the inhabited globe. I am of it. It is of me. Man made it to rule mankind. Can we revolt from it . . . if perhaps it is the best arrangement? My little family is one unit. My children are only children, may be killed by others, may kill others. The One State is poised towards possible futures. Something was always locked out of somewhere.'"

He was silent. The Interrogator still paced up and down.

I said, "A disconnected train of thought. Maybe I have it all wrong."

"You question the functioning of the State?"

"I was questioning my own functioning."

"You have every right to question the State. It is there to serve you as much as you to serve it. You are not at Tilich because you are a traitor."

We were silent. The room was whitewashed. The shadows were grey. I remembered how I had run through the trees after falling from my grey pony. The pallor of the trees, the boldness of uncoloured things.

"180, do you recall why you are here?"

I did not answer.

"You are here because you paid for it, paid for a month's course of suffering. Right?"

I nodded.

"Why did you need it?"

"We've been over all this."

"Why did you need it?"

"Some are born with the y-chromosome, which gives them criminal tendencies. I was born with the k-chromosome; I have a tendency towards guilt."

"So that punishment is a therapy for you?"

"This place used to be a spa." Miserable attempt at a joke.

Précis: Of the many tendencies and traits in a man, few – sometimes none – work on behalf of the individual. Even the drivers are often the driven.

"'All arts try to recreate one dawn.' What did you mean or intend to mean by that?"

"I'm not a writer. I may remember in another dawn."

A sight of the baton. "What do you think you intended to mean?"

"I've been trying to work out what I am. What people are. What you are."

"And?"

"Perhaps – this is an old-fashioned view . . . perhaps all society is a psycho-drama. We're . . . acting something out. Something we don't comprehend."

"Religious?"

"Huh! No, anti-religious, I suppose. Anti-human. I can't explain it, but I've had glimpses of it here. . . ."

A long silence. The smell of the pony was like a colour or a face seen a long time ago, perhaps when standing at the top of a flight of steps.

"Do I have to remind you that you have only three more days

before your month is up and you are returned to your family in One
State City?"

"I've lost track of time. Is it only three more days?"

"Is that why you tried to escape?"

I hung my head. He came and stood in front of me. I was
trembling again. "I wanted to think . . . You can't really think in
the City, with a job of work and a family. . . ."

Précis: I believe that at this point 180 was questioning me, rather
than vice versa.

"You have to go back to the City, unless . . . This is the second
time you have volunteered for a spell of punishment. Very few
volunteer a second time."

With an effort, I raised my eyes to his. In my ears was a great
uproar, the accompaniment of a flash of insight. "But you did!"

He smiled: "I did. . . ."

Then he turned and left the room. As he went, a curt gesture to
the Witness. The Witness rose and followed him.

I lay back against the wall and closed my eyes. Suffering,
mortification, was it a way to understanding? Did I understand?
How much did I understand? Were they just offering me a job?

At length, I rose and went over to a small window, of which there
were two. Outside the window was a sloping roof, beneath which a
guard sheltered. Beyond was nothing but the plain, the flat and
dusty plain, dominant factor in life at Tilich. The mountains in the
distance. Meaningless. Insoluble. Eternal. As transitory as everything else. Take your pick.

Précis: When someone begins to wonder what "meaningless"
means in terms of human lives, he is coming to understand the
question of what human lives mean.

On the hard bench, I slept comfortably until a maid with a tray of
lunch woke me. I recognised the woman. Her face was wrinkled
and her hands were puffy. As she set the tray down, she said, "Red
wine today, 180"

"Thank you."

"A pleasure." Was it really a pleasure for her to do this menial
work? Why should it not be?

I ate without thinking, and drank the wine. When my lunch was
finished, I returned to the window and looked across at the

mountains. Far in the distance, I could see one of the mounted guards.

While I was standing staring, the Interrogator returned.

Précis: Speech. Human contact. Lunch. Red wine. Mountains. Plain. Place in order of importance. Possible question for next interrogation course.

The Interrogator had no baton. Nor did the Witness accompany him, but I saw he switched on a recording instrument as he entered. He came and sat down on my bench.

"What do you know of Jesus Christ?"

"He was a man who died about thirty-seven centuries ago."

"He wanted people to pretend less to each other. He established a religion, once forbidden, now almost extinct. Did you know that?"

"I suppose I must have known it once. Isn't there a nursery rhyme about him?"

"In the course of the last ten centuries, the One State has made many mistakes. Mankind always makes uncertain progress. One of those mistakes – not necessarily the gravest – lay in ignoring the diversity of human kind. That has been remedied. Once on a time, a man with your craving for punishment would have sought it through anti-societal channels because no other channels existed for its assuagement. Now the State is remedying another of its mistakes – or let's say its short-sightednesses."

He looked askance at me. "If I tell you what it is, you may not wish to go home to your family. You may not wish to leave here."

I sat down on the bench beside him. "What is it?" I did not look at him.

"The State recognises that human consciousness is changing. That a quantal step is being taken by the human animal. That we are coming into a period when more and more individuals – finally the whole race – will . . . evolve into a being with a greater capacity for consciousness."

The word eluded me. Then I got it out in a whisper. "Supermen?"

"It's not a term I would use. We know there are different levels of awareness. Not just the conscious. The below-conscious as well, with more than one level. They are merging into a new integrated consciousness."

". . . And the State wants individuals with such awareness to be on its side. . . ."

"It wants to be on their side."

My awareness throughout this conversation was expanding in a totally strange way. It exhilarated me. I rode through our sentences as if through sparse trees, seeking the true scent. Was every conversation the shadow, greatly diminished by distance, of bygone ancestral hunts on which life depended? If so, could discourse have other than shadow quarries? Or could it be that in among the verbal shadows a real new goal lay in the ghostland of this psychic chase?

Could we have found it?

Here, in Tilich?

And where else, simultaneously?

Never to be suppressed?

As I saw he read the mistrust in my eyes, I said, "Who can trust the State?"

He spread his hands in one of his rare gestures. "Not even the State itself. But over the centuries, it has built safeguards to its own power."

"Which it could smash. . . ."

"180, none of us forget that once there were centuries of blood-shed when the old Age of Religion met its close, when the One State crushed and obliterated Capitalism, Christianity, and Communism. Since those terrible times, the State has learned not to demand the loyalties the cruel Cs demanded – loyalty is the most dangerous of all human attributes. The State has grown enough – so I, one of its servants, believe – to encourage a consciousness greater than its own."

Could we really have stumbled through the last of the psychic forests? Even as I posed the question to myself, I could perceive that its answer lay buried in the strata of the future. First, many smaller questions had to be asked – the chase was far from over.

"May I ask, Interrogator, what role you play in all this?"

"A humble one. Such 'spas' as this have existed for many generations. They take care of the State's misfits. Equally, misfits have to run them. That is the actual level on which we meet, you and I. Only comparatively recently was it realised that men with a new awareness would naturally be misfits in society. So the State knew where to go to find such men . . . And it knew it had a forcing ground ready for them.

"We form part of a small but growing nucleus, you understand."

Précis: He asked questions. But not the obvious one. He saw the obvious answer. From this point on, I considered that 180 had

graduated. He is what he believes himself to be. For complete-
ness's sake, the rest of his statement is appended, together with
my précis.

He rose. I did the same and we stood looking at each other. I
recalled the mounted guard, bearing down on me with his slanting
eyes steady behind the rifle.

"I shall leave you now, 180. You have plenty to think about. You
will be escorted back to the hotel very shortly. Do not forget that
one thousand words will be expected of you as usual. What you
have written so far has been restored to your room. Till we meet
again!" He gave a curt bow and left.

Alone, I stood staring at the stout wooden door set in the whitened
stones of the wall. That man – did he imagine himself some kind of
superman too? Did he imagine I would work with him?

Already, I saw how living would be altered, and man's world with
it, when the new dizzy spans of awareness were used and acknowledged. But there would still be a place for the old antagonisms. Like
the plain outside, they could never be made fertile. My Interrogator
remained my enemy although he had brought me to the pitch of
recognising my own potential. He smelt of torture and midnight
sulphur. Hatred was all I had for him.

Précis: He forgets for the moment that even the plain knows its
summer and its winter season.

One of the house-guards came and escorted me back to the hotel. I
sank down on my bed, falling immediately into a deep sleep.

Précis: His brain reshuffled its generations of evidence.

When I roused, I went across to the tap in the outer chamber and
dashed cold water over my head. Still battered. My mirror showed
a distortion in the familiar outline of my face. And my eyes?
Knowledge is no more visible than air. My walk, the breath I drew
– these told me.

Darkness had fallen. Of the wilderness of garden, nothing was
left. But in the sky, low down, bars of light, the lees of day, still
stood. This day! Dark grey sky, bright lemon line of light. In the
other direction, the mountains still unextinguished. I switched on
my small table lamp and began to write by the wooden sill. What I
put was: $2n\,(x{-}me)^2$. The jest from my fevered period.

Beneath it I wrote: "Living had to be on the textbook level. Now the directions have all been read. Throw away the book. Change metaphors. Life and art become one. The performance goes on but now players, critics, and audience unite on a wider stage. Abandon metaphors. Live them."

Over that paper I sat a long time. Paper no longer held the answer.

I climbed back on to my bed and slept again.

My interrogations began at two in the morning. At two, the usual grim guard came to awaken me. I dressed and went with him. The long corridors were silent and in darkness – he carried a lantern. As always before, in that dreadful repetition, we went downstairs. The old lovely smell of sulphurous waters. In the hall, he turned in a different direction from his accustomed one and led me out of the front door, past the armed guard.

He carried the lantern above his head. Instinctively, I looked up at the blank windows with their lines of bars, half-visible.

We went to the stable. Men were smoking there, drinking quietly, playing dice, before a small fire in the saddle room. I was handed over to an officer.

The officer gave me a heavy cloak and a woollen hat. A pony was already saddled. I was helped into the saddle. A groom led me to the stable door. He gave an ironic salute.

Grasping the reins, I urged the animal forward and we clip-clopped easily over the courtyard.

Once out of the shelter of the buildings, I was aware of a keen night breeze, coming with ice on its breath. A thin moon shone overhead. The plain was featureless. Limitless. I rode. The animal and I were one.

It was on such a night and such a night . . . countless countless nights, that men went forth, solaced by movement for the division in their own minds, as night was divided from day. In the new order arising, movements would still have value.

Précis: Movement. Change. Fluidity. Hitherto they have been contained in unmoving man-forged forms. Soon the forms will begin to move. Not only will we know ourselves. We will see that all the lost generations of ignorance were caused by a protective fixity. Barriers were set up. We no longer fear infinite knowledge. The barriers are going down.

I could ride to the end of the plain if I wished. Never return. I did not wish. To know that the possibility existed was sufficient. Soon I would ride back to the hotel, fortified by the symbolism of this gallop (just as the directors of the hotel well knew I would). Now I understood why I had written the message for myself, "All arts try to comprehend one dawn".

And I was riding in that dawn! Made mysterious by night and distance, an echo of my steed's drumming hooves came to me as we headed rapidly back towards the cluster of buildings.

(1971)

The Dark Soul of the Night

As Cordron continued across the plain, he became aware of a line in the ground, scrawled like a snake across old paving. He continued to walk. He ignored the boom-boom-boom boom-boom-boom in his head.

He kept heading due south as always, checking direction occasionally by the compass on the arm of his suit. After another kilometre, the line in the ground was still beside him. Now it was drawn more boldly.

Cordron did not look back. His ears gave him all the data he needed regarding the disposition of his family. Over the months, he had trained himself not to look back, except at long measured intervals, even when the quarrels of the children were at their most shrill.

At present, his two older boys were staying fairly close behind him. The rest of the family spread back over perhaps half a kilometre, with Katti in the middle by the sledge, interfering in the quarrels and generally managing to exacerbate them. Behind her straggled the younger members of the family, with the exception of the wandering girl of the party, who was keeping up with the biggest boys for a while, and the sick member, who rode on the sledge. It had become a convention of the Journey that one child should be sick each day and ride on the underpowered sledge.

Their voices came clearly to Cordron. He took no notice of what they were saying, merely using the sounds as weather-gauges for morale and possible trouble. He could effectively still arguments by slowing or hastening his own pace, depending on the time of day to decide which would be more immediately effective. So long had it been on the move that the family responded automatically to his pace-setting, even in the heat of a quarrel.

He heard a piping dispute on whether hopping animals could be taught to walk. He heard a continuation of the endless saga of the imaginary Eegey Bumptoe, who had set out to swim round the galaxy, after first flooding it with H_2O provided by a sentient hosepipe nebula. He heard the low conversation concerning the difficulty of getting to know – *really* getting to know – other people in starflight. He heard the older boys speculating on what the natives of this planet would do and look like if there were any natives. All this Cordron heard and did not listen to. He kept walking towards the south. Sooner or later, they must reach the equatorial guardian posts. Such posts had been soft-landed on every deserted planet.

As the hours passed, the talk became more intermittent, the family more strung out. The line in the ground widened into a crack. It widened only gradually, sometimes changing direction or sending out tributary cracks which crossed their path.

There was nothing to be seen ahead except the dull mist, which closed in at two hundred paces in all directions. Cordron generally kept his gaze on the mist, still watchful after all these months. Just in case something came charging out of the mist at them, or there was a sudden change in the nature of the terrain. Morn or night, he never forgot the heavy responsibility he carried.

The continual boom-boom-boom boom-boom-boom was still audible in the background. They had heard it as soon as they crawled out of the wrecked ship; it had been so continuously with them that they heard it now only with conscious effort. Like the labouring of blood in their inner ears, the boom-boom-boom boom-boom-boom was part of them.

At first they had believed the noise to be the sound of immense but distant machinery. There was something about the planet – so large yet so lacking in mass, so distant from the inhabited galaxy, so near to annihilation – that made it seem unlikely and therefore artificial. The machine-sound might have been coming from some cavernous alien-forged interior.

During the early weeks of the Journey, the boom-boom-boom boom-boom-boom had slowly increased in volume. The mist had been thicker then. As it intensified, the sound increased; mist and sound had grown to become the presence of the planet. Some titanic thing ahead laboured at its existence, not caring who knew of it. Their sleep was shot through with dreadful speculations as to what shape it took.

Katti had come to him and begged that they might proceed in a different direction. He refused. In their perilous situation, logic must be sole arbiter. Their only hope lay to the south. They could not waste their lives in desolation; if there was anything of intelligence controlling the machinery – if it was machinery they could hear – then they must try to establish rapport with it; their salvation lay no other way. So he said, assembling them together. They went ahead on unaltered compass reading. That night, she crept close to him, weeping in his arms for fear. All the while, the boom-boom-boom boom-boom-boom continued unaltered, unchanging in its tedious rhythm. The nights were the worst: at night, when the mists blew away, they saw both the Phantom and that terrible thing which ruled over all their troubles.

Days later, they were walking in their normal formation when the ground became broken and sloped downwards into the mist. Cordron called a halt and went forward with one of the boys. They came to a place where the ground tumbled away into an abyss. Its depths were filled with mist, swirling uneasily in updrafts. The rest of the party gathered cautiously on the lip of the land, staring uneasily down.

Finally, the mists had parted for a time. Not far below their feet lay a foamless cavern-dark ocean, its uncapped waves moving in steady progression towards the shore. Every wave was the same size as the one before, as the one after, as the one after that. Each came in briskly, yet without haste, as if it had crossed many thousands of miles of open and unpunctuated sea – as it undoubtedly had – to cast itself into formlessness again as it delivered its particular boom to the perpetual boom-boom-boom boom-boom-boom.

The family stood for a long while staring at that fish-free vat of planetary waters. Even Cordron could not pull himself away.

"It's the primordial ocean," one of the younger boys said. He repeated the phrase at intervals. Uncertain whether he had the correct word, he occasionally varied the phrase, remarking instead, "It's the primordinal ocean."

The time came when they turned away. The compass was reset on a new bearing and Cordron got them all into action again with the aid of Alouette. Since then, they had moved parallel to the coast, hoping for a way due south. The incessant mist and the incessant boom-boom-boom boom-boom-boom accompanied them.

Where the mist parted ahead, Cordron saw that the crack in the ground widened sharply. He stopped and inspected the increased division, over which he could still tread with a full pace. The rocky ground, which appeared parched despite the prevailing mists, showed sheer sides where it parted; as yet, the gap was only a metre deep.

He summoned Alouette and told her to round up the party. They straggled towards him, waiting indifferently on either side of the crack. None of them showed curiosity, he noted, although one of the smaller girls climbed down into the crack with little shrieks, perching on its edge and calling to another sister to join her.

"The crack is getting wider by the kilometre," Cordron said. "There's no danger, but you must all stay on this side of it. Otherwise you will eventually become cut off from the rest of the family and have to make a long detour. So stay on this side of the crack. Okay? On we go again."

And off they went. As the party again began to string out, he heard their comments without looking back. As usual, they resented the mildest guidance. Everyone grumbled about him. He bore them no resentment. He was the leader of the party, a natural target for their anxieties, and their dislike of him helped to unite them. He walked steadily on, noting when the widening crack forced them to deviate slightly from southwest. He wondered if the mist was dispersing, but the unhurried boom-boom-boom boom-boom-boom continued unfalteringly as ever. He told himself that he would endure as the noise endured; sometimes he became confused in his thoughts and believed the noise to be the regular impulse of starflier engines.

The older boys were close behind him once more. He estimated them to be some hundred metres behind. His oldest son said, "He's mad, he's parablasting mad. Poor old *shoat* believes he's still walking across that deadly planet."

He heard one of the others saying, "Too much responsibility – broke his mind. Just broke his mind. Doesn't know where he is. . . ."

They had said it before, he recalled. Cordron risked a glance back over his shoulder, trying not to meet their gaze. Then he looked ahead again, bewildered. The boys appeared very close, almost leaning over him in some impossible manner; yet they were also far away.

Rannaroth, he thought; Rannaroth bears a curse with it.

The boys were losing their grip on reality. He did not allow himself to wonder if he could deliver them before everyone lost his sanity. The journey must occupy his whole mind. Just concentrate on getting to the equator; ignore the boys – and Rannaroth.

Nevertheless, the concept of the planet they traversed oppressed him. Cordron was an agriculturalist, specialising in protein mutagenesis, and he knew very little about the universe across which he and his family were being shipped. What he had managed to learn had been gleaned from lifeboat read-outs as the little ship lunged from its doomed mother and hurtled down to crash-land, its electronics burnt out in the stratosphere. Planet X was large and largely non-metallic, with a small eccentric iron core. It pursued a narrow elliptical orbit about its sun, Wexo, in a year as long as ten Earth-years.

Planet X had just passed perihelion. Now it was slowing and heading away from Wexo. The long winter was setting in, a winter that would mean the death of every living thing. Spring would not come again for another six or so Earth-years. The family had signalled its position as they fled from the starflier; but space was vast. They were far from civilisation and civilisation's outposts; if rescue did not come soon, the family would die. The thought of that long slow winter, of death by starlight, came very close to Cordron's mind, so he kept his party on the move for almost as long as Wexo burned in the shrouded skies.

Night came stealthily. Just as the seasons moved sluggishly from one phase to the next, so did the day, expiring in wreaths of brown, grey and purple. They pitched camp on the endless plain, erecting the inflatable tents stashed away on the sledge. Katti supervised the heating of the evening meal. When the meal was eaten, one of the boys read from a poem – the telecoders were useless – after which all the family joined in a singsong.

As they settled down for sleep, the usual night wind rose, whining about the tents as it drove the mist away. Cordron stood for a while, arms wrapped round his chest, watching the night clear; the sense of claustrophobia which assailed him in daylight hours eased a little.

He was about to turn in when Katti joined him, slipping an arm about his waist. Cordron was impatient, he hardly knew why. Ever since the Journey began, she seemed incongruous, almost irrelevant. Just as the Journey brought out his qualities, he could not help feeling that it obliterated hers.

"How long have we been on the move?" she asked, in a tone meant to ingratiate. Annoyed by the question, he answered her gruffly.

"What happens when we've walked right round the planet once? Do we start again?"

"Don't be silly, dear. There will be automatic posts at the equator."

They stood in silence. He thought with regret that she must feel as isolated as he, yet he could do nothing about it. He loved her; he could do nothing about that either, until they had escaped from Planet X.

"I dread the nights," she said. 'Rannaroth will be visible soon. And the – the phantom. . . .'

Every evening, she told him she dreaded the nights. Most evenings, they stood together and watched for the phantom; it was their only contact throughout the day.

When they slept, the phantom hung over them, heavy, louring, a dead weight on their spirits, as if the night had a dark soul. While the wind rose and the persistent afterglow, debris from ancient worlds, fluttered overhead, Cordron felt again the oppression he never shook off. He had trained himself not to voice his thoughts to any of the family. They straggled back over the plain, through the mist, and involuntarily he uttered a groan.

"It's all right, David," she said. "It's all over, the Journey's over. We're safe, they picked us up, we reached the guardian post." She mopped his forehead. Wexo was a pallid disc like a sickbay emergency light.

He struggled to grasp what she was saying. All he could hear was that machine-like noise, boom-boom-boom boom-boom-boom.

He shook his head. "It's getting you down, Katti. The boys are the same. Never fear – we'll see it through. I'll see you through. The Journey isn't endless."

He could hardly make out her face. It was distorted, as if affected by the endless boom-boom-boom boom-boom-boom.

Pushing her away, he stared up at the sky. The afterglow was clearing as the planetary penumbra washed across it. There in the sky the terrible darkness of Rannaroth was revealed, boring its great circle out of the stars.

Here on the edge of the galaxy, he was looking back into the pearly heart of it. The outline of the black hole was easily visible. It seemed to pulsate slightly, to wear a halo – an atmospheric effect, he thought, every night uncertain whether or not he was correct. Every night, that terrible gravitational well dominated the sky of Planet X, ascending towards zenith as the planet forged towards its autumn solstice. Every night, it dominated his wakeful sleep, permeated his dreams. It was comparatively close, so that in his nightmares he saw Wexo slipping into it.

From Rannaroth they had escaped, if it counted as escape. The starflier's trajectory towards a new world had been miscalculated to few seconds of arc, and it had been drawn into that maw. The lifeboats had blasted free just in time to escape annihilation, as the mother ship sank below the event horizon.

For the family in the lifeboat, existence beckoned. For the starflier, life and time had ceased, both wiped off the slate of possibility. Other lifeboats, too, had been drawn into the trap.

Cordron stared up at the black hole in the stars, wrestling with vaguely formed relativistic ideas in his head. Up *there*, in some bizarre way, the starflier's crew were definitively dead to the outside world – yet within their own skulls they would still be falling inwards towards Rannaroth's nucleus for years. But years, like space and sanity, were meaningless terms beyond the event horizon of the hole.

True night came. Up *there*, it was perpetual night. And now Cordron could make out the image of the starflier. The ship itself had been sucked into the whole. Its image remained, isolated at the frozen point where light became stationary. The image hung there like a hollow fly in an old spider's web.

He shook his head to see it clearly. There it was, the Phantom, the ghost of a brilliant ship with some five thousand passengers and crew, dead months ago! Every night, the Phantom grew as the hole grew, occupying all his mind.

In the morning, they took the usual instrumental scan for metallic objects ahead of them on the planetary surface. Every morning, nothing. The guardian post established somewhere on the equator was still beyond range of their detectors. They loaded all the equipment on to the sledge and started off again.

It was a matter of walking beside the crack. The fissure was all of a half-kilometre wide and almost as deep, as far as could be discerned through the mists. They went on south-west, the weary column extending as the morning progressed and Wexo rose higher.

"I'll get you there if we go on for ever," Cordron said.

He heard his wife say something and did not turn his head. She was many metres behind him, lagging with the wandering child, he knew, yet it was as if she spoke in his ear.

"It's all right," she said. "The Journey's over, David. We're almost home. We're safe!"

He kept on, ignoring their voices, eyes staring ahead, jaw set.

(1976)

An Appearance of Life

Something very large, something very small: a galactic museum, a dead love affair. They came together under my gaze.

The museum is very large. Less than a thousand light years from Earth, countless worlds bear constructions which are formidably ancient and inscrutable in purpose. The museum on Norma is such a construction.

We suppose that the museum was created by a species which once lorded it over the galaxy, the Korlevalulaw. The spectre of the Korlevalulaw has become part of the consciousness of the human race as it spreads from star-system to star-system. Sometimes the Korlevalulaw are pictured as demons, hiding somewhere in a dark nebula, awaiting the moment when they swoop down on mankind and wipe every last one of us out in reprisal for having dared to invade their territory. Sometimes the Korlevalulaw are pictured as gods, riding with the awfulness and loneliness of gods through the deserts of space, potent and wise beyond our imagining.

These two opposed images of the Korlevalulaw are of course images emerging from the deepest pools of the human mind. The demon and the god remain with us still.

But there were Korlevalulaw, and there are facts we know about them. We know that they had abandoned the written word by the time they reached their galactic-building phase. Their very name comes down to us from the single example of their alphabet we have, a sign emblazoned across the façade of a construction on Lacarja. We know that they were inhuman. Not only does the scale of their constructions imply as much; they built always on planets inimical to man.

What we do not know is what became of the Korlevalulaw. They must have reigned so long, they must have been so invincible to all but Time.

Where knowledge cannot go, imagination ventures. Men have supposed that the Korlevalulaw committed some kind of racial suicide. Or that they became a race divided, and totally annihilated themselves in a region of space beyond our galaxy, beyond the reach of mankind's starships.

And there are more metaphysical speculations concerning the fate of the Korlevalulaw. Moved by evolutionary necessity, they may have grown beyond the organic; in which case, it may be that they still inhabit their ancient constructions, undetected by man. There is a stranger theory which places emphasis on Mind indentifiable with Cosmos, and supposes that once a species begins to place credence in the idea of occupying the galaxy, then so it is bound to do; this is what mankind has done, virtually imagining its illustrious predecessors out of existence.

Well, there are many theories, but I was intending to talk about the museum on Norma.

Like everything else, Norma possesses its riddles.

The museum demarcates Norma's equator. The construction takes the form of a colossal belt girdling the planet, some sixteen thousand kilometres in length. The belt varies curiously in thickness, from twelve kilometres to over twenty-two.

The chief riddle about Norma is this: is its topographical conformation what it always was, or are its peculiarities due to the meddling of the Korlevalulaw? For the construction neatly divides the planet into a northern land hemisphere and a southern oceanic hemisphere. On one side lies an endless territory of cratered plain, scoured by winds and bluish snow. On the other side writhes a formidable ocean of ammonia, unbroken by islands, inhabited by firefish and other mysterious denizens.

On one of the widest sections of the Korlevalulaw construction stands an incongruous huddle of buildings. Coming in from space, you are glad to see that huddle. Your ship takes you down, you catch your elevator, you emerge on the roof of the construction itself, and you rejoice that – in the midst of the inscrutable symmetrical universe (of which the Korlevalulaw formed a not inconsiderable part) – mankind has established an untidy foothold.

For a moment I paused by the ship, taking in the immensity about me. A purple sun was rising amid cloud, making shadows race across the infinite-seeming plane on which I stood. The distant sea pounded and moaned, lost to my vision. It was a solitary spot, but I was accustomed to solitude – on the planet I called home, I hardly met with another human from one year's end to the next, except on my visits to the Breeding Centre.

Wind tugged me and I moved on.

The human-formed buildings on Norma stand over one of the enormous entrances to the museum. They consist of a hotel for visitors, various office blocks, cargo handling equipment, and gigantic transmitters – the walls of the museum are impervious to the electromagnetic spectrum, so that any information from inside the construction comes by cable through the entrance, and is then transmitted by second-space to other parts of the galaxy.

"Seeker, you are expected. Welcome to the Norma Museum."

So said the android who showed me into the airlock and guided me through into the hotel. Here as elsewhere, androids occupied all menial posts. I glanced at the calendar clock in the foyer, punching my wrisputer like all arriving travellers to discover where in time Earth might be now.

Gently sedated by alpha-music, I slept away my light-lag, and descended next day to the museum itself.

The museum was run by twenty human staff, all female. The Director gave me all the information that a Seeker might need, helped me to select a viewing vehicle, and left me to move off into the museum on my own.

Although we had many ways of growing unimolecular metals, the Korlevalulaw construction on Norma was of an incomprehensible material. It had no joint or seam in its entire length. More, it somehow imprisoned or emanated light, so that no artificial light was needed within.

Beyond that, it was empty. The entire place was equatorially empty. Only mankind, taking it over a thousand years before, had turned it into a museum and started to fill it with galactic lumber.

As I moved forward in my vehicle, I was not overcome by the idea of infinity, as I had expected. A tendency towards infinity has presumably dwelt in the minds of mankind ever since our early ancestors counted up to ten on their fingers. The habitation of the void has increased that tendency. The happiness which we experience as a species is of recent origin, achieved since our maturity; it also contributes to a disposition to neglect any worries in the present to concentrate on distant goals. But I believe – this is a personal opinion – that this same tendency towards infinity in all its forms has militated against close relationships between individuals. We do not even love as our planet-bound ancestors did; we live apart as they did not.

In the museum, a quality of the light mitigated any intimations of infinity. I knew I was in an immense space; but, since the light absolved me from any sensations of clausagrophobia, I will not attempt to describe that vastness.

Over the previous ten centuries, several thousand hectares had been occupied with human accretions. Androids worked perpetually, arranging exhibits. The exhibits were scanned by electronic means, so that anyone on any civilised planet, dialling the museum, might obtain by second-space a three-dimensional image of the required object in his room.

I travelled almost at random through the displays.

To qualify as a Seeker, it was necessary to show a high serendipity factor. In my experimental behaviour pool as a child, I had exhibited such a factor, and had been selected for special training forthwith. I had taken additonal courses in Philosophicals, Alpha-humerals, Incidental Tetrachotomy, Apunctual Synchronicity, Homoöntogenesis, and other subjects, ultimately qualifying as a Prime Esemplastic Seeker. In other words, I put two and two together in a situation where other people were not thinking about addition. I connected. I made wholes greater than parts.

Mine was an invaluable profession in a cosmos increasingly full of parts.

I had come to the museum with a sheaf of assignments from numerous institutions, universities, and individuals all over the galaxy. Every assignment required my special talent – a capacity beyond holography. Let me give one example. The Audile Academy of the University of Paddin on the planet Rufadote was working on a hypothesis that, over the millennia, human voices were gradually generating fewer phons or, in other words, becoming quieter. Any evidence I could collect in the museum concerning this hypothesis would be welcome. The Academy could scan the whole museum by remote holography; yet only to a rare physical visitor like me was a gestalt view of the contents possible; and only to a Seeker would a significant juxtapositioning be noted.

My car took me slowly through the exhibits. There were nourishment machines at intervals throughout the museum, so that I did not need to leave the establishment. I slept in my vehicle; it was comfortably provided with bunks.

On the second day, I spoke idly to a nearby android before beginning my morning drive.

"Do you enjoy ordering the exhibits here?"

"I could never tire of it." She smiled pleasantly at me.

"You find it interesting?"

"It's endlessly interesting. The quest for pattern is a basic instinct."

"Do you always work in this section?"

"No. But this is one of my favourite sections. As you have probably observed, here we classify extinct diseases – or diseases which would be extinct if they were not preserved in the museum. I find the micro-organism beautiful."

"You are kept busy?"

"Certainly. New exhibits arrive every month. From the largest to the smallest, everything can be stored here. May I show you anything?"

"Not at present. How long before the entire museum is filled?"

"In fifteen and a half millennia, at the current rate of intake."

"Have you entered the empty part of the museum?"

"I have stood on the fringes of emptiness. It is an alarming sensation. I prefer to occupy myself with the works of man."

"That is only proper."

I drove away, meditating on the limitations of android thinking. Those limitations had been carefully imposed by mankind; the androids were not aware of them. To an android, the android *umwelt* or conceptual universe is apparently limitless. It makes for their happiness, just as our umwelt makes for our happiness.

As the days passed, I came across many juxtapositions and objects which would assist clients. I noted them all in my wrisputer.

On the fifth day, I was examining the section devoted to ships and objects preserved from the earliest days of galactic travel.

Many of the items touched me with emotion – an emotion chiefly composed of nosthedony, the pleasure of returning to the past. For in many of the items I saw reflected a time when human life was different, perhaps less secure, certainly less austere.

That First Galactic Era, when men – often accompanied by "wives" and "mistresses", to use the old terms for love-partners – had ventured distantly in primitive machines, marked the beginnings of the time when the human pair-bond weakened and humanity rose towards maturity.

I stepped into an early spaceship, built before second-space had been discovered. Its scale was diminutive. With shoulders bent, I moved along its brief corridors into what had been a relaxation room for the five-person crew. The metal was old-fashioned refined; it might almost have been wood. The furniture, such as it was, seemed scarcely designed for human frames. The mode aimed at an illusionary functionalism. And yet, still preserved in the air, were attributes I recognised as human: perseverance, courage, hope. The five people who had once lived here were kin with me.

The ship had died in vacuum of a defective recycling plant – their micro-encapsulation techniques had not included the implantation of oxygen in the corpuscles of the blood, never mind the genetosurgery needed to make that implantation hereditary. All the equipment and furnishings lay as they had done aeons before, when the defect occurred.

Rifling through some personal lockers, I discovered a thin band made of the antique metal, gold. On the inside of it was a small but clumsily executed inscription in ancient script. I balanced it on the tip of my thumb and considered its function. Was it an early contraceptive device?

At my shoulder was a museum eye. Activating it, I requested the official catalogue to describe the object I held.

The reply was immediate. "You are holding a ring which slipped on to the finger of a human being when our species was of smaller stature than today," said the catalogue. "Like the spaceship, the ring dates from the First Galactic Era, but is thought to be somewhat older than the ship. The dating tallies with what we know of the function – largely symbolic – of the ring. It was worn to indicate married status in a woman or man. This particular ring may have been an hereditary possession. In those days, marriages were expected to last until progeny were born, or even until death. The human biomass was then divided fifty-fifty between males and females, in dramatic contrast to the ten-to-one preponderance of females in our stellar societies. Hence the idea of coupling for life was not so illogical as it sounds. However, the ring itself must be regarded as a harmless illogic, designed merely to express a bondage or linkage – "

I broke the connection.

A wedding ring . . . It represented symbolic communication. As such, it would be of value to a professor studying the metamorphoses of nonverbality who was employing my services.

A wedding ring . . . A closed circuit of love and thought.

I wondered if this particular marriage had ended for both the

partners on this ship. The items preserved did not answer my
question. But I found a flat photograph, encased in plastic windows,
of a man and a woman together in outdoor surroundings. They
smiled at the apparatus recording them. Their eyes were flat,
betokening their undeveloped cranial reserves, yet they were not
unattractive. I observed that they stood closer together than we
would normally care to do.

Could that be something to do with the limitations of the
apparatus photographing them? Or had there been a change in the
social convention of closeness? Was there a connection here with the
decibel-output of the human voice which might interest my clients
of the Audile Academy? Possibly our auditory equipment was more
subtle than that of our ancestors when they were confined to one
planet under heavy atmospheric pressure. I filed the details away for
future reference.

A fellow-Seeker had told me jokingly that the secret of the
universe was locked away in the museum if only I could find it.

"We'll stand a better chance of that when the museum is
complete," I told her.

"No," she said. "The secret will then be too deeply buried. We
shall merely have transferred the outside universe to inside the
Korlevalulaw construction. You'd better find it now or never."

"The idea that there may be a secret or key to the universe is in
any case a construct of the human mind."

"Or of the mind that built the human mind," she said.

That night, I slept in the section of early galactic travel and
continued my researches there on the sixth day.

I felt a curious excitement, over and above nosthedony and simple
antiquarian interest. My senses were alert.

I drove among twenty great ships belonging to the Second Galactic
Era. The longest was over five kilometres in length and had housed
many scores of women and men in its day. This had been the epoch
when our kind had attempted to establish empires in space and
extend primitive national or territorial obsessions across many light-
years. The facts of relativity had doomed such efforts from the start;
under the immensities of space-time, they were put away as childish
things. It was no paradox to say that, among interstellar distances,
mankind had become more at home with itself.

Although I did not enter these behemoths, I remained among

them, sampling the brutal way in which militaristic technologies expressed themselves in metal. Such excesses would never recur.

Beyond the behemoths, androids were arranging fresh exhibits. The exhibits slid along in transporters far overhead, conveyed silently from the museum entrance, to be lowered where needed. Drawing closer to where the new arrivals were being unloaded, I passed among an array of shelves.

On the shelves lay items retrieved from colonial homes or ships of the quasi-imperial days. I marvelled at the collection. As people had proliferated, so had objects. A concern with possession had been a priority during the immaturity of the species. These long-dead people had seemingly thought of little else but possession in one form or another; yet, like androids in similar circumstances, they could not have recognised the limitations of their own *umwelt*.

Among the muddle, a featureless cube caught my eye. Its sides were smooth and silvered. I picked it up and turned it over. On one was a small depression. I touched the depression with my finger.

Slowly, the sides of the cube clarified and a young woman's head appeared three-dimensionally inside them. The head was upside down. The eyes regarded me.

"You are not Chris Mailer," she said. "I talk only to my husband. Switch off and set me right way up."

"Your 'husband' died sixty-five thousand years ago," I said. But I set her cube down on the shelf, not unmoved by being addressed by an image from the remote past. That it possessed environmental reflexion made it all the more impressive.

I asked the museum catalogue about the item.

"In the jargon of the time, it is a 'holocap'," said the catalogue. "It is a hologrammed image of a real woman, with a facsimile of her brain implanted on a collapsed germanium-alloy core. It generates an appearance of life. Do you require the technical specifics?"

"No. I want its provenance."

"It was taken from a small armed spaceship, a scout, built in the two hundred and first year of the Second Era. The scout was partially destroyed by a bomb from the planet Scundra. All aboard were killed but the ship went into orbit about Scundra. Do you require details of the engagement?"

"No. Do we know who the woman is?"

"These shelves are recent acquisitions and have only just been catalogued. Other Scundra acquisitions are still arriving. We may find more data at a later date. The cube itself has not been properly

examined. It was sensitised to respond only to the cerebral emissions
of the woman's husband. Such holocaps were popular with Second
Era women and men on stellar flights. They provided life-mimicking
mementoes of partners elsewhere in the cosmos. For further details,
you may – "

"That's sufficient."

I worked my way forward, but with increasing lack of attention
to the objects about me. When I came to where the unloading was
taking place, I halted my vehicle.

As the carrier-platforms sailed down from the roof, unwearying
androids unloaded them, putting the goods in their translucent
wraps into nearby lockers. Larger items were handled by crane.

"This material is from Scundra?" I asked the catalogue.

"Correct. You wish to know the history of the planet?"

"It is an agricultural planet, isn't it?"

"Correct. Entirely agricultural, entirely automated. No humans
go down to the surface. It was claimed originally by Soviet India
and its colonists were mainly, although not entirely, of Indian stock.
A war broke out with the nearby planets of the Pan-Slav Union. Are
these nationalist terms familiar to you?"

"How did this foolish 'war' end?"

"The Union sent a battleship to Scundra. Once in orbit, it
demanded certain concessions which the Indians were unable or
unwilling to make. The battleship sent a scoutship down to the
planet to negotiate a settlement. The settlement was reached but, as
the scout re-entered space and was about to enter its mother-ship, it
blew up. A party of Scundran extremists had planted a bomb in it.
You examined an item preserved from the scoutship yesterday, and
today you drove past the battleship concerned.

"In retaliation for the bomb, the Pan-Slavs dusted the planet with
Panthrax K, a disease which wiped out all human life on the planet
in a matter of weeks. The bacillus of Panthrax K was notoriously
difficult to contain, and the battleship itself became infected. The
entire crew died. Scout, ship, and planet remained incommunicado
for many centuries. Needless to say, there is no danger of infection
now. All precautions have been taken."

The catalogue's brief history plunged me into meditation.

I thought about the Scundra incident, now so unimportant. The
wiping out of a whole world full of people – evidence again of that
lust for possession which had by now relinquished its grip on the
human soul. Or was the museum itself an indication that traces of

the lust remained, now intellectualised into a wish to possess, not merely objects, but the entire past of mankind and, indeed, what my friend had jokingly referred to as "the secret of the universe"? I told myself then that cause and effect operated only arbitrarily on the level of the psyche; that lust to possess could itself create a secret to be found, as a hunt provides its own quarry. And if once found? Then the whole complex of human affairs might be unravelled beneath the spell of one gigantic simplification, until motivation was so lowered that life would lose its purport; whereupon our species would wither and die, all tasks fulfilled. Such indeed could have happened to the unassailable Korlevalulaw.

To what extent the inorganic and the organic universe were unity could not be determined until ultimate heat-death brought parity. But it was feasible to suppose that each existed for the other, albeit hierarchically. Organic systems with intelligence might achieve unity – union – with the encompassing universe through knowledge, through the possession of that "secret" of which my friend joked. That union would represent a peak, a flowering. Beyond it lay only decline, a metaphysical correspondence to the second law of thermodynamics.

Breaking from this chain of reasoning, I realised two things immediately: firstly, that I was well into my serendipitous Seeker phase, and, secondly, that I was about to take from an android's hands an item he was unloading from the carrier-platform.

As I unwrapped it from its translucent covering, the catalogue said, "The object you hold was retrieved from the capital city of Scundra. It was found in the apartment of a married couple named Jean and Lan Gopal. Other objects are arriving from the same source. Do not misplace it or our assistants will be confused."

It was a "holocap" like the one I had examined the day before. Perhaps it was a more sophisticated example. The casing was better turned, the button so well-concealed that I found it almost by accident. Moreover, the cube lit immediately, and the illusion that I was holding a man's head in my hands was strong.

The man looked about, caught my eye, and said, "This holocap is intended only for my ex-wife, Jean Gopal. I have no business with you. Switch off and be good enough to return me to Jean. This is Chris Mailer."

The image died. I held only a cube in my hands.

In my mind questions flowered.

Sixty-five thousand years ago. . . .

I pressed the switch again. Eyeing me straight, he said in unchanged tones, "This holocap is intended only for my ex-wife, Jean Gopal. I have no business with you. Switch off and be good enough to return me to Jean. This is Chris Mailer."

Certainly it was all that was left of Chris Mailer. His face made a powerful impression. His features were generous, with high forehead, long nose, powerful chin. His grey eyes were wide-set, his mouth ample but firm. He had a neat beard, brown and streaked with grey. About the temples his hair also carried streaks of grey. His face was unlined and generally alert, although not without melancholy. I resurrected him up from the electronic distances and made him go through his piece again.

"Now I shall reunite you with your ex-wife," I said.

As I loaded the holocap into my vehicle and headed back towards the cache of the day before, I knew that my trained talent was with me, leading me.

There was a coincidence and a contradiction here – or seemed to be, for both coincidences and contradictions are more apparent than real. It was no very strange thing that I should come upon the woman's holocap one day and the man's the next. Both were being unloaded from the same planetary area, brought to the museum in the same operation. The contradiction was more interesting. The woman had said that she spoke only to her husband, the man that he spoke only to his ex-wife; was there a second woman involved?

I recalled that the woman, Jean, had seemed young, whereas the man, Mailer, was past the flush of youth. The woman had been on the planet, Scundra, whereas Mailer had been in the scoutship. They had been on opposing sides in that "war" which ended in death for all.

How the situation had arisen appeared inexplicable after six hundred and fifty centuries. Yet as long as there remained power in the submolecular structure of the holocap cells, the chance existed that this insignificant fragment of the past could be reconstructed.

Not that I knew whether two holocaps could converse together.

I stood the two cubes on the same shelf, a metre apart. I switched them on.

The images of two heads were reborn. They looked about them as if alive.

Mailer spoke first, staring intensely across the shelf at the female head.

"Jean, my darling, it's Chris, speaking to you after all this long time. I hardly know whether I ought to, but I must. Do you recognise me?"

Although Jean's image was of a woman considerably younger than his, it was less brilliant, more grainy, captured by an inferior piece of holocapry.

"Chris, I'm your wife, your little Jean. This is for you wherever you are. I know we have our troubles but . . . I was never able to say this when we were together, Chris, but I do love our marriage – it means a lot to me, and I want it to go on. I send you love wherever you are. I think about you a lot. You said – well, you know what you said, but I hope you still care. I want you to care, because I do care for you."

"It's over a dozen years since we parted, my darling Jean," Mailer said. "I know I broke up the marriage in the end, but I was younger then, and foolish. Even at the time, a part of me warned that I was making a mistake. I pretended that I knew you didn't care for me. You cared all the time, didn't you?"

"Not only do I care, but I will try to show more of my inner feelings in future. Perhaps I understand you better now. I know I've not been as responsive as I might be, in several ways."

I stood fascinated and baffled by this dialogue, which carried all sorts of overtones beyond my comprehension. I was listening to the conversation of primitive beings. The image of her face had vivacity; indeed, apart from the flat eyes and an excess of hair she passed for pretty, with a voluptuous mouth and wide eyes – but to think she took it for granted that she might have a man for her own possession, while he acted under similar assumptions! Whereas Mailer's mode of speech was slow and thoughtful, but without hesitation, Jean talked fast, moving her head about, hesitating and interrupting herself as she spoke.

He said, "You don't know what it is like to live with regret. At least, I hope you don't, my dear. You never understood regret and all its ramifications as I do. I remember I called you superficial once, just before we broke up. That was because you were content to live in the present; the past or the future meant nothing to you. It was something I could not comprehend at the time, simply because for me both past and future are always with me. You never made reference to things past, whether happy or sad, and I couldn't stand that. Fancy, I let such a little matter come between our love! There was your affair with Gopal, too. That hurt me and, forgive me, the fact that he was black added salt in my wound. But even there I should have taken more of the blame. I was more arrogant then than I am now, Jean."

"I'm not much good at going over what has been, as you know," she said. "I live each day as it comes. But the entanglement with Lan Gopal – well, I admit I was attracted to him – you know he went for me and I couldn't resist – not that I'm exactly blaming Lan . . . He was very sweet, but I want you to know that that's all over now, really over. I'm happy again. We belong to each other."

"I still feel what I always did, Jean. You must have been married to Gopal for ten years now. Perhaps you've forgotten me, perhaps this holocap won't be welcome."

As I stood there, compelled to listen, the two images stared raptly at each other, conversing without communicating.

"We think differently – in different ways, I mean," Jean said, glancing downwards. "You can explain better – you were always the intellectual. I know you despise me because I'm not clever, don't you? You used to say we have non-verbal communication . . . I don't quite know what to say. Except that I was sad to see you leave on another trip, going off hurt and angry, and I wished – oh well, as you see, your poor wife is trying to make up for her deficiencies by sending you this holocap. It comes with love, dear Chris, hoping – oh, everything – that you'll come back here to me on Earth, and that things will be as they used to be between us. We do belong to each other and I haven't forgotten."

During this speech, she became increasingly agitated.

"I know you won't want me back, Jean," Mailer said. "Nobody can turn back time. But I had to get in touch with you when the chance came. You gave me a holocap fifteen years ago and I've had it with me on my travels ever since. When our divorce came through, I joined a fleet of space-mercenaries. Now we're fighting for the Pan-Slavs. I've just learnt that we're coming to Scundra, although not with the best of motives. So I'm having this holocap made, trusting there'll be a chance to deliver it to you. The message is simple really – I forgive anything you may think there is to forgive. After all these years, you still mean a lot to me, Jean, though I'm less than nothing to you."

"Chris, I'm your wife, your little Jean. This is for you wherever you are. I know we have our troubles but . . . I was never able to

say this when we were together, Chris, but I do love our marriage –
it means a lot to me, and I want it to go on."

"It's a strange thing that I come as an enemy to what is now, I
suppose, your home planet since you married Gopal. I always knew
that bastard was no good, worming his way in between us. Tell him
I bear him no malice, as long as he's taking care of you, whatever
else he does."

She said: "I send you love wherever you are. I think about you a
lot . . ."

"I hope he's made you forget all about me. He owes me that. You
and I were once all in all to each other, and life's never been as
happy for me again, whatever I pretend to others."

"You said – well, you know what you said, but I hope you still
care. I want you to care, because I do care for you . . . Not only do
I care, but I will try to show more of my inner feelings in future.
Perhaps I understand you better now."

"Jean, my darling, it's Chris, speaking to you after all this long
time. I hardly know whether I ought to, but I must."

I turned away. At last I understood. Only the incomprehensible
things of which the images spoke had concealed the truth from me
for so long.

The images could converse, triggered by pauses in each other's
monologues. But what they had to say had been programmed before
they met. Each had a role to play and was unable to transcend it by
a hairsbreadth. No matter what the other image might say, they
could not reach beyond what was predetermined. The female, with
less to say than the male, had run out of talk first and simply begun
her chatter over again.

Jean's holocap had been made some fifteen years before Mailer's.
She was talking from a time when they were still married, he from a
time some years after their divorce. Their images spoke completely
at odds – there had never been a dialogue between them . . .

These trivial resolutions passed through my mind and were gone.

Greater things occupied me.

Second Era man had passed, with all his bustling possessive
affairs.

The godly Korlevalulaw too had passed away. Or so we thought.
We were surrounded by their creations, but of the Korlevalulaw
themselves there was not a sign.

We could no more see a sign of them than Jean and Mailer could see a sign of me, although they had responded in their own way . . .

My function as a Prime Esemplastic Seeker was more than fulfilled. I had made an ultimate whole greater than the parts. I had found what my joking friend called "the secret of the universe".

Like the images I had observed, the galactic human race was merely a projection. The Korlevalulaw had created us – not as a genuine creation with free will, but as some sort of reproduction.

There would never be proof of that, only intuition. I had learned to trust my intuition. As with those imprisoned images, the human species was gradually growing fainter, less able to hear the programmed responses. As with those imprisoned images, we were all drifting further apart, losing definition. As with those imprisoned images, we were doomed to root through the debris of the past, because copies can have no creative future.

Here was my one gigantic simplification, here my union with the encompassing universe! This was the flowering before the decline.

No, my idea was nonsense! A fit had seized me! My deductions were utterly unfounded. I knew there was no ultimate "secret of the universe" – and in any case, supposing humanity to be merely a construct of the Korlevalulaw: who then "constructed" the Korlevalulaw? The prime question was merely set back one step.

But for every level of existence there is a key to its central enigma. Those keys enable life-forms to ascend the scale of life or to reach an impasse – to flourish or to become extinct.

I had found a key which would cause the human species to wither and die. We possessed merely an *umwelt*, not a universe.

I left the museum. I flew my ship away from Norma. I did not head back to my home world. I went instead to a desolate world on which I now intend to end my days, communicating with no one. Let me assume that I caught a personal blight instead of detecting a universal one. If I communicate, the chance is that the dissolution I feel within me will spread.

And spread forever.

Such was my mental agony that only when I reached this barren habitation did I recall what I neglected to do in the museum. I forgot to switch off the holocaps.

There they may remain, conducting their endless conversation, until power dies. Only then will the two talking heads sink into blessed nothingness and be gone.

Sound will fade, images die, silence remain.

(1976)

Last Orders

The alphameter indicated that two people, perhaps more, were somewhere in the block. The Captain took his ACV slowly down the street. There was a canal to his left; its waters churned as if they were living.

He kept the vehicle window open. Gusts of rain, by turns icy and hot, beat against the narrow battlements of his face. They helped him stay awake. His was one of the last rescue parties and he had gone without sleep for over three days.

At the end of the foul little street, a light showed. Oil, probably: electric power had failed long before the city emptied. He sounded his hooter, peering through the murk, through a bar window. A small figure gesticulated in shadow.

The Captain stopped his engine; the craft sank on to cobbles. He waited. The man inside was still talking, or whatever the thing was he was doing. The Captain felt for a pill in his oilskin jacket and squirted it down his throat with a spray from the drink-tube on his dash. Then he climbed out and made his way to the bar. His movements were stiff with controlled weariness. A slate whirled past his head and dashed itself to bits against a bollard by the canal-side. He did not blink.

Pushing the bar door open, he went in. A dim light on a counter revealed the outlines of shambles. The last earth tremor had broken most of the furniture and the bottles behind the bar. Mirrors were cracked. He picked his way forward between shattered floorboards.

At the bar stood a stocky man of indeterminate age, dressed with incongruous neatness in an old-fashioned suit. His round head was covered in a fuzz of colourless hair. Oyster eyes sat in his round face. He was talking with a jovial animation to a thin old lady dressed in black who perched on a high stool, her hands folded together on her lap. A beer stood by her elbow, half finished. The man had a neat little liqueur by him which he had not touched.

Taking all this in at a glance, the Captain said, "You're supposed to have been out of here hours ago. How come the patrols missed you? In a very few minutes – "

"Yes, yes," said the stocky man, "we're just drinking up, we're fully aware of the seriousness of the situation. You look a bit tired – have one with us while we're finishing ours. We'll go together."

"Leave your drinks. We've got to get to Reijkskeller Field. The last ferry is almost due to leave." The Captain took the stocky man by the elbow.

"Just a moment. Have a beer. This lady here says it's very good. No, no trouble, won't take a minute. We'll all travel better for another drink."

He ducked behind the bar and came up smiling with a foaming glass.

"I've got to get you out of here, both of you," the Captain said. "Our lives are in danger. You don't seem to realize. The Moon, as you must know, is about to – "

"My dear man," said the stocky man, coming back round the bar and striking a positive attitude before his untouched liqueur, "you need not remind us of the gravity of the situation. I was telling this lady here that I was right there on the Moon, in Armstrong, when the first fissure began. I saw it with my own eyes. It was a funny thing, really – you see, I'm a xenobalneologist, specializing in off-Earth swimming pools with all their attendant problems, and you'd never believe how many! – Do you know that there are – or were, I suppose I should say – more swimming pools on Luna than in the USA? And I'd just been over to see Wally Kingsmill, who owns – well, his family owns – one of the biggest and most splendid pools in Armstrong, and as I was pavrunning down Ordinary, I could hear people shouting and screaming. First thing you think of on Luna is always that the dome might be damaged. As it happened, I had all my breathing equipment by me – I'd used them in Wally Kingsmill's pool, you see – and I said to myself, 'Right,' but it wasn't the dome at all – though that went a couple of hours later and it was curious how that happened, but this time it was the crack, it came snaking along, travelling fast in erratic fashion, and zip, it ran under the pavrunner, which stopped. Just stopped dead, just like that – "

"The Moon has been evacuated. Now it's our turn. Now we've got to go. At once," said the Captain. He felt mist gathering in his brain. "At once," he repeated. He took up his beer and sipped it.

"It's a lovely beer," said the old lady. "Seems such a shame to waste it." Her gaze returned to the stocky man on whose every word she fastened avidly.

The stocky man poised himself before his daintily shaped liqueur glass, lifted it, drank it off at a gulp, poured himself another from a green bottle, and resumed his vigil over the glass, all in one movement.

"So of course I climbed off, and it's a curious thing, but that crack reminded me of one on the ceiling of the Sistine Chapel, you know, where Michelangelo painted his – of course, it's in Houston now, and I've studied it many times, being interested in art – in fact, about five years ago, about the time that the President visited Venusberg, I was commissioned – "

"That was seven years ago next month," said the Captain. "The President visiting Venusberg. I know because I was on Venus at the time, on a posting to the Space Police. Anyhow, that's immaterial, sir. I must insist you come along now."

"Immediately." He trotted behind the counter and poured the old lady another beer. "You're right, it was seven years ago, because at that time I was under contract to the planetoids. Funnily enough, I was just saying about Michelangelo and, in fact, the grandest pool we put in at the planetoids was finished with a mosaic, consisting of almost a million separate pieces, of Michelangelo's 'Creation', with God reaching out his finger to Adam, you know, covering the entire bottom of the pool. Beautiful. You should go and see it. At least the planetoids will be unaffected by all the gravitational disturbances, or so one hopes."

Having finished his beer, the Captain could not tell whether he felt worse or better for it. "Not only are we all three in grave danger, sir, but you and this lady are contravening martial law established ten days ago. I shall be fully within my rights to shoot you down unless you accompany me to my vehicle immediately."

The stocky man laughed. "Don't worry, I'm a strong supporter of martial law in the circumstances. What else can you do? I think it's marvellous – a credit to all concerned – the way the evacuation of Earth has gone so smoothly. I just wish that more attention could have been paid to the art treasures; not that I'm criticizing, because I know how little warning we've had, but all the same . . . You can build more swimming pools, but you can't resurrect Michelangelo from the dead to paint his masterpieces again, can you?"

As he spoke, he stared more and more fixedly at his liqueur glass, which gleamed in the yellow glow of the oil lamp. Suddenly, he pounced on it and drained its contents as swiftly as before, immediately pouring himself another tot. The old lady, meanwhile, climbed down from her stool and was threading her way through debris over to the window.

"Where are you going, ma'am?" the Captain asked, following her. "I told you to leave."

"Oh, I won't go away, officer," she said, laughing at the thought. "I am as upset about it all as you are. Poor old Earth, after all these millions of years. It's Earth I worry about, not the Moon. The Moon was never much use to us in the first place. I just wanted to see if I could see it out of the window."

Her words were drowned by a tremendous buffet of wind which shook the whole building and set doors banging and weakened walls collapsing. The window shattered as she reached it; luckily, the shards of glass were swept outwards.

"Oh, dear, it's dreadful, what are we coming to? Anyone would think it was the end of the world."

"It is the fucking end of the world, ma'am," the Captain said. "Are you coming, or do I have to carry you?"

"Of course you don't have to carry me. I'm not drunk, if that's what you suspect. You look absolutely worn out. Look, there it is! How I hate it!"

She pointed into the darkness and the Captain stared where she pointed. Furious winds had blown away the cloud. In the night sky, fuming in silver and crimson, was the biggest mountain ever invented, one side of it curved, the other ragged, looming almost to the zenith of the heavens. Gutted lunar cities could clearly be seen across its shattered face. They wondered that it did not fall down upon them as they looked.

Grasping the old lady roughly by the elbow, the Captain said, "You're getting out of here at once. That's an order. Do you know this guy? Is he your husband?"

When she looked up at him, smiling ruefully, he could trace faded youth among the lines and blemishes of her skin.

"My husband? I only met him today – or yesterday, I suppose. What time is it? Though I wouldn't mind a husband like that, old as I am. I mean, he's so fascinating to talk to. We have a lot in common, despite a few years' difference in age. A very sympathetic man. Do you know, officer, he was telling me a few hours ago, before we came in here – "

"Never mind what he was telling you, we've got to get him out of here. This is a rescue operation, understand? It's urgent, understand? Look at the damned thing out there, arriving fast. What's his name?"

She laughed nervously and looked down at her neat little feet. "You're going to think this is plain crazy after what I said just now, but I've never married. Not legally married, you understand. My life really hasn't been – this may sound as if I'm terribly sorry for myself, still, you have to face facts – but it hasn't been fortunate as far as the other sex is concerned. Goodness knows what his name is. When I was younger, I was often in despair. Very often. After almost every man left – despair again. Yet I wasn't ugly, you know, or possessive . . . I'm sorry, officer, I realize this heart-searching may not interest you – I'm not a particularly introspective person – "

"Lady, it's not a question of interest, it's a question of desperation. We're going to get ourselves killed if we aren't away from Earth within the next hour – "

"Oh, I know, officer, but that's exactly what I'm complaining about. Don't think I don't feel as bad as you do. As I was saying, I never had luck – you know what I mean? – with men. I was telling our friend here, and he was so sympathetic, that my flat was partially destroyed in the first of the earth tremors, when they first told us that Earth might have to be evacuated. And I couldn't bear to think that my little home, and my garden, and the town where I've lived for over forty years, should have to be left behind. I wept, I'm not ashamed to say it, and I wasn't the only one to weep, by any means – "

"We've all wept, lady, every one of us. This was the planet we were born on, and this is the planet we are going to die on, unless we move fast. Now, come on, for the last time – out!"

The stocky man had put down another dose of liqueur. He came across the broken floor, carrying two beers, his plain face wrinkled in a smile.

"Have a quick one, both of you, before we go. It'll only be wasted. I shouldn't stand by that broken window, it isn't safe. Come back to the bar."

"Nowhere's safe. Everywhere's doomed. That's why – "

The old lady said, "I was telling this officer how my flat was partially destroyed and – "

"It'll be totally flattened with every other building on Earth, in a short while. Now, I appeal to you both for the last time – all right,

I'll just drink this beer, all right – look, I'm exhausted, and I know your flat was ruined, but I'm appealing to you both – "

"You know my flat was ruined!" the old lady exclaimed with anger. "What do you care about my flat? You just don't listen to what I'm trying to say. I told you about this first earth tremor, when my chest-of-drawers fell over, flat on its face. I was in bed at the time – "

The Captain, with a certain weary sense of unreality, drew his gun, stepping back a pace to cover them both. He clutched his half-finished beer in his other hand.

"That's enough. Silence, both of you. Vehicle outside. Out of here, move!"

"You've got a funny way of going about things, I must say," the stocky man said, shaking his head in regret. "What's the point of violence at a time like this? At any time, really, but particularly at a time like this, when the whole world is about to be crushed out of existence?"

In his stance and gestures, he presented a vitality which the Captain experienced as an assault on his own depleted resources. He found himself saying apologetically, "I don't want violence, I'm just trying to do my duty and – "

"We've heard that one before, haven't we?" said the stocky man to the old lady, but in such a jovial way that even the Captain could not take offence. "Duty, indeed! You ought to hear this lady's story, it's an extremely nice little anecdote – far more than an anecdote, really, a – what's the word?"

"An epic?" the Captain suggested. "No time left for epics."

"Not an epic, man – a vignette, that's the word, a vignette of a life. You see, when her chest-of-drawers crashed over, the lady was in bed, as she has related – "

"It was two o'clock in the morning – of course I was in bed," said the old lady, as if something improper had been suggested.

"And this chest-of-drawers had belonged to her mother." As he talked, the stocky man led the way back to the bar, giving the old lady a chance to say to the Captain, *sotto voce*, "In fact, it's been in the family for several generations. It was a very valuable piece, dating from the mid-nineteenth century."

The stocky man lifted a full liqueur glass from the counter, drained it swiftly, refilled it instantly from the bottle, standing with his plump hands palm-down on the bar, one on either side of the brimming glass, and managed to complete these manoeuvres almost without a break in his speech.

"So she put on the light – still working fortunately because, if you remember, the first tremor was not severe – in fact a good many people, myself included, I might add, slept right through it. In fact, I'd only just gone to bed, being a bit of a night bird – it was early for me – and she climbed out to see what damage had been done and bless me if the chest hadn't split right down the back, revealing a secret drawer. She had known about the secret drawer but she had forgotten it, the way you do, quite unpredictably, just as you can unpredictably remember something. You see how this ceiling is cracked? We were talking about the cracks in the Sistine Chapel ceiling, but you notice on this ceiling that the cracks mostly run in pretty straight lines. When I was telling you both about the Michelangelo painting, I happened to notice these cracks here, and even as I was speaking I saw that they form a perfect map of a sector of this city which I used to live in when I was an engineering student, and that's going back some thirty years."

At this point, he made a swoop on his liqueur glass and downed its contents. Seizing her opportunity, the old lady said smoothly, "And it must have been thirty years since I had used that secret drawer. I put something in that drawer thirty years ago and some trick of the mind – as you say, it's quite unpredictable what you forget and what you remember, particularly when you're getting on in years – some trick of the mind made me forget it entirely until the tremor. And what do you think I'd put in there?"

The Captain went behind the bar and helped himself to another beer.

"I'll put it to you another way," he said. "If you aren't out of here by the time I've finished this beer, I'm going to shoot myself." He set the service revolver down solemnly on the counter and raised the glass to his lips.

"Cheers! I hid a secret diary in that drawer. Mind you, I was no chicken, even then. It dated from my late thirties . . ." She paused to sob.

"Don't fret," the stocky man said, passing her another beer. "I used to keep a diary for years, and much good it did me. One day, I said to my brother, 'Look at all these dreary old – ' Ah, wait, yes – there you are, another instance of how memory is unpredictable! I believe I've got an engagement diary in my pocket which contains a map – yes, here we are!"

He brought a little diary out and begun thumbing his way towards the back of it.

"I've nearly finished this beer – " cautioned the Captain.

"Let me get you another," said the old lady, coming round behind the counter with him, "because I would like to tell you this rather romantic story before you go."

"I say, isn't this pleasant?" exclaimed the stocky man, spreading open his diary with a heavy hand and looking up with a smile as he did so. "You'd never think this was the end of the world, would you? I can't see myself being happy on any other world – not really happy, I mean. Anyhow, here you are, here's the map. I thought I'd find it. Better get my reading spectacles . . ." He began a search of his pockets and then, catching sight of the liqueur glass with a meniscus of drink crowning it, seized that instead, to pause with it half way to his lips. He pressed his lips with the fingers of his other hand and set the glass down on the counter again. "You know, I believe I'll join you in a glass of beer," he said, amazed at his own whim.

"Coming up," said the old lady. "You know, I think you're right. It *is* nice here. I haven't been up so late in years – well, not since I was in Norfolk, staying with my cousin Beth last May – and I don't feel a bit tired. You don't happen to have a cigarette, do you?"

"There are some packets on this shelf," said the Captain, reaching for them. "I'd just spotted them myself. Let's all light up! I'm not supposed to smoke on duty but, after all, these are rather special circumstances . . ."

They all laughed, suddenly happy, lighting up cigarettes, puffing away, pulling at their beers, instinctively moving closer in the warm light of the oil lamp. Wind whistled outside. Somewhere nearby there was the escalating rumble of a building collapsing under the weight in the sky.

"It's moments like this that make life, don't you agree?" said the stocky man. "Far too few of them, that must be admitted. Poor old Earth, I wonder if it'll miss mankind, just a little bit?"

"'Course it won't," said the Captain, drinking deeply. "Mankind has just been a sort of parasite on the face of the Earth, despoiling it, ravishing its fair face. Those stupid gravity experiments on the Moon – they've brought us to this miserable pass, but we're only leaving a world we've ruined steadily, century by century – "

"Oh, I'm afraid I can't agree with that at all, really I can't," said the old lady, puffing at her cigarette. "I have a lovely garden at my flat – I wish you could see it – it'll be spoilt, of course, when the Moon crashes – though the roses are very hardy – I've got a lovely show of Queen Elizabeths, I wonder if perhaps they won't survive? And just opposite, there's the park – "

"Quite agree," said the stocky man. He patted her arm. "I think we improved the place. It was nothing but jungle till mankind got going. I love cities, theatres, music – swimming pools, naturally, but you'd expect me to say that – and all these snug little bars where you can get together with a few kindred spirits and talk. Take this dear old city – well, here's a map, very small scale, but let me show you where the roads take on the exact configuration of the cracks over our heads . . . It's not a very good diary."

"I was saying about my old diary," said the old lady. "Actually, I didn't find it till the morning after the tremor, and there it was, exactly where I'd left it thirty years earlier. And I opened it, and on the last page, after December 31st – just fancy, no more December 31sts . . . you can hardly imagine it, can you?"

"That's one day I can do without," said the Captain, and laughed.

"Ah, but it's the day before New Year's Day," said the stocky man, "when everyone makes merry! I've seen some New Year's Days, believe me – "

"What I'd written where New Year's Day should have been was rather a desolate little sentence. I hope you won't laugh when I tell you, officer."

"Jim," said the Captain. "My friends call me Jim."

"Jim, then." She fluttered her eyelids, and lifted her glass to him before drinking. "Don't laugh – I was thirty-eight when I wrote it – I put 'My long quest for love – I realize now that it will never be fulfilled' . . ." She began to weep.

Both the stocky man and the Captain put their arms round her. "Don't cry, love," they said. "Have another drink."

"While there's life there's hope," said the Captain.

"We all have our disappointments," said the stocky man. "You have to laugh them off . . . I know when I was twenty-five I was all ready to throw myself in that canal out there – no, I'm wrong, it wasn't that canal. It was – well, look, it's the spur of the canal that ends at Fisher's Wharf, where Kayle Bridge Street comes in. Let me show you on the map, or you can see it in these cracks on the ceiling. See? There's the end of the canal, at Fisher's Wharf, just by the old chapel, and Kayle Bridge Street comes in here, and on this corner there used to be an old man with a stall selling hot dogs, year in, year out – '

"I'm weeping now," said the old lady, laughing. "And I wept

when I read what I'd written in the diary, and I remember that I wept when I was thirty-eight and wrote the words down, and yet within a week – well, I'd hidden the diary by then – I met a man called – what was his name? I remembered it not a week ago – "

"The old man with the hot dogs was at the other end of Kayle Bridge Street, where the railway station used to be," said the Captain. "Had a big walrus moustache. On the corner you're speaking of, there was – "

A resounding crash made him stop. Part of the ceiling, including the interesting cracks, collapsed, showering them with flakes which fell in their beers. The building next door collapsed. Dust and grit billowed in through the open window.

"The vehicle!" exclaimed the Captain in horror. He set his glass down, removed his other hand from the old lady's clutches and staggered across to the door. Outside, the ACV had half disappeared under rubble which still slid and bounced across the road into the boiling canal.

"Come and look at this!" he called. They joined him at the door.

"We'll have to walk to Reijkskeller Field," he said. He looked at his watch. 'We'd better get going."

"It's raining. I'm not going out in that," said the old lady. "What time is it?"

"Look at that horrible thing in the sky. Makes you shudder," said the stocky man. "What are the chances that it will miss Earth and just swan off into space?"

"Nil, absolutely nil," said the Captain. "Let me just fetch my gun and we'd better get going, rain or no rain. The last ferry's waiting for us. Once we hear the siren, we've got five minutes and then they blast off, and we'll be stuck here, alone on Earth. Better hurry."

He turned back, muttering, into the bar. The stocky man went with him, brushing white dust from his suit. "I suppose you're right. Let's just have a last drink. One for the road. But you know you're wrong about that hot-dog stall. I was so poor when I was a student that I used to live off hot dogs, so I went to that stall just about every evening for two or more years, so I ought to know, and I remember – "

"All round the wharf was part of my patrol area when I first joined the force, so I ought to remember. The canal finished – hey, where's my gun? I left it on the bar."

"Perhaps it fell down behind. Look behind."

"You haven't got it, have you?"

"I loathe guns. Fist fights, no guns. You wouldn't really have shot yourself, would you?"

"Look, it's not here. Are you sure you didn't take it? You could be jailed for that, I'm warning you. God, I feel so exhausted."

"I told you, I have not touched your gun. The last people left on Earth and you think I'd steal your gun!"

"Don't you two quarrel, just when we're having a nice time," said the old lady brightly, bustling behind the bar and bringing out three new glasses. "I always fancied myself as a barmaid. What'll it be, gentlemen?"

"That's the stuff, love," said the stocky man, rubbing his hands in delight. "You're a woman after my own heart. I wish I'd bumped into you thirty years ago, that's all I can say. I'll have another beer and perhaps I'll just have a quick liqueur too while you're pouring it. Keeps the cold out."

"Mind if I try that stuff?" asked the Captain.

"Help yourself." He pushed the liqueur bottle over. "On the house."

"Your bonny blue eyes, lady!" said the Captain, lifting his drink with trembling hands.

"You're darlings, both of you," she said, adding, as she lifted her own glass, 'and here's to Earth, the best planet in the whole universe!"

They all three drank. Distantly, a siren wailed.

They winked at each other. "Time for one more," said the Captain.

"*His* name was Jim too," said the old lady, "and it was really funny how I bumped into him."

As she lit another cigarette and passed the packet round, the stocky man said, "We'll go and inspect Fisher's Wharf in the morning and you'll see that I'm right. I can remember exactly the very pattern of the cobbles. Anyhow, as I was saying, Michelangelo – "

The siren died away. A new and more insistent wind sprang up outside.

"I know," said the Captain, "let's take our drinks and go into the back parlour. There's bound to be a back parlour, and we'll be cosier in there. Bring the lamp."

"Good idea, Jim," said the stocky man. "These little back parlours take some beating. I know once – "

(1976)

Door Slams in Fourth World

They flew to Frankfurt by the July plane.

Officials in green dungarees filled the airport, far outnumbering travellers. The officials were German and Chinese, and seemed completely uninterested in the three visitors, or in their baggage, their passports, their antanthrax certificates. They stood almost unmoving as the visitors shuffled by. The heat sealed off the world of action behind plate glass.

"No air-conditioning. I warned you," Hemingway said triumphantly to his two companions. "It's gonna be rough!"

The hectares of car park were deserted. Their yellow directional signs, printed on the asphalt in orthogonal lettering, were ideographs of an extinct culture.

". . . 'All the pomp of yesterday is one with Nineveh and Ur'," quoted Mirbar Azurianan, with relish. This desolation they had journeyed all the way from Detroit to see. There was some rebuilding going on, but no workmen moved among the scaffolding.

Mirbar Azurianan was large, burly, bearded like his Armenian ancestors, and, in his early thirties, already running to fat. Under his loosely flapping shirt, his stomach swung before him, imitating the movements of the pack dangling over one shoulder. He wore a large leather hat, considered suitable for travel in the Fourth World. Beneath its brim, his heavy young face was pasty. His blue eyes darted nervously across the European distances.

Azurianan's size and presence proclaimed him the most important personage of the three-person company. Jeremy Hemingway and his silent wife, Peggy, walked behind him, like mere appendages. They looked at him more often then he glanced at them.

They came to a kiosk labelled INFORMATION. A Chinese attendant directed them to a cab-rank. Obediently, they traversed hot tarmac to where a thin line of people stood, emitting the squarking noise common in tourists visiting less favoured parts of the world.

Battered BMWs with biogas envelopes lashed to their roofs drew up and bore the travellers away. Azurianan and the Hemingways climbed into a vehicle with a German driver. He stowed their luggage in the boot. Beside the steering wheel on the dash was his photograph, with a notice assuring passengers in the four international languages that he was a morally irreproachable person.

Soon they were rolling through a complex of feed-roads and major routes which had hardly been repaired since the day the twentieth century died, back in the nineteen-eighties. The pattern of autobahns held no more meaning than the astrobahns overhead, where zeepees rode the energy zone above Earth.

"Well, here's what we paid for – local colour. They sure got local colour here," Hemingway said, gazing out at the drained landscape. Hemingway was making one of his attempts to be expansive, slapping his knee as he spoke. His wife said nothing. She sat limply under her pale linen hat, under her pale linen suit, staring at nothing.

"*Wie viele kilometre nach Wurzburg?*" Azurianan asked the driver.

"*Nur ein hundert.*"

"What did you say?" Hemingway asked the psychoanalyst.

Must you deliver yourself up to him continually, in every small detail? Could you not have guessed that hundert *meant hundred – or else held your tongue? The simplest remark you make betrays the kind of jerk you are.*

Hemingway spent most of the slow journey flicking through his guide book, announcing all the sights they might visit in Wurzburg. The two that particularly excited him – as he had informed them on the airship over – were Cologne cathedral and Milan railway station.

"The Chinese are doing a fantastic job on rehabilitating Europe. They're short on materials, they're short on energy, they're short on just about everything, and how do they manage it? Why, the way they always got by in the past – by teamwork. Teamwork, yeah. They're a great nation, a great nation, and I hand it to them. A great nation, no doubt about that. Eh, Mirbar?"

"They're a great nation," Azurianan said.

Not one hundred per cent satisfied with this level of response, Hemingway turned to his wife.

"They're a great nation, don't you think, Peggy? The way they came right into the Fourth World when everyone else was scared off by anthrax, right?"

"Mmm."

"You still got your headache?" He wrinkled his eyes to look better at her.

"It's on the mend." She turned her dark and heavily-lashed eyes to stare out of the window.

"That's good. We're really on vacation now, really – on – vacation. Yeah, no shirking now." He laughed, did a little swagger with head and shoulders. "Got to go through with it now."

She did not laugh, though a ghost of a smile was conjured about her lips. Azurianan looked at her, grinning sympathetically. "We'll get you a drink and one of your pills as soon as we're in the hotel, Peggy, don't worry."

"I'll be okay, thanks. Just don't bug me."

You will never possess me as you possess Hem. I know that at the back of all this is your desire to possess me utterly – no, not for my sake, but merely in order to destroy Hem more entirely. I know that you cannot be deflected, and that your desires rule your world like lines of latitude. But my fear is at least equal to your obsessions, thank god.

He leaned forward and clutched her narrow waist, saying, "Sure you'll be okay. I'll see to that. And don't let Jeremy get you down. He's just excited, and that's absolutely right and proper. Fourth World's big stuff."

A pulse throbbed under her zygomatic arch.

A number of barriers were staggered across the road as they entered Wurzburg. The BMW trailed behind ancient trucks loaded with hay. Smoke lay heavy ahead, tinting the sunlight with lead. They were stopped at several guard posts while their papers were examined. Wurzburg was more difficult to get into than Europe. Each German soldier was doubled by a Chinese; the Germans looked amateurish and unsmart, the Chinese correct, unflustered. Ahead, they glimpsed the Arc de Triomphe, still unfinished.

"We're here," Hemingway said, and he read off a large notice, lettered in the four international languages, Chinese, Arabic, German and English, "'Welcome to Premier Tourist Centre of Fourth World. Welcome to Wurzburg, the Home of the Equator of the White Sausage'. Now what you imagine that happens to mean, eh?"

A smiling young Chinese stuck his face through the open window of the automobile and said, "You have been allocated to the Hotel of Fourth World Peoples, nearby to the Residenz. We hope you will have a happy vacation here." He handed the driver a docket.

Hemingway began to search in his Fodor for the hotel. He read off a list of symbols to the others. "No pets. Telephone. Bar. Goldfish pond. *Goldfish pond*! Swim Pool. Sun Lounge. No Nudity.

I've heard it said they're pretty puritanical in China and the Fourth World. I guess a bit of sex is allowed in the bedrooms." He laughed and hugged his wife. "Vacation, eh, Peggy! I guess a bit of sex is allowed in the bedrooms."

"What does it say in your guide book on the subject?"

No Nudity meant she would be spared the sight of Mirbar Azurianan naked, lying luxuriously, his smooth brown body with its heavy belly and dark penis trailing, the yellowy soles of his feet. He was a man who stripped naked whenever conditions permitted; one of his basic assumptions in life was that nobody could mind anything he did. If they did mind, then it was time their particular phobia was examined fairly rigorously.

The Hotel of Fourth World Peoples was a two-storey building, practical and inelegant, built in front of the Residenz in what had once been a coach park. Two Chinese army lorries were parked there. Nobody was about. Inside the building, it was similarly deserted. It seemed that no one else was delegated to visit the hotel at present. Carp turned lazily in a concrete pond set in the floor perilously near the reception desk.

A woman clerk with short hair came and registered them. She had a way of looking at their mouths instead of their eyes when speaking. Her own mouth was crushed against her face, as if distorted by social pressures.

After the hectic traffics and tartan wallpapers of Detroit's hotels, the Wurzburg hotel was like a dried gourd, its walls badly distempered, its carpets thin, its perspectives tinny. There were no potted plants.

As if she read their minds, the crushed woman said, when unlocking their bedroom doors, "We hope you will be happy here, and apologise if conditions in the Fourth World are not as you are accustomed at home."

"It'll be all right," Peggy Hemingway said, smiling at her. The smile she received back was perfunctory.

Hemingway ran right in and checked the toilet and shower, to see if water flowed. His wife stood in the middle of the room; she removed her hat and let her rich dark hair escape. He bumped into her as he emerged from the bathroom, laughing.

"Grab a look at the plumbing . . . Place sure has *character*!"

"I was thinking how little character. . . ."

"You know what I mean."

As he tried out the bed, she moved over to the window, pushed it open and stepped on to a shallow balcony. Below lay a paved area, trapped between three sides of hotel and, in the middle of the paved area, a swimming pool. Three women and a man lay as if dead by the side of the pool. The water was almost without ripple. Down its length, it reflected a cable which ran overhead, making it resemble a big enigmatic parcel, treacherously wrapped in a gangrene coloured foil.

A man passed on the far side of the pool, walking briskly, ignoring the recumbent forms, and went into the hotel. He glanced up at Peggy Hemingway as he went, one expert appraising glance, taking her in from eyebrows to ankles. He was dark, sharp-faced. His suit was light and as uncrumpled as the surface of the pool. Something in his stride set him apart from anyone else in the hotel. She was immediately curious about him.

He's an interloper, too. He doesn't belong . . . We none of us belong, to be honest, but at least I realise that. There is nowhere I belong, even within myself. Perhaps it'll be easier for me here in the Fourth World than anywhere; the disaster has happened, and pretending otherwise can't be managed . . . If only it wasn't for Hem, making an obscenity over testing out – pretending to test out – pretending to be enjoying testing out – the bed . . . Why this constant pretence? Was it originally his fault or mine?

"Go and look see how Mirbar is making out, Hem," she said. "I'll check the natives aren't stealing our baggage."

Both her sentences were designed to evoke a needed response from him. As he marched down the ochre corridor whistling "Hail to the Chief", she whispered downstairs like a ghost. The reception hall was empty. Viewing it again as she descended the last steps, she saw its ugliness. An electrician knelt in a corner by the desk, trying to prize up marble tiles with a screwdriver.

The man she had observed in the pool area was standing looking at a small exhibition beside a drinks bar. The bar was closed. The man stood with his arms folded judiciously regarding the objects on the wall. She got the impression of someone poised for flight. He was conspicuously neat and cool.

Anxious lest he disappeared, she went straight over to him and said the first thing that came into her head. "Are you the manager?"

He turned to scrutinise her. She saw she was recognised. The girl on the balcony. Her mistake had been to take his rapid walk for that of an outgoing man. This stranger was deeply sorrowful; the lean planes of his face were so set in melancholy that she was shocked into losing her own smile.

"I'm not the manager, no. You might think I was one of the mismanagers." He spoke in a light, accented English, gesturing as he did so at the exhibition on the wall.

She did not understand. Her casual glance at what he indicated became a stare. The exhibition, mounted near the bar so that none could miss it, was entitled

ISLAMIC ATROCITIES

In photographs and crudely blown-up newsprint, it showed a few details of the Islamic strike against Israel and Europe, the present Fourth World. Most of the stills of dead cities – Rome, Bonn, Strasbourg, Amsterdam – were familiar to her, as were the pictures of dead animals. The centrepiece of the exhibit was a mummified corpse of an eight-year old child. It was at this that Peggy fixed her gaze. The child was parcelled in glass. It still wore some shreds of clothes. Its toes were curled up in an agony which death had frozen rather than releasing.

Oh, Rachel, Rachel, it was all so sudden. I'll never forgive myself about Patricia, never, never, that I swear – or Hem either, the bastard . . . It was all so sudden, the way they struck. They'd learnt from us, from the Israelis. First bombs, then chemicals, then random anthrax strikes . . . When are we ever going to break these endless cycles of retribution. . . .

Only when he turned as if dismissed did she recall there was some shadow of the present in which she still felt need for human contact.

"I didn't understand your meaning."

"It's my improper speech of English. Excuse me." He bent the full melancholy force of his attention on her. "I know we must not expect justice, but I am sad for this heading where we read, 'Islamic Atrocities'. It was not all of the Islamic World that brought destruction to the Fourth World." When she still looked blank, he said, "Madam, forgive me, I speak without heed because I am troubled all the while here. I am a Saudi. From Saudi Arabia, you know? Our kingdom always stood out against the great European jihad."

"It was the effect of this dead child. . . ."

"Although I am not the manager, we might use his office, if you care to sit down and talk. Come along, please."

She walked beside him, trying to deal with the shadows of the past and those of the present. He exuded a faint aroma of *eau de cologne*. She had never encountered an Arab before. Should she admit that she was born Israeli and was American only by marriage? Why was she walking meekly with him, following him as for years she had followed Jeremy Hemingway?

Patricia, I swear I loved you – love you still. I just could not cope with so much grief. It's always with me . . . And Hem, too, I guess. . . .

In the office, empty of people and very nearly empty of furniture, she sat down. The Saudi brought her a glass and poured into it a measure of warm red wine. He poured himself a similiar glass, raising it to his lips without tasting.

"Your health," she said automatically. His name, he told her, was Fahd al-Moghrabi. He was here on reconstruction work, advising the Chinese. He travelled all over the Fourth World, from conference to conference. His profession, he said with a smile, was really communication.

If only someone invented a way of true communication between humans . . . Since I failed you, dear child, I am stricken silent. What can I possibly say to this man, what can I possibly do, except give myself to him?

Looking searchingly at her, al-Moghrabi said, "Saudi Arabia does advise the Chinese continually, and give them financial aid. We mediate between them and the rest of the Arab world. You may have observed that the new airport at Frankfurt, although it appears in material aspect a traditional Communist Chinese construction, faces towards Mecca and has a religious environment for the convenience of pilgrims."

"We only just got here."

"You are with a party?"

"Yes."

"But otherwise you are on your own?"

" . . . Yes."

"That is a disgrace for such a beautiful lady." The sad sensuous eyes regarded her, as much in sympathy as calculation. "Would you do me the honour of dining with me this evening? I don't mean here, in this hotel. I will drive you somewhere tolerable."

"I'd like that. My name. You don't even know my name. My name is Peggy Schmidt."

"Schmidt? But you are American, isn't it?"

"Yes."

There could just be a time for confession this evening, feller, if you

play your cards right. I could do with a good cry. And a good screw.
Thank god he doesn't drink – that's a promising sign, it really is.

They spent the afternoon doing the sights. Smoke hung heavily over
the city. The Chinese nourished a belief that smoke warded off any
untoward effects – exactly what effects was never specified. They
were shown some of the old sights and some of the new.

The Residenz had escaped destruction and was a great attraction.
Here, several dozen tourists walked up Neumann's great staircase
and gazed at the whitewashed walls and ceilings. The new government had painted out Tiepolo's murals; their frivolity was not in
keeping with the times. The oppressive austerities of Peking and
the Koran met where once Beatrice had been sportively conducted
by the gods to Barbarossa's side. The delicacies of the Holy Roman
Empire were extinguished by an army of crude brush strokes.
Jeremy Hemingway read the details from his guide.

He laughed. "Well, that's what history's all about."

They comforted themselves by purchasing with hard currency
mango ice creams from a stall in the chapel. The men bought jolly
paper hats saying I LOVE THE FOURTH WORLD. Peggy refused to wear
one, and held on to her pale linen hat while the men capered
tauntingly before her.

The great baroque church of Melk had been reconstructed at a
point overlooking the river. They visited it, as well as a rather half-
hearted attempt at the Lascaux caves, also destroyed in the early
nuke attacks; the replica had been improvised in a series of old
cellars. Rather better – three stars in Fodor – was von Erlach's
Schönbrunn, authentic in every detail outside, a shell within.

Exhausted but uplifted, the three sat in the coach that took them
back to the hotel.

"Hand it to the Chinese, they're going to have one of the best
tourist centres in the world, time they're finished," Azurianan said.
"What do you say, Peggy?"

"It's a privilege, no less, to be among the first to see what they're
planning," Hemingway said. He had been holografting all afternoon, and his face shone beneath the white paper hat. "They sure
know how to lay out the money, I hand them that."

"The Saudis have invested heavily in the reconstruction programme," Peggy said. "Islam is richer than China."

"Islam, Islam, that's all we hear about in the States nowadays,"
Hemingway said. "Give me the good old days of US-USSR confron-

tation. That I could understand. Anyhow, what you know about the Saudis, Peg?"

"Are your zeepees also contributing to the reconstruction programme?" she asked him in return.

Azurianan laughed. "Those lazy sons of bitches up in the zodiacal planets? What do they care what goes on on Earth? My brother went up there fifteen years ago, made a packet out of alternative environment facilities, and once is precisely, but precisely, how many times I heard from him in all that while."

"Do you write to him?" Peggy asked.

"Too damn right I don't." He and Hemingway laughed. He snapped his fingers. "They figure things out in different ways up there. Earth isn't good enough for them up there."

They began talking over plans for the rest of the day, and were still discussing when the coach arrived at the Fourth World Peoples' Hotel. The general idea was to have a few drinks, use the pool to cool off and sober up, eat dinner, go to the movie the hotel was showing, and then seek out whatever night-life Wurzburg had to offer before midnight curfew.

"How's that sound to you, honey?" Hemingway asked, clutching his wife's arm. "Know what, you need a few martinis to give you a lift, right, Mirbar? We can't have you moping all the vacation, can we? Then we'll have a splash around in their pool. Then the evening can just sort of close in around us, all nice and gentle."

"Yes, Hem. But I have to see if I can turn up that item of baggage I'm missing." She had hidden a small grip in a cupboard in the manager's office. It gave her an excuse to leave her husband's side when al-Moghrabi arrived to collect her in his car.

Hemingway paused, detaining her in the foyer as Azurianan trudged ahead with his heavy panther walk. He looked anxiously at her.

"Peggy – you're not brooding, are you? We're here to have fun, hon. That's why we quit the States for two weeks, remember. Just don't be so uptight, just for once. I'm asking now."

She looked at him coldly, at his hangdog expression, his air of pleading, his pathetic hat, lowering her head so that her velvet eyes regarded him under the white linen brim.

"Who's uptight? Will you relax and quit bugging me, Hem? Have you seen this goddam exhibition they have here of Islamic atrocities? A fine way to greet visitors!"

"Yeah, well, come on, Peggy, I took a look at it, but what the hell . . . I mean, what'm I supposed to do about it? Just don't look at it. I mean, we know it all happened, right, but it's all over and done with, eight years and more ago."

"Hem, have you gotten so insensitive that that mummified kid doesn't remind you of Patricia? Have you gotten that fucking insensitive?"

He looked anxiously about him. She was raising her voice.

"No, that mummified kid did not remind me of Patricia. I refuse to be reminded of Patricia, particularly when I am on vacation abroad with my wife."

"Yeah, with your wife and your shrink."

"My shrink does not remind me of Patricia either, Peg, and you'd best take the same line. We can't remedy what happened in the past, any more than the Germans can. Now, snap out of it, and let's see if we can't rustle up some alcohol, damn it."

"I don't aim to get smashed with you and have you tongue me all over, if that's what you're hoping."

He showed his teeth and, with a sudden anger, bunched a fist under her lip. "I long ago ceased hoping anything with you. Now, get back in line, will you?"

"Oh god, Hem, why is life so awful? Why do we have to go on living like this? Can't you do something?"

"I did something. I brought you to this motherfucking city. So enjoy, woman, enjoy."

Fahd al-Moghrabi's room had an austerity she liked, an austerity that spoke of wealth, not poverty. Mysterious music, tuned low, filled its tiled spaces. The lights were well-placed. An enormous cactus flowered in a pot, its blooms like rosy shark's teeth. The one incongruous note, she thought, was a calendar showing a carnival in Rio de Janeiro. Al-Moghrabi explained that his bank enjoyed considerable trade with Brazil. *His bank*. Peggy noted that.

She had not cried, though she still considered the possibility. Instead, she had played the mother role. He had been unexpectedly shy, resisting her desire to scrutinise his body. He had giggled and looked vexed. Then, covering himself with the sheet, he had lectured her on money.

In the middle of a lecture on how many million rials Saudi Arabia was investing in the Chinese reconstruction of the Fourth World – to the public disgust of many Arab fellow-nations – she had put forth a tentative hand, to find him clutching a strong erection. From then on, he had proved himself an enthusiastic lover.

His hotel was in a part of town where other foreigners did not go. Even Germans were not allowed here – only Chinese and their business partners, Arabs, Russians, Brazilians, South Africans. Al-Moghrabi hated the Chinese. He seemed to hate most races. He hated Europeans, he hated Americans. He hated blacks, as the Chinese did. He liked Chinese women. Chinese women were good in bed.

Peggy began to dislike his arrogance. To her obvious question, he answered frankly, yes, they were better in bed than she was. No, not more abandoned. More skilled. Saudis preferred skill in their women.

As she sat undecided on the edge of the bed, he ran a finger up the range of her vertebrae and told her a complicated story about Arab temperament and pride, and a girl of sixteen he knew in Riyadh, and the prodigies she had performed on the living and the dying. Peggy Hemingway was torn between the wish to believe his story and the wish not to. She was also realising that she would soon have to disentangle herself from this man. So often in the past it had proved unexpectedly difficult to disentangle herself from a mere stranger. Then she would have to lie to Hem, maybe for days, until he dropped the subject.

Tension built up inside her. She knew the feeling well. It was almost like letting blood collect in the mouth. Sooner or later, you were forced to spit.

"How old did you say this little whore was?"

"Fatima is sixteen years."

"Patricia is sixteen, Patricia, worth a hundred Fatimas. Patricia – Patricia, my niece." She turned on him savagely. "She's locked up, you know that, certified insane, behavioural problems, severe emotional instability?"

He lay defenceless, no longer shy about his nakedness. "One may be in prison and still have freedom of mind."

"Freedom of mind? Patricia has no mind. She lives out her days in a slammer. No one can get through to her any more. And you know what? You did it, you are responsible."

"I have no privilege to meet you or your interesting family before this day," he protested.

She stood naked before him, face livid. It was blood-spitting time.

"Oh, you can mock me. You don't feel, do you? Directly I saw you by the pool, I knew you had no feelings. Why do I always seek out men without feelings?"

To make him feel, she told him about Patricia.

Peggy and Rachel Schmidt were sisters. They were born and grew up in Israel. Rachel was the older of the two. She married into a wealthy family; her husband was some years her senior, a scholar at Tel Aviv University who achieved international acclaim for his recreation of ancient music and musical instruments of the Middle East. He had friends even in Cairo, and was a frequent visitor to the States. Rachel bore him a daughter, Patricia, on whom both parents doted.

Rachel worked in Jerusalem, managing the head offices of a travel agency owned by her husband's family. Peggy was working in one of the agency's branches when she encountered Jeremy Hemingway. He was young, amusing, diffident, virginal, and she had never met an American before. He worked for a petro-chemical firm in Detroit. The name Detroit was magic to Peggy. She seduced him in Eilat, and a week later – amid storms of protest from her family – was flying back to the States with him.

Just in time, as it transpired.

Israeli aggro. Libyan paranoia. Palestinian obsessions. The Pakistani bomb. The sequence of events had been long foreseen. The Islamic Strike hit six days after Jeremy and Peggy were married. Rachel had fallen ill at the last moment, and lay in a hospital in Tel Aviv while the wedding took place in Detroit. Her daughter had been sent over to act as bridesmaid.

The grief of that eight-year-old kid! You'd never think an eight-year-old could contain so much grief. An adult, okay – a kid, no. Christ, how she howled when she heard that Israel had been wiped off the slate, just like that. There was no one for her to go back to, no place. Jeremy and I were still on honeymoon. Patricia was seeing the States with his sister. We hurried back. I tried to comfort her. He tried to comfort her. Yes, he really did, poor ineffectual bastard, he really tried to comfort Patricia. We'd never seen grief like that. It frightened us. It frightened the shit out of us. It really frightened the shit out of us. We didn't love each other like that. We didn't love anyone the way she loved Rachel.

You couldn't grasp the kid. She was all sort of elbows and knees and flailing limbs. You couldn't get near her to wash her or mop her snotty face. Like trying to get near a windmill, that's what it was like. A windmill in a storm. . . .

The grief. It just went on. Old Hebrew grief out of a well. It ate us up. She struck at us when we tried to comfort her. No substitutes for Patricia. Not like me. Hem hit her first. He hit back. I was glad when he did it. Jesus, I'll never forget that evening. Maybe she had already fucked our lives up. She attacked him and he hit her right in the mouth. Maybe he was scared.

"You goddamned slut, suffer in silence like the rest of us!" That was what he said. I went wild. I hit him. Then Patricia got her breath and started screaming real bad. I hit her. The pleasure of it. I followed it up, too. I hated that selfish miserable mourning windmill of bones. I wanted to kill her. I wished she'd been wiped out along with her parents, her country.

She crawled back to her room, all bloody.

Hem and I got slammed that night. Neat gin. I never touch the poison, but that night it so happened it was neat gin. Bottle after bottle. I guess the hating really began then. We couldn't speak to each other. We hated each other. I hated myself – I hate myself more than I hate him.

We had to call the doctor to Patricia. We got her committed.

I still go and see her once a month. Conscience visits. She doesn't recognise me. Sixteen. Still waiting for her mother to come back. Still pissing the bed every night.

"I'll drive you home, Peggy," Fahd al-Moghrabi said. He kissed her lightly on the lips.

Punctuating the night, the fake buildings flashed by. The fake Arc de Triomphe, the fake Schönbrunn, the fake Escorial, the fake Colosseum, the fake Milan railway station, the fake this, the fake that, huddling close as if space had puckered in some unexpected cosmic contraction.

Once they passed a long line of Chinese, four abreast, marching along the road in their green dungarees. Al-Moghrabi spat out of the car window. Smoke hung everywhere, shifty as a cat. Curfew was a few minutes away.

He kissed her farewell at the door of the Hotel of the Fourth World Peoples. She was frightened by his correctness, fancying it grew like a tumour from some deep inexpressible anger; or was she, as Azurianan would say, projecting?

"You hate me. I gave you only ashes."

"You gave me all you had to give," he said. "How should I make complaint of such a gift? This world makes us all suffer. Goodnight, Peggy." He walked briskly back to the car.

She remembered to retrieve her concealed baggage from the

office. She staggered as if tipsy among the sharp reflecting surfaces of the reception area. The encounter was over; once more, she had missed something hoped for.

The hotel was airless. Peggy thought she heard someone moving in the dark, but saw no one. In skirting the ornamental fish pond, she kicked something. It rolled over the tiles. A tool – a screwdriver. It tinkled down among the fish. After a pause she moved to the side entrance, trying to breathe the air. It was stale, flat with a taint of smoke.

The pool lay shimmering under its cellophane surface. She listened to catch the sound of al-Moghrabi's car, chugging beneath its biogas envelope, but it had gone. There was no sound. No sound from countryside or town. The whole of Europe was now as silent as China itself after dark. DOOR SLAMS IN FOURTH WORLD could have made a shock headline, if newspapers still existed.

Above the patchy walls of the hotel loomed the skeleton of the fake Eiffel Tower.

The deserted pool reminded her of a painting by David Hockney hanging in the penthouse back home in Detroit. A present from Hem's parents. If she ever got back to that damned First World, she'd sell that painting. Reminders of grief and silence people didn't need.

Did Fahd care anything for her? Was she just one more – unsatisfactory – woman for him, as he was just one more man for her? Was it possible for real – real genuine – contact to exist between two people? Hem, you bastard, thank god you've failed me as much as I fail you. . . .

Despite the dead warmth of the night, a shivering fit overcame her. She turned, and immediately a hand was clamped about her mouth. Immediately she was terrified of death, although only a moment earlier the idea had wooed her from the shadows of her mind.

"You're back, then. I gave your husband a grammy and he's asleep. Don't scream." Words hot in her ear.

When he saw she would not scream, he removed his paw. Abstractedly, she thought, in all hotels I've ever been in, even in the Fourth World, there's always enough light to see who is attacking you.

"Where've you been this time?" Azurianan asked.

She looked into his vague Armenian eyes. He was no more

frightening now than when being consolatory. She laughed, pretending drunkenness.

"Where've you been, you bitch?" He shook her.

"I'm going to bed, Mirbar, thanks so much. I just may take a grammy myself, okay. I've had the bother of going all the way back to the airport to check out this hunk of missing baggage."

She swung the grip forward and hit him in the chest with it.

Totally unconvinced, he said, "I'll see you upstairs."

"I'm not drunk, as you are."

"I'm never drunk."

"More's the fucking pity."

She heard shots distantly. Who were they shooting? Germans? Tourists? Each other? She staggered as she advanced towards the stairwell as if drunkenness were truth. The wall was rough under her steadying palm.

Outside his door, she said, "By the way, Mirbar, *darling*, I am going to fix it, if it's the last thing I do, that Hem gives you the push. I can't take you getting between us any longer. We might have a chance again if you weren't around. From this day forth, Hem is going to have to do without his lousy shrink."

His face was against hers. She could feel the sagging young belly pressing against her grip, smell spice on his breath, as if he were stuffed with dead sweet things.

He said, "Peggy, I'm not Jeremy's shrink. I'm yours. He pays me to see after you."

Her anger came back. She hit him across his cheek, feeling his bones and teeth unyielding under her yielding palm.

"Lies, lies, you liar! Get out of here! Get lost!"

He grasped her and flung his door open. "Come in here, you neurotic little whore, I'll teach you a thing or two. I'll show you something that won't shrink. Maybe I'll fuck a little sanity into you tonight."

He was unzipping his flies. She broke from him and ran for her room, slamming the door behind her and shooting the bolt into place.

Azurianan whispered her name once from the corridor, and then no more. She stood where she was, listening. There was no further sound.

Hemingway had not roused. His heavy breathing was disturbed, then it became more regular. On the ceiling of the room, light rippled, reflected from the surface of the pool outside. That stifling silence again.

She stood for a long time, her back to the door. Then she flung off her soiled clothes and climbed into bed beside her husband.

There was more shooting outside before dawn. Neither of the Americans heard it.

(1982)

The Gods in Flight

Behind the hotel, cliffs rose sheer. The steps which had been cut into the rock long ago made their ascent easy. Kilat climbed them slowly, hands on knees, and his small brother Dempo followed, chattering as he went.

At the top of the climb, the boys were confronted by huge stones, fancifully carved in the likenesses of human beings, water buffalo, and elephants, all squatting among the foliage crowning the island. Kilat clapped his hands with pleasure. A hornbill fixed Kilat with its pebble eyes, flapped away, and glided towards the sea. Kilat watched it till it was out of sight, pleased. The bird was popularly supposed to be a messenger from the Upper World, and was associated with the beginnings of mankind.

"That hornbill can be a sign that the world is not destroyed," Kilat told his brother. Dempo tried to climb up a negroid face, planting his bare brown feet on the negroid lips. He still carried baby fat, but Kilat was eight and so lean that his ribs showed.

Kilat stood on the edge of the precipice and stared in a north-easterly direction across the gleaming waters. The sea looked calm from this vantage point, one of the highest on the island; silvery lanes wound across it reflecting the morning sun. Further out, a leaden haze absorbed everything.

Shielding his eyes, Kilat searched in the haze for sight of Kerintji. Generally, the peak was visible, cloud-wreathed, even when the long coast of Sumatra remained hidden. Today, nothing could be seen. Kilat loved Kerintji and thought of it as a god. Sometimes he slept up here under the stars, just to be near Kerintji.

Although he stood for a long time, Kilat saw nothing in the haze. Finally he turned away.

"We'll go down to town now," he called to Dempo. "Kerintji is angry with the behaviour of men."

Still he lingered. It had always been his ambition to get on a ship or, better still, a plane, one of the big white planes which landed on the new airfield, and go north to see the world. Not just the nearby world, but that huge world of affairs where white people travelled about in their white birds as if they were gods. He had already started saving his rupiahs.

The two boys made their way back down the steps. His mother sat on the front steps of her hotel, smoking and chattering to her servants. There were no tourists, no white people, although it was the season for them to arrive, so there was no reason to work.

When Kilat was not made to do small jobs about the hotel, he sold rugs and watches down by the waterfront. Today, it was not worth the effort, but he stuffed some watches in his pocket, just in case.

"You can stay here with me," their mother told the boys. But they shook their dark heads. It was more interesting down in town, now that they were growing up. Kilat took his brother's hand to show his mother how responsible he was.

The road into town wound round the hill. Going on foot, the boys took a shorter route. They walked down flights of stone steps which, according to legend, the gods had built to allow the first man and woman to climb out of the sea. Every stone was carved; did not steps too have souls, waiting to find expression through the soles of man?

The sun was already hot, but the boys walked in the occasional shade of trees. They had a fine view of the airstrip at one point, stretched like a sticking plaster on one of the few flat areas of the whole of Sipora. All was quiet there. Heat rippled over the runway so that its white lines wriggled like the worms dogs spewed.

"Why aren't the white planes flying?" Dempo asked.

"Perhaps the gods are not coming to Sipora any more."

"You mean the devils. It's better if they don't come, Kilat. No work for you and mother, isn't that a fact?"

"It's better if they come."

"But they spoil our island. Everyone says it."

"Still it's better if they come, Dempo. I can't tell you why but it is."

He knew that it was something to do with that huge world of affairs which began over the horizon. The schoolmistress had said as much.

As they negotiated the next section of stairs, the airport was hidden behind a shoulder of rock. Butterflies sailed between Upper World and Earth. The stairs twisted and they could see the little town, with its two big new hotels which were rivals to his mother's hotel. The Tinggi Tinggi had only six wooden rooms and no air-conditioning. The new hotels were of concrete; one had twelve bedrooms and the other sixteen little bungalows in its grounds. Among the trees behind the bungalows a part of the old village was preserved; its saddlebacked longhouses stood almost on the shore among the palm trees. Their roofs were no longer of thatch but corrugated iron which shone in the sun.

"The old village is excitingly beautiful," Kilat told his brother. He kept some brochures under his mattress which he saved when his mother's tourists threw them away. One of them had described the village – he had asked the schoolmistress what the English words meant – as "excitingly beautiful". It had completely changed Kilat's appreciation of the longhouses. Not that he believed them to be beautiful; he preferred the sixteen little concrete bungalows; but the words had mysteriously distanced him from what had once been familiar. In the photograph in the brochure, the longhouses on their sturdy stilt legs did look excitingly beautiful, as if they no longer formed a part of Sipora.

The steps finished where the slope became easier. Cultivation began immediately. Water buffalo were working in the fields, together with men, women, and some children. A Chinese tea-seller walked along the top of an irrigation dyke, his wares balanced at either end of a pole. Everything looked as normal, except that the tourist stalls which dotted the sides of the sandy road to town were shuttered and padlocked.

"This is where the white gods buy film for their cameras," Kilat said, indicating a stall where a Kodak sign hung. He spoke crisply, with assumed contempt – yet in a curious way he did feel contempt for these rich people who came for a day or two and then disappeared for ever. What were they after? They made so much noise and became angry so easily. They were always in a hurry, although they were supposed to be on a "holiday". It was beyond Kilat to understand what a "holiday" was. The elders said that the tourists from the north came to steal Sipora's happiness.

"They won't need any film now," Dempo said. "Perhaps they have taken enough pictures."

"Perhaps their own gods have stopped them flying in their planes."

They had both watched tourists photographing, jumping up and down and laughing as they watched, to see the way these lumpy people always pointed their cameras at the same things, and the most boring ones. Always the water buffalo, always the longhouses, always the tumbledown coffeeshop. Never the sixteen little concrete bungalows or the airport.

In the market square, they met other boys. Dempo played with his friend in a ditch while Kilat talked and joked with his. The weekly boat from Padang should have arrived this morning at nine, but had not done so – Kilat had looked for it from the mountainside and noted that it was missing. The world was mad. Or possibly it was dead. Just as the gods had created Sipora first, perhaps they had left it till last. Everyone laughed at the idea.

Later, George strolled by, as usual wearing nothing but a pair of rolled-up jeans and a battered hat. He was German or American or something, and he lived in a cheap *penginapan* called Rokhandy's Accommodation. George was known locally as The Hippie, but Kilat always called him George. George was about as thin as Kilat.

"I'm heading for the airport, Kilowatt. Like taking my morning constitutional. Want to come along?"

"Kilowatt" was just George's joke – not a bad one either, since Kilat's name meant "lightning". Kilat always enjoyed the joke, and he started walking beside George, hands in pockets, leaving Dempo to look after himself. He took long strides, but George never moved fast. George did not even have a camera.

They skirted the shore, where the wind-surfers lay forlorn with their plastic sails on the sand. Rokhandy himself, bored with the failure of his business, was sailing out on the strait, almost to where the wall of purple cloud began. George waved, but received no response.

"Seems like the good ole Western world has finally done itself in for sure. For fifty years they been shaping up for a final shoot-out. There's the lore of the other West, Kilowatt, old son, the one where the cowboys ride the range. Two brave men walking down Main Street in the noonday sun, one playing Goodie, one playing Baddie. They git nearer, and they don't say a thing and they don't change their expressions. And then – bang, bang – the fucking idiots shoot each other dead, 'stead of skedaddling off down a side alley, like what I'd have."

"Were you a cowboy once, Georgie?" Kilat asked. The Hippie went right on with his monologue.

"I feel kind of bad if that's like what's happened in real life. I'd say *our* president and *their* president seen too many them cowboy films, they finally put pride before common horse sense once too often – 'n' this time all the bystanders they got themselves killed as well. Serve 'em right trusting the sheriff. So I feel kind of bad, but let me tell you, Kilowatt, old son, I also feel kind of good, because I used to warn 'em and they took not a damned bit of notice, so finally I skedaddled down this here side-alley. And here I still am while bits of them are flying up in the clouds like snowflakes." He made a noise like a laugh and shook his head.

Some of this Kilat understood. But he was more interested in the lizards climbing over the cowling of the tourists' speedboats, beached like dead sharks. The man who ran the speedboats was sitting in the shade of a tree. He called to Kilat.

"Why don't you take a ride yourself, like Mr Rokhandy's doing?" Kilat asked him. "I'll come with you. I'd like a ride."

"Got no fuel," the man said, shaking his head. "No power. The oil tanker didn't come from Bengkulu this week. Pretty soon, everyone is going to be in trouble."

"He's always complaining, that man," Kilat told George, as they walked on.

The haze was creeping over the water from the north, where the sky was a livid purple.

The Hippie said nothing. He kept wiping his face with a dirty rag.

"I'm feeling low. I never trusted no sheriff . . . Jesus. . . ."

The airport was close now. They had merely to cut through the Holy Grove to reach the broken perimeter fence. But once they were in the shade of the trees, George uttered a sound like a muffled explosion, staggered to a carved stone, and threw himself down on it at full length.

"Rokhandy's wine is really bad," he said. "Not that I complain, and after all Rokky drinks it too, so fair's fair. All the same . . . Jesus. . . ." He sat up, rolling himself a joint from a purse full of the local *ganja*. "Suppose those cats have truly done for themselves this time round. Those big political cats. . . ."

Kilat sat and watched him with some concern. There were many things The Hippie did not understand.

"You're sitting on the tomb of King Sidabutar, George. Watch out he does not wake up and grab you! He's still got power, that old man. You're one of his enemies, after all."

"I'm nobody's enemy but my own. Jesus, I love old Sidabutar." George gave a slap to the warm stone on which he sat.

The stone formed the lid of an immense sarcophagus, shaped somewhat like a primitive boat, terminating in a brutal carved face.

The blind eyes of this face gazed towards the new airport and the mountain behind. Other tombs and menhirs stood among the trees. None was so grand as the king's tomb. Yet almost all had been overcome by the spirits of the trees.

These tombs were ancient. Some said they had existed since the dawn of the world. But the story of King Sidabutar was as solid as if itself carved in stone.

The people who lived on Sipora had once been part of a great nation. The nation lived far to the north, even beyond Sumatra, beyond Singapore, away in the Other Hemisphere. The nation had then been prosperous and peaceful; even the poor of the nation lived in palaces and ate off gold plate. So said the legend, so Kilat told it to George.

George had learnt patience. He lay on Sidabutar's grave and stared into the shimmering distance.

Powerful enemies came from further north. The nation fought them bravely, and the names of the Twelve Bloody Battles were still recalled. But the nation had to yield to superior numbers. Led by King Sidabutar, it left its homes and moved south in search of peace. Thousands of people, women and children along with the men, deserted their ancestral grounds and fled with their animals and belongings. The cruel invaders from the north pursued them.

There was no safety for them in the south. Wherever the beaten nation went, it was assailed. But the great-hearted king always encouraged his people; by force and guile he persuaded them to remain united against everything. They came at last to the sea. They crossed the sea, thanks to intervention by the gods, and settled in Sumatra, the Isle of Hope. Even in Sumatra, headhunters and other ferocious tribes made life miserable for the king's people. While some of the nation moved into the forests and mountain ranges of the interior, the king himself, accompanied by the ladies and gentlemen of his court, again crossed over the seas. So he came at last to the peaceful and fruitful island of Sipora.

By this time, King Sidabutar was an old man. Most of his life had been spent on the great journey, whose epic story would never be forgotten on Earth. When he reached the shelter of what is now the Holy Grove, he fell dying. His queen tended him and wept. The old King blessed the land and proclaimed with his dying breath that if the enemies of his people ever landed on Sipora, then he would rise up again in majesty, bringing with him all the Powers of the Upper World in vengeance.

"What a guy to have for a hero!" exclaimed George. He lay smoking his joint and looking up into the branches of the *hariara*, or sacred oak. The oak's roots had spread and widened, taking a grip on the king's sarcophagus with arms like veins of petrified lava.

"Sidabutar is the greatest hero in the world," Kilat said. "You ought to get off his grave."

"Sidabutar was a bum, a real bum. One of the defeated. He got his gang kicked out of wherever it was – somewhere up on the borders of China, I guess – and spent his whole life on the run, right? Always heading further south, out of trouble, right? Finally he freaked out here, on this little dump of an island in the Indian Ocean . . . Jesus, Kilowatt, that's the story of my life. Do you think some cat's going to be looney enough to raise up a stone tomb for me? No way. Old Sidabutar is just a plain bum, like me. A plain bum."

Kilat jumped up and started pummelling George in the chest. "You bastard! Just because you screw old Rokky's daughter every night, I know! Don't you say a word against our king. Otherwise he will fly right up and destroy you *flat*, just like America and Russia have been destroyed."

George rolled out of his way and laughed. "Yeah, maybe, maybe – and destroyed for the same good reason. Talking too much. Okay, man, I'll keep my trap shut, and you keep Rokky's daughter out of it, right."

Kilat was not satisfied. He was convinced he could sense King Sidabutar's spirit in the Grove. The curious thing was, he felt the same uncomfortable mixture of admiration and contempt for Sidabutar as he did for the white gods. If they were so clever, how come they ruined everything? If the king was so great, how come he let them ruin everything? They had brought gonorrhoea and other diseases to Sipora – the old king did nothing about it.

But he said no more, because Dempo came running through the trees. Between complaints that his big brother had left him, Dempo had a long story to tell about a *beruk* monkey escaping while climbing a coconut tree.

"Never mind," Kilat told him. "We are going with George to the airport. It's excitingly beautiful."

George nipped out his joint and they made their way through the sacred oaks, each one of which looked sinuous enough to contain a living spirit.

Since there was no traffic, the airport guards had gone home.

Nobody was about. They were able to walk right across the runway, across the magic white lines. The asphalt was hot to bare feet. Lizards scuttled away into holes as they went.

In the foyer of the airport building, two rows of floor tiling had been taken up and a trough chiselled in the concrete beneath, deep enough to take a new electric cable. But the cable had not materialised, and the trough lay like a wound across the empty space. Upstairs, a good many locals were gathered, to admire the view, to chat and pass the time. The kiosk was open, selling beer.

In the side window of the kiosk, a two-month-old newspaper had been hung. The paper was yellowing, the edges curling like an old leaf.

Under a headline reading SUPER POWERS END IT!!! was a report from Manila, describing how the long-anticipated nuclear war had broken out between the countries of the Warsaw Pact and the NATO Alliance. It was believed that Europe was destroyed. The Soviet Union had also fired its SS20s against China, who had not retaliated. The USA had made a massive retaliation, but was herself destroyed. The entire northern hemisphere was blanketed in radioactive dust-clouds. Manila was suffering. Nobody had any idea how many people had died or were dying. The monsoons were bringing death to India.

George glanced at this document and laughed bitterly. "If the poor old kicked-about planet can fix its circulation system properly, odds are on staying safe here in the Southern Hemisphere. Just don't let them ship in any of that radiation muck down here."

They talked to a lot of people, but only rumours could pass between them. Some said that Australia had been destroyed, some mentioned South Africa. Others said that South Africa was sending hospital teams to Europe. Kilat enjoyed just being in the lounge, with its map of world communications in marquetry on the wall. He felt powerful in the airport. This was the escape route to other lands, if they still existed.

"Will we be wiped out?" Dempo asked. "The white gods hate us, don't they?"

"No, nonsense. We are the lucky ones. The great body of Sumatra lies between us and all that destruction. Kerintji and the other giants will keep infection away from us."

He thought about his watches, and walked among the crowd trying to sell them. Nobody was in the mood for buying. One smartly dressed merchant said, shaking his head, "Watches are no good any more, my son. Time has run out." He looked very sad.

The airport siren sounded. An official in the uniform of Merpati marched into the lounge and addressed them. He held his hands up, palms forward, for silence.

"Attention. We are receiving radio messages from a plane in trouble in the area. We have signalled it to land in Bengkulu, but there is trouble in the plane – illness of some sort – and they are running out of fuel. The plane will land here."

A babble of questions greeted the statement. Men pressed forward on the official. He was a middle-aged man with greying hair. He smiled and waved his hands again as he backed away.

"Do not worry. We shall deal with the emergency." His words were drowned by the siren of an ambulance, swinging out of its garage on to the tarmac just beyond the reception lounge. "We ask all those who have no official business here please to quit the airport premises for their own safety. The plane is larger than the types officially designated to land here. We may have a little trouble, since the runway is too short in this instance. Please vacate the premises immediately."

More questions and excitement. The official held his ground and said, "Yes, yes, I understand your worries. No worries if you do not panic. Please evacuate the building peacefully. We understand the plane is American, bringing high-ranking officials from San Diego."

At the word "American", the panic got under way in earnest. Everybody started to run, down the stairs or simply round the lounge.

Kilat grasped Dempo's hand and charged downstairs. They elbowed their way out through the double glass doors. They had lost The Hippie, but Kilat did not care about that. He ran with Dempo, aiming for the airport fence. The fire engine went by. When he looked up, he saw the sky had hazed over. It felt suddenly cold.

Someone whistled. The boys looked and saw George leaning against the open doors of the ambulance garage. He beckoned them over.

They ran to him; he stooped to put his arms around them.

"Sounds like there might be a little excitement. Let's wait here. I want to get a look at these guys getting off this plane." He stared hard at Kilat, saying, "Heap bad medicine, Kilowatt."

He relit his joint, his soft face unusually grim. Kilat and Dempo squatted in the dust. They could look right across the airport to the Holy Grove, and through the grove to the sea, its surface sullen, no longer glittering.

"To see a plane come in from here will be excitingly beautiful. Have you ever been to San Diego, George?"

"If these cats survived, they have been underground, out of harm's way."

Kilat did not understand, and allowed himself to be cuddled only a minute. But he remained close to George.

After a while, George said, "Listen, Kilowatt, these cats are going to bring trouble. Plenty trouble. If they survived the holocaust and they've grabbed a plane, then they are bigwigs, that's sure. And if they come this far – like why not some place nearer home? – then it figures that some other guys along the way would not let them land, right? I'm telling you, these cats may be loaded with marines and god-knows-what, like bodyguards. They bring trouble."

"They'll – perhaps they'll be grateful to us. . . ."

"Grateful, shit. Cats with guns aren't grateful. They'll be looking for one last shoot-out."

"Maybe it's the President of the United States coming to visit us," Dempo said, hoping for reassurance. He looked frightened and clung to George's leg.

Kilat said in a small voice, "You think they might take Sipora over?"

"Why not? Why the hell not? I know these cats, think they own the world. Maybe your police should gun them all down as they cross the tarmac."

Kilat looked concernedly up into The Hippie's face. He could tell George was frightened. Overhead, the engine-roar grew slowly louder. The plane remained hidden in the overcast.

"We've only got six police and they've only got one gun between them. They're just for controlling tourists, that's all."

George looked wildly about. "Maybe the damned bird will crash if the runway's too short. Blow itself up and good riddance. We need those cats here like we need the clap."

Dempo started to jump up and down. "Oh, I hope it crashes! I hope it crashes! That would be really excitingly beautiful."

The airport was now a scene of wild action. Sirens were blaring, and people and cars were moving about the runways. The island's one police car was trying to hustle them out of the way. Centreline lights came on along the landing strips; high-density approach lights, white touchdown zonelights, winked on. Flags were rushed up masts. More people were running up from the direction of the town.

Suddenly the noise of the plane was louder. The craft emerged from the low cloud. It was enormous, silver, predatory, its under-carriage unfolding. It made the universe vibrate. Anyone sleeping anywhere on the island would have been awakened.

Dempo and Kilat fell over in awe.

The plane came roaring down, aiming straight for the ambulance shed, or so it appeared. Then, with a gust of wind which curled the dust off the airport, it was gone again. They saw its glaring jets before it vanished back into the cloudcover.

"Oh, it's gone away," cried the boys. "It's gone to Bengkulu after all."

All the people out on the airport ground had flung themselves flat. Now they got up and ran for safety, while the cars drove off in all directions, revving their engines and skidding to avoid collision.

"It'll be back," George said. He spat on the ground. "Pilot just took a look. His instruments must be malfunctioning. Who the hell could those guys be up there? Oh, I don't like this, I don't like this one little bit."

"It's the President, I know it," Kilat shouted. He had to shout. The noise was greater. The plane had turned over the strait and was coming in again.

"Run slap into the mountain, you bastard!" George called, raising a fist to the sky. "Leave us in peace."

They saw it then. This time it was much lower, spoilers up, ailerons going down, nose lifting. The undercarriage appeared to brush the tossing palms at the far end of the field. It looked too enormous and fast possibly to stop in the length of the island.

"Crash, you bastard!" George yelled as it rushed by, monstrous, bouncing, jarring. Grit whipped up into their faces. The scream of the tyres hit them. Then it was past.

It was slowing. Only a few hundred yards to go to the far fence. Both the ambulance and the fire engine were roaring along behind it.

The plane juddered as it braked while the fence came nearer. Now it might stop in time. But momentum carried it on. Stones flew.

Still thundering, the silver monster ran over the threshold mark-ings, bumped off the end of the asphalt, and crunched through a row of flashers. The people watching through the wire fence broke and ran.

The machine swerved, rammed a wing against the fencing and ploughed in a leisurely way through the side fence, striking its nose and one engine against palm trees. Part of the undercarriage snapped. The plane sank to one side as if going down on one knee. Smoke, steam and dust covered the scene.

"Jesus," said George.

"Jesus," said the boys in imitation.

The scene seemed to hold as if time had frozen. The diffused sunlight made everything shadowless. Then one of the emergency exits opened in the side of the plane. A yellow escape chute billowed out.

Passengers began to slide down the chute, one every one and a half seconds. They came down like dolls, only returning to life at the bottom as they picked themselves up. The smashed engine was smoking. Suddenly it burst into flame. Flames ran along the wing, rose up over the cockpit. Shouts came from the plane, another exit opened forward of the wing, uniformed men jumped out and fell.

"Wouldn't you know it – soldiers!" yelled George. "The Yanks are coming."

He started hurling abuse at the men lining up beside the yellow chute. They wore battle dress, helmets, and were armed with machine carbines.

The two boys could see that most of the men were in bad condition. Their faces were pale, their hair patchy. Some were bandaged. Some fell to the ground directly they exchanged the air-conditioning of the plane for the muggy atmosphere of Sipora. Although the fire was gaining hold, and their movements were panicky, the newcomers moved slowly and stiffly.

"They are ill," Kilat said. "They are bringing their diseases here. Let's skedaddle down a side-alley. . . ."

"There ain't no more side-alleys, son."

As the fire-engine drove up, the soldiers stopped it, aiming their weapons at the crew. Black smoke billowed across the tarmac.

Older men were now deplaning. They walked painfully towards the airport buildings. Most of them wore peaked caps with braid, and medal ribbons on their chests. An armed escort fell in and accompanied them, carbines at the ready.

"It's the fucking Chiefs of Staff!" George yelled. "Those are the bastards that started this war, and they think they can hide out in some damned bolthole in the Indian Ocean."

"They have the sickness," Kilat called, but George was already running out of the shelter, running across the concrete towards the approaching column of decrepit figures, swerving to avoid the oily smoke.

Kilat saw it happening, saw the muzzles of the guns go up, saw the faces of the soldiers. He never forgot the faces of those soldiers. They tightened their mouths, froze, became expressionless, and fired. Fired at George as he charged towards them, shouting.

The bullets came spanging in the direction of the boys. Kilat pulled Dempo to the floor as one smacked into the back of the garage. When he looked up, George had fallen and was rolling over and over in a curious way, kicking his legs. Then he stopped and lay still.

Even as George ceased to move, another noise added itself to the roar of fire.

It was a quite distinctive sound, like a whistle, like a giant's exhalation. The ground shook with it.

Among the trees opposite where the boys lay, clouds of steam billowed up. They concealed something rising from the earth itself, from a gaping tomb. A great figure grew taller. It came up like a rocket. Its head emerged above the crowns of the trees in the Holy Grove.

Smoke and steam wreathed that countenance like whiskers, but the expression of an anger implacable in intent was clear to see.

King Sidabutar had woken at last from his long sleep. He rose like vengeance, to summon up the Powers of the Upper World. Science was dead: now he was free to wreak destruction on his enemies.

(1984)

My Country 'Tis Not Only of Thee

The little lieutenant from Chicago said. "Remember, guys, the folk in the South are on our side. We're fighting for them. You can exploit 'em but you mustn't shoot 'em. Don't go getting no wrong ideas."

Huddled together, the troops laughed.

Lieutenants had been saying things like that for many years. Troops had been laughing like that for any years. At thirty-five thousand feet, when you are heading for action in an alien land way across the wide ocean, you laugh. It helps with the nerves.

People get hurt looking after Democracy.

From outside the craft, the scene must have appeared beautiful. The big troop carriers look so good with their heavy bellies and stub wings. As the planes came down towards a landing through the blue evening air, cloud layers floated up to meet them, layers burnished with gold. No sign, no whisper, of the catastrophe being played out below.

Nor was there in the troop carriers much sign of the sense of purpose, the vision, which had involved the American people in this distant struggle.

As the planes entered the cloud layer, the troops inside the heavy bellies fell silent. A lid was coming down on them. The thick moisture beyond the ports made the distance to the US almost tangible.

Then we were through the cloud.

Little could be seen. The sun was obscured. All below us was shadow.

We altered course, sinking. Suddenly the ground was close, dark, without detail. It promised nothing, said nothing, was silent under an ancient sense of outrage.

As we came in to land, a brief glimpse of ocean, with sun split wide like a split egg between cloud curtain and horizon. Tension, no speech. Smooth landing.

Amazing silence as the jets cut. Muzak: "Everything's Coming

Up Roses" for reassurance. By the look on some of the guys' faces, they were expecting to be fired on straight away. The approach and touchdown lights died. The glow around the perimeter indicated we were on a large base.

An officer in a jeep was waiting for me. The troops moved off under shouted orders. They became anonymous, war statistics. I remembered that eleven per cent of all our casualties were killed without actual combat, killed in enemy booby-traps: just part of the price of involvement in someone else's civil war. At least I was not Infantry.

The jeep drove me around to the far side of the air base. A helicopter gunship was waiting, big and clumsy, floodlights trained on its camouflaged flank. The lights turned the evening to total darkness. I inhaled before stepping aboard, trying to orient myself after several hours of dislocating flight. All I could smell was ozone and gasoline.

Two men searched me without interest or hope. I was then free to greet a tall hollow-chested man with greying hair cut short. He had a leathery countenance, thick eyebrows, and a belligerent jaw. Half-moon spectacles gave him a curiously mild look, despite contra-indications.

"My name is Gratinelli. I'm in Intelligence. You are James Lambard?"

When I said I was, he wanted to see my identification. Then he relaxed.

"Okay, Jim, take a seat right here. We'll be airborne soonest. Welcome to the war zone. We know you're special and we're glad you came over. You were born here, I understand?"

He must have known. He had seen my papers. He must have heard by my accent. He just wanted to hear it for himself.

"Okay, Jim. That's great. We're going to see to it that your mission is made as safe as can be."

He intended reassurance. I found him creepy. When he smiled, he showed a gold-capped tooth. My feelings were still ruffled from the journey. I felt it as a snub that an ally – that's what I was – should have been made to travel with infantry in a troop carrier when on a special mission. The gold tooth might have been planted just to annoy me.

The gunship lifted almost at once. Gratinelli told me to relax. We were flying ten miles along the coast to a R&R base where I would be properly briefed.

"You won't come across any VCs in this area."

Since I had no small talk, Gratinelli, speaking above the roar of the engines, gave me a lecture on how the war was necessary to defend the Free World. An expenditure of fire-power was the only effective argument the enemy understood. And in fact the war would have been won at least a year ago had it not been for the support coming in to the North from the outside. He let the word "outside" linger like a threat between us.

When I said nothing, he eyed me, I thought, with hostility, and began on another tack.

"Also, we would have less difficulty if the goddamned slimeys – I mean, sorry, I mean the South – was not so corrupt. Corruption is everywhere. You probably heard the President's speech. We are pledged to win not only a military victory over here, but a moral victory against hunger, disease, and despair. Vast quantities of material have been airlifted into your country, Mr Lambard. We have increased food relief for the countryside as well as the towns. Vehicles, machinery to build highways." He ticked the items off on his thumb. "Pharmaceutical factories, steel plants, garbage trucks. A massive aid program. What happens? They all disappear. Just vanish. Might as well pour the money down the sink."

"Too bad," I said.

"*Too bad . . .*" he echoed, scornfully. "Widespread corruption. We're after the hearts and minds of these people. What do we get? This shit."

I sat with my hands on my knees, avoiding his gaze.

The helicopter sank on to its landing pad. Brilliant lights showed round us. A reluctance to leave the machine overwhelmed me, so sure was I that I was on the fringe of some humiliating experience; although his condemnation was couched in familiar terms, it remained oppressive. Gratinelli gestured impatiently. I climbed out with him close behind me.

As we got into the waiting jeep, he said, "You're assigned to the Metro. Quite a comfortable hotel, if old-fashioned. Get a night's rest, and the men who will escort you on your mission will be round at eight in the morning. Be ready for them." He gave me an Army pass.

"Where are we, exactly?"

"The troops call this Sugar City. It's where they come for R&R." He gave a dry laugh, showing the gold-capped tooth again.

The Metro proved to be a large hotel almost on the waterfront.

Its grand crumbling façade stretched upward into the night, seemingly without termination, since a garish neon sign with kicking dancing girls over the main foyer dazzled the eyes, making the darkness darker.

I slung my pack over one shoulder and jumped on to the pavement. The jeep bore Gratinelli away into the night.

A crowd of GIs, garishly dressed local girls, and kids swarmed about the steps of the Metro. Youths roared about on Hondas, miraculously avoiding running into anyone. Beggars and vendors were everywhere. A boy tried to sell me a watch. All along the front by the Metro were hotel signs, dance signs, bar signs, massage signs. American music blared, pops. competing with blue grass, country, jazz. I stood there in a mood of dull amazement before pushing through the crowd and entering the hotel.

The foyer was as disorderly as the front.

Military police were on duty, too busy with girls to take any notice of new arrivals. Couples were coming and going everywhere. Raucous laughter sounded from a lounge bar, where a sailor could be glimpsed, dancing on a table. Going up in the elevator after I had checked in, I pushed among men kissing and feeling girls who could scarcely have been more than thirteen.

My room was at the back, small, uninviting. I sat on the bed. The whole hotel pulsed with its transitory life like a coral reef. A painful anguish seized me. Anything was better than solitude, trapped in one cell of this labyrinth. I had to get a girl myself.

She was young and said her name was Velvet. I picked her up in the foyer. Rather, she chose me. She generally worked with a friend, but the friend was ill tonight. She opened her legs and invited me in.

Afterwards, as she washed herself, she did not wish to talk. She knew very little, but she said a general had told her that Sugar City's population of a half-million had swollen to three million since the Americans had arrived. Surrounding the central area was a city of refugees and derelicts from the war further north. Velvet grew spiteful when I questioned her further. I let her go.

After a restless night, I rose and showered. I watched the TV intermittently while I dressed and drank a cup of coffee. There were only American stations, run by local US Armed Forces Networks. The news concerned the capture of a VC General, Tom Gardale, apparently the most brilliant general fighting for the North. There was also a one-minute burst of hate for the IRA, fighting against the South, and responsible for blowing up a US naval frigate in Plymouth harbour, with the loss of nine lives. The Irish government was being denounced by Washington for supporting the IRA.

These news items were perfunctorily done. An incest case in San Antonio got more coverage. There were old cartoons and the customary pap, shovelled out in the usual half-joking American way, all interspersed by items from home: how rain persisted in the Detroit area and a high pressure ridge was stable over Seattle and the Pacific Northwest.

In came my two American escorts. One went straight over and switched off the television without invitation.

"Sure thing, American wealth and technology allows us our own little enclaves over here," one of them said, in answer to a comment I made. "You don't expect us to exist on their standard of living, for god's sake. The local culture has nothing to offer."

"A thousand years of history?"

"Forget history. This dump is falling apart at the seams. If you want my personal opinion, we should hand it over to the VCs. But the US always honours its treaties. Worse luck."

At that they both laughed. The men were in their early twenties. Solid energetic young men with pale heavy faces. Hair short, uniform casual. One wore a big cowboy hat. Both were army officers and carried revolvers. One of them had the Stars and Stripes tattooed on his biceps. They told me their names were Pedro and Len. Pedro was the one with the cowboy hat and the tattoo. Their manner towards me was a mixture of friendliness and insult: I was familiar with it from my years in Florida.

We ate a quick breakfast in the hotel dining room. The windows looked out across the sea. The sun shone as if disaster never happened. With the tide out, the beach glittered in the sunlight.

Already there were guys about, soldiers on R&R, stumbling along, clutching girls. Pedro and Len made a hearty breakfast of pancakes with sausages and hash browns. They complained about the quality of the food as they devoured it. It was better back home. I drank coffee, listening to their contempt.

"You despise this place," I said to the one who had last spoken. He was Len.

"No offence, Jim, but what else? Look, we have to be over here putting things to rights. We don't have to like it. See, I'm well-informed on the general picture. The country was divided, North and South. It's poor up North, real poor, so they turned to Communism. Those sons of bitches will not stay put in the North. They keep infiltrating across the frontier. It's like a contagion, and the slimeys in the South just don't have the motivation to kill the VCs in any whole-hearted way."

"We try to slam a little spirit into them," Pedro said. He smiled a lot more than his partner. "Like you know why they are called VCs? Because their leader is a Southerner. He got started in a town called Ventnor on an island out in that ocean there." He pointed through the window with his fork. "VC stands for Ventnor Commies. Maybe you know. Somehow the name stuck – nostalgia, maybe. But when the US weighed in, one of the first things we did was take out Ventnor and the island, so that at least the South was safe in our hands. I suppose you saw that on TV back in Florida, but I was here on my first tour of duty and I saw it happen. It's history. You feel proud to be part of history."

He gave a drum-roll with two heavy fingers on the edge of the table.

"History," Len said thoughtfully. "Give me Atlanta, Georgia, every time. Stuff history. History is for heroes."

"What do I have to do?" I asked, when they finally got to the coffee and cigarette stage. They sized me up and Pedro gave a secret smile.

"You went to school at a place called Christ Church College. That right?"

"Not a school. University. A college at a University. What about it?"

"Okay." He exaggerated his patience. "You went to University at a place called Christ Church College?"

"Just called Christ Church. It is a college but it is just called Christ Church. That's the tradition."

Smiling even more heavily, Pedro slammed his fist to the table. "Don't give me that slimey shit. From now on it's Christ Church College, okay? Let's be clear, okay?"

"The foundation dates back to the time of Henry VIII. You can't simply change things overnight that – "

He interrupted with another bang on the table. "Listen, we don't have to take crap, Lambard. Just so you know this dump we're talking about, that's enough. Screw history. How long were you there?'

"Three years. The statutory period."

"Three years. So you would remember your way around?"

"Of course. If the college is still intact."

"Jesus. Henry the Eighth," Len said, belatedly. "You slimeys really are a caution. Didn't he have seven or eight wives?"

Ignoring him, Pedro said, "The VCs have got a VIP locked up in Christ Church College. We want that guy. He is valuable to both sides and we need him. You are going to help us. Understand?"

"Who is this guy? A secret agent?"

"There won't be much danger. The less you know, the better," Pedro said. He stubbed out his cigarette forcefully, as if illustrating his point.

"Who is he?"

"Code name Hawk," Len said. "We need him, okay? Let's move. We're going to get you into local clothing and then we'll hit the trail. It isn't going to be dangerous."

They had both told me that. It did not make me feel happier. Nor did the underlying assumption that because of my nationality I must be a coward. I followed them from the dining room.

We took a route north from Sugar City. I could see for the first time what had become of the land in which I had been born.

The disaster which had overtaken it had been twofold.

Firstly, during the eighties, high rates of unemployment, an indifferent government, and inner city decay, coupled with inevitable problems of racism, had led to demonstrations and ferocious rioting in the North, that part of the country worst hit by the poverty trap. The rioting was met by increasingly repressive measures from a police force once renowned throughout the world for its restraint. Several pitched battles were fought, notably in Leeds, Liverpool and Sheffield. Liverpool had become the HQ of a rebel army, supplied with war material coming from the country's traditional enemies in the Marxist camp. As the news bulletin I had seen admitted, the IRA was also active. There are always many who wish to see society destroyed.

In the nineties, decline was rapid. Police were defeated at the Battle of Warrington, with three hundred of them mowed down by machine-gun fire. The government in the affluent South decided to divide the country, leaving the North to its own increasingly anti-establishment devices. Despite trails of refugees wending north and south, a wall – the infamous Cotswold Wall – for many miles little more than a few strands of barbed wire – marked a physical division between the two halves of the country.

Secondly, the USA had moved to the aid of its ancient democratic ally, the land from which so many of its own traditions, legal and cultural, had come. Many voices urged the President not to take such a step. The parallels with the Vietnam War, still a scar in many minds, were stressed. But the military argued that all that was needed was an increased presence. American bases had to be defended. There were treaty obligations through NATO. And there was, as there had been in World War II, strategic value to an island lying off the coast of a Europe also undergoing a series of violent disruptions in many major cities. So a presence was maintained, and increased. Pressure induces counter-pressure. Islamic insurgency was added to Marxist strength in the North. Infiltration into the South continued. Month by month, the American presence in the South was increased. There was no pulling back.

"We're after the hearts and minds of these people," Gratinelli had said, echoing his President's words. But those in the South, in the old capital of London, had seen the corruption that American wealth brought in its wake. They watched hungrily as sky-cranes flew in meat and beer for the daily barbecues behind defended US enclaves. They became sucked into the dirty trades that black-marketeering brings. About the US bases grew tatty tinsel towns constructed from waste, the non-bio-degradables of plastic packing cases and wrappings from which brothels, cafes, bars, dope-shops and the rest could be constructed. Goods and equipment from the base made their way through the wire in a steady stream, paying for services which a ruined country readily supplies. And every weekend, the casualties – the men with AIDS and the new quick-syph and chancres and hepatitis cases with dirty needles and the poisoned and the maimed who had driven drunkenly off the winding local roads – every weekend, these casualties were shipped back to the States on special hospital flights, or flown to secret recovery bases in the Mediterranean, away from the investigative eye of reporters. The States itself was torn apart by this new overseas war.

The route from the south coast northwards ran over downland. Apart from some encampments, the country looked much as ever. There were few people about. Those who walked by the road froze as we passed. The sight of a US uniform was enough to stop them in their tracks. They knew GIs fired at moving targets, in a war where they could not tell one side from the other.

Over the downs, towards the outskirts of London, change was more apparent. Sprawling shanty towns had gone up. By Purley, these makeshift quarters were visible on either side. The road became fenced and roofed with electrified fencing, so that civilians could not interfere with troop movements. Beyond the fencing people stood, looking into the road, sullen, unmoving. They were in the main the people who had fled from the North and found no shelter, no trust, in the homes of relations.

"Slimeys! Lost the gift of movement," Pedro said. I thought I disliked him more than Len. It was something to do with his sunny smile.

Our vehicle and the two vehicles escorting us were halted at a barrier. Our credentials were checked. Someone had blown up a lorry a mile ahead and the road was blocked. We were sent on a detour.

So we drove through the heart of London.

Everywhere were stamped the insignia of decay. No building had been maintained. Paint had come near no dwelling in the last fifteen years. Gutters and roofs had not been repaired. Many of the streets we drove through were boarded up, perhaps by the military to facilitate their movements. As we drove along Millbank, burnt-out buildings confronted us on either side of the Thames. Military traffic could be seen patrolling on the river.

Some of the famous landmarks had gone.

The House of Commons, that individual gothic building, had disappeared, and Big Ben along with it. The entire structure had been bought by a consortium of billionaires, and shipped to Arizona stone by stone where, with the aid of computers, it had been assembled just as before, to stand on the lip of the Grand Canyon, an object of reverence and curiosity for the tourist trade. It housed an unrivalled collection of old pin-table machines.

"We got to many of the old art treasures before the VCs ruined them," Len said. "The entire contents of the National Gallery are now safe in an annexe of the Smithsonian, as maybe you heard. Worth millions. Millions." He repeated the word with satisfaction.

The Stars and Stripes flew over Buckingham Palace, dominating the Union Jack. An immense battery of tanks and weaponry was drawn up in front of the palace. There were no tourists, no guards in scarlet uniforms and bearskins.

"That's where we have your royal family, Jim," Len said.

"They're safe as long as they are there, and we take good care of them."

Pedro laughed. "Imagine – the Canadians wanted to take them over. Some chance. . . ."

We drove on, to stop for a break in a new barracks area in Hyde Park. Then through Paddington to the Oxford road.

Paddington was in ruins. The whole area had been reduced to rubble. The IRA had been at work. Later, a wide road had been bulldozed through the rubble. Again, the local population was kept off the road by electrified fencing. Behind the fencing, clusters of stalls had been set up. I saw men and women climbing over piles of bricks to see what trade was to be had. All were thin and crudely dressed. As our cars went by they froze.

I noted that Len and Pedro kept carbines ready in case of trouble, but there was none.

Vegetation had sprung up among the ruins. Beds of a pink flower, rose-bay willow-herb, created a little beauty among the blackened debris.

Driving up the Thames Valley was no longer the pleasant experience it had been when I had first gone to the University of Oxford. Here were more indicators of the disaster which had overtaken my country. Whole towns evacuated, prison camps set up, immense fortifications, airfields, mobile guns on the move, convoys, once a wood on fire. The only moving figures we saw were Americans. They were everywhere: marching, directing the traffic, swarming over vehicles, drinking. Old Glory hung everywhere, limp in the mild afternoon sun. I was in an occupied country.

Before Henley, we had to detour to avoid a pitched battle. The US forces, perhaps out of contempt for the opposition, were careless. They commanded heavy armour but not vigilance. The average GI had no stomach for defending Europe. So the guerillas from the North, with a few well-placed mines, were often able to raid camps for supplies or capture whole convoys.

Three Tomcats screamed overhead, cannons blazing. The noise went straight through to the very fibres of being.

"Give it to the bastards!" Len shouted after them. He went into a story about how he had been on a patrol outside Norwich when one of the men triggered an IRA mine of the kind known as a Jumping Jenny. When a boot touched a concealed prong, the mine jumped a metre in the air before exploding. Len's friends were reduced to an area of raw shredded meat around the spot, with red tissue and

white bone splinters sprayed everywhere. Len was lucky. He had
just skipped behind a big tree to urinate. He was the only one to
survive. Len seemed more friendly after he had told me this.

"I'm sorry about your friends."

"Forget it."

I remembered when I had first gone up to Oxford, to Christ
Church, that most beautiful of colleges. The start of my first
academic year. Oxford seemed to me a peaceful and civilised place.
True, there was much talk of the country's economy declining, with
manufacturing industry closing down; and there were strikes and
the occasional riot. Troop movements increased, along with demonstrations. But none of it touched Oxford. Oxford had been there
since the thirteenth century. It was impossible to imagine its green
lawns besmirched, its welcoming libraries looted. Wrapped up in
our own little lives, we had not taken alarm.

But my father had. My father ran a successful chain of trendy
clothes stores, some in high streets, some within department stores.
He often visited his shops in the North.

At the Glasgow store, he received a threatening letter. Someone
did not approve of the way the profits of the branch went south. My
father ignored the letter. On his next visit, he was attacked by three
men in a side street when returning to his hotel. He carried an
illegally purchased British Army revolver. As the men came up, he
drew the gun and fired. One man fell. Panic seized my father. As
the other two froze, he shot them too. I remember his return home
in a state of shock.

The incident changed our lives. My father became a haunted
man. He saw the civil war coming, sold up the clothes chain and
our house, and took us over to live in the States, in Florida, where
many other English were settling. I managed to get a porter's job on
the local air base.

In Florida we are the poor whites. Why are we so unpopular?
Because the war is unpopular. American viewers are tired of seeing
their boys being blown up outside Leicester and Stow-on-the-Wold.
Escalating costs, escalating deaths: for these we are in some way
responsible.

I believe it. We are responsible. We didn't care enough in the
good years. We didn't care when millions of people went on the
scrap pile of unemployment. We thought all the American talk
about Democracy and Eternal Vigilance was crap. So it may be. But
we tried to live without Democracy and Eternal Vigilance and it

finished us. Throughout the eighties our divided society had ceased to believe in the idea of equal rights for the individual.

Oxford was only a few miles south of the Cotswold Wall. Big US air bases lay nearby, together with a store of missiles and nuclear weapons – so far unused but kept perpetually on the ready for the next stage of the war, which many saw as inevitable. Infiltration from the North was constant. Both sides saw that when London was blotted out, Oxford would make a suitable second capital for government. Hitler had had the same idea long ago, refraining from bombing the ancient city in consequence.

Now it was less privileged. Evidence of damage was clear, as we studied the city through binoculars from an adjacent hill. I wondered as I viewed it, Did you teach us aright?

Pedro and Len gave me a casual briefing. By now I had the two of them separate and distinct. Their manner was basically sullen, perhaps of a cultivated sullenness in order to keep me in my place but more likely an attitude fostered by their resentment at being here at all. But Len, I now perceived, was the stronger of the two. He was a stolid individual, even likeable in a way. His cold, deliberate manner was part of his approach to life – a life which, from various hints he let fall, seemed to have been spent surviving in the tougher districts of Atlanta, Georgia. He did not like England, but to Len it was merely an extension of back-street existence.

In some curious way, Len – neither he nor Pedro would reveal their surnames – wanted to secure my liking. He explained to me with care that the US was in my country legally, in response to treaty obligations and the obligations of a long-standing relationship between our two nations.

Pedro laughed when he heard this. I did not laugh.

Pedro was from Detroit. His real name was Peter, but his wife was Mexican. Watching him as we travelled – for my life might depend on understanding the two officers – I saw his nervousness. His sullen manner hid fear. He took his cues from Len and tried to imitate his manners. He was a minor academic in civilian life, now trying to be one of the bunch. Perhaps his tattoo was another of his bids to be thought something other than he was; he had acquired it in Sugar City. As he saw that Len and I were reaching a kind of tacit understanding, Pedro became more personally edgy.

Our vehicles were drawn up in what had been the garden of a private house. The house had been hastily fortified at one time, since it commanded a good view of Oxford. It was now deserted, with that woebegone look of a building for whom maintenance is a forgotten word. Sycamore seedlings sprouted in its gutters. Its roof sagged and there were damp stains on its stuccoed walls.

With friendly insults, the soldiers dispersed themselves about the garden, negligently keeping watch. Lighting cigarettes, they adopted casual poses. The radio operator took messages back and forth between the officers and his set. Why was it all like a play? I asked myself. Had Americans so far embraced unreality that they did not believe in death?

The three vehicles were drawn up on what had once been lawn. We looked over shaggy hedges of *lonicera* and laurel towards the old city.

"There's Christ Church," I said. "You can see Tom Tower." The famous tower gleamed in the afternoon sun. Something seemed to flutter in my throat as I stared at it. I was looking back at the peaceful past we had lost, which could never return.

The Cumnor Hills to the west of Oxford were yellow, not with autumn but with Agent Orange defoliant. Near at hand, the trees were blighted and woebegone. It was as if we stood on the edge of a bowl of rotting salad.

As we stared, tracer bullets came spanging through the hedge just to the left of us. They hit the side of the house behind us and went ricocheting off into space. We dropped immediately, faces in early summer buttercups.

My first experience of being under fire was immensely exciting. I was not frightened. Rather, it occurred to me that the experience was right and just. Everything that had gone before had prepared me for being shot at in my own native land.

Pedro retrieved his cowboy hat. He jumped up and was peering through cover. There was nothing to be seen. He thrust his fists into his pockets.

"Some bastards got the approaches covered," he muttered.

"All those towers down there make great snipers' posts," Len said. He was very calm. He looked at me almost with approval, one eyebrow raised, as if to say, See what we're up against?

Shivering fits began inside me, although I remained unfrightened. I hid them as best I could, wishing I were back in bed with Velvet, her arms about me.

The two officers lit a joint and shared it between them.

Sheltered by hedge, our backs against the wall of the house, they gave me the rest of my orders, one sitting one side of me, one the other.

Half of Oxford was in enemy hands – that is, held by the North. The South, after initial resistance, had accepted the situation. Separated only by no-go areas, the two sides lived in truce together, thus proving the American hypothesis that both were rotten with Communism. It was left to the States to stir things up in the old city and awaken British fighting spirit now and again.

"We go get Hawk as soon as we get the signal over the air," Pedro said, leaning his head against the wall behind and inhaling deeply.

"When do we get the signal?"

He shrugged. Neither he nor Len answered me. Pedro's smile had become a grimace. I could not look at him. The soldiers were reappearing from various hiding places, sheepishly lighting up fresh cigarettes.

No more shots sounded. Perhaps the firing had been random. We sat mute.

After a while, Len rose and went across to the radio operator. Pedro followed. Opening his hand, Len took over the operator's headphones.

He stood tethered to the vehicle by the headphones.

"No decision," he said finally to Pedro. They lit another joint. When it grew dark, Len kicked in the door of the house. We established occupancy, taking the radio with us. Screens were put up against the window of a downstairs room. There was no electricity, but a battery light was lit.

After a while, we ate sausages and beans from self-heating cans, followed by ice-cream and coffee.

Consultations with the men were intermittent. Although they were there to protect us, the arrangements appeared casual. A machine gun was mounted in the grounds of the house, and a sentry posted. Pedro and Len brought out collapsible beds. I slept beside them, rolled in a khaki army blanket.

Towards dawn, I was woken by their boots on the bare floor and their subdued voices. The other men were in the room, and all were in a state of suppressed excitement. I propped myself on one elbow.

"Get up, Jim," Len said. "We're on the move."

"What is it?"

"Signal came through, that's all. Get up."

They were looking at each other from under eyebrows, with

pleased, eager expressions. I was excluded from their circle of quiet triumph.

"Operation Hawk," Pedro said, with relish. He shaved with a cordless razor.

Dawn was seeping from behind the blackout. I peered round the screen. The garden was grey, with a discarded look, as if it were an old indoor film set. Nothing moved there. Everything had gone away.

One of the drivers hustled in with a canister of coffee and mugs. We drank standing up. Still the Americans talked in low voices full of expectation, their occasional glances in my direction debarring me from their secrets.

We pissed in the garden before climbing into the vehicles. As we rolled forward, Pedro opened up a bag and passed me over a revolver. He grinned at me without showing his teeth.

"Stick this in your pocket. Listen to orders. We're aiming to halt before we hit this college of yours, okay? You're to go on on foot. You're an ordinary civilian. Remember, the college is in the hands of the VC, so you say you are from the North. Get inside, ask for a job. Hawk is kept in an upstairs room, so Intelligence says. Get him out of there. We'll be outside to give you support."

"How do I do that? How do I get him out?"

"We'll be outside with the cars. The quick getaway. First, you bring him out. He's in the Bursary, according to our Intelligence."

I found myself waving my hands at him.

"Who is this Hawk? What's his real name? This is crazy!"

Len leaned forward and said, reassuringly, "He's no one. We need him, Lambard, and we trust you." Here he gripped my knee to steady my resolve. "We'd join you, happen we didn't look so American."

That being undeniable, I sat tight as we bumped down the neglected road, trying to rehearse what I might do. After all, I was going to be among my own people, in my own College. Although I had been out of touch with events, except as reflected through the distorting lens of American TV, I could rely on my native wits to see me through.

The revolver helped my courage. The memory of my father's bravery in killing three attacking Northerners put spirit into me.

As we rolled into the town, past a check point set up by the forces of the South, a dull roar like that of an earthquake filled the air.

Like the roar of an earthquake, it seemed to come from all sides at once.

Overhead in the pale blue sky planes were flying. Pedro pointed upwards with the muzzle of a carbine and let out a cheer. The planes moved steadily, lines of them, high, heading westwards.

At the bridge over the Isis called Folly Bridge stood another check-point. Here our small convoy stopped; the vehicles were backed into a concealing side lane. Christ Church loomed on the rise a short way ahead. The venerable foundation made an ornamental kind of fortress. The flag of the North, the Red Rose, flew from its towers.

People I passed in the street harboured a skulking look, a tendency to hide their chins behind their shoulders. The old and the very young were represented only. Several carried boxes or bore bundles of sticks. Most of the women walked with dogs. Their clothes were neutral in colour, their eyes downcast but mobile in their set faces. I thought, They scarcely look English.

A woman with an old tartan rug over her shoulders went to the great gate of Christ Church, under Tom Tower. She carried a basket of goods, possibly laundry, her manner anxious. Someone opened the door set in the gate and she slipped in.

Momentarily uncertain, I paused, glancing round. Len was following, some way back down the street. He made no gesture when he saw me looking at him. I went ahead under the shadow of the portal and knocked on the worn door.

When the door opened, I explained to the eye presenting itself that I was looking for work. A porter dragged the door wider and admitted me. I was immediately seized. Two men in camouflage jackets pinned me to the inside of the great gate. They searched me roughly. My revolver was removed from my pocket.

I stood with my face pressed to the rough timber, listening as one of the men examined the weapon. "No firing pin," he said, contemptuously. I heard my revolver thrown into a nearby bin. They both laughed and stood back.

They let me go without question, motioning me away.

What had been a spacious quadrangle – Mercury – was now filled with sheds containing the vehicles of mobile units, battered lorries and Land Rovers. Under the cloisters surrounding Mercury, stalls had been established – to sell what I could not see. People were coming and going, mainly young men in a kind of uniform and young women scantily dressed. A sense of unreality possessed me as

I witnessed this degradation of a revered seat of learning. It might all have been a strange charade enacted for my benefit, a parable of folly.

To add to the feeling of unreality, planes were still droning overhead on their westward path. The sky was now full of them. Nobody in the quad was paying them any attention.

A few people were casting glances in my direction. The influence of American propaganda caused me in part to regard the VC as enemies; yet, since I had not been personally involved in the civil war, I felt in part that they were merely fellow-countrymen. All the same, I began to walk as if with innocent purpose towards where the Bursar's office had been situated in my day.

Discreet windows which had once been closed were now thrown wantonly open. Glass was missing in many cases. Trousers, skirts, long-johns, hung over the sills to dry. I reached a stone staircase and ascended to the upper level. Looking back, I saw that one of the soldiers who had frisked me was following me.

This decided me to act fast. I would enter the bursar's office and ask for work. Perhaps I should demand to join the VC. Perhaps I should reveal that I was an old student of Christ Church. Perhaps there would be some clue as to who or where Hawk was.

The door still bore a small brass plate saying Bursar. I knocked and went in.

An elderly man, very square, sat with arms folded against the window. Nearer at hand was a tough black sergeant in a red beret and green uniform, pointing a sub-machine-gun at me. In that frozen moment, I heard the planes still passing overhead, wave after wave. The Red Rose hung over the stone fireplace.

I turned too late. The soldier who had been following me ran up and stuck a gun into my spine. I did as I was told, moving reluctantly into the room. The door was slammed behind us. The three men regarded me with satisfaction.

The man in the window came over to inspect me. He had an immense expanse of face, most of it whiskered or wrinkled, with a great nose and a mouth that remained slightly open, as if he were about to bite. He scrutinised me unblinkingly, almost as if I were a piece of furniture.

"Papers," he said, holding out a hand.

"Are you Hawk?"

"Papers."

I handed them over.

"James Malcolm Lambard. Good. Sit in that chair."

I did as I was told and the tension in the room eased.

"Your father, Arthur Lambard, is a war criminal."

"My father is dead. And he was certainly no criminal."

"His name remains registered as a war criminal with the Government of the North. Three deaths to answer. His anti-Communist activities are well-known."

Terrible confusion ran through me. Among the old college photographs and engravings on the wall was a portrait of Lenin. It disoriented me.

"There's been a misunderstanding," I said. "I have come just to meet a man called Hawk."

"We'll be sending you to a prisoner-of-war camp near Bootle, Lambard. A tribunal will try you and adjudge your classification. There is no Hawk. It's a code name. Once you step into Christ Church with a revolver with no firing pin and ask for Hawk, you are delivered. Like a parcel."

He was turning away as he spoke, throwing my papers on his desk and motioning to the armed men to march me off. I jumped up. Before I could take a step towards him, I was seized roughly and held.

"This is all crazy. I've done nothing wrong. Let me go at once." I shouted madly until the sergeant punched me in the ribs.

"You're co-operating with the American enemy." The man at the window spoke without looking round at me.

"But if I understand you, you are co-operating with them too."

"Not co-operation. It's an arrangement on a war footing." He turned round to me as if suddenly pleased and said, "We collect little men like you, Lambard. The Yanks are happy to hand you over. When we get enough of you we exchange you for a Big Name the Yanks are holding. There's another war going on – a diplomatic war – and it looks good for both sides if we exchange a few bodies we don't need. The United Nations approves of that sort of thing. Keeps the Third World quiet. You may be part of a deal for our General Gardale, held by the Yanks. Just behave yourself, you'll be okay."

As the guards led me from the room, I shouted, "I thought you people hated the Yanks. You're in league with them."

He had returned to the window, to stand looking out at the planes overhead, and did not reply. The door slammed.

As they led me away, the black sergeant said, "You want to keep your mouth shut, mate, or you'll be in trouble. Course we hate the bloody Yanks, but the real enemy's the South. The Yanks'll have to go away in the end, same as they did in Vietnam. Pack up and go."

"They'll never go. They believe they have a duty to this country. They still have a vision of saving the world."

We came out into Mercury. Armed vehicles were revving up. I could see other prisoners, a dejected bunch, standing handcuffed behind a lorry.

The sergeant gave me a push from behind. "Saving the world from what? That persistence of vision will ruin them – and us. You know nothing, Lambard. You bloody chose to clear off – into their camp. The Yanks will over-reach themselves, like they did before. Then the US public'll get pissed off of the whole shooting match. They won't want to know about Europe, will they? – won't want to stump up the taxes necessary to save the world."

A fit of trembling made me weak. I staggered, and the stone buildings seemed to whirl about me. I fought not only to keep my balance but to fend off the extent of my betrayal.

"They saved the world before . . . Europe . . . World War II. . . ."

His hand was tight round my arm, steadying me and shaking me at the same time. His big face came close to mine.

"They're too stinking rich to go through that stuff again. Too stinking rich. Now stop blowing your mouth and move it."

"Listen – when I get back – if I'm exchanged . . . I'm going to tell this whole rotten Hawk story to the world. Then you'll – "

He hit me with his fist in the stomach, so that I doubled up, gasping for breath. So much fury at the injustice of things rose in me that it burst out as hot tears, springing from my eyes to the stones below my feet.

The sergeant straightened me up, saying, quite gently, "Who's going to believe what you say? No one will listen – on our side, or on their side. You're discredited, Lambard. Now, come on, move it, man."

His words were lazily delivered, without malice, and he stood there a moment while I got my breath back, thinking there was rough justice in what the sergeant said. Much had been discredited by war – not I alone. The planes still roared overhead.

"Saving the world for Democracy, shit!" he said, and laughed.

I said nothing. He was producing a chit and signing me over. As a corporal took me into custody, the sergeant said, almost pityingly,

"You're dumb, Lambard. What price their latest move? Didn't the Yanks tell you before they sold you down the river? They're re-enacting Cambodia now."

Seeing that I didn't immediately take his meaning, he said, "Washington has just decided to attack the IRA direct. The loonies have begun the strategic bombing of Ireland. A neutral country. . . ."

Raising my eyes, I saw the long-range bombers crossing a sky that was now a clear hard blue.

As we prisoners were herded into the waiting trucks, loudspeakers round the quadrangle blared forth the martial noise of the national anthem, "There'll Always Be North England".

(1986)

Infestation

This is what Marigold Amery did, that morning when the Amery family's *jaskiferianni* returned.

She got breakfast for her bedridden mother, Doris Meszoly, before presiding over the breakfast table downstairs, at which her husband, Hector Amery, and her widowed younger sister, Viola Parkinson-Hill, were present. It was Saturday, so neither Hector nor Viola was at work. Marigold met and kissed Hector when he came in from the garden pool. She then went shopping in the village supermarket, taking the Porsche, and joining her friend Mary-Rose Cargill for coffee. She returned home, phoned her son in Manchester, and sat in the garden in the sunshine reading Hesse's *Steppenwolf* for the fifth time.

She had read the novel first some years back, in a Spanish translation in Buenos Aires; Marigold was then living with a musician older than she who had taught her many things. Hesse's book was one of the musician's heritages. Marigold read again of the steppenwolf and its indifference to the life of the bourgeois, and of that "last extremity of loneliness which rarefies the atmosphere of the bourgeois world". She thought, How true, and wondered why this bitter knowledge comforted her. It was then that the *jaskiferianni* materialised inside her, almost knocking her out of her lounger with a cold dose of surprise.

"Enter, you vile poison," she said, as if uttering whatever kind of welcome took off somewhat from the violation of her privacy. By this time, Marigold was more intrigued by it than frightened.

She put a hand over her eyes as cold parts of the thing slipped in among her consciousness. The alien made her get up and walk about the garden, staring at plants, before it flung her back into the chair again. It held her motionless for half-an-hour while she tried to hum Mozart's 39th at it. But was it listening?

Marigold lay there with the book beside her. The *jaskiferianni* left with no signal of departure beyond a cryptic picture of endless coiled piled grey things. What were they? The thing itself? Its world? There was no clue to scale. Perhaps she looked down momentarily on a mighty structure within which it lived. Perhaps she had glimpsed only a small area of its skin. If it had a skin. The glimpse was wonderful in its very mystery.

She put aside both her repulsion and her attraction, to marvel at life: not simply here, but also somewhere unreachable . . . at the galactic heart, beyond even the flight of Hermann Hesse's thought.

And because the *jaskiferianni* were so unimaginable, every government on Earth was uniting clumsily to think of ways of destroying them. And probably destroying the Amery family too, if necessary.

At twelve-thirty, Marigold heard the sound of her sister's Toyota in the drive. No doubt Viola was returning from a trip to see her latest friend, a creative older man; Marigold approved of the liaison. Jeremy had proved a stabilising influence on poor Viola.

Marigold was wearing a green-and-gold caftan. She picked up her book and sailed indoors. The two sisters went into Marigold's conservatory-studio, where her latest painting stood unfinished on an easle. They talked inconsequentially while Marigold drank vodka and Viola Perrier water. Hector emerged from his study and called; they went to greet him. He stood smiling from one to the other on the threshold, nervously fingering the wart under his right ear. Preparations for lunch got under way. Marigold's mother's bell sounded, Marigold took herself slowly upstairs to see what the old lady wanted.

Marigold Amery was a sturdy person with a wide, honest face. Her colour was in general golden, including her freckles. She was generally admired, and had many acquaintances, though few close friends. She liked to dress grandly. Her father, now dead, was Hungarian by birth. She had celebrated her fortieth birthday the previous week. Her name as a painter was not well known, although the Tate Gallery had recently bought a painting from her.

She felt the *jaskiferianni* beginning to work in her again, even as she sat with her dying mother.

This is what Viola Parkinson-Hill did, that morning when the Amery family's *jaskiferianni* returned.

She woke with a start at five in the morning, aware that the alien was back and tunnelling away inside her, drinking up her every experience as a cat laps milk. Viola lay there naked in her bed, stuck between revulsion and a kind of pleasure which transcended any she had known.

The *jaskiferianni* drove her out of bed and made her put on some clothes. Viola did not choose the clothes. She was powerless to do anything but the alien's bidding. On some matters – some trivial matters, even, like which pair of shoes she should put on – it was firm; on other matters, it seemed vague or indifferent.

Morning light was still milk-dim. The Regency house was wrapped in silence and birdsong. A Siamese cat sat watchful on the landing; even it had been infested.

She went down through the house, and got her car from the garage, and drove recklessly to the coast. The sea was only twenty miles away. All the while, she wrestled in her mind with the cold thing there, saying to it, No, she would not go in the sea, No, she could not swim, No, she hated the sea and would probably drown. To no effect. The *jaskiferianni* drove her just as she drove the Toyota, without consultation, often crashing gears.

And there was the humiliation of having to undress on the public beach, to strip nude, and to plunge into the water. Fortunately only two distant diggers for lug-worms shared the gleaming sand with her.

The *jaskiferianni* loved water. It loved big waves. She had to sport in and out of the breakers, almost drowned, for half an hour. With the alien in her, she swam perfectly. The North Sea was chilly, grey, salty, restless.

Finally, she was allowed to dry herself, dress, and drive home. The *jaskiferianni* disappeared when she was only a mile along the road, as if impatient at such slow means of travel. It left a nugget of blackness in her mind. Viola called it blackness, although she knew it was something different. Perhaps it was a gift the alien wanted to give her.

She steered the Toyota into a lay-by, and sat back to recover from her experience. It had been fun in a way, the bastard. Perhaps it fancied her. My Ardent Lover from the Stars. When the *jaskiferianni* had first invaded the Amery family and the government had placed the Amerys under surveillance, a scientist – himself showing some interest in Viola – had propounded the theory that the *jaskiferianni* had evolved, over millions of years, away from consciousness into a form of higher automatism, much as the human foetus makes its journey upwards from molecular levels. It could be that the aliens were rediscovering in humanity something they had lost long ago.

Viola thought, Maybe we should try staging some sort of big spectacular show for them, instead of hoping to drive them away. Magic Theatre – For Madmen Only. Maybe they're just bored like the rest of us, the bastards. She longed for a drink. A tumblerful of a rough whisky would do the trick . . .

It was a relief to see Marigold's house again, standing among its pine trees. The hour was still early, but her sister was worrying about her. They comforted each other. Hector appeared in a towelling robe, unshaven, and the three of them sat down to breakfast. Viola poured herself a strong black coffee.

After a shower and a change of clothes, she drove over to visit her current lover, a senior producer who worked at the BBC. He was attractive and loneliness had coaxed her to him. They had recently collaborated on a successful triptych of plays, and were hatching a sequel. The *jaskiferianni* returned when they were in mid-discussion. Jeremy was sympathetic and envious – he would have liked to leap into Viola's little psyche himself.

Back home, she went upstairs to sit with her mother, with whom she had never got on as well as had her stronger-minded sister. She passed an hour with Marigold in her studio until it was time for lunch and Hector emerged from his study. Viola could not think how she had once fancied Hector, even allowing for her drink problem. The *jaskiferianni* ferreted out all the details of that involvement. She imagined that this breed of alien had asexual reproduction and were forever croggled by the human way of doing it, the bastards.

Viola Parkinson-Hill was of more slender build than her older sister, more like her Hungarian father, and with something of his dash. She had a wide face, the family face, with golden eyes which had got her a long way in life. Otherwise, she was as dark as her sister was marigold-coloured. She suffered from a devouring loneliness. It was a year since her husband had been killed, when the *jaskiferianni* made him drive his car straight over a cliff; it suited her to live temporarily with Hector and Marigold. They got on well; but getting on well was one of Viola's specialities. She was thirty-five.

Even as they ate lunch, she could feel that infernal thing inside her, tasting each mouthful. Viola knew that when it disappeared she would want it back, the bastard.

This is what Doris Meszoly did, that morning when the Amery family's *jaskiferianni* returned.

She awoke feeling very ill as usual, and imagined that someone was standing beside the bed. Slowly bringing her head round on the pillow, she discovered that it was not a personage but the curtain, which Marigold had drawn back slightly last thing on the previous night. She dimly remembered moonlight. The curtain hung from pelmet to floor. The old lady admired its graceful folds, trying to think what it reminded her of.

Her ormolu clock, bought by her husband in pre-war Vienna, chimed nine o'clock from the mantelpiece.

When Marigold entered with a tray, Doris gulped down her medicines greedily. They tasted neither good or bad. The noise was in her ears again. The alien, when it came, seemed a familiar presence, more intimate than doctor. She had no fear of it. It was funny to think that only two years ago, the aliens had never visited Earth; now they were a part of everyone's environment, although only six families in England had been infested – and they on and off, at unpredictable intervals.

The *jaskiferianni* was rather like a visitation from Death.

The teaspoon rattled harshly in the saucer as she sipped at her tea.

Doris lay back when she had sampled the breakfast Marigold brought. The alien was tunnelling into the decaying storehouse of her memories – perhaps making better sense of them than she could, the old woman reflected.

"Is it with you, mother?" Marigold asked.

"Death it likes," Doris said faintly, gazing up at her golden daughter. "It's excited. I feel that it's excited by my. . . ." After a while, she said, "Perhaps where they come from, they don't die."

"Then they're lucky."

The old woman mustered her strength to reply. "No, that's not lucky. Ageing, that's the trouble . . . Not death."

She lay back after Marigold had washed her, staring out of the window, barely able to see a distant church spire, bright in summer sun. Her thoughts drifted. Perhaps she would get up for an hour later, to sit in the chair by the window.

"Why don't you speak to me?" she said aloud, once, twice. No reply.

Viola came up before lunch and talked about her writing plans. Doris had secretly been shocked by the sexual explicitness of Viola's previous plays, and let her thoughts wander while her younger daughter talked. Both she and Marigold were so creative. . . .

She wondered what it must be like out in the heart of the galaxy, unimaginable distances away, where all those varieties of strange life-forms went on incredible journeys. Did they basically make anything *more* of life than humble Earth-people, who had travelled no farther than Mars? Was the texture of their lives richer, more intricate?

Occasionally, she thought, the *jaskiferianni* told her something, as it did not do with the other members of its chosen family. Not that it liked her in any way, she remained certain of that; it communicated only to draw on her response. It had told her once, she felt sure, that it was on a long journey between two distant star-clusters. Its infestation of the Amery family was its way of passing time until it reached its destination. The Amerys were merely parts of its soap opera. It had no belief in their reality.

Doris could not remember if she had rung her bell for Marigold. But lunch came up just the same, served on a familiar tray.

She did not want it. After tasting the celery soup, she lay back and closed her eyes. Doris tried to remember what celery looked like, growing, but was unable to do so.

Doris Meszoly was the daughter of an actress once famous for her roles in musical comedy, a soubrette who had broken many hearts in her time before being ruined by her third husband, a horse-racing Scot. Doris was the only fruit of the first marriage, a neglected child who grew into a difficult adolescent. She followed her mother on to the stage, had one success, and then married a romantic Hungarian who might have stepped out of her mother's musicals, except that he was not a count and was broke. Meszoly, however, won the confidence of some London backers, and went into films in a big way, with successes like *He Who Thinks* and *The Passionate Pretenders*, in which his wife played the female lead. They had two daughters, Marigold and Viola, both strong-willed and pretty girls. Doris, in the last year of her life, was seventy-nine.

This is what Hector Amery did, that morning when the Amery family's *jaskiferianni* returned.

He woke to find that his wife Marigold was already up, and sauntered down into the garden in his bathing shorts. He swam ten lengths of the pool slowly. He then took a net and executed his daily ten minutes maintainance of the pool, scooping the water surface free of drowned insects. The contact with a large silent body of water always refreshed him; it did so even this morning, when he had the worry of the company closure hanging over him.

Hector was returning the net to the filter room when the filthy thing arrived inside him again. It took him and flung him back into the pool. He wrestled with it, and surfaced nearly drowned. The *jaskiferianni* seemed to relish the fear in his mind. Or did it simply play with him, like a cat with a bird? He understood the thing even less than he understood women.

"Get the hell out of there," Hector said. He signalled unnecessarily to one of the scanners which watched over all the Amery estate. Like the other five English families also irregularly possessed by these particular aliens, all the activities of the Amerys were subject to international scrutiny. They had long become used to it.

Yet Hector felt profoundly depressed. Angry and depressed. The Amerys had been free of the invader for a month, ever since it had forced his brother to step into a busy road and be struck by a passing motor cycle. His brother was still in a nursing home, learning to walk with a prosthetic leg.

He ate a perfunctory breakfast with Marigold and Viola, the golden sister and the dark. There was no need to announce that the *jaskiferianni* was back. They knew. You could smell *jaskiferianni*. Well, not smell exactly, but detect their proximity by some interior nose the humans had not known they possessed.

"They flung me into the pool just now," he told his wife.

"Are you all right?"

"Some day we'll get those fuckers."

Once Marigold had disappeared on her shopping expedition to the village, Hector tried to talk to Viola, but without much luck. When Viola had come to live with them after her husband died, she had been practically alcoholic. Hector had got himself into bed with her. It was hard to resist that slender body, that vulnerable smile. Now that she was on the wagon, she would not look his way. As aloof as her sister.

Hector was sure Viola still wanted him, and that only scruples towards her sister kept her away. All the same, he suspected she was having an affair with the boring BBC chap who helped her with her plays.

He deliberately wasted his morning, shutting himself in his study, studying the company reports on his computer terminal – they looked worse every time – and making a long phone call to the company secretary.

Just four years earlier, Hector had taken a daring decision, selling all but a small share interest in his own company and investing the capital in his brother's mushrooming firm, which was assembling and marketing ESRSs. They had made a fortune between them; everyone wanted to receive pictures from the Mars station and to own a better communications system into the bargain. The infestation of people all over the world by galactic aliens had changed the situation abruptly. Sales were now approaching zero. The arrival of the galaxy had driven everyone back to their native hearths.

It looked as if the company would have to be wound up while Hector's brother was still immobilised.

Hector sat slumped for a long while, glaring at the figures in his VDU.

He did not emerge from his study even when he heard the chink of glasses, and Marigold and Viola talking together.

The *jaskiferianni* visited him once more. He felt himself being taken over. This time, he was forced to play a video cassette of Viola's first TV play, *The Yearning Fox-Trot*, forced to turn the volume high, forced to watch once more. It was his theory that this alien thing, from whatever awful utilitarian culture it came, could not distinguish between fact and fiction. Inevitably, its view of life would be bizarre in the extreme: like vision without perspective.

But when one gave it thought, how curious was the human obsession with fantasies, lies, and fictions of all kinds. Perhaps you had to come to Earth to savour such richness.

Hector heard Marigold's mother's bell ring for attention as the *jaskiferianni* left him. He remained where he was in the study, doing nothing until lunch, brooding.

Hector Amery had been a well-known athlete, strong in swimming and running. His lean, tanned face was youthful, his fair hair did not show its grey. After breaking an ankle at the age of twenty-three, he went into the marketing of sports clothes, rejigging his father's ageing shirt business. By thirty, he was able to bring in a younger partner and to travel. At a party for expatriate British given by the Parkinson-Hills in Buenos Aires – Sir Kendal Parkinson-Hill was in the diplomatic service – Hector had met the post-expressionist painter, Marigold Meszoly. She was his miracle. Hector lured her away from the Swedish musician she was living with and married her.

He was now forty-three years of age. The marriage, like life itself, had not given Hector all he expected. That, he told himself, was because he had expected too much. And then the *jaskiferianni* had arrived unexpectedly, and fouled up his life.

★

Marigold, Viola and Hector gathered for lunch. Hector took a luncheon tray up to his mother-in-law and then poured glasses of Rioja wine for his wife and himself; his sister-in-law kept to Perrier water. He switched off the wall-screen which, this being Saturday, was mainly occupied by sports he no longer wished to know about.

The scanners that covered them from different points of the room could not be turned off. The lens watched as Marigold sliced a pizza in three.

"Well, they're back all right," Hector said, lifting his glass. "And I take it that we were all occupied in turn?" The *jaskiferianni* were always "they". "The bastards nearly drowned me."

"They nearly drowned me in the sea," Viola said. "They like to play rough."

Hector said, "They're back, we don't know for how long. I hate those accursed things as I've never hated anything else in my life. I would willingly blow my brains out when they are in there, if anyone thought that that would rid us of the things." He thumped his fist on the table so that the cutlery rattled.

"Oh, they're rather amusing in their way," Viola said, driven into one of her teasing fits by Hector's solemn, flushed face. "They certainly make solitude easy. You could advertise the *jaskiferianni* as complete substitutes for all forms of sociability. They scare you sometimes, but it is rather a thrill to have something so completely intimate with one, knowing all one's naughtiest secrets."

"It disgusts me," Hector said. "I simply feel infested."

"Perhaps your secrets are naughtier than mine," Viola said, with a laugh, hoping it was not so.

He hit the table again. "These things are just having a holiday and using us for their fun. They killed your husband, Viola, they nearly killed my brother, they have bankrupted us, they made you an alcoholic – we're all under threat of death from their whims. How can you take it so lightly? It's unbearable, degrading."

"They used to enjoy my alcoholic bouts. They lead very dull teetotal lives. Adultery and circuses are not known among them. It must be incredibly boring, having to travel through space. What are they, exponents of a super-civilisation or some sort of glorified commercial travellers?"

Marigold finished a mouthful of salad and said, "It's true that our lives are in danger. I suppose I am terrified of the *jaskiferianni*, yet I'm more curious than terrified. For all their powers, they seem simple and brutal things – almost elemental. As subtle as a brick. Yet they show a fascination with art."

"I don't think they know what art is," Hector said. "They come from some horrible authoritarian culture in the stars – perhaps the galactic centre is just a kind of gigantic anthill – and they cannot distinguish between what is real and what is imaginary. That's why they want to run *The Yearning Fox-Trot* so often. They can't make it out."

"Those unbearable journeys among the stars," Viola exclaimed. "One light-year must be terribly like another. It sounds to me as if they are longing to escape from the unendurable quality of their own existence, and they find the life of an ordinary family like ours endlessly fascinating. As mother suggested, they may be immortal – that's another kind of burdensome journey. After all, one year's much like another."

"Immortal or not, some day we're going to get those fuckers," Hector said.

At that moment, as if on cue, Doris's bell rang. The meal broke up. Afterwards, Viola served coffee.

Hector took his cup from her and wandered over to the window to glare moodily out at the sunlit garden. He would have to go and see his brother this afternoon. This house would probably have to be sold up. What a disgrace!

The fact had to be faced. No one wanted to buy the company's ESRSs. One common factor among the six English families infested by the *jaskiferianni* was that each owned an Earth Satellite Receiving Station. Not that that proved anything. But people were frightened. He was frightened. And when you suddenly learned that there were almost magical ways of communicating – really communicating – then you were not going to invest in an expensive chunk of home-technology like a receiving station.

If only he had stayed in sports gear. . . .

Those fuckers. . . .

Marigold took her coffee alone into her studio. She contemplated the Picasso sketch on her wall. She switched on her personal stereo, and her head was filled with the music of Mozart's *Don Giovanni*, the passage heralding the approach of the guest of stone.

She spoke into the room, confident that her face, her words, were being picked up in the JIC, the *Jaskiferianni* Information Centre in Birmingham.

"I know you are all thinking like Hector. You would love to blow all these aliens to kingdom come. Yet they are visitors, here voluntarily, and the *jaskiferianni* at least seem less malevolent than curious. They do not even require rare metals, like some of the other galactic species infesting people elsewhere. I want to suggest to you a different approach to the problem, one involving no bloodshed."

She was silent a moment, letting the music flow. After all – but that one could hardly say aloud, certainly not to the uniformed men in Birmingham – was there any great difference between human and *jaskiferianni* loneliness? Did they offer a unique, priceless way of communication, if it could be understood? Weren't all human art-forms infestations of the material world, designed to overcome it?

The *jaskiferianni* must be trapped.

She said into the flowered silence of her studio, "I presume you are prepared to give the Amerys financial aid on a large scale, if we arrive at a bright idea?"

She knew the answer. The Controller's face would be up on her wall-screen soon enough. She said, "Viola and I will create a complex work of art – with a little help from our friends. The work will be a marathon play, showing in minutest detail the complexity of relationships in an ordinary family like ours; but that family will be in communication with a galactic culture, which will be depicted as immense, crushingly powerful, philistine, bleak, sexless, death-less – and therefore lifeless. . . . The very opposite of our vulnerable and transitory little family groupings . . . Permanent but without hope of joy. . . ." She was improvising as she talked. "Perhaps these galactic races are the descendants of insect communities, worms, wasps, ants, internal parasites – I don't know. I tend to visualise them as hot-rodding maggots tunnelling through the cheese of hyperspace. They have a power of single-mindedness beyond our comprehension. But we have something beyond their comprehension, and there's the trap by which we catch them: a sort of super science-fiction epic so finely imagined and portrayed that they will not be able to tell if it is real or not. *Then* perhaps a real dialogue will begin.

"I believe they need our help and we theirs."

Marigold trembled as she spoke. There was no race on Earth without its art. But to take art to an entire species – maybe dozens of species – without art . . . perhaps it would destroy them. At the least it would alter them entirely.

Maybe Mozart would be more effective than nuclear warheads.

She thought of how English culture had enriched the globe – and of how England depended for its enrichment on contributions from all over the globe. Perhaps the galaxy might become dependent on Earth in the same way.

Her thoughts made her dizzy. She sat down in her favourite creaking rattan chair.

Then the *jaskiferianni* was back, suddenly in place, like chill coins dropping into her interior. She gripped the arms of the chair. *Don Giovanni* still washed over her.

Maybe it could read her plan. Yet these galactic conquerors were, and she knew it intuitively, stupid in all sorts of human ways she was not. She was not to be defeated by a worm.

Even if they killed her, Pablo was waiting, and Mozart too.

They stole something they could never have.

They could be caught.

And civilised.

(1986)

The Difficulties Involved in Photographing Nix Olympica

It was unprecedented for anyone stationed on Mars to refuse home leave. Ozzy Brooks refused. He secretly wanted to photograph Olympus Mons.

For his whole two-year tour of duty, Sgt Brooks had saved money and hoarded material. Had made friends with the transport section. Had ingratiated himself with the officer in charge of rations. Had gone out of his way to be nice to practically everyone in Atmosphere Control. Had wooed the guys in the geological section. Had made himself indispensable in Engineering.

Almost everyone in Fort Arcadia knew and, within their lights, liked little Sgt Brooks.

Brooks was small, dark-skinned, lightly built, neat-boned – ideal fodder for Mars. He had nondescript sandy hair which grew like lichen over his skull, with eyes to match. He had what are often referred to as ageless looks, and the rather blank stare that goes with those looks.

Behind that blank and inoffensive gaze lay ambition. Brooks was an intellectual. Brooks never drank. He rarely watched the TV screenings from Earth. Instead, he could be seen reading old books. He went to bed early. He never complained or scratched his armpits. And he seemed to know everything. It was amazing that the other troops stationed in Fort Arcadia liked him nevertheless: but Brooks had another qualification.

Ozzy Brooks was Fort Arcadia's Martian *t'ai chi* master. He taught two classes of *mar t'ai chi*, as he himself called it: an elementary class from eight to ten in the morning and an advanced class from eight to eleven in the evening. Even men for whom *mar t'ai chi* was not compulsory joined Brooks's classes, for they agreed that Brooks was a brilliant teacher; all felt better when each session was finished. Brooks's teaching was an antidote to the monotony of Mars.

After dismissing one of his morning classes, Brooks slipped out of his costume, put on denims, and strolled across the dome to Engineering, to work on the larger format camera he was building.

"What do you need a camera for on Mars?" Sgt Al Shapiro asked.

"I want to photograph Martian women if any turn up," Brooks said.

Shapiro laughed, with contempt in the sound.

Brooks's secret in life was that he did not hate anything. He hated no man. He did not hate the Army, he did not hate Mars. All the rest of the men, his friends, spent long hours trying to decide whether they hated the Army or Mars most. Sometimes Mars won, sometimes the Army.

"It's the boredom. The monotony," they said. Referring to both or either.

Brooks was never bored. In consequence, he did not find life monotonous. He did not dislike Army discipline, since he had always strictly disciplined himself. Certainly he missed women; but he consoled himself by saying that instead he had this unique opportunity to know the Red Planet.

He loved Mars. Mars was the ideal place on which to do *t'ai chi*. Despite his ordinary name, Brooks was an exotic. While his grandmother, a refugee from Vietnam, had had the fortune to marry a seventh-generation American, his great-grandparents were Chinese from Szechwan Province. A *t'ai chi* tradition had been passed down in the family from generation to generation. Ozzy Brooks hugged this knowledge to himself: Mars, with its lighter gravity, was the perfect planet on which to develop his art. Some wise Chinese ancestor, many generations ago, had invented the postures of the White Crane *with Mars in mind*.

Under Brooks's American-ness ran a strong delight in his oriental heritage. He believed that it was a Chinese who had discovered the perfect way to live on another planet, in harmony with its elements, using those elements to become more perfect in oneself. Mars – he had realised this almost as soon as he had disembarked from the military spaceship – was the most Chinese of planets, even down to the *sang-de-boeuf* tint of its soil, the colour of ancient Chinese gateways and porcelains.

In Brooks's mind, Mars became an extension of China, the China of long ago, crammed with warriors, maidens as fair as white willows, and tombs loaded high with carvings and treasure. Beyond the dome of Arcadia, he thought he saw Cathay.

It was some while before he realised he had a friend in Sgt Al Shapiro.

He was working in the engineering laboratories, inserting the shutter mechanism in the 8x10 camera now rapidly nearing completion, when Shapiro strolled up. Shapiro was small, light on his feet, and darker in complexion than Brooks. He smiled at Brooks through a hank of black hair which hung across his face.

"What are you going to use that camera for, Ozzy?" he asked, as before.

"I take pictures, of course, what else?"

"You're not going to be able to take it back to Earth in your kit. It's too heavy."

"What a nuisance," said Brooks, blandly.

Shapiro paused, then said, "You should photograph Mars with it."

The remark took Brooks aback. He had intended to do nothing else. To hear someone else state his intention was to feel himself somehow robbed, as if a precious stone had been stolen.

He looked open-mouthed at Shapiro.

Mistaking his surprise, Shapiro lowered his voice and said, "Most guys see nothing in Mars, nothing at all. Except the officers. Do you notice when we're out doing manoeuvres, Colonel Wolfe always says, 'Mars is fine fighting country'? That's how a professional soldier sees it, I guess. What do the men say about it? 'The dustbowl' – that's what they call Mars, the squaddies. They can't see it except as a torn-off chunk of America's Badlands. They've got no imagination."

"How do you see Mars, Al?" Brooks asked, very calm and in control again.

Shapiro gave his flitting smile.

"How do I see it? Why, when I take a look out there, I see it as a fantastic piece of natural engineering. Uncluttered by trees and all the vegetation that hides Earth. Mars is honest, a great series of cantilevers and buttresses and platforms. God's naked handiwork. I'm the only guy I know who'd like to get out there among it all."

"Some of the men like to go out for the pigeon shoots," Brooks said.

There were Mars jeeps which toured nearby gulleys firing off clay pigeons in all directions. These shoots formed one of the few outdoor recreations available. But no one ever ventured more than a mile from the fort.

Shapiro shrugged. "Kid stuff . . . I'd just like to figure on doing something memorable with my time on Mars. I've only got a month before they ship me back to Chicago."

Brooks put out his hand.

"That's the way I think too. I wish to do something memorable."

And so they came to draw up plans to photograph Olympus Mons from the ground.

Al Shapiro was as resourceful as Ozzy Brooks in getting what he wanted. He actually enjoyed the Army, and knew how to exploit all the weaknesses of that organisation. They indented for a week's base leave, they set about bribing Captain Jeschke in Transport to secure the unauthorised loan of a Mars jeep, they bartered services in return for supplies.

"I should be a general – I could run Mars single-handed!" Shapiro said, laughing.

And all the while, he went ahead with his work in Engineering, and Brooks taught *mar t'ai chi*, instructing his squads how to love Mars as the ally of all their muscular exertions – thus, in his quiet way, subverting the army's purpose, which was to make the men hate the planet and anything on it which moved and was not capitalist.

Occasionally, manoeuvres were undertaken in conjunction with the EEC dome in Eridania. The men had to fire missiles on the arctic ranges, or crawl around, cursing, in the red dust. Brooks saw then that his subversion had not had much effect. Everyone wanted to go back to Earth. They had no vision. He longed to give them one.

"Before we leave here, we must make a model of Nix Olympica, and study it from all angles, so that we decide the ideal position to which to drive." Brooks nodded sagely as he spoke and looked sideways at Shapiro.

"Cartography," said Shapiro. "Lou Wright owes me a favour. Let's try Cartography."

They obtained more than maps and photographs. As the most prominent physical feature on Mars, the extinct volcano had warranted a plastic model, constructed by a bygone officer in the Army Geological survey. Brooks inspected it with interest before rejecting it.

"It's too small. We can make a much better one between us," he said.

What he felt was that this army model of Olympus was contaminated by its source; it had no poetry. Whoever had ordered it had probably been concerned with how the sides of the crater could be scaled, or how the caldera itself might provide a base for ground-to-space missiles.

Brooks moulded his model of the gigantic volcano in plastic, colouring it with acrylics. Shapiro occasionally came over to admire his work.

"You see, the formation is about the size of the state of Missouri. It rises to all of fifteen miles high," Brooks said. "The best idea is to approach it from the east. The lighting will be best from the east."

"What's your lens?"

"I'm taking a selection. The point about an 8x10 camera is that it will give terrific definition – though it feeds on sheet film, and I'll need a tripod to keep it steady."

"I can make you a tripod."

They surveyed the model of Olympus critically when it was finished. Brooks shook his head.

"It's a good model," Shapiro said. "Photograph it here against a black background and we can save ourselves a trip."

Although Brooks rarely laughed, he laughed now. Laughed and said nothing.

He was serenely happy drawing up his own map, entering the sparse names of features in fine calligraphic style, precision-drawing contour lines. The most dangerous aspect of the trip was its distance. They were contemplating a drive of almost seven hundred and ninety miles, with no filling stations on the way, and then the journey back. They would be unlikely to see anyone the whole trip, except possibly a patrol moving between the Arcadia base and the hemisphere of the planet held by the enemy.

No possible danger could deter Brooks. His mind was filled with his delight in having found a friend and in the prospects ahead. Ever since Mariner 9 had executed its fly-over back in 1971, Olympus Mons, the largest volcano in the solar system, had frequently been photographed, by both satellites and rockets. But never from the ground. Never as *he* would photograph it, with all the skill of an Ansel Adams.

He could visualise the prints now. They would be majestic, expressing both the violence and the deadness of the Martian landscape; he would create a serenity out of the conflicting tensions. He would create such an image that it would remain definitive: through the elusive art of photography, he would create a monument not only to the sublimity of the universe, but also to the greatness and the insignificance of mankind in the scheme of things.

With such exalted thoughts in his mind, Brooks had no room for fear.

The two men left Arcadia early one morning. Clad in suits, they slipped through one of the personnel locks in the main dome and made their way over to the transport hanger. There a stretched Mars jeep was waiting, loaded with fuel and supplies. As it rolled into the dim dawn light, the half-tracked vehicle resembled a cumbrous beetle.

There was little room to move in the cab. When they slept, their hammocks would be strung overhead. The ironically named Fort Arcadia was situated close to 50° North, in the veined recesses of the Arcadia Planita. It was summer in the northern hemisphere of Mars, and they had a straightforward drive southwards to the giant volcano, according to the maps.

They reckoned on travelling for fourteen hours a day, and averaging something close to twenty-seven miles per hour, the best they could hope for over trackless terrain. They nodded with pleasure as the shabby collection of prefabricated buildings disappeared behind them, and they were alone with Mars. Shapiro was driving.

A chill, shrunken sun had pierced through the mists of the eastern horizon, where layers of salmon pink dissolved into the sky. The shadow of their vehicles spread across a terrain which resembled Earth's Gobi Desert. Dust lay in sculptured terraces, punctuated here and there by rocks of pumice. In the far distance to the right, a series of flat-topped escarpments suggested a kind of order completely lacking nearer at hand; they made their way through a geological rubbish dump.

This formless landscape was familiar to them from their military exercises. They had crawled through it, dressed in camouflaging sand-robes. Nothing moved but dusts and rusts; the rest – unlike Earth's restless territories – had endured without change for billions of years. It had no more life to offer than the Geological Survey map of the route pinned to the dash.

There was no cratering here, as in the southern hemisphere, to lend interest. Their one concern was to steer south, avoiding rocks and dust drifts. After the first hour of travel, with Al Shapiro at the wheel, Brooks began to want to talk.

Shapiro, however, had gone silent. As the sun climbed in the pinkish sky, he became more silent. He offered the information that his family came from the Cicero area of Chicago, and then gave up entirely. Brooks, tired of trying to make conversation, resorted to whistling.

The sun arced overhead. The two sergeants took the wheel by turns, driving till the suns sloped to the west, to sink behind a low dust cloud. They had covered three hundred and seventy miles, and were pleased with their good progress. With nightfall, Shapiro found his voice again and was more cheerful; they ate a companionable supper from their rations before climbing into their hammocks and sleeping.

Once in the night, Brooks woke and peered out of the window. The stars and the Milky Way were there in glory, remote yet curiously intimate, as if they shone only for him, like a hope at the back of his mind. He was caught between the tensions of awe and enjoyment, like a troglodyte before its god, unable to tear his gaze away from the glitter until an hour had passed. He climbed back into his hammock, smiling into the fuggy darkness, and slept.

Next dawn revealed no sign of the dust storm glimpsed at sunset – to Brooke's secret relief. Joy came to him. He sang. Shapiro looked doleful.

"Are you okay?" Brooks asked.

"I'm fine, sure."

"Anything worrying you? You wanted to get out among it all, and here we are."

"I'm fine."

"The Tharsis Bulge should be in view in an hour or two. Tomorrow we'll be within sight of Nix Olympica."

"Its name's Olympus," Shapiro said, sourly.

"I like to call it by the old name, Al. Nix Olympica . . . That was the name bestowed on it before anyone had ever set foot on the planet, or even left Earth. Nix Olympica is the old name, the name of mystery, of remoteness. I like it best. I'm going to photograph Nix Olympica and give a new image to Earth, before they come and build a missile site in the crater. Let's hope the atmosphere stays clear of dust."

Shapiro shrugged and brushed his hair from his eyes. He said nothing.

They were rolling by six-thirty. By eight, the terrain was changing. Petrified lavas created a series of steps over the ancient sandrocks. Their gravimeter began to show fluctuations in the gravity field.

Brooks pointed ahead.

"There's the Tharsis Bulge," he said. "From here it stretches to south of the equator."

"I can see it," Shapiro said, without responding to Brook's excitement.

They began to steer south-east until the low wizened lips of Alba Patera lay distinctly to their left. The view ahead became increasingly formidable.

The Tharsis Bulge distorted half a hemisphere. Earth held no feature as majestic. At its north-western bastion stood the grim sentinel shape of Olympus, its cone rising sheer fifteen and a half miles above the surrounding plain. As yet, they were too distant to see more than a pimpled shoulder of the Bulge rising above the ancient lands like a great bruise. Black clouds of dust rolled above the bruise. From the clouds, lightning showered, flickered like burning magnesium wire, died, flickered elsewhere. High above both Bulge and dust clouds, wispy white clouds formed a halo in the dark sky.

They climbed. The engine throbbed. The hours passed, the landscape took on power. It was as though the ancient rock breathed upwards. Despite the jeep, Brooks could feel the strength of the great igneous upthrust through the soles of his feet – the "Bubbling Well", as t'ai chi had it.

He breathed air deep into his hora centre. But Shapiro sank back in his seat.

"You are suffering agoraphobia, Al," Brooks said. "Don't worry. Now we have something marvellous to distract your mind."

Brooks's intention was to drive some way up into the Bulge until Nix Olympica lay to the west; from there, he estimated he could photograph the formation at its most dramatic, with falling ground behind it.

The terrain which had been merely rutted now became much more difficult to drive. Long parallel fractures, remarkably uniform in spacing and orientation, ran downhill in their path. There was no way of avoiding the fracturing; as the map indicated, the faults extended for at least a hundred miles on either side of their course. Each fracture had straight, almost vertical, cliffs and reasonably flat bottoms. They found a point where a landslide had destroyed a cliff. By working their tracks on alternate sides, they contrived to slip down a small landslide to the bottom of the fracture, after which it was simple to drive along it. It was the width of an eight-lane highway.

Cliffs boxed them in on either side. The sky above was leaden, relieved by a strip of white cloud low ahead. It was just a matter of proceeding straight. No canyon on Earth was ever like this one.

Brooks pointed into the shadowed side of the fracture at the foot of the cliff. A trace of white lay across small boulders.

"It's a mixture of frost and snow, by the look of it," he said.

The sight delighted him. At least there was one natural process still functioning on the dead surface of the planet.

"How're we going to get out of this fault?" Shapiro asked.

"We're in a crack at least two and a half billion years old," Brooks said, more or less to himself. Even Cathay was not that old.

"And the satellites can't pick us up while we're down here," Shapiro said.

But Brooks would have nothing of misgivings. They would emerge somehow. He had never enjoyed himself so much.

"Just imagine it – once a great torrent rushed along here, Al. We're on an old river bed."

"No, this wasn't formed by water," Shapiro said expertly. "It's the result of stresses in the Martian lithosphere. You'll be looking out for fish-bones next."

Although Brooks was silenced by this rejoinder, he spent the next hour alert for signs of departed life. What a triumph to see a fossil in the fracture walls! Once he cried out and stopped the jeep, to peer more closely at the cliff; there was nothing to be seen but a pattern of splintering in the rock.

"Nothing living has ever lived here – not ever," Shapiro said, and began to shiver.

It was impossible to say anything sympathetic, but Brooks understood how Shapiro felt. These unknown spaces chilled Shapiro as much as they excited Brooks; it was what came of being born in a crowded Chicago slum. Besides, he understood intellectually how absurd it was to be experiencing such intense pleasure in such a forbidding place. The mountains of Western Szechwan Province, from which his Chinese ancestors had come, might be almost as unwelcoming as this.

It turned out that Brooks's light-heartedness was not misplaced. The fracture cut into another at an oblique angle. Vast ramps, as smooth as if designed by mortal architect, led up to the general level of the Bulge. The jeep climbed with ease, and they emerged onto the rainless elevations of the Tharsis Bulge. They were 1.3 miles above the datum, Mars's equivalent of sea level. The read-out also showed a free-air gravity anomaly of 229 mgals. The wall of yellowish black dust had disappeared. Visibility was good in the thin atmosphere. The sun shone as if encased in lucite. There was a glazed aspect, too, to the great smooth features of the inclined plain about them, where strange bumps and undulations suggested bones under the basaltic skin.

"Wonderful!" Brooks said. He began to tease himself. "All we need now is for a devil to emerge and dance before us. A devil with a red and white face."

"For god's sake . . ." Shapiro protested. "Take your photographs and let's get home."

But Brooks wanted to climb out and dance. He was sick of being cooped in the cab of the vehicle, sick of the perpetual noise of the engine and air-purifier. It would be a time for the t'ai chi solo dance, even with the space suit on. He would celebrate Mars as no one else had done.

He controlled himself. A few more hours' driving and they would see Nix Olympica itself. The sun was already descending. They had to make as much distance as they could before dark.

With nightfall, an electrical storm swept down from the heights. They stopped the jeep beside a corroded boulder. Flicking light surrounded them. Shapiro spent an hour checking through all the equipment, climbing restlessly about, and muttering to himself.

"One failure and we're dead," he said, catching Brooks's eye. "No one could get to us in time if anything went wrong. We embarked on this caper far too thoughtlessly. We should have planned it like a military operation."

"We shall see Nix Olympica tomorrow. Don't worry. Besides, imagine – wouldn't this spot really make a dramatic tomb?"

Shapiro was apologetic next morning. He did not realise that the desolate spaces of Mars would have such a bad effect on him. He knew he was acting foolishly. It was his determination to take a grip on himself. He was looking forward to seeing Olympus, and would be fine, he felt sure, on the way home. There was just – well, the realisation that their lives balanced on a knife-edge.

Clapping him affectionately on the shoulder, Brooks said, "Life is always lived on a knife-edge. Don't worry."

By ten that morning, when the sun was shining through its blue glaze, they caught sight of a dark crust beyond the curve of the horizon. It was the volcano.

Both men cheered.

The volcano grew throughout the day, arising from behind the humps of the Bulge. Hour by hour, they gained a clearer impression of its size. It was a vast tomb of igneous rock which would have dominated any continent on Earth. It would have stretched from Shapiro's Chicago to Buffalo, obliterating Lake Erie. It would have stretched from Switzerland to London, obliterating Paris and most of Belgium. It would have stretched from Lhasa in Tibet to Calcutta, obliterating Mount Everest like a molehill on its way.

Above its shoulders, where the sky was indigo, little demons of lightning danced, corkscrewing their way down into its scarred crust.

It could not be imagined or described. Only photographed.

Brooks brought his films from the refrigerator. He had three SLR cameras beside his home-made "tank". He went to work with cameras, lenses, and filters when they were still over four hundred miles from the giant caldera of Olympus. In the thin air, it appeared deceptively close.

Talking excitedly as he worked, Brooks tried to explain what he felt to Shapiro, who drove with his gaze on the ridged ground ahead.

"Back in the eighteenth century, painters discriminated between the beautiful, the picturesque, and the sublime. You'd need to dream up another category for most of Mars, particularly the dull bits round Arcadia. You wouldn't find much that would square with definitions of 'beautiful' or 'picturesque', but here we have the sublime and then some . . . This monster has all the elements of awfulness and grandeur which the sublime requires. I wonder what the great painters would have made of Nix Olympica. . . ."

The sun climbed to zenith, and then began to slope away down the western sky.

"Turn direct south, Al. Speed it up, if you can. I want to catch the sunset behind Nix. It should be wonderful."

Shapiro managed a laugh. "I'm doing my best, Ozzy. Don't want to shake the buggy to pieces."

Brooks began loading low-grain fast film into his cameras.

They were travelling over ground composed of flow after flow of lava, one wave upon another, slags, powders, and ejecta cast upon the previous outpourings in grotesque patterns, as if the almost indestructible material had been bent on destroying itself, to the depth of hundreds of fathoms.

Whatever ferment had taken place over eons of time, those eons were themselves now eons past; since then, only silence covered the forbidding highlands – silence without motion, without so much as a wisp of steam from a solitary fumarole.

"Stop here!" Brooks exclaimed suddenly. "Where's that tripod? Oh, god . . . I must get on top of the jeep and film from there."

Grunting, Shapiro did as he was told. Brooks screwed his helmet on, draped his cameras and telescopic lenses over one shoulder, and climbed to the ground. He stood for a while, staring at the ground sloping towards the distant formation, and the sky, in which thin cloud curled like feather some five miles overhead. He took several shots at various shutter speeds almost without thought.

Looking back on his modest life, without distinction of any kind, he could hardly believe his luck. Night was descending on Mars, and he was here to photograph it. Even if Earth soon blew itself up, still he was here, and could record the moment.

His luck was crowned as he started to photograph from the top of the vehicle, using the 8x10 tank, steadying it with the tripod.

Phobos, the innermost moon, appeared to rise from the west – its orbital period being less than Mars's rotation period.

It glittered above the barricades of Nix Olympica. An ice cloud tailed like a pennant above the great volcano. The setting sun emerged from under a band of mist, spilling its light like broken egg along the horizon. The volcano was black in silhouette against the sky. The tank's shutter clicked, as moment by moment the light enriched itself.

Totally engrossed, Brooks slotted a polarising filter over the lens. Click. Wonderful.

The universe closed down like an oyster on the strip of brightness. The sun seemed to flare and was gone, leaving Nix Olympica to prop up its sky. Brooks opened up his aperture and kept shooting. He knew he would never witness anything like this again. Tomorrow night, they would be on their way home, racing the sinking gauge on the oxygen cylinders. Then it would be up to him to try and recreate this moment in his darkroom, where the hard work would be done.

Next morning, both sergeants were stirring before dawn.

"I've got to capture the first ray of light to touch those crater walls," Brooks said. "Let's try to get fifty miles nearer."

"How about something to eat first, Ozzy?"

"We can eat for the rest of our lives. You drive, okay?"

Shapiro drove while Brooks fussed over his equipment. He threw the vehicle recklessly forward, caught by Brooks's excitement. He laughed.

"This'll be something to tell people about."

"No mistake there," Brooks said. "Maybe I'll publish an album of the best shots. Hey, Al, maybe we should climb the crater while we're here!"

"Forget it. Fifteen miles up in a space suit, with no climbing gear! I'm not mad even if you are."

They were racing across the bulbous incline. A worn stump of rock loomed ahead.

"Stop and I'll climb that," Brooks said.

When they got to it, the rock proved to be a small cone, a hundred yards across and several feet high. Unmoved by Shapiro's protests, Brooks unclamped the portable ladder from the jeep and climbed to the top. The crater was plugged with ancient magma and covered with dust. He got the tripod and the cameras in place just as the sun rose from behind a shoulder of Tharsis.

Click. This time, the fortress of Olympus was bright against a dark sky. For a moment, the outline of Tharsis was printed in shadow on its eastern flank. Click. Then like an iceberg of untold mass, it was floating on a sea of shadow. Click. The shadow withdrew across the plain towards the men. Mists rose. Click. For no more than five minutes, the great mesa was softened by evaporating carbon dioxide fumes. Click.

"Wonderful, wonderful!" said Brooks. He found that Shapiro had followed him up the ladder. Rapture was on both their faces. They hugged each other and laughed. They took shots of each other standing by the volcanic cone.

They forgot to eat and, throughout the morning, drove as fast as they could towards the volcano. It was a magnet, bathed in light.

At midday, they stopped to drink ham and green pea soup.

They were still over one hundred and fifty miles from Olympus. It spread grandly before them: its great shield, its summit caldera – not a vent as in Earth's familiar stratovolcanoes but a relapse of the summit region – its flanking escarpments, its pattern of frozen lava runs, which from this distance resembled tresses of hair. From above, as Brooks knew, Nix Olympica resembled the nipple of a Martian Juno.

They gazed out at this brilliant formation as they slurped down their soup. It occupied one hundred and twelve degrees of their vision, although it was still so distant.

Shapiro turned from the sight and checked their instruments.

"We're doing okay, but getting near the safety margin on both fuel and oxygen. Are you almost ready to turn homewards, Ozzy?"

Brooks hesitated, then spoke in a nonchalant manner. "I'm almost ready. There's just one thing left to do. We've got some fine photographs in the bag, and by the time I bring the negatives up, there just could be a masterpiece or two among them. The only problem is the question of scale. Since there's no means of comparison in any of the pictures, you can't get an idea of the magnitude of Nix."

They looked at each other. Shapiro said. "You want me to leave you here and then drive the jeep nearer, so that you can have it in the foreground?"

"I don't want the truck in. Besides, I need to be mobile myself. I want you in it, Al – the human figure. I want to put you forward in the landscape. Then I move around taking shots."

Shapiro became rigid.

"I won't do that, Ozzy."

"Why not?"

"I won't do it."

"Tell me why."

"Because I just won't."

"Look, Al, we'll never be out of sight of each other. We'll be in radio contact. You'll be able to see the jeep all the while. All you have to do is stand where I put you. It'll take an hour, no more."

"No, I said. I'm not standing out in that landscape alone. That's flat, okay?"

They glowered at each other.

"You go out there. I'll take the damned pictures."

"I'm not afraid to go out there. Come on, Al, we've come all this way. There's nothing to be scared of, for Christ's sake. One hour, that's all I ask."

Shapiro dropped his gaze, clenching his fists together.

"You can't make me do it."

"I'm not making you. What's so difficult? You just do it."

"Suppose something happens?"

"Nothing has happened here for century after century. Not a thing."

Shapiro expelled a sigh. His face showed the tension inside him. His skin gleamed in the flat light.

"Okay. I'll do it, I guess."

"Okay." Brooks hesitated then said, "I appreciate it, Al. The medics haven't yet got round to naming a fear of wide open alien spaces, but they will. I know it must take some fighting."

"I'll conquer it. Just don't talk about it," said Al, his teeth chattering, as Brooks helped him secure the helmet of his suit.

"Sometimes there's need for talk. Remember, the same demons and spirits haunt the wide open spaces of Mars as those of Earth. No difference really, since all apparitions are in the mind. If we import demons, then we can conquer them, because they must obey our laws."

"I'll try and bear that in mind," said Shapiro, forcing his teeth to stop chattering. "Now let me out before I think better of it."

All the while Brooks drove back and forth about that portion of the Bulge, taking his historic shots of Nix Olympica, he was aware of what the distant white figure was undergoing as it stood alone in the grotesque landscape. He proceeded without haste, but he worked as fast as possible, concentrating now on his wide-angle lenses.

The end result of the men's endeavour was the series of photographs which became historic records of mankind's expansion through the solar system. They rank as works of art. As for Brooks, despite a period of fame, he eventually died in penury. General Shapiro ended up as Officer Commanding, Mars Base; his memoirs, in four volumes, contain an account of his first reconnaissance of Olympus – which differs considerably from the facts as set down here.

(1986)

Brian W. Aldiss has over the last thirty years established an enviable reputation as one of this generation's most versatile writers. His novels *The Hand-Reared Boy* and *A Soldier Erect* were both international bestsellers, and, most recently, *Life in the West* was chosen by Anthony Burgess as one of his 99 Best Novels. For his critically acclaimed works of science fiction, including *The Long Afternoon of Earth*, *The Saliva Tree*, and the *Helliconia* Trilogy, he has received both the Hugo and Nebula Awards as well as the Prix Jules Verne and the Ditmar Award. In addition to his distinguished career as a novelist, Aldiss has also established himself as one of today's foremost science fiction critics: in 1987 he was honored with the Hugo Award for *Trillion Year Spree: The History of Science Fiction* (written with David Wingrove). Born in Norfolk, England, Brian Aldiss now lives on the outskirts of Oxford with his wife, Margaret, and various children.